Almost every mystery story I write belongs to the "armchair detective" variety. Our hero listens to a puzzling story of some kind that seems to have no solution and, taking into account only what he is told, comes up with the answer in so cogent a fashion that every other character in the story (and the reader, too) is at once convinced of its legitimacy. . . .

My stories are, in short, not exercises in violence, not thrillers, not psychological suspense stories. They are, generally speaking, puzzles, and rather intellectual ones.

THE BEST MYSTERIES OF
ISAAC ASIMOV

Isaac Asimov

FAWCETT GOLD MEDAL • NEW YORK

To Marty and Rosalind,
for making each other happy.

ACKNOWLEDGMENTS

PART I THE BLACK WIDOWER MYSTERIES

1 "The Obvious Factor," *Ellery Queen's Mystery Magazine (EQMM)*, May 1973, © 1973 by Isaac Asimov, from *Tales of the Black Widowers*.

2 "The Pointing Finger," *EQMM*, July 1973, © 1973 by Isaac Asimov, from *Tales of the Black Widowers*.

3 "Out of Sight," *EQMM*, December 1973, under the title of "The Six Suspects," © 1973 by Isaac Asimov, from *Tales of the Black Widowers*.

4 "Yankee Doodle Went to Town," © 1974 by Isaac Asimov, from *Tales of the Black Widowers*.

5 "Quicker Than the Eye," *EQMM*, May 1974, © 1974 by Isaac Asimov, from *More Tales of the Black Widowers*.

6 "The Three Numbers," *EQMM*, September 1974, under the title of "All in the Way You Read It," © 1974 by Isaac Asimov, from *More Tales of the Black Widowers*.

7 "The One and Only East," *EQMM*, March 1975, © 1975 by Isaac Asimov, from *More Tales of the Black Widowers*.

8 "The Cross of Lorraine," *EQMM*, May 1976, © 1976 by Isaac Asimov, from *Casebook of the Black Widowers*.

9 "The Next Day," *EQMM*, May 1978, © 1978 by Isaac Asimov, from *Casebook of the Black Widowers*.

10 "What Time Is It?" © 1980 by Isaac Asimov, from *Casebook of the Black Widowers*.

11 "Middle Name," © 1980 by Isaac Asimov, from *Casebook of the Black Widowers*.

12 "Sixty Million Trillion Combinations," *EQMM*, May 5, 1980, © 1980 by Isaac Asimov, from *Banquets of the Black Widowers*.

13 "The Good Samaritan," *EQMM*, September 10, 1980, © 1980 by Isaac Asimov, from *Banquets of the Black Widowers*.

14 "Can You Prove It?" *EQMM*, June 17, 1981, © 1981 by Isaac Asimov, from *Banquets of the Black Widowers*.

15 "The Redhead," *EQMM*, October 1984, © 1984 by Isaac Asimov, from *Banquets of the Black Widowers*.

PART II THE UNION CLUB MYSTERIES

16 "He Wasn't There," *Gallery*, February 1981, under the title of "The Spy Who Was Out of Focus," copyright © 1980 by Montcalm Publishing Corporation, from *The Union Club Mysteries*.

17 "Hide and Seek," *Gallery*, May 1981, copyright © 1981 by Montcalm Publishing Corporation, from *The Union Club Mysteries*.

18 "Dollars and Cents," *Gallery*, January 1982, under the title of "Countdown to Disaster," copyright © 1982 by Montcalm Publishing Corporation, from *The Union Club Mysteries*.

19 "The Sign," *Gallery*, April 1982, under the title of "The Telltale Sign," copyright © 1982 by Montcalm Publishing Corporation, from *The Union Club Mysteries*.

20 "Getting the Combination," *Gallery*, June 1982, under the title of "Playing It by the Numbers," copyright © 1982 by Montcalm Publishing Corporation, from *The Union Club Mysteries*.

21 "The Library Book," *Gallery*, July 1982, under the title of "The Mystery Book," copyright © 1982 by Montcalm Publishing Corporation, from *The Union Club Mysteries*.

22 "Never Out of Sight," *Gallery*, March 1983, under the title of "The Amusement Lark," copyright © 1983 by Montcalm Publishing Corporation.*

23 "The Magic Umbrella," *Gallery*, May 1983, under the title of "Stormy Weather," copyright © 1983 by Montcalm Publishing Corporation.*

24 "The Speck," *EQMM*, December 1983, © 1983 by Isaac Asimov.*

PART III MISCELLANEOUS MYSTERIES

25 "The Key," October 1966, *The Magazine of Fantasy and Science Fiction*, © 1966 by Mercury Press, Inc., from *Asimov's Mysteries*.

26 "A Problem of Numbers," May, 1970, *EQMM*, © 1970 by Isaac Asimov.*

27 "The Little Things," May 1975, *EQMM*, © 1975 by Isaac Asimov.*

28 "Halloween," October 1975, *American Way*, © 1976 by American Way.*

29 "The Thirteenth Day of Christmas," July 1977, *EQMM*, © 1977 by Isaac Asimov, from *The Key Word and Other Mysteries*.

30 "The Key Word," copyright © 1977 by Isaac Asimov, from *The Key Word and Other Mysteries*.

31 "Nothing Might Happen," December 1973, *Alfred Hitchcock's Mystery Magazine*, © 1983 by Davis Publications, Inc.*

*Story has not appeared in any previous collection.

CONTENTS

PART III   MISCELLANEOUS MYSTERIES

Introduction

When I was younger than I am now, and began reading mystery novels in the 1930s, the field was going through its "classic" phase.

The most prominent writers of the time were British men and women of the intellectual classes, and this was reflected in the novels themselves. They dealt for the most part with educated men and women of the type that thought of themselves as "gentlemen" and "ladies." People of the lower and middle classes were rarely allowed entrance, except as comic relief or as semibarbaric threats.

Generally, a crime (usually a murder) was committed under conditions that permitted a closed circle of suspects. It took place in a locked room, or in any case, in such a way that no one else could have gotten into the place of the murder. (If, in fact, an outsider proved to be the criminal, the author was cheating and would have to face an enraged public.)

What is more, the detective, either a stolid (or possibly brilliant) member of the police force or a lighthearted amateur, was compelled to solve the murder by shrewd observation and closely reasoned logic. It would again be cheating if he stumbled upon the solution by accident, and it was distinctly beneath such a detective's dignity to have to search for clues on his hands and knees with a magnifying glass, after the fashion of Sherlock Holmes.

The generally accepted monarch of the classic detective story was, of course, Agatha Christie, and the most indefatigable and best detective (with all apologies to the great Sherlock) was Hercule Poirot. Certainly, I read all the Christies I could find and, as it happens, I have now read every mystery novel or short story she has ever written, without exception, many of them three or four times.

This is not to say I find Christie perfect, or that I even found her perfect in my green teenage years. She had a peculiar attitude toward foreigners, which she carefully blamed upon her characters whom she presented as naturally xenophobic since any Briton would know that any non-Briton was an inferior and, possibly, immoral person. Furthermore, she included Americans among the foreigners and, especially in her early books, had them speak with a dialect of a type that I had never encountered and that I don't believe anyone living could speak without bursting his or her vocal cords. Finally, she was as matter-of-factly anti-Semitic as most of the British upper classes were at that time (and, for all I know, still are). At least she was openly anti-Semitic before World War II; afterward she tried to hide the fact.

Since I was a foreigner by her standards, and a Jewish-American one at that, I didn't really appreciate Christie's narrow-minded view of the human race, and yet for the sake of her fascinating mysteries I had to overlook the matter (which didn't exactly make me feel good then—or now, either).

Then came a time when the classic mystery came to be outmoded. All things evolve and few contemporary mysteries meet the old Christie criteria. Instead, the mystery novel has now split into two dominant subgenres. There is the "tough-guy detective," where the hero is constantly drinking without destroying his liver, constantly having his skull cracked with a pistol butt without destroying his brain, and constantly solving the mystery by shooting down all the characters but one and then pinning the crime on the survivor.

There is also the "psychological mystery," where you

know who did the crime and why, and find that there is no difficulty in pinning that crime upon him. What you are expected to do, however, is to follow, in great detail, the tortuous and muddled pathology of the criminal's emotional life. You find yourself involved, therefore, with a large number of very unpleasant people, a great many of them uneducated and rather drearily stupid.

This change of emphasis hasn't pleased me. I don't enjoy scenes of gruesome violence in books. I hold with the ancient Greeks that all deeds of violence should take place offstage. To be sure, there *is* such violence in real life—and worse than anything described in fiction—but, oddly enough, I don't enjoy it in real life, either. Nor do I enjoy immersion in psychopathology.

What do I do, then? I read those few writers who turn out the old classical stuff, and I re-read, whenever desperate, the old masters and mistresses of the genre. And I note that on the paperback racks the Agatha Christies are spread out in wild profusion so that one can be quite sure that the old girl is still read without stint.

There came a time when I became involved in this matter as something more than a dissatisfied reader yearning for the vanished days of yore.

I am, you must understand, a science fiction writer primarily, and have been a prominent professional in the field since I was eighteen.

And yet—and yet—I have an urge to write mysteries. What's more, the urge has grown stronger with the years. Occasionally, I would even write one, though without remarkable success.

Beginning in 1972, however, I threw caution to the winds and began to write mystery short stories in great numbers. In the last thirteen years, in fact, I have written over a hundred of them.

What's more, I have refused to compromise. There is no way I can force other writers to turn out stories à la Christie, but I made up my mind that my stories were going to be of the classic variety.

In fact, I decided to be even purer than the pure. I was going to try to have no violence at all in my stories. My stories rarely involve murder and, when they do, the murder takes place offstage and preferably before the story begins. And that murder, if it takes place at all, is the only one. I do not kill someone else the minute the tension seems to flag. For the most part, though, the detective must find a missing object, or choose one correct alternative among many, or foil a spy, and so on.

What's more, almost every mystery story I write belongs to the "armchair detective" variety. Our hero listens to a puzzling story of some kind that seems to have no solution and, taking into account only what he is told, comes up with the answer in so cogent a fashion that every other character in the story (and the reader, too) is at once convinced of its legitimacy.

Naturally, the story under such conditions must be a fair one. The detective must know only what the reader knows so that there is nothing to stop a particularly ingenious reader from beating the detective to the solution. And, indeed, my stories openly challenge the reader to do so; and often enough, the reader does.

My stories are, in short, not exercises in violence, not thrillers, not psychological suspense stories. They are, generally speaking, puzzles, and rather intellectual ones.

Christie used to say she didn't have lower-class characters in her stories because she had never associated with them and therefore didn't know how they talked and acted.

So it is with me, too. A writer should remain in those milieus in which he feels at home, and so my characters tend to be professional men who are cerebral and, if anything, overeducated. Every one of them (I suspect) has a little of myself in him. Or a lot of myself, perhaps.

As it happens, I have published half a dozen or so collections of my short stories, but what I want to do here is to put out an omnibus volume, larger than the ordinary ones, and pile into it thirty-one of my favorite mystery stories. This has not been an easy job for me, for I am the kind of fortunate writer who enjoys everything he writes, without exception. I have, however, managed and I have placed before each story a short explanation as to why I have chosen it.

PART I

BLACK WIDOWER MYSTERIES

1

The Obvious Factor

In many a classic mystery, the crime is described as having occurred under conditions where no one can seem to have committed it. The fun then consists in showing how the "impossible" can be made possible. Naturally, to enhance the suspense an author sometimes throws a pall of the possible-supernatural over the whole thing. I love stories like that.

It is tempting, though, for an author to conclude with an intimation that something supernatural has happened, after all. Agatha Christie and John Dickson Carr have each written stories of the supernatural, for instance.

I include this story, then, because I set up a situation that seems to make no solution possible that doesn't involve the paranormal. And then I produce my solution—the one solution that is almost always overlooked in stories of this type.

Thomas Trumbull looked about the table and said, with some satisfaction, "Well, at least you won't get yourself pen-and-inked into oblivion, Voss. Our resident artist isn't here. . . . Henry!"

Henry was at Trumbull's elbow before the echo of the

bellow had died, with no sign of perturbation on his bright-eyed and unlined face. Trumbull took the scotch and soda the waiter had on his tray and said, "Has Mario called, Henry?"

"No, sir," said Henry calmly.

Geoffrey Avalon had reduced his second drink to the half-way point and swirled it absently. "After last month's tale about his murdered sister, it could be that he didn't—"

He did not complete the sentence, but put down his glass carefully at the seat he intended to take. The monthly banquet of the Black Widowers was about to begin.

Trumbull, who was host, took the armchair at the head of the table and said, "Have you got them all straight, Voss? At my left is James Drake. He's a chemist and knows more about pulp fiction than about chemistry, and that probably isn't much. Then Geoffrey Avalon, a lawyer who never sees the inside of a courtroom; Emmanuel Rubin, who writes in between talking, which is practically never; and Roger Halsted. . . . Roger, you're not inflicting another limerick on us this session, are you?"

"A limerick?" said Trumbull's guest, speaking for the first time. It was a pleasant voice, light and yet rich, with all consonants carefully pronounced. He had a white beard, evenly cut from temple to temple, and white hair, too. His youthful face shone pinkly within its fence of white. "A poet, then?"

"A poet?" snorted Trumbull. "Not even a mathematician, which is what he claims to be. He insists on writing a limerick for every book of the *Iliad*."

"And *Odyssey*," said Halsted, in his soft, hurried voice. "But, yes, I have my limerick."

"Good! It's out of order," said Trumbull. "You are not to read it. Host's privilege."

"Oh, for heaven's sake," said Avalon, the flat lines of his well-preserved face set in disappointment. "Let him recite the poor thing. It takes thirty seconds and I find it fun."

Trumbull pretended not to hear. "You've all got it straight about my guest now? He's Dr. Voss Eldridge. He's a Ph.D. So is Drake, Voss. We're all doctors, though, by virtue of membership in the Black Widowers." He then raised his glass, gave the monthly invocation to Old King Cole, and the meal was officially begun.

Halsted, who had been whispering to Drake, passed a paper to him. Drake rose and declaimed:

> "Next a Lycian attempted a ruse
> With an arrow—permitted by Zeus.
>   Who will trust Trojan candor, as
>   This sly deed of Pandarus
> Puts an end to the scarce-proclaimed truce?"

"Damn it," said Trumbull. "I ruled against reading it."

"Against *my* reading it," said Halsted. "Drake read it."

"It's disappointing not to have Mario here," said Avalon. "He would ask what it means."

"Go ahead, Jeff," said Rubin. "I'll pretend I don't understand it and you explain."

But Avalon maintained a dignified silence while Henry presented the appetizer and Rubin fixed it with his usual suspicious stare.

"I hate stuff," he said, "that's so chopped up and drowned in goop that you can't see what the ingredients are."

Henry said, "I think you'll find it quite wholesome."

"And you know Henry's honesty," said Drake. "It wouldn't hurt a fly if he says it's wholesome."

"Try it; you'll like it," said Avalon.

Rubin tried it, but his face showed no signs of liking it. It was noted later, however, that he had finished it.

Dr. Eldridge said, "Is there a necessity of explaining these limericks, Dr. Avalon? Are there tricks to them?"

"No, not at all, and don't bother with the doctorate. That's only for formal occasions, though it's good of you to humor the club idiosyncrasy. It's just that Mario has never read the *Iliad;* few have, these days."

"Pandarus, as I recall, was a go-between and gives us the word 'pander.' That, I take it, was the sly deed mentioned in the limerick."

"Oh, no, no," said Avalon, unsuccessfully hiding his delight. "You're thinking now of the medieval Troilus tale, which Shakespeare drew on for his *Troilus and Cressida*. Pandarus was the go-between there. In the *Iliad* he was merely a Lycian archer who shot at Menelaus during a truce.

That was the sly deed. He is killed in the next book by the Greek warrior Diomedes."

"Ah," said Eldridge, smiling faintly, "it's easy to be fooled, isn't it?"

"If you want to be," said Rubin, but he smiled as the London broil arrived. There was no mistaking the nature of the components there. He buttered a roll and ate it as though to give himself time to contemplate the beauty of the meat.

"As a matter of fact," said Halsted, "we've solved quite a few puzzles in recent meetings. We did well."

"We did lousy," said Trumbull. "Henry is the one who did well."

"I *include* Henry when I say 'we,' " said Halsted, his fair face flushing.

"Henry?" asked Eldridge.

"Our esteemed waiter," said Trumbull, "and honorary member of the Black Widowers."

Henry, who was filling the water glasses, said, "You honor me, sir."

"Honor, hell. I wouldn't come to any meeting if you weren't taking care of the table, Henry."

"It's good of you to say so, sir."

Eldridge remained thoughtfully quiet thereafter, as he followed the tide of conversation that, as was usual, grew steadily in intensity. Drake was making some obscure distinction between Secret Agent X and Operator 5, and Rubin, for some reason known only to himself, was disputing the point.

Drake, whose slightly hoarse voice never rose, said, "Operator 5 may have used disguises. I won't deny that. It was Secret Agent X, however, who was 'the man of a thousand faces.' I can send you a Xerox of a contents page of a magazine from my library to prove it." He made a note to himself in his memo book.

Rubin, scenting defeat, shifted ground at once. "There's no such thing as a disguise, anyway. There are a million things no one can disguise, idiosyncrasies of stance, walk, voice; a million habits you can't change because you don't even know you have them. A disguise works only because no one *looks*."

"People fool themselves, in other words," said Eldridge, breaking in.

"Absolutely," said Rubin. "People *want* to be fooled."

The ice-cream parfait was brought in, and not long after that, Trumbull struck his water glass with his spoon.

"Inquisition time," he said. "As Grand Inquisitor I pass, since I'm the host. Manny, will you do the honors?"

Rubin said, at once, "Dr. Eldridge, how do you justify the fact of your existence?"

"By the fact that I labor to distinguish truth from folly."

"Do you consider that you succeed in doing so?"

"Not as often as I wish, perhaps. And yet as often as most. To distinguish truth from folly is a common desire; we all try our hands at it. My interpretation of Pandarus' deed in Halsted's limerick was folly and Avalon corrected me. The common notion of disguise you claimed to be folly and you corrected it. When I find folly, I try to correct it, if I can. It's not always easy."

"What is your form of folly correction, Eldridge? How would you describe your profession?"

"I am," said Eldridge, "Associate Professor of Abnormal Psychology."

"Where do you . . . ?" began Rubin.

Avalon interrupted, his deep voice dominating, "Sorry, Manny, but I smell an evasion. You asked Dr. Eldridge's profession and he gave you a title. . . . What do you do, Dr. Eldridge, to occupy your time most significantly?"

"I investigate parapsychological phenomena," said Eldridge.

"Oh, God," muttered Drake, and stubbed out his cigarette.

Eldridge said, "You disapprove of that, sir?" There was no sign of annoyance on his face. He turned to Henry and said, "No, thank you, Henry, I've had enough coffee," with perfect calmness.

Henry passed on to Rubin, who was holding his cup in the air as a signal of its emptiness.

"It's not a question of approval or disapproval," said Drake. "I think you're wasting your time."

"In what way?"

"You investigate telepathy, precognition, things like that?"

"Yes. And ghosts and spiritual phenomena, too."

"All right. Have you ever come across something you couldn't explain?"

"Explain in what way? I could explain a ghost by saying, 'Yes, that's a ghost.' I take it that's not what you mean."

Rubin broke in. "I hate to be on Drake's side right now, but he means to ask, as you well know, whether you have ever come across any phenomenon you could not explain by the accepted and prosaic laws of science."

"I have come across many such phenomena."

"That you could not explain?" asked Halsted.

"That I could not explain. There's not a month that passes but that something crosses my desk that I cannot explain," said Eldridge, nodding his head gently.

There was a short silence of palpable disapproval and then Avalon said, "Does that mean that you are a believer in these psychic phenomena?"

"If you mean: Do I think that events take place that violate the laws of physics? No! Do I think, however, that I know all there is to know about the laws of physics? Also, no. Do I think anyone knows all there is to know about the laws of physics? No, a third time."

"That's evasion," said Drake. "Do you have any evidence that telepathy exists, for instance, and that the laws of physics, as presently accepted, will have to be modified accordingly?"

"I am not ready to commit myself that far. I well know that in even the most circumstantial stories, there are honest mistakes, exaggerations, misinterpretations, outright hoaxes. And yet, even allowing for all that, I come across incidents I cannot quite bring myself to dismiss."

Eldridge shook his head and continued, "It's not easy, this job of mine. There are some incidents for which no conceivable run-of-the-mill explanation seems possible; where the evidence for something quite apart from the known rules by which the universe seems to run appears irrefutable. It would seem I *must* accept—and yet I hesitate. Can I labor under a hoax so cleverly manipulated, or an error so cleverly hidden, that I take for the gold of fact what is only the brass of nonsense? I can be fooled, as Rubin would point out."

Trumbull said, "Manny would say that you *want* to be fooled."

"Maybe I do. We all want dramatic things to be true. We want to be able to wish on a star, to have strange powers, to be irresistible to women—and would inwardly conspire to believe such things no matter how much we might lay claim to complete rationality."

"Not me," said Rubin flatly. "I've never kidded myself in my life."

"No?" Eldridge looked at him thoughtfully. "I take it then that you will refuse to believe in the actual existence of parapsychological phenomena under all circumstances?"

"I wouldn't say that," said Rubin, "but I'd need damned good evidence—better evidence than I've ever seen advanced."

"And how about the rest of you gentlemen?"

Drake said, "We're all rationalists. At least I don't know about Mario Gonzalo, but he's not here this session."

"You, too, Tom?"

Trumbull's lined face broke into a grim smile. "You've never convinced me with any of your tales before this, Voss. I don't think you can convince me now."

"I never told you tales that convinced *me*, Tom. . . . But I have one now; something I've never told you and that no one really knows about outside my department. I can tell it to you all and if you can come up with an explanation that would require no change in the fundamental scientific view of the universe, I would be greatly relieved."

"A ghost story?" said Halsted.

"No, not a ghost story," said Eldridge. "It is merely a story that defies the principle of cause and effect, the very foundation stone on which all science is built. To put it another way, it defies the concept of the irreversible forward flow of time."

"Actually," said Rubin, at once, "it's quite possible, on the subatomic level, to consider time as flowing either—"

"Shut up, Manny," said Trumbull, "and let Voss talk."

Quietly, Henry had placed the brandy before each of the diners. Eldridge lifted his small glass absently and sniffed at it, then nodded to Henry, who returned a small, urbane smile.

"It's an odd thing," said Eldridge, "but so many of those

who claim to have strange powers, or have it claimed for them, are young women of no particular education, no particular presence, no particular intelligence. It is as though the existence of a special talent has consumed what would otherwise be spread out among the more usual facets of the personality. Maybe it's just more noticeable in women.

"At any rate, I am speaking of someone I'll just call Mary for now. You understand I'm not using her real name. The woman is still under investigation and it would be fatal, from my point of view, to get any kind of publicity hounds on the track. You understand?"

Trumbull frowned severely. "Come on, Voss, you know I told you that nothing said here is ever repeated outside the confines of these walls. You needn't feel constrained."

"Accidents happen," said Eldridge equably. "At any rate, I'll return to Mary. Mary never completed grade school and has earned what money she could earn by serving behind a counter at the five-and-ten. She is not attractive and no one will sweep her away from the counter, which may be good, for she is useful there and serves well. You might not think so, since she cannot add correctly and is given to incapacitating headaches, during which she will sit in a back room and upset the other employees by muttering gibberish to herself in a baleful sort of way. Nevertheless, the store wouldn't dream of letting her go."

"Why not?" asked Rubin, clearly steeling himself to skepticism at every point.

"Because she spots shoplifters, who, as you know, can these days bleed a store to death through a thousand small cuts. It isn't that Mary is in any way shrewd or keen-eyed or unrelenting in pursuit. She just knows a shoplifter when he or she enters the store, even if she has never seen the person before, and even if she doesn't actually see the person come in.

"She followed them herself at first for brief intervals; then grew hysterical and began her muttering. The manager eventually tied the two things together—Mary's characteristic behavior and the shoplifting. He started to watch for one, then the other, and it didn't take long for him to find out that she never missed.

"Losses quickly dropped to virtually nothing in that particular five-and-ten despite the fact that the store is in a bad neighborhood. The manager, of course, received the credit. Probably, he deliberately kept the truth from being known lest anyone try to steal Mary from him.

"But then I think he grew afraid of it. Mary fingered a shoplifter who wasn't a shoplifter but who later was mixed up in a shooting incident. The manager had read about some of the work my department does, and he came to us. Eventually, he brought Mary to us.

"We got her to come to the college regularly. We paid her, of course. Not much, but then she didn't ask for much. She was an unpleasant not-bright girl of about twenty, who was reluctant to talk and describe what went on in her mind. I suppose she had spent a childhood having her queer notions beaten out of her and she had learned to be cautious, you see."

Drake said, "You're telling us she had a gift for precognition?"

Eldridge said, "Since precognition is just Latin for seeing-things-before-they-happen, and since she sees things before they happen, how else can I describe it? She sees unpleasant things only, things that upset or frighten her, which, I imagine, makes her life a hell. It is the quality of becoming upset or frightened that breaks down the time barrier."

Halsted said, "Let's set our boundary conditions. What does she sense? How far ahead in time does she see things? How far away in space?"

"We could never get her to do much for us," said Eldridge. "Her talent wasn't on tap at will and with us she could never relax. From what the manager told us and from what we could pick up, it seemed she could never detect anything more than a few minutes ahead in time. Half an hour to an hour at the most."

Rubin snorted.

"A few minutes," said Eldridge mildly, "is as good as a century. The principle stands. Cause and effect is violated and the flow of time is reversed.

"And in space, there seemed no limits. As she described

it, when I could get her to say anything at all, and as I interpreted her rather clumsy and incoherent words, the background of her mind is a constant flickering of frightening shapes. Every once in a while, this is lit up, as though by a momentary lightning flash, and she sees, or becomes aware. She sees most clearly what is close by or what she is most concerned about—the shoplifting, for instance. Occasionally, though, she sees what must be taking place farther away. The greater the disaster, the farther she can sense things. I suspect she could detect a nuclear bomb getting ready to explode anywhere in the world.''

Rubin said, ''I imagine she speaks incoherently and you fill in the rest. History is full of ecstatic prophets whose mumbles are interpreted into wisdom.''

''I agree,'' said Eldridge, ''and I pay no attention—or at least not much—to anything that isn't clear. I don't even attach much importance to her feats with shoplifters. She might be sensitive enough to detect some characteristic way in which shoplifters look and stand, some aura, some *smell*—the sort of thing you talked about, Rubin, as matters no one can disguise. But then—''

''Then?'' prompted Halsted.

''Just a minute,'' said Eldridge. ''Uh—Henry, could I have a refill in the coffeecup after all?''

''Certainly,'' said Henry.

Eldridge watched the coffee level rise. ''What's *your* attitude on psychic phenomena, Henry?''

Henry said, ''I have no general attitude, sir. I accept whatever it seems to me I must accept.''

''Good!'' said Eldridge. ''I'll rely on you and not on these prejudiced and preconcepted rationalists here.''

''Go on, then,'' said Drake. ''You paused at the dramatic moment to throw us off.''

''Never,'' said Eldridge. ''I was saying that I did not take Mary seriously, until one day she suddenly began to squirm and pant and mumble under her breath. She does that now and then, but this time she muttered 'Eldridge. Eldridge.' And the word grew shriller and shriller.

''I assumed she was calling me, but she wasn't. When I responded, she ignored me. Over and over again, it was

'Eldridge! Eldridge!' Then she began to scream, 'Fire! Oh, Lord! It's burning! Help! Eldridge! Eldridge!' Over and over again, with all kinds of variations. She kept it up for half an hour.

"We tried to make sense out of it. We spoke quietly, of course, because we didn't want to intrude more than we had to, but we kept saying, 'Where? Where?' Incoherently enough, and in scraps, she told us enough to make us guess it was San Francisco, which, I need not tell you, is nearly three thousand miles away. There's only one Golden Gate Bridge after all, and in one spasm, she gasped out, 'Golden Gate,' over and over. Afterward it turned out she had never heard of the Golden Gate Bridge and was quite shaky as to San Francisco.

"When we put it all together, we decided that there was an old apartment house somewhere in San Francisco, possibly within eyeshot of the Bridge, that had gone up in fire. A total of twenty-three people were in it at the time it burst into fire, and of these, five did not escape. The five deaths included that of a child."

Halsted said, "And then you checked and found there *was* a fire in San Francisco and that five people had died, including a child."

"That's right," said Eldridge. "But here's what got me. One of the five deaths was that of a woman, Sophronia Latimer. She had gotten out safely and then discovered that her eight-year-old boy had not come out with her. She ran wildly back into the house, screaming for the boy, and never came out again. The boy's name was Eldridge, so you can see what she was shouting in the minutes before her death.

"Eldridge is a very uncommon first name, as I need not tell you, and my feeling is that Mary captured that particular event, for all that it was so far away, entirely because she had been sensitized to the name, by way of myself, and because it was surrounded by such agony."

Rubin said, "You want an explanation, is that it?"

"Of course," said Eldridge. "How did this ignorant girl see a fire in full detail, get all the facts correct—and believe me, we checked it out—at three thousand miles."

Rubin said, "What makes the three-thousand-mile distance so impressive? These days it means nothing; it's one sixtieth of a second at the speed of light. I suggest that she heard the tale of the fire on radio or on television—more likely the latter—and passed it on to you. That's why she chose that story; because of the name Eldridge. She figured it would have the greatest possible effect on you."

"Why?" asked Eldridge. "Why should she put through such a hoax?"

"Why?" Rubin's voice faded out momentarily, as though with astonishment, then came back in a shout. "Good God, you've been working with these people for years and don't realize how much they *want* to hoax you. Don't you suppose there's a feeling of power that comes with perpetrating a good hoax; and money, too, don't forget."

Eldridge thought about it, then shook his head. "She doesn't have the brains to put something like this across. It takes brains to be a faker—a good one, anyway."

Trumbull broke in. "Well, now, Voss. There's no reason to suppose she's in it on her own. A confederate is possible. She supplies the hysteria, he supplies the brains."

"Who might the confederate be?" asked Eldridge softly.

Trumbull shrugged. "I don't know."

Avalon cleared his throat and said, "I go along with Tom here, and my guess is that the confederate is the manager of the five-and-ten. He had noted her ability to guess at shoplifters, and thought he could put this to use in something more splashy. I'll bet that's it. He heard about the fire on television, caught the name Eldridge, and coached her."

"How long would it take to coach her?" asked Eldridge. "I keep telling you that she's not very bright."

"The coaching wouldn't be difficult," said Rubin quickly. "You say she was incoherent. He would just tell her a few key words: Eldridge, fire, Golden Gate, and so on. She then keeps repeating them in random arrangements and you intelligent parapsychologists fill it in."

Eldridge nodded, then said, "That's interesting, except that there was no time at all to coach the girl. That's what precognition is all about. We know exactly what time she had her fit and we know exactly what time the fire broke out in San Francisco. It so happens the fire broke out at just about the minute that Mary's fit died down. It was as though once the fire was actual, it was no longer a matter of precognition, and Mary lost contact. So you see, there could be no coaching. The news didn't hit the network TV news programs till that evening. That's when *we* found out and began our investigation in depth."

"But wait," said Halsted. "What about the time difference? There's a three-hour time difference between New York and San Francisco, and a confederate in San Francisco—"

"A confederate in San Francisco?" said Eldridge, opening his eyes wide, and staring. "Are you imagining a continental conspiracy? Besides, believe me, I know about the time difference also. When I say that the fire started just as Mary finished, I mean allowing for the time difference. Mary's fit started at just about one-fifteen P.M. Eastern Standard Time, and the fire in San Francisco started at just about ten forty-five A.M. Pacific Standard Time."

Drake said, "I have a suggestion."

"Go on," said Eldridge.

"This is an uneducated and unintelligent girl—you keep saying that over and over—and she's throwing a fit, an epileptic fit, for all I know."

"No," said Eldridge firmly.

"All right, a prophetic fit, if you wish. She's muttering and mumbling and screaming and doing everything in the world but speaking clearly. She makes sound which *you* interpret, and which you make fit together. If it had occurred to you to hear her say something like 'atom bomb,' then the word you interpreted as 'Eldridge' would have become 'Oak Ridge,' for instance."

"And Golden Gate?"

"You might have heard that as 'couldn't get' and fitted it in somehow."

"Not bad," said Eldridge. "Except that we know that it is hard to understand some of these ecstatics and we are bright enough to make use of modern technology. We routinely tape-record our sessions and we tape-recorded this one. We've listened to it over and over and there is no question but that she said 'Eldridge' and not 'Oak Ridge,' 'Golden Gate' and not 'couldn't get.' We've had different people listen and there is no disagreement on any of this. Besides, from what we heard, we worked out all the details of the fire before we got the facts. We had to make no modifications afterward. It all fit exactly."

There was a long silence at the table.

Finally Eldridge said, "Well, there it is. Mary foresaw the fire three thousand miles away by a full half-hour and got all the facts correct."

Drake said uneasily, "Do *you* accept it? Do *you* think it was precognition?"

"I'm trying not to," said Eldridge. "But for what reason can I disbelieve it? I don't want to fool myself into believing it, but what choice have I? At what point am I fooling myself? If it wasn't precognition, what was it? I had hoped that perhaps one of you gentlemen could tell me."

Again a silence.

Eldridge went on. "I'm left in a position where I must refer to Sherlock Holmes's great precept: 'When the impossible has been eliminated, then whatever remains, however improbable, is the truth.' In this case, if fakery of any kind is impossible, the precognition must be the truth. Don't you all agree?"

The silence was thicker than before, until Trumbull cried out, "Damn it all, Henry is grinning. No one's asked *him* yet to explain this. Well, Henry?"

Henry coughed. "I should not have smiled, gentlemen, but I couldn't help it when Professor Eldridge used that quotation. It seems the final bit of evidence that you gentlemen *want* to believe."

"The hell we do," said Rubin, frowning.

"Surely, then, a quotation from President Thomas Jefferson would have sprung to mind."

"What quotation?" asked Halsted.

"I imagine Mr. Rubin knows," said Henry.

"I probably do, Henry, but at the moment I can't think of an appropriate one. Is it in the Declaration of Independence?"

"No, sir," began Henry, when Trumbull interrupted with a snarl.

"Let's not play Twenty Questions, Manny. Go on, Henry, what are you getting at?"

"Well, sir, to say that when the impossible has been

eliminated, whatever remains, however improbable, is the truth, is to make the assumption, usually unjustified, that everything that is to be considered has indeed been considered. Let us suppose we have considered ten factors. Nine are clearly impossible. Is the tenth, however improbable, therefore true? What if there were an eleventh factor, and a twelfth, and a thirteenth . . ."

Avalon said severely, "You mean there's a factor we haven't considered?"

"I'm afraid so, sir," said Henry, nodding.

Avalon shook his head. "I can't think what it can be."

"And yet it is an obvious factor, sir; the *most* obvious one."

"What is it, then?" demanded Halsted, clearly annoyed. "Get to the point!"

"To begin with," said Henry, "it is clear that to explain the ability of the young lady to foretell, as described, the details of a fire three thousand miles away except by precognition is impossible. But suppose precognition is also to be considered impossible. In that case—"

Rubin got to his feet, straggly beard bristling, eyes magnified through thick-lensed glasses, staring. "Of course! The fire was *set*. The woman could have been coached for weeks. The accomplice goes to San Francisco and they coordinate. She predicts something she *knows* is going to happen. He causes something he *knows* she will predict."

Henry said, "Are you suggesting, sir, that a confederate would deliberately plan to kill five victims, including an eight-year-old boy?"

"Don't start trusting in the virtue of mankind, Henry," said Rubin. "You're the one who is sensitive to wrongdoing."

"The minor wrongdoings, sir, the kind most people overlook. I find it difficult to believe that anyone, in order to establish a fancied case of precognition, would deliberately arrange a horrible multi-murder. Besides, to arrange a fire in which eighteen of twenty-three people escape and five specific people die requires a bit of precognition in itself."

Rubin turned stubborn. "I can see ways in which five people can be trapped; like forcing a card in conjuring—"

"Gentlemen!" said Eldridge peremptorily, and all turned to look at him. "I have not told you the cause of the fire."

He went on, after looking about the table to make sure he had the attention of all, "It was a stroke of lightning. I don't see how a stroke of lightning could be arranged at a specific time." He spread out his hands helplessly. "I tell you. I've been struggling with this for weeks. I don't want to accept precognition, but . . . I suppose this spoils your theory, Henry?"

"On the contrary, Professor Eldridge, it confirms it and makes it certain. Ever since you began to tell us this tale of Mary and the fire, your every word has made it more and more certain that fakery is impossible and that precognition has taken place. If, however, precognition is impossible, then it follows of necessity, Professor, that you have been lying."

Not a Black Widower but exclaimed at that, with Avalon's shocked "Henry!" loudest of all.

But Eldridge was leaning back in his chair, chuckling. "Of course I was lying. From beginning to end. I wanted to see if all you so-called rationalists would be so eager to accept parapsychological phenomena that you would overlook the obvious rather than spoil your own thrill. When did you catch me out, Henry?"

"It was a possibility from the start, sir, which grew stronger each time you eliminated a solution by inventing more information. I was certain when you mentioned the lightning. That was dramatic enough to have been brought in at the beginning. To be mentioned only at the very end made it clear that you created it on the spot to block the final hope."

"But why was it a possibility from the start, Henry?" demanded Eldridge. "Do I *look* like a liar? Can you detect liars the way I had Mary detect shoplifters?"

"Because this is *always* a possibility and something to be kept in mind and watched for. That is where the remark by President Jefferson comes in."

"What was that?"

"In 1807, Professor Benjamin Silliman of Yale reported seeing the fall of a meteorite at a time when the existence of meteorites was not accepted by scientists. Thomas Jefferson, a rationalist of enormous talent and intelligence, on hearing the report, said, 'I would sooner believe that a Yankee professor would lie than that a stone would fall from heaven.' "

"Yes," said Avalon at once, "but Jefferson was wrong. Silliman did *not* lie and stones *did* fall from heaven."

"Quite so, Mr. Avalon," said Henry, unruffled. "That is why the quotation is remembered. But considering the great number of times that impossibilities have been reported, and the small number of times they have been proven possible after all, I felt the odds were with me."

2

The Pointing Finger

In each of my Black Widowers, I try to bring up some different subject concerning which each of my members can wax erudite and eloquent about. The plays of Shakespeare are an obvious example and I feel at home with them, for at about the time I had begun my Black Widower series I had also written a two-volume dicussion of those plays. The books were entitled Asimov's Guide to Shakespeare.

Frankly, I have as much fun involving myself in such discussions as in working up the conclusion. Of course, I keep thinking with a shiver: What happens when I run out of subjects for competing erudition?

However, it hasn't happened yet, and I present this story as a successful example (in my opinion) of this sort of thing.

It was a rather quiet Black Widowers banquet until Rubin and Trumbull had their nose-to-nose confrontation.

Mario Gonzalo had been first to arrive, subdued and with the shadow of trouble upon him.

Henry was still setting up the table when Gonzalo arrived. He stopped and asked, "How are you, sir?" in quiet and unobtrusive concern.

Gonzalo shrugged. "All right, I guess. Sorry I missed the last meeting, but I finally decided to go to the police and I wasn't up to much for a while. I don't know if they can do anything, but it's up to them now. I almost wish you hadn't told me."

"Perhaps I ought not to have done so."

Gonzalo shrugged. "Listen, Henry," he said. "I called each of the guys and told him the story."

"Was that necessary, sir?"

"I had to. I'd feel constrained if I didn't. Besides, I didn't want them to think you had failed."

"Not an important consideration, sir."

The others came one by one, and each greeted Gonzalo with a hearty welcome that ostentatiously ignored a murdered sister, and each then subsided into a kind of uneasy quiet.

Avalon, who was hosting the occasion, seemed, as always, to add the dignity of that office to his natural solemnity. He sipped at his first drink and introduced his guest, a young man with a pleasant face, thinning black hair, and an amazingly thick mustache which seemed to be waiting only for the necessary change in fashion to be waxed at the end.

"This is Simon Levy," said Avalon. "A science writer and a splendid fellow."

Emmanuel Rubin promptly said, "Didn't you write a book on the laser, *Light in Step?*"

"Yes," said Levy with the energetic delight of an author greeting unexpected recognition. "Have you read it?"

Rubin, who was carrying, as he always did, the self-conscious soul of a six-footer in his five-foot-four body, looked solemnly at the other through his thick glasses and said, "I did, and found it quite good."

Levy's smile weakened, as though he considered a judgment of "quite good" no good at all.

Avalon said, "Roger Halsted won't be with us today. He's out of town on something or other. Sends his regrets and says to say hello to Mario if he shows up."

Trumbull said with his mouth down-curved in a sneer, "We're spared a limerick."

"I missed last month's," said Gonzalo. "Was it any good?"

"You wouldn't have understood it, Mario," said Avalon gravely.

"That good, eh?"

And then things quieted down to a near whisper until somehow the Act of Union came up. Afterward, neither Rubin nor Trumbull could remember exactly how.

Trumbull said, in what was considerably more than an ordinary speaking voice, "The Act of Union forming the United Kingdom of England, Wales, and Scotland was made law at the Treaty of Utrecht in 1713."

"No, it wasn't," said Rubin, his straw-colored and straggly beard wagging indignantly. "The Act was passed in 1707."

"Are you trying to tell me, you dumb jackass, that the Treaty of Utrecht was signed in 1707?"

"No, I'm not," shouted Rubin, his surprisingly loud voice reaching a bellow. "The Treaty of Utrecht was signed in 1713. You guessed that part right, though God only knows how."

"If the Treaty was signed in 1713, then that settles the Act of Union."

"No, it doesn't, because the Treaty had nothing to do with the Act of Union, which was 1707."

"Damn you, five dollars says you don't know the Act of Union from a union suit."

"Here's my five dollars. Where's yours? Or can you spare a week's pay at that two-bit job you've got?"

They were standing up now, leaning toward each other over James Drake, who philosophically added a fresh dollop of sour cream and chives to the last of his baked potato, and finished it.

Drake said, "No use shouting back and forth, my fellow jackasses. Look it up."

"*Henry!*" roared Trumbull.

There was the smallest of delays and then Henry was at hand with the third edition of the *Columbia Encyclopedia*.

"Host's privilege," said Avalon. "I'll check, as an impartial observer."

He turned the pages of the fat volume, muttering, "Union, union, union, ah, Act of." He then said, almost at once, "1707. Manny wins. Pay up, Tom."

"What?" cried Trumbull, outraged. "Let's see that."

Rubin quietly picked up the two five-dollar bills which had been lying on the table and said in a ruminating voice, "A good reference book, the *Columbia Encyclopedia*. Best one-volume all-round reference in the world and more useful than the *Britannica*, even if it does waste an entry on Isaac Asimov."

"On whom?" asked Gonzalo.

"Asimov. Friend of mine. Science fiction writer and pathologically conceited. He carries a copy of the *Encyclopedia* to parties and says, 'Talking of concrete, the *Columbia Encyclopedia* has an excellent article on it only 249 pages after their article on me. Let me show you.' Then he shows them the article on himself."

Gonzalo laughed. "Sounds a lot like you, Manny."

"Tell him that and he'll kill you—if I don't first."

Simon Levy turned to Avalon and said, "Are there arguments like that all the time here, Jeff?"

"Many arguments," said Avalon, "but they generally don't get to the wager and reference book stage. When it does happen, Henry's prepared. We have not only the *Columbia Encyclopedia*, but copies of the Bible, both the King James and the New English; Webster's unabridged—second edition, of course; *Webster's Biographical Dictionary; Webster's Geographical Dictionary; The Guinness Book of Records; Brewer's Dictionary of Phrase and Fable;* and *The Complete Works of Shakespeare*. It's the Black Widowers' library and Henry is the custodian. It usually settles all arguments."

"I'm sorry I asked," said Levy.

"Why?"

"You mentioned Shakespeare and I react to that, right now, with nausea."

"To Shakespeare?" Avalon gazed down at his guest with lofty disapproval.

"You bet. I've been living with him for two months, reading him backward and forward till one more 'Why, marry' or 'fretful porpentine' and I'll throw up."

"Really? Well, wait. . . . Henry, is dessert coming up?"

"Directly, sir. *Coupe aux marrons.*"

"Good! . . . Simon, wait till dessert's finished and we'll carry on."

Ten minutes later, Avalon placed spoon to water glass and

tinkled the assemblage to silence. "Host's privilege," he said. "It is time for the usual inquisition, but our honored guest has let it slip that for two months past he has been studying Shakespeare with great concentration, and I think this ought to be investigated. Tom, will you do the honors?"

Trumbull said indignantly, "Shakespeare? Who the hell wants to talk about Shakespeare?" His disposition had not been improved by the loss of five dollars and by the look of unearthly virtue upon Rubin's face.

"Host's privilege," said Avalon firmly.

"Humph. All right. Mr. Levy, as a science writer, what is your connection with Shakespeare?"

"None, as a science writer." He spoke with a distinct Brooklyn accent. "It's just that I'm after three thousand dollars."

"In Shakespeare?"

"Somewhere in Shakespeare. Can't say I've had any luck, though."

"You speak in riddles, Levy. What do you mean three thousand dollars somewhere in Shakespeare that you can't find?"

"Oh, well, it's a complicated story."

"Well, *tell* it. That's what we're here for. It's a long-standing rule that nothing that is said or done in this room is ever repeated outside under any circumstances, so speak freely. If you get boring, we'll stop you. Don't worry about that."

Levy spread out his arms. "All right, but let me finish my tea."

"Go ahead, Henry wrill bring you another pot, since you aren't civilized enough to drink coffee. . . . Henry!"

"Yes, sir," murmured Henry.

"Don't start till he comes back," said Trumbull. "We don't want him to miss any of this."

"The waiter?"

"He's one of us. Best man here."

Henry arrived with a new pot of tea and Levy said, "It's a question of a legacy, sort of. It's not one of those things where the family homestead is at stake, or millions in jewels, or anything like that. It's just three thousand dollars which I don't really need, but which would be nice to have."

"A legacy from whom?" asked Drake.

"From my wife's grandfather. He died two months ago at the age of seventy-six. He'd been living with us for five years. A little troublesome, but he was a nice old guy and, being on my wife's side of the family, she took care of most of it. He was sort of grateful to us for taking him in. There were no other descendants and it was either us or a hotel for old people."

"Get to the legacy," said Trumbull, showing some signs of impatience.

"Grandpa wasn't rich but he had a few thousand. When he first came to us, he told us that he had bought three thousand dollars' worth of negotiable bonds and would give them to us when he died."

"Why when he died?" asked Rubin.

"I suppose the old guy worried about our getting tired of him. He held out the three thousand to us as a reward for good behavior. If he was still with us when he was dying, he would give the bonds to us, and if we kicked him out, he wouldn't. I guess that was what was in his mind."

Levy went on, "He hid them in various places. Old guys can be funny. He'd change the hiding place now and then whenever he began to fear we might find them. Of course, we usually did find them before long, but we'd never let on and we'd never touch them. Except once! He put them in the clothes hamper and we had to give them back to him and ask him to put them elsewhere, or sooner or later they would get into the washing machine.

"That was about the time he had a small stroke—no connection, I'm sure—and after that he was a little harder to handle. He grew morose and didn't talk much. He had difficulties in using his right leg and it gave him a feeling of mortality. After that, he must have hidden the bonds more efficiently, for we lost track of them, though we didn't attach much importance to that. We assumed he would tell us when he was ready.

"Then two months ago, little Julia, that's my younger daughter, came running to us to tell us that Grandpa was lying on the couch and looking funny. We ran to the living room, and it was obvious that he had had another stroke. We called the doctor, but it was clear that his right side was gone entirely. He couldn't speak. He could move his lips and make sounds, but they came to no words.

"He kept moving his left arm and trying to speak and I said, 'Grandpa, are you trying to tell me something?' He could just about tremor his head into a small nod. 'About what?' I asked, but I knew he couldn't tell me, so I said, 'About the bonds?' Again a small nod. 'You want us to have them?' Again a nod and his hand began to move as though he were trying to point.

"I said, 'Where are they?' His left hand trembled and continued to point. I couldn't help but say, 'What are you pointing at, Grandpa?' but he couldn't tell me. His finger just kept pointing in an anxious, quivering way, and his face seemed in agony as he tried to talk and failed. I was sorry for him. He wanted to give the bonds to us, to reward us, and he was dying without being able to.

"My wife, Caroline, was crying and saying, 'Leave him alone, Simon,' but I *couldn't* leave him alone. I couldn't let him die in despair. I said, 'We'll have to move the couch toward whatever it is he's pointing to.' Caroline didn't want to, but the old man was nodding his head.

"Caroline got at one end of the couch and I at the other and we moved it, little by little, trying not to jar him. He was no lightweight, either. His finger kept pointing, always pointing. He turned his head in the direction in which we were moving him, making moaning sounds as though to indicate whether we were moving him in the right direction or not. I would say, 'More to the right, Grandpa?' 'More to the left?' And sometimes he would nod.

"Finally, we got him up against the line of bookcases, and slowly his head turned. I wanted to turn it for him, but I was afraid to harm him. He managed to get it round and stared at the books for a long time. Then his finger moved along the line of books till it pointed toward one particular book. It was a copy of *The Complete Works of Shakespeare*, the Kittredge edition.

"I said, 'Shakespeare, Grandpa?' He didn't answer, he didn't nod, but his face relaxed and he stopped trying to speak. I suppose he didn't hear me. Something like a half-smile pulled at the left side of his mouth and he died. The doctor came, the body was taken away, we made arrangements for the funeral. It wasn't till after the funeral that we went back to the Shakespeare. We figured it would wait for us and it didn't seem right to grab for it before we took care of the old man.

"I assumed there would be something in the Shakespeare volume to tell us where the bonds were, and that's when the first shock came. We turned through every page, one by one, and there was nothing there. Not a scrap of paper. Not a word."

Gonzalo said, "What about the binding? You know, in between the stuff that glues the pages and the backstrip?"

"Nothing there."

"Maybe someone took it?"

"How? The only ones who knew were myself and Caroline. It isn't as though there were any robbery. Eventually, we thought there was a clue somewhere in the book, in the written material, in the plays themselves, you know. That was Caroline's idea. In the last two months, I've read every word of Shakespeare's plays; every word of his sonnets and miscellaneous poems—twice over. I've gotten nowhere."

"The hell with Shakespeare," said Trumbull querulously. "Forget the clue. He had to leave them somewhere in the house."

"Why do you suppose that?" said Levy. "He might have put it in a bank vault for all we know. He got around even after his first stroke. After we found the bonds in the clothes hamper, he might have thought the house wasn't safe."

"All right, but he still might have put them in the house somewhere. Why not just search?"

"We did. Or at least Caroline did. That was how we divided the labor. She searched the house, which is a big, rambling one—one reason we could take in Grandpa—and I searched Shakespeare, and we both came out with nothing."

Avalon untwisted a thoughtful frown and said, "See here, there's no reason we can't be logical about this. I assume, Simon, that your grandfather was born in Europe."

"Yes. He came to America as a teen-ager, just as World War I was starting. He got out just in time."

"He didn't have much of a formal education, I suppose."

"None at all," said Levy. "He went to work in a tailor shop, eventually got his own establishment, and stayed a tailor till he retired. No education at all, except for the usual religious education Jews gave each other in Tsarist Russia."

"Well, then," said Avalon, "how do you expect him to indicate clues in Shakespeare's plays? He wouldn't know anything about them."

Levy frowned and leaned back in his chair. He hadn't touched the small brandy glass Henry had put in front of him some time before. Now he picked it up, twirled the stem gently in his fingers, and put it down again.

"You're quite wrong, Jeff," he said, a little distantly. "He may have been uneducated but he was quite intelligent and quite well-read. He knew the Bible by heart, and he'd read *War and Peace* as a teen-ager. He read Shakespeare, too. Listen, we once went to see a production of *Hamlet* in the park and he got more out of it than I did."

Rubin suddenly broke in energetically, "I have no intention of ever seeing *Hamlet* again till they get a Hamlet who looks as Hamlet is supposed to look. Fat!"

"Fat!" said Trumbull indignantly.

"Yes, fat. The Queen says of Hamlet in the last scene, 'He's fat and scant of breath.' If Shakespeare says Hamlet is fat—"

"That's his mother talking, not Shakespeare. It's the typical motherly oversolicitousness of a not-bright woman—"

Avalon banged the table. "Not now, gentlemen!"

He turned to Levy. "In what language did your grandfather read the Bible?"

"In Hebrew, of course," Levy said coldly.

"And *War and Peace?*"

"In Russian. But Shakespeare, if you don't mind, he read in English."

"Which is not his native tongue. I imagine he spoke with an accent."

Levy's coolness had descended into the frigid. "What are you getting at, Jeff?"

Avalon harumphed. "I'm not being anti-Semitic. I'm just pointing out the obvious fact that if your wife's grandfather was not at home with the language, there was a limit to how subtly he could use Shakespeare as a reference. He's not likely to use the phrase 'and there the antick sits' from *Richard II* because, however well-read he is, he isn't likely to know what an antick is.''

"What is it?" asked Gonzalo.

"Never mind," said Avalon impatiently. "If your grandfather used Shakespeare, it would have to be some perfectly obvious reference.''

"What was your father's favorite play?" asked Trumbull.

"He liked *Hamlet* of course. I know he didn't like the comedies," said Levy, "because he felt the humor undignified, and the histories meant nothing to him. Wait, he liked *Othello.*''

"All right," said Avalon. "We ought to concentrate on *Hamlet* and *Othello.*''

"I read them," said Levy. "You don't think I left them out, do you?''

"And it would have to be some well-known passage," Avalon went on, paying no attention. "No one would think that just pointing to Shakespeare would be a useful hint if it were some obscure line that were intended.''

"The only reason he just pointed," said Levy, "was that he couldn't talk. It *might* have been something very obscure which he would have explained if he could have talked.''

"If he could have talked," said Drake reasonably, "he wouldn't have had to explain anything. He would just have told you where the bonds were.''

"Exactly," said Avalon. "A good point, Jim. You said, Simon, that after the old man pointed to Shakespeare, his face relaxed and he stopped trying to speak. He felt that he had given you all you needed to know.''

"Well, he didn't," said Levy morosely.

"Let's reason it out, then," said Avalon.

"Do we have to?" said Drake. "Why not ask Henry now? . . . Henry, which verse in Shakespeare would suit our purpose?''

Henry, who was noiselessly taking up the dessert dishes, said, "I have an average knowledge of the plays of Shakespeare, sir, but I must admit that no appropriate verse occurs to me.''

Drake looked disappointed, but Avalon said, "Come on, Jim. Henry has done very well on past occasions but there's no need to feel that we are helpless without him. I flatter myself I know Shakespeare pretty well."

"I'm no novice, either," said Rubin.

"Then between the two of us, let's solve this. Suppose we consider *Hamlet* first. If it's *Hamlet*, then it has to be one of the soliloquies, because they're the best-known portions of the play."

"In fact," said Rubin, "the line 'To be or not to be, that is the question' is the best-known line of Shakespeare. It epitomizes him as the 'Quartet' from *Rigoletto* typifies opera."

"I agree," said Avalon, "and that soliloquy talks of dying, and the old man was dying. 'To die: to sleep; No more; and by a sleep to say we end the heart-ache and the thousand natural shocks that flesh is—' "

"Yes, but what good does that do?" said Levy impatiently. "Where does it get us?"

Avalon, who always recited Shakespeare in what he insisted was Shakespearean pronunciation (which sounded remarkably like an Irish brogue), said, "Well, I'm not sure."

Gonzalo said suddenly, "Is it in *Hamlet* where Shakespeare says, 'The play's the thing'?"

"Yes," said Avalon. " 'The play's the thing wherein I'll catch the conscience of the king.' "

"Well," said Gonzalo, "if the old man was pointing out a book of plays, maybe that's the line. Do you have a picture of a king, or a carving, or a deck of cards, maybe."

Levy shrugged. "That doesn't bring anything to mind."

"What about *Othello*?" asked Rubin. "Listen. The best-known part of the play is Iago's speech on reputation, 'Good name in man and woman, dear any lord . . .' "

"So?" said Avalon.

"And the most famous line in it, and one which the old man was sure to know because it's the one everyone knows, even Mario, is 'Who steals my purse steals trash; 'tis something, nothing; 'twas mine, 'tis his . . .' and so on."

"So?" said Avalon again.

"So it sounds as though it applies to the legacy. ''Twas

mine, 'tis his,' and it also sounds as though the legacy were gone. 'Who steals my purse steals trash.' ''

''What do you mean, 'gone'?'' said Levy.

''After you found the bonds in the clothes hamper, you lost track of them, you said. Maybe the old man took them off somewhere to be safe and doesn't remember where. Or maybe he mislaid them or gave them away or lost them to some confidence scheme. Whatever it was, he could no longer explain it to you without speech. So to die in peace, he pointed to the works of Shakespeare. You would remember the best-known line of his favorite play, which tells you that his purse is only trash—and that is why you have found nothing.''

''I don't believe that,'' said Levy. ''I asked him if he wanted us to have the bonds and he nodded.''

''All he could do was nod, and he *did* want you to have them, but that was impossible. . . . Do you agree with me, Henry?''

Henry, who had completed his tasks and was quietly listening, said, ''I'm afraid I don't, Mr. Rubin.''

''I don't, either,'' said Levy.

But Gonzalo was snapping his fingers. ''Wait, wait. Doesn't Shakespeare say anything about bonds?''

''Not in his time,'' said Drake, smiling.

''I'm sure of it,'' said Gonzalo. ''Something about bonds being nominated.''

Avalon said, ''Ah! You mean 'Is it so nominated in the bond?' The bond is a legal contract, and the question was whether something was a requirement of the contract.''

Drake said, ''Wait a bit. Didn't that bond involve a sum of three thousand ducats?''

''By Heaven, so it did,'' said Avalon.

Gonzalo's grin split his head from ear to ear. ''I think I've got something there: bonds involving three thousand units of money. That's the play to look into.''

Henry interrupted softly. ''I scarcely think so, gentlemen. The play in question is *The Merchant of Venice* and the person asking whether something was nominated in the bond was the Jew, Shylock, intent on a cruel revenge. Surely the old man would not enjoy this play.''

Levy said, ''That's right. Shylock was a dirty word to him—and not so clean to me, either.''

Rubin said, "What about the passage that goes: 'Hath not a Jew eyes? hath not a Jew hands, organs, dimensions, senses, affections, passions . . .?"

"It wouldn't appeal to my grandfather," said Levy. "It pleads the obvious and cries out for an equality my grandfather would not, in his heart, be willing to grant, since I'm sure he felt superior in that he was a member of God's uniquely chosen."

Gonzalo looked disappointed. "It seems we're not getting anywhere."

Levy said, "No, I don't think we are. I went through the entire book. I read all the speeches carefully; all the passages you mentioned. None of them meant anything to me."

Avalon said, "Granted they don't, but you may be missing something subtle—"

"Come on, Jeff; you're the one who said it couldn't be subtle. My grandfather was thinking of something tailored for the mind of myself and my wife. It was something we would get, and probably get at once; and we didn't."

Drake said, "Maybe you're right. Maybe some in-joke is involved."

"I've just said that."

"Then why don't you try it backward? Can you think of something, some gag, some phrase? . . . Is there some expression he used every time?"

"Yes. When he disapproved of someone he would say, 'Eighteen black years on him.' "

"What kind of an expression is that?" asked Trumbull.

"In Yiddish it's common enough," said Levy. "Another one was 'It will help him like a dead man cups.'"

"What does that mean?" asked Gonzalo.

"It refers to cupping. You place a lighted piece of paper in a small round glass cup and then put the open edge against the skin. The paper goes out but leaves a partial vacuum in the cup and circulation is sucked into the superficial layers. Naturally, cupping can't improve the circulation of a corpse."

"All right," said Drake, "is there anything about eighteen black years, or about cupping dead men, that reminds you of something in Shakespeare?"

There was a painful silence and finally Avalon said, "I can't think of anything."

"And even if you did," said Levy, "what good would it do? What would it mean? Listen, I've been at this for two months. You're not going to solve it for me in two hours."

Drake turned to Henry again and said, "Why are you just standing there, Henry? Can't you help us?"

"I'm sorry, Dr. Drake, but I now believe that the whole question of Shakespeare is a false lead."

"No," said Levy. "You can't say that. The old man pointed to *The Collected Works* without any question. His fingertip was within an inch of it. It couldn't have been any other book."

Drake said suddenly, "Say, Levy, you're not diddling us, are you? You're not telling us a pack of lies to make jackasses out of us?"

"What?" said Levy in amazement.

"Nothing, nothing," said Avalon hastily. "He's just thinking of another occasion. Shut up, Jim."

"Listen," said Levy. "I'm telling you exactly what happened. He was pointing exactly at Shakespeare."

There was a short silence and then Henry sighed and said, "In mystery stories—"

Rubin broke in with a "Hear! Hear!"

"In mystery stories," Henry repeated, "the dying hint is a common device, but I have never been able to take it seriously. A dying man, anxious to give last-minute information, is always pictured as presenting the most complex hints. His dying brain, with two minutes' grace, works out a pattern that would puzzle a healthy brain with hours to think. In this particular case, we have an old man dying of a paralyzing stroke who is supposed to have quickly invented a clue that a group of intelligent men have failed to work out; and with one of them having worked at it for two months. I can only conclude there is no such clue."

"Then why should he have pointed to Shakespeare, Henry?" asked Levy. "Was it all just the vague delusions of a dying man?"

"If your story is correct," said Henry, "then I think he was indeed trying to do something. He cannot, however, have been inventing a clue. He was doing the only thing his dying mind could manage. He was pointing to the bonds.''

"I beg your pardon," said Levy huffily. "I was there. He was pointing to Shakespeare."

Henry shook his head. He said, "Mr. Levy, would you point to Fifth Avenue?"

Levy thought a while, obviously orienting himself, and then pointed.

"Are you pointing to Fifth Avenue?" asked Henry.

"Well, the restaurant's entrance is on Fifth Avenue, so I'm pointing to it."

"It seems to me, sir," said Henry, "that you are pointing to a picture of the Arch of Titus on the western wall of this room."

"Well, I am, but Fifth Avenue is beyond it."

"Exactly, sir. So I only know that you are pointing to Fifth Avenue because you tell me so. You might be pointing to the picture or to some point in the air before the picture, or to the Hudson River, or to Chicago, or to the planet Jupiter. If you point, and nothing more, giving no hint, verbal or otherwise, as to what you're pointing at, you are only indicating a direction and nothing more.''

Levy rubbed his chin. "You mean my grandfather was only indicating a direction?"

"It must be so. He didn't *say* he was pointing to Shakespeare. He merely pointed."

"All right, then, what was he pointing at? The—the—" He closed his eyes and fingered his mustache gently, as he oriented the room in his house. "The Verrazano Bridge?"

"Probably not, sir," said Henry. "He was pointing in the direction of *The Collected Works*. His finger was an inch from it, you said, so it is doubtful that he could be pointing at anything in front of it. What was behind the book, Mr. Levy?"

"The bookcase. The wood of the bookcase. And when you took the book out, there was nothing behind it. There was nothing pushed up against the wood, if that's what you have in mind. We would have seen it at once if anything at all had been there."

"And behind the bookcase, sir?"

"The wall."

"And between the bookcase and the wall, sir?"

Now Levy fell silent. He thought a while, and no one interrupted those thoughts. He said, "Is there a phone I can use, Henry?"

"I'll bring you one, sir."

The phone was placed in front of Levy and plugged in. Levy dialed a number.

"Hello, Julia? What are you doing up so late? . . . Never mind the TV and get to bed. But first call Mamma, dear. . . . Hello, Caroline, it's Simon. . . . Yes, I'm having a good time, but listen, Caroline, listen. You know the bookcase with the Shakespeare in it? . . . Yes, *that* Shakespeare. Of course. Move it away from the wall. . . . The bookcase. . . . Look, you can take the books out of it, can't you? Take them all out, if you have to, and dump them on the floor. . . . No, no, just move the end of the bookcase near the door a few inches; just enough to look behind and tell me if you see anything. . . . Look about where the Shakespeare book would be. . . . I'll wait, yes."

They were all frozen in attitudes. Levy was distinctly pale. Some five minutes passed. Then, "Caroline? . . . Okay, take it easy. Did you move . . . ? Okay, okay, I'll be home soon."

He hung up and said, "If that doesn't beat everything. The old guy had them taped to the back of the bookcase. He must have moved that thing sometime when we were out. It's a wonder he didn't have a stroke then and there."

"You did it again, Henry," said Gonzalo.

Levy said, "Agent's fee is three hundred dollars, Henry."

Henry said, "I am well paid by the club, and the banquets are my pleasure, sir. There is no need for more."

Levy reddened slightly and changed the subject. "But how did you get the trick of it? When the rest of us—"

"It was not difficult," said Henry. "The rest of you happened to track down all the wrong paths, and I simply suggested what was left."

3

Out of Sight

The Black Widowers, as a club, is modeled after a real-life club of which I am a member. What's more, each of the Black Widowers (except Henry, who is an invention out of thin air) is modeled—as far as physical appearance is concerned—on members of the real-life club. (They all know this and don't mind, so I'm putting myself in no danger in saying this.)

I am often asked which of the Black Widowers is me, and the answer is "None of them." However, I sometimes make my appearance as a guest or as a character in the story within the story. In this tale, for instance, I am the character "Smith." He is not described in very complimentary fashion, but then I never describe myself in very complimentary fashion. More to the point, Mrs. Smith is modeled on my dear wife, Janet, and the incident with the hot chocolate described in the story happened in real life in that precise fashion.

Because Janet and I are both in it, I can't help but have a warm spot in my heart for this story.

The monthly banquet of the Black Widowers had reached the point where little was left of the mixed grill save for an occasional sausage and a markedly untouched piece of liver on the plate of Emmanuel Rubin—and it was then that voices rose in Homeric combat.

Rubin, undoubtedly infuriated by the presence of liver at all, was saying, even more flatly than was usual for him, "Poetry is *sound*. You don't *look* at poetry. I don't care whether a culture emphasizes rhyme, alliteration, repetition, balance, or cadence, it all comes down to sound."

Roger Halsted never raised his voice, but one could always tell the state of his emotions by the color of his high forehead. Right now, it was a deep pink, the color extending past the line that had once marked hair. He said, "What's the use of making generalizations, Manny? No generalization can hold generally without an airtight system of axiomatics to begin with. Literature—"

"If you're going to tell me about figurative verse," said Rubin hotly, "save your breath. That's Victorian nonsense."

"What's figurative verse?" asked Mario Gonzalo lazily. "Is he making that up, Jeff?" He added a touch to the tousled hair in his careful caricature of the banquet guest, Waldemar Long, who, since the dinner had begun, had eaten in a somber silence, but was obviously following every word.

"No," said Geoffrey Avalon judiciously, "though I wouldn't put it past Manny to make something up if that were the only way he could win an argument. Figurative verse is verse in which the words or lines are arranged typographically in such a way as to produce a visual image that reinforces the sense. 'The Mouse's Tail' in *Alice in Wonderland* is the best-known example."

Halsted's soft voice was unequal to the free-for-all and he methodically beat his spoon against the water goblet till the decibels had simmered down.

He said, "Let's be reasonable. The subject under discussion is not poetry in general, but the limerick as a verse form. My point is this—I'll repeat it, Manny—that the worth of a limerick is not dictated by its subject matter. It's a mistake to think that a limerick has to be dirty to be good. It's easier—"

James Drake stubbed out his cigarette, twitched his small grizzled mustache, and said in his hoarse voice, "Why do you call a dirty limerick dirty? The Supreme Court will get you."

Halsted said, "Because it's a two-syllable word with a meaning you all understand. What do you want me to say? Sexual-excretory-blasphemous-and-miscellaneous-generally-irreverent?"

Avalon said, "Go on, Roger. Go on. Make your point and don't let them needle you." And, from under his luxuriant eyebrows, he frowned austerely at the table generally. "Let him talk."

"Why?" said Rubin. "He has nothing to . . . Okay, Jeff. Talk, Roger."

"Thank you all," said Halsted, in the wounded tone of one who has finally succeeded in having his wrongs recognized. "The worth of a limerick rests in the unpredictability of the last line and in the cleverness of the final rhyme. In fact, irreverent content may seem to have value in itself and re-quire less cleverness—and produce a less worthwhile limer-ick, as limerick. Now it is possible to have the rhyme masked by the orthographical conventions."

"What?" said Gonzalo.

"Spelling," said Avalon.

"And then," said Halsted, "in seeing the spelling and having that instant of delay in getting the sound, you intensify the enjoyment. But under those conditions you have to *see* the limerick. If you just recite it, the excellence is lost."

"Suppose you give us an example," said Drake.

"I know what he means," said Rubin loudly. "He's going to rhyme M.A. and C.D.—Master of Arts and Caster of Darts."

"That's an example that's been used," admitted Halsted, "but it's extreme. It takes too long to catch on and amuse-ment is drowned in irritation. As it happens, I've made up a limerick while we were having the argument—"

And now, for the first time, Thomas Trumbull entered this part of the discussion. His tanned and wrinkled face twisted into a dark scowl and he said, "The hell you did. You made it up yesterday and you engineered this whole silly nonsense so you could recite it. If it's one of your *Iliad* things, I'll personally kick you out of here."

"It's not the *Iliad*," said Halsted. "I haven't been working on that recently. It's no use my reciting this one, of course. I'll write it down and pass it around."

He wrote in dark block letters on an unused napkin:

> YOU CAN'T CALL THE BRITISH QUEEN MS.
> TAIN'T AS NICE AS ELIZABETH IS.
> BUT I THINK THAT THE QUEEN
> WOULD BE EVEN LESS KEEN
> TO HAVE HERSELF MENTIONED AS LS

Gonzalo laughed aloud when it came to him. He said, "Sure, if you know that MS is pronounced Miz, then you pronounce LS as Liz."

"To me," said Drake scornfully, "LS would have to stand for 'lanuscript' if it's going to rhyme with MS."

Avalon pursed his lips and shook his head. "Using TAIN'T is a flaw. You ought to lose a syllable some other way. And to be perfectly consistent, shouldn't the rhyme word IS be spelled simply S?"

Halsted nodded eagerly. "You're quite right, and I thought of doing that, but it wouldn't be transparent enough and the reader wouldn't get it fast enough to laugh. Secondly, it would be the cleverest part of the limerick and would make the LS anticlimactic."

"Do you really have to waste all that fancy reasoning on a piece of crap like this?" asked Trumbull.

"I think I've made my point," said Halsted. "The humor can be visual."

Trumbull said, "Well, then, drop the subject. Since I'm host this session, that's an order. . . . Henry, where's the damned dessert?"

"It's here, sir," said Henry softly. Unmoved by Trumbull's tone, he deftly cleared the table and dealt out the blueberry shortcake.

The coffee had already been poured and Trumbull's guest said in a low voice, "May I have tea, please?"

The guest had a long upper lip and an equally long chin. The hair on his head was shaggy but there was none on his face and he had walked with a somewhat bearlike stoop.

When he was first introduced, only Rubin had registered any recognition.

He had said, "Aren't you with NASA?"

Waldemar Long had answered with a startled "Yes" as though he had been disturbed out of a half-resentful resignation to anonymity. He had then frowned. He was frowning now again as Henry poured the tea and melted unobtrusively into the background.

Trumbull said, "I think the time has come for our guest to enter the discussion and perhaps add some portion of sense to what has been an unusually foolish evening."

"No, that's all right, Tom," said Long. "I don't mind frivolity." He had a deep and rather beautiful voice that had a definite note of sadness in it. He went on, "I have no aptitude for badinage myself, but I enjoy listening to it."

Halsted, still brooding over the matter of the limericks, said, with sudden forcefulness, "I suggest Manny *not* be the grill master on this occasion."

"No?" said Rubin, his sparse beard lifting belligerently.

"No. I put it to you, Toni. If Manny questions our guest, he will surely bring up the space program since there's a NASA connection. Then we will go through the same darned argument we've had a hundred times. I'm sick of the whole subject of space and whether we ought to be on the moon."

"Not half as sick as I am," said Long, rather unexpectedly, "I'd just as soon not discuss any aspect of space exploration."

The heavy flatness of the remark seemed to dampen spirits all around. Even Halsted seemed momentarily at a loss for any other subject to introduce to someone connected with NASA.

Then Rubin stirred in his seat and said, "I take it, Dr. Long, that this is a recently developed attitude of yours."

Long's head turned suddenly toward Rubin. His eyes narrowed. "Why do you say that, Mr. Rubin?"

Rubin's small face came as close to a simper as it ever did. "Elementary, my dear Dr. Long. You were on the cruise that went down to see the Apollo shot last winter. I'd been invited as a literary representative of the intellectual community, but I couldn't go. However, I got the promotional literature and noticed you were along. You were going to lecture on some aspect of the space program, I forget which, and that was voluntary. So your disenchantment with the subject must have arisen in the six months since the cruise.''

Long nodded his head very slightly a number of times and said, ''I seem to be more heard of in that connection than in any other in my life. The damned cruise has made me famous, too.''

''I'll go farther,'' said Rubin enthusiastically, ''and suggest that something happened on the cruise that disenchanted you with space exploration, maybe to the point where you're thinking of leaving NASA and going into some other field of work altogether.''

Long's stare was fixed now. He pointed a finger at Rubin, a long finger that showed no signs of tremor, and said, ''Don't play games.'' Then, with a controlled anger, he rose from his chair and said, ''I'm sorry, Tom. Thanks for the meal, but I'll go now.''

Everyone rose at once, speaking simultaneously; all but Rubin, who remained sitting with a look of stunned astonishment on his face.

Trumbull's voice rose above the rest. ''Now wait a while, Waldemar. God damn it, will all of you sit down? Waldemar, you too. What's the excitement about? Rubin, what *is* all this?''

Rubin looked down at his empty coffeecup and lifted it as though he wished there were coffee in it so that he could delay matters by taking a sip. ''I was just demonstrating a chain of logic. After all, I write mysteries. I seem to have touched a nerve.'' Then, gratefully, he said, ''Thanks, Henry,'' as the cup before him sparkled black to the brim.

''What chain of logic?'' demanded Trumbull.

''Okay, here it is. Dr. Long said, 'The damned cruise has made me famous, too.' He said 'too' and emphasized the word. That means it did something else for him and since we were talking about his distaste for the whole subject of space exploration, I deduced that the something else it had done was to supply him with that distaste. From his bearing I guessed it was sharp enough to make him want to quit his job. That's all there is to it.''

Long nodded his head again, in precisely the same slight and rapid way as before, and then settled back in his seat. "All right. I'm sorry, Mr. Rubin. I jumped too soon. The fact is I *will* be leaving NASA. To all intents and purposes, I *have* left it—and at the point of a shoe. That's all. . . . We'll change the subject. Tom, you said coming here would get me out of my dumps, but it hasn't worked that way. Rather, my mood has infected you all and I've cast a damper on the party. Forgive me, all of you."

Avalon put a finger to his neat, graying mustache and stroked it gently. He said, "Actually, sir, you have supplied us with something we all like above all things—the opportunity to exert our curiosity. May we question you on this matter?"

"It's not something I'm free to talk about," said Long, guardedly.

Trumbull said, "You can if you want to, Waldemar. You needn't mention sensitive details, but as far as anything else is concerned, everything said in this room is confidential. And, as I always add when I find it necessary to make that statement, the confidentiality includes our esteemed friend Henry."

Henry, who was standing at the sideboard, smiled briefly.

Long hesitated. Then he said, "Actually, your curiosity is easily satisfied and I suspect that Mr. Rubin, at least, with his aptitude for guessing, has already deduced the details. I'm suspected of having been indiscreet, either deliberately or carelessly, and, either way, I may find myself unofficially, but very effectively, blocked off from any future position in my field of competence."

"You mean you'll be blackballed?" said Drake.

"That's a word," said Long, "that's never used. But that's what it will amount to."

"I take it," said Drake, "you weren't indiscreet."

"On the contrary, I was." Long shook his head. "I haven't denied that. The trouble is they think the story is worse than I admit."

There was another pause and then Avalon, speaking in his most impressively austere tone, said, "Well, sir, *what* story?

Is there anything you can tell us about it or must you leave it at no more than what you have already said?''

Long passed a hand over his face, then pushed his chair away from the table so that he could lean his head back against the wall.

He said, ''It's so damned undramatic. I was on this cruise, as Mr. Rubin told you. I was going to give a talk on certain space projects, rather far-out ones, and planned on going into detail on exactly what was being done in certain fascinating directions. I can't give you *those* details. I found that out the hard way. Some of the stuff had been classified, but I had been told I could talk about it. Then, on the day before I was to give my lecture, I got a radiophone call saying it was all off. There was to be no declassification.

''I was furious. There's no use denying I have a temper and I also have very little gift for spontaneous lecturing. I had carefully written out the lecture and I had intended to read it. I know that's not a good way of giving a talk, but it's the best I can do. Now I had nothing left to give to a group of people who had paid considerable money to listen to me. It was a damned embarrassing position.''

''What did you do?'' asked Avalon.

Long shook his head. ''I held a rather pathetic question-and-answer session the next day. It didn't go over at all well. It was worse than just not having a talk. By that time, you see, I knew I was in considerable trouble.''

''In what way, sir?'' said Avalon.

''If you want the fun story,'' said Long, ''here it is. I'm not exactly talkative at meals, as you may perhaps have noticed, but when I went in to dinner after getting the call, I suppose I put on a passable imitation of a corpse that had died with an angry look on its face. The rest tried to draw me into the conversation, if only, I suppose, to keep me from poisoning the atmosphere. Finally one of them said, 'Well, Dr. Long, what will you be talking about tomorrow?' And I blew up and said, 'Nothing! Nothing at all! I've got the paper all written out and it's sitting there on the desk in my cabin and I can't give it because I just found out the material is still classified.'''

''And then the paper was stolen?'' said Gonzalo excitedly.

"No. Why steal anything these days? It was photographed."

"Are you sure?"

"I was sure at the time. When I got back to my cabin after dinner the door was not locked and the papers had been moved. Since then, it's become certain. We have proof that the information has leaked."

There was a rather depressed silence at that. Then Trumbull said, "Who could have done it? Who heard you?"

"Everyone at the table," said Long despondently.

Rubin said, "You have a strong voice, Dr. Long, and if you were as angry as I think you were, you spoke forcefully. Probably a number of the people at adjoining tables heard you."

"No," said Long, shaking his head. "I spoke through clenched teeth, not loudly. Besides, you don't realize what the cruise was like. The cruise was badly undersubscribed, you see—poor promotion, poor management. The ship was carrying only forty percent capacity and the shipping company is supposed to have lost a packet."

"In that case," said Avalon, "it must have been a dreary experience apart from your misadventure."

"On the contrary, up to that point it was very pleasant for me, and it continued to be very pleasant for all the rest, I imagine. The crew nearly outnumbered the passengers and the service was excellent. All the facilities were available without crowding. They scattered us through the dining room and gave us privacy. There were seven of us at our dining table. Lucky seven, someone said at the beginning." For a moment Long's look of grimness deepened. "None of the tables near us were occupied. I'm quite certain that nothing any of us said was heard anywhere but at our own table."

"Then there are seven suspects," said Gonzalo thoughtfully.

"Six, since you needn't count me," said Long. "I knew where the paper was and what it was. I didn't have to hear myself to know that."

"You're under suspicion, too. Or you implied that," said Gonzalo.

"Not to myself," said Long.

Trumbull said peevishly, "I wish you had come to me with

this, Waldemar. I've been worrying over your obvious green-and-yellow attitude for months.''

"What would you have done if I had told you?"

Trumbull considered. "Damn it, I'd have brought you here. . . . All right. Tell us about the six at the table. Who were they?"

"One was the ship's doctor; a good-looking Dutchman in an impressive uniform."

Rubin said, "He would be. The ship was one of the Holland-American liners, wasn't it?"

"Yes. The officers were Dutch and the crew—the waiters, stewards, and so on—were mostly Indonesian. They'd all had three-month cram courses in English, but we communicated mostly in sign language. I don't complain, though. They were pleasant and hard-working—and all the more efficient since there was considerably less than the ordinary complement of passengers."

"Any reason to suspect the Doctor?" asked Drake.

Long nodded. "I suspected them all. The Doctor was a silent man; he and I were the two silent ones. The other five made a continuous uproar, much as you do here at this table. He and I listened. What I've brooded about in connection with him was that it was he who asked me about my talk. Asking a personal question like that was uncharacteristic."

"He may have been worried about you medically," said Halsted. "He may have been trying to draw you out."

"Maybe," said Long indifferently. "I remember every detail of that dinner; I've gone over and over it in my mind. It was an ethnic dinner, so everyone was supplied with little Dutch hats made out of paper and special Indonesian dishes were supplied. I wore the hat but I hate curried food and the Doctor asked about my speech just as a small dish of curried lamb was put before me as an hors d'oeuvre. Between fuming over official stupidity and sickening over the smell of curry, I just burst out. If it hadn't been for the curry, perhaps—

"Anyway, after dinner I discovered that someone had been in my cabin. The contents of the paper weren't so important, classification or not, but what was important was that some-one had taken action so quickly. Someone on the ship was part of a spy network and that was more important than the actual coup. Even if the present item were not important, the next might be. It was important to report the matter and, as a loyal citizen, I did.''

Rubin said, ''Isn't the Doctor the logical suspect? He asked the question and he would be listening to the answer. The others might not have. As an officer, he would be used to the ship, know how to get to your cabin quickly, perhaps have a duplicate key ready. Did he have an opportunity to get to your cabin before you did?''

''Yes, he did,'' said Long. ''I thought of all that. The trouble is this. Everyone at the table heard me, because all the rest talked about the system of classification for a while. I kept quiet myself but I remember the matter of the Pentagon Papers came up. And everyone knew where my cabin was because I had given a small party in it for the table the day before. And those locks are easy to open for anyone with a little skill at it—though it was a mistake not to close it again on leaving, but whoever it was had to be in a hurry. And, as it happened, everyone at the table had a chance to get to the cabin during the course of the meal.''

''Who were the others, then?'' asked Halsted.

''Two married couples and a single woman. The single woman—call her Miss Robinson—was pretty, a little on the plump side, had a pleasant sense of humor, but had the bad habit of smoking during the meal. I rather think she liked the Doctor. She sat between us—we always had the same seats.''

''When did she have a chance to reach your cabin?'' asked Halsted.

''She left shortly after I made my remark. I was brooding too deeply to be aware of it at the time but of course I remembered it afterward. She came back before the fuss over the hot chocolate came up because I remember her trying to help.''

''Where did she say she went?''

''Nobody asked her at the time. She was asked afterward and she said she had gone to her cabin to go to the bathroom. Maybe she did. But her cabin was reasonably near mine.''

''No one saw her at all?''

''No one would. Everyone was in the dining room and to the Indonesians all Americans look alike.''

Avalon said, "What's the fuss over the hot chocolate you referred to?"

Long said, "That's where one of the married couples comes in. Call them the Smiths and the other one the Joneses, or the other way around. It doesn't matter. Mr. Smith was the raucous type. He reminded me, in fact, of—"

"Oh, Lord," said Rubin. "Don't say it."

"All right, I won't. He was one of the lecturers. In fact, both Smith and Jones were. Smith talked fast, laughed easily, turned everything into a double-entendre, and seemed to enjoy it all so much he had the rest of us doing it, too. He was a very odd person. The kind of fellow you can't help but take an instant dislike to and judge to be stupid. But then, as you get used to him, you find you like him after all and that under the surface nonsense, he's extremely intelligent. The first evening, I remember, the Doctor kept staring at him as if he were a mental specimen, but by the end of the cruise, he was clearly pleased with Smith.

"Jones was much quieter. He seemed horrified, at first, by Smith's outrageous comments but eventually he was matching him, I noticed—rather, I think, to Smith's discomfiture."

Avalon said, "What were their fields?"

"Smith was a sociologist and Jones a biologist. The idea was that space exploration was to be viewed in the light of many disciplines. It was a good concept but showed serious flaws in the execution. Some of the talks, though, were excellent. There was one on Mariner 9 and the new data on Mars that was superb, but that's beside the point.

"It was Mrs. Smith who created the confusion. She was a moderately tall, thin girl. Not very good-looking by the usual standards but with an extraordinarily attractive personality. She was soft-spoken and clearly went through life automatically thinking of others. I believe everyone quickly grew to feel quite affectionate to her and Smith himself seemed devoted. The evening I shot my mouth off, she ordered hot chocolate. It came in a tall glass, very top-heavy, and, of course, as a mistaken touch of elegance, it was brought on a tray.

"Smith, as usual, was talking animatedly and waving his arms as he did so. He used all his muscles when he talked.

The ship swayed, he swayed—well, anyway, the hot chocolate went into Mrs. Smith's lap.

"She jumped up. So did everyone else. Miss Robinson moved quickly toward her to help. I noticed that and that's how I know she was back by then. Mrs. Smith waved help away and left in a hurry. Smith, looking suddenly confused and upset, tore off the paper Dutch hat he was wearing and followed. Five minutes later he was back, talking earnestly to the head steward. Then he came to the table and said that Mrs. Smith had sent him down to assure the steward that she was wearing nothing that couldn't be washed, that she hadn't been hurt, that it wasn't anyone's fault, that no one was to be blamed.

"He wanted to assure us she was all right, too. He asked if we could stay at the table till his wife came back. She was changing clothes and wanted to join us again so that none of us would feel as though anything very terrible had happened. We agreed, of course. None of us were going anywhere."

Avalon said, "And that means she had time to get to your cabin."

Long nodded. "Yes, I suppose so. She didn't seem the type but I suppose in this game you disregard surface appearances."

"And you all waited?"

"Not the Doctor. He got up and said he would get some ointment from his office in case she needed it for burns, but he came back before she did by a minute or so."

Avalon said, tapping his finger on the table slowly to lend emphasis, "And he might have been at the cabin, too, then. And Miss Robinson might, when she left before the hot-chocolate incident."

Rubin said, "Where do the Joneses come in?"

Long said, "Let me go on. When Mrs. Smith came back she denied having been burned and the Doctor had no need to give her the ointment, so we can't say if he even went to get it. He might have been bluffing."

"What if she had asked for it?" said Halsted.

"Then he might have said he couldn't find what he had been looking for but if she came with him he'd do what he could. Who knows? In any case, we all sat for a while almost as though nothing had happened and then, finally, it broke up. By that time, we were the last occupied table. Everyone left, with Mrs. Jones and myself lingering behind for a while.''

"Mrs. Jones?" asked Drake.

"I haven't told you about Mrs. Jones. Dark hair and eyes, very vivacious. Had a penchant for sharp cheeses, always taking a bit of each off the tray when it was brought round. She had a way of looking at you when you talk that had you convinced you were the only object she saw. I think Jones was rather a jealous type in his quiet way. At least, I never saw him more than two feet fom her, except this one time. He got up and said he was going to the cabin and she said she would be there soon. Then she turned to me and said, 'Can you explain why those terraced icefields on Mars are significant? I've been meaning to ask you all during dinner and didn't get a chance.'

"It had been that day that we had had the magnificent talk on Mars and I was rather flattered that she turned to me instead of to the astronomer who had given the talk. It seemed as though she were taking it for granted I knew as much as he did. So I talked to her for a while and she kept saying, 'How interesting.'"

Avalon said, "And meanwhile, *Jones* could have been in your cabin."

"Could be. I thought of that afterward. It was certainly atypical behavior on both their parts."

Avalon said, "Let's summarize, then. There are four possibilities. Miss Robinson might have done it when she left before the hot-chocolate incident. The Smiths might have done it as a team, Mr. Smith deliberately spilling the hot chocolate, so that Mrs. Smith could do the dirty work. Or the Doctor could have done it while going for the ointment. Or the Joneses could have done it as a team, with Jones doing the dirty work while Mrs. Jones kept Dr. Long out of action."

Long nodded. "All this was considered and by the time the ship was back in New York, security agents had begun the process of checking the background of all six. You see, in cases like this, suspicion is all you need. The only way any secret agent can remain undetected is for him or her to remain unsuspected. Once the eye of counterintelligence is upon him, he must inevitably be unmasked. No cover can survive an investigation in depth.''

Drake said, ''Then which one did it prove to be?''

Long sighed. ''That's where the trouble arose. None of them. All were clean. There was no way, I understand, of showing any of them to be anything other than what they seemed.''

Rubin said, ''Why do you say you 'understand.' Aren't you part of the investigation?''

''At the wrong end. The cleaner those six are, the dirtier I appear to be. I told the investigators—I *had* to tell them—that those six are the only ones who could possibly have done it, and if none of them did, they must suspect me of making up a story to hide something worse.''

Trumbull said, ''Oh, hell, Waldemar. They can't think that. What would you have to gain by reporting the incident if you were responsible?''

''That's what they don't know,'' said Long. ''But the information did leak and if they can't pin it on any of the six, then they're going to pin it on me. And the more my motives puzzle them, the more they think those motives must be very disturbing indeed. So I'm in trouble.''

Rubin said, ''Are you sure those six are indeed the only possibilities. Are you sure you really didn't mention it to anyone else?''

''Quite sure,'' said Long dryly.

''You might not remember having done so,'' said Rubin. ''It could have been something very casual. Can you be *sure* you didn't?''

''I can be sure I didn't. The radiophone call came not long before dinner. There just wasn't time to tell anyone before dinner. And once I got away from the table, I was back in the cabin before I as much as said anything to anybody. Anything at all.''

''Who heard you on the phone? Maybe there were eavesdroppers.''

''There were ship's officers standing around, certainly. However, my boss expressed himself Aesopically. I knew what he meant, but no one else would have.''

''Did you express *your*self Aesopically?'' asked Halsted.

"I'll tell you exactly what I said. 'Hello, Dave.' Then I said, 'God damn it to hell.' Then I hung up. I said those seven words. No more.''

Gonzalo brought his hands together in a sudden, enthusiastic clap. "Listen, I've been thinking. Why does the job have to be so planned? It could be spontaneous. After all, everybody knows there's this cruise and people connected with NASA are going to talk and there might be something interesting on. Someone—it could have been anyone—kept searching various rooms during the dinner hour each day and finally came across your paper—''

"No," said Long sharply. "It passes the bounds of plausibility to suppose that someone would, just by chance, find my paper just in the hour or two after I had announced that a classified lecture was sitting on my desk. Besides, there was nothing in the paper that would have given any idication of importance to the nonexpert. It was only my own remark that would have told anyone it was there and that it was important.''

Avalon said thoughtfully, "Suppose one of the people at the table passed on the information, in perfect innocence. In the interval they were away from the table, they might have said to someone, 'Did you hear about poor Dr. Long? His paper was shot out from under him?' Then that someone, anyone, could have done the job.''

Long shook his head. "I wish that could be so, but it can't. That would only happen if the particular individual at my table were innocent. If the Smiths were innocent when they left the table, the only thing on their minds would be the hot chocolate. They wouldn't stop to chat. The Doctor would be thinking only of getting the ointment. By the time Jones left the table, assuming he was innocent, he would have forgotten about the matter. If anything, he would talk about the hot chocolate, too.''

Rubin said suddenly, voice rising, "All right. What about Miss Robinson? She left before the hot-chocolate incident. The only interesting thing in her mind would have been your dilemma. She might have said something.''

"Might she?" said Long. "If she is innocent, then she was really doing what she said she was doing, going to the bathroom in her cabin. If she had to desert the dinner table to do so, there would have had to be urgency; and no one under those conditions stops for idle gossip."

There was silence all around the table.

Long said, "I'm sure investigation will continue and eventually the truth will come out and it will be clear that I'm guilty of no more than an unlucky indiscretion. By then, though, my career will be down the drain."

"Dr. Long?" said a soft voice. "May I ask a question?"

Long looked up, surprised. "A question?"

"I'm Henry, sir. The gentlemen of the Black Widowers organization occasionally allow me to participate—"

"Hell, yes, Henry," said Trumbull. "Do you see something the rest of us don't?"

"I'm not certain," said Henry. "I see quite plainly that Dr. Long believes only the six others at the table might possibly be involved, and those investigating the matter apparently agree with him—"

"There's no way not to," said Long.

"Well, then," said Henry. "I am wondering if Dr. Long mentioned his views on curry to the investigators."

Long said, "You mean that I didn't like curry?"

"Yes," said Henry. "Did that come up?"

Long spread his hands and then shook his head. "No, I don't think it did. Why should it? It's irrelevant. It's just an additional excuse for my talking like a jackass. I tell it to you here in order to collect sympathy, I suppose, but it would carry no weight with the investigators."

Henry remained silent for a moment, and Trumbull said, "Does the curry have meaning to you, Henry?"

"I think perhaps it does," said Henry. "I think we are in rather the position Mr. Halsted described earlier in the evening in connection with limericks. Some limericks to be effective must be seen; sound is not enough. And some scenes to be effective must be seen."

"I don't get that," said Long.

"Well, Dr. Long," said Henry. "You sat there in the ship's restaurant at a table with six other people and therefore only those six other people heard you. But if we could see the scene instead of having you describe it to us, would we see something clearly that you have omitted?"

"No, you wouldn't," said Long doggedly.

"Are you sure?" asked Henry. "You sit here with six other people at a table, too, just as you did on the ship. How many people hear your story?"

"Six—" began Long.

And then Gonzalo broke in, "Seven, counting you, Henry."

"And was there no one serving you at table, Dr. Long? You said the Doctor had asked you about the speech just as curried lamb was put before you and it was the smell of curry that annoyed you to the point where you burst out with your indiscretion. Surely, the curried lamb didn't place itself before you of its own accord. The fact is that at the moment you made your statement, there were six people at the table before you, and a seventh standing just behind you and out of sight."

"The waiter," said Long in a whisper.

Henry said, "There's a tendency never to notice a waiter unless he annoys you. An efficient waiter is invisible, and you mentioned the excellence of the service. Might it not have been the waiter who carefully engineered the spilling of the hot chocolate to create a diversion; or perhaps he who took advantage of the diversion, if it was an accident? With waiters many and diners few, it might not be too noticeable if he vanished for a while. Or he could claim to have gone to the men's room if it were indeed noticed. He would know the location of the cabin as well as the Doctor did, and be as likely to have some sort of picklock."

Long said, "But he was an Indonesian. He couldn't speak English."

"Are you sure? He'd had a three-month cram course, you said. And he might have known English better than he pretended. You would be willing to conceive that Mrs. Smith was not as sweet and thoughtful underneath as on the surface, and that Mrs. Jones's vivacity was pretense, and the Doctor's respectability and Smith's liveliness and Jones's devotion and Miss Robinson's need to go to the bathroom. Might not the waiter's ignorance of English also be pretense?"

"By God," said Long, looking at his watch. "If it weren't so late, I'd call Washington now."

Trumbull said, "If you know some home phone numbers,

do call now. It's your career. Tell them the waiter ought to be investigated, and for heaven's sake, don't tell them you got the notion from someone else."

"You mean, tell them I just thought of it? They'll ask why I didn't think of that before."

"Ask them why *they* didn't. Why didn't *they* think a waiter goes with a table?"

Henry said softly, "No reason for anyone to think of it. Only very few are as interested in waiters as I am."

4

Yankee Doodle
Went to Town

This story was written in Rochester. I was giving a talk there the following night, but on this particular night I was at a loss. Janet was sleeping in the other room, and I was not sleepy. I desperately wanted to write a story, but I had not brought my typewriter.

Finally, the yearning grew to the point where I collected the stationery in the drawer and began to write in pen and ink. I didn't think I could endure it long, but I grew interested and continued to scribble and scribble till I was finished. (I was fascinated by the fact that writing a story without a typewriter was a noiseless exercise.)

At home, I typed the handwritten story and found it as good as any other. Since then, I have written at least one story almost every time I have been forced to be somewhere for a period of at least two days without my typewriter. It makes such times bearable and ''Yankee Doodle Went to Town,'' as the first to be written in this manner, is a favorite of mine, in consequence.

It was general knowledge among the Black Widowers that Geoffrey Avalon had served as an officer in World War II

and had reached the rank of major. He had never seen active
service, as far as any of them knew, however, and he never
talked about wartime experiences. His stiff bearing, however,
seemed suited to the interior of a uniform, so that it never
surprised anyone to know that he had once been Major Avalon.

When he walked into the banquet room with an army
officer as his guest, it seemed, therefore, entirely natural.
And when he said, "This is my old army friend Colonel
Samuel Davenheim," everyone greeted him cordially without
so much as a raised eyebrow. Any army buddy of Avalon's
was an army buddy of theirs.

Even Mario Gonzalo, who had served an uneventful hitch
in the army in the late fifties, and who was known to have
acerbic views concerning officers, was pleasant enough. He
propped himself on one of the sideboards and began sketch-
ing. Avalon looked over Gonzalo's shoulder briefly, as though
to make sure the artist member of the Black Widowers would
not, somehow, draw the Colonel's head upward into a crown
of ass's ears.

It would have been most inappropriate for Gonzalo to have
done so, for there was every indication of clear intelligence
about Davenheim. His face, round and a little plump, was
emphasized by outmoded hair, short above and absent below.
His mouth curved easily into a friendly smile, his voice was
clear, his words crisp.

He said, "I've had you all described to me, for Jeff, as you
probably all know, is a methodical man. I ought to be able to
identify you all. For instance, you're Emmanuel Rubin since
you're short, have thick glasses, a sparse beard—"

"Straggly beard," said Rubin, unoffended, "is what Jeff
usually calls it because his own is dense, but I've never found
that density of facial hair implies—"

"And are talkative," said Daveheim firmly, overriding the
other with the calm authority of a colonel. "And you're a
writer. . . . You're Mario Gonzalo, the artist, and I don't
even need your description since you're drawing. . . . Roger
Halsted, mathematician, partly bald. The only member without a full head of hair, so that's easy. . . . James Drake, or,
rather, Dr. James Drake—"

"We're all doctors by virtue of being Black Widowers," said Drake from behind a curl of cigarette smoke.

"You're right, and Jeff explained that carefully. You're Doctor Doctor Drake because you smell of tobacco smoke at ten feet."

"Well, Jeff should know," said Drake philosophically.

"And Thomas Trumbull," said Davenheim, "because you're scowling, and by elimination. . . . Have I got everyone?"

"Only the members," said Halsted. "You've left out Henry, who's all-important."

Davemheim looked about, puzzled. "Henry?"

"The waiter," said Avalon, flushing and staring at his drink. "I'm sorry, Henry, but I didn't know what to tell Colonel Davenheim about you. To say you're the waiter is ridiculously insufficient and to say more would endanger Black Widower confidentiality."

"I understand," said Henry agreeably, "but I think it would be well to serve the Colonel. What is your pleasure, sir?"

For a moment the Colonel looked blank. "Oh, you mean drinks? No, that's all right. I don't drink."

"Some ginger ale, perhaps?"

"All right." Davenheim was plainly grasping at straws. "That will be fine."

Trumbull smiled. "The life of a non-drinker is a difficult one."

"Something wet must be pressed on one," said Davenheim wryly. "I've never managed to adjust."

Gonzalo said, "Have a cherry put in your ginger ale. Or better yet, put water in a cocktail glass and add an olive. Then drink and replace the water periodically. Everyone will admire you as a man who can hold his liquor. Though, frankly, I've never seen an officer who could—"

"I think we'll be eating any minute," said Avalon hastily, looking at his watch.

Henry said, "Won't you be seated, gentlemen?" and placed one of the bread baskets directly in front of Gonzalo as though to suggest he use his mouth for that purpose.

Gonzalo took a roll, broke it, buttered one half, bit into it, and said in muffled tones, "—keep from getting sloppy drunk on one martini," but no one listened.

Rubin, finding himself between Avalon and Davenheim, said, "What kind of soldier was Jeff, Colonel?"

"Damned good one," said Davenheim gravely, "but he didn't get much of a chance to shine. We were both in the legal end of matters, which meant desk work. The difference is that he had the sense to get out once the war was over. I didn't."

"You mean you're still involved with military law?"

"That's right."

"Well, I look forward to the day when military law is as obsolete as feudal law."

"I do, too," said Davenheim calmly. "But it isn't as yet."

"No," said Rubin, "and if you—"

Trumbull interrupted. "Damn it, Manny, can't you wait for grilling time?"

"Yes," said Avalon, coughing semi-stentorially, "we might as well let Sam eat before putting him through his paces."

"If," said Rubin, "millitary law applied the same considerations to those—"

"Later!" roared Trumbull.

Rubin looked through his thick-lensed glasses indignantly, but subsided.

Halsted said, in what was clearly intended to be a change of topic, "I'm not happy with my limerick for the fifth book of the *Iliad*."

"The what?" said Davenheim, puzzled.

"Pay no attention," said Trumbull. "Roger keeps threatening to put together five lines of crap for every book of the *Iliad*."

"And the *Odyssey*," said Halsted. "The trouble with the fifth book is that it deals chiefly with the feats of the Greek hero Diomedes, and I feel I ought to have him part of the rhyme scheme. I've been at it, off and on, for months."

"Is that why you've spared us limericks the last couple of sessions?" asked Trumbull.

"I've had one and I've been ready to read it, but I'm not quite satisfied with it."

"Then you've joined the great majority," said Trumbull.

"The thing is," said Halsted quietly, "that both 'Diomedes' and its legitimate variant 'Diomed' cannot be rhymed seriously. 'Diomedes' rhymes with 'Wheaties' and 'Diomed' rhymes with 'shy-a-bed' and what good are those?"

"Call him Tydeides," said Avalon. "Homer frequently used the patronymic."

"What's a patronymic?" asked Gonzalo.

"A father-name, which is the literal translation of the word," said Halsted. "Diomedes' father was Tydeus. Don't you think I've thought of that? It rhymes with 'didies' or, if you want to go Cockney, with 'lydies.'"

"How about 'ascites'?" asked Rubin.

"Or 'iron pyrites'?" said Drake.

"Wit seeks its own level," said Halsted. "How about this? All I need do is distort the stress and give 'Diomed' accents on first and last syllables."

"Cheating," said Rubin.

"A little," admitted Halsted, "but here it is:

> "In courage and skill well ahead,
> Into battle went brave Diomed.
>   Even gods were his quarries,
>   And the war-loving Ares
> He struck down and left nearly for dead."

Avalon shook his head. "Ares was only wounded. He had enough strength left to rise, roaring, to Olympus."

"I must admit I'm not satisfied," said Halsted.

"Unanimous!" said Trumbull.

"Veal parmesan!" said Rubin enthusiastically, for, with his usual agility, Henry was already placing the dishes before each.

Colonel Davenheim said, after he had devoted considerable time to the veal, "You do yourselves well here, Jeff."

"Oh, we do our poor best," said Avalon. "The restaurant charges in proportion, but it's only once a month."

Davenheim plied his fork enthusiastically and said, "Dr. Halsted, you're a mathematician—"

"I teach mathematics to reluctant youngsters, which isn't quite the same thing."

"But why, then, limericks on the epic poems?"

"Precisely because it is not mathematics, Colonel. It's a mistake to think that because a man has a profession that can be named, all his interests must bear that name."

"No offense," said the Colonel.

Avalon stared at a neatly cleaned plate and pushed thoughtfully at his untouched last half-glass of liquor. He said, "As a matter of fact, Sam knows what it is to have an intellectual hobby. He is an excellent phoneticist."

"Oh, well," said Davenheim, with heavy modesty, "in an amateur way."

Rubin said, "Does that mean you can tell jokes in accent?"

"In any accent you wish—within reason," said Davenheim. "But I can't tell jokes even in natural speech."

"That's all right," said Rubin, "I'd rather hear a bad joke in an authentic accent than a good one with a poor one."

Gonzalo said, "Then how do you account for the fact that you laugh only at your own jokes when they fail in both respects?"

Davenheim spoke quickly to cut off Rubin's rejoinder. He said, "You've got me off the subject." He leaned to one side to allow Henry to place the rum cake before him. "I mean, Dr. Halsted—very well, Roger—that perhaps you switch to the classics to get your mind off some knotty mathematics problem. Then, while your conscious mind is permutating rhymes, your unconscious mind is—"

"The funny thing about that," said Rubin, seizing his own chance to cut in, "is that it works. I've never been so stymied by a plot that I couldn't get it worked out by going to a movie. I don't mean a *good* movie that really absorbs me. I mean a bad one that occupies my conscious mind just sufficiently to allow my unconscious free reign. A spy-action film is best."

Gonzalo said, "I can't follow the plot of those things even when I'm paying attention."

"And yet they're aimed at the twelve-year-old mind," said Rubin, striking back at last.

Henry poured the coffee, as Davenheim said, "I agree with what Manny says. I happen to think that a day spent on phonetics is sometimes the best way of contributing to a problem at work. But isn't there another aspect to this? It's easy to see that by keeping the conscious mind occupied, we leave the unconscious free to do as it wislies underground. But will it stay underground? Might it not obtrude above-ground? Might it not make itself seen or heard, if not to the person himself—the person who is thinking—then to others?''

"Exactly what do you mean, Colonel?" asked Trumbull.

"Look," said Davenheim, "if we're on first-name terms, let it be first names all round. Call me Sam. What I mean is this. Suppose Manny is working on a plot involving an undetectable poison—"

"Never!" said Rubin strenuously. "Tarantulas are out, too, and mystic Hindus, and the supernatural. That's all nineteenth-century romanticism. I'm not sure that even the locked-room mystery hasn't become a matter of—"

"Just for *example*," said Davenheim, who had momentary trouble breasting the tide. "You do other things to let your unconscious work and as far as you yourself are concerned you can swear that you have completely forgotten the mystery, that you're not thinking about it, that it's completely wiped out. Then, when you're hailing a cab, you call, 'Toxic! Toxic!''

Trumbull said thoughtfully, "That's farfetched and I don't accept it, but I'm beginning to get a notion. Jeff, did you bring Sam here because he has a problem on his mind?"

Avalon cleared his throat. "Not really. I invited him last month for many reasons—the most important of which was that I thought you would all like him. But he stayed over at my house last night and—may I tell them, Sam?"

Davenheim shrugged. "This place is as quiet as the grave, you say."

"Absolutely," said Avalon. "Sam knows my wife almost as long as he knows me, but twice he called her Farber instead of Florence."

Davenheim smiled dimly. "My unconscious forcing its way through. I could have sworn I had put it out of my mind."

"You weren't aware of it," said Avalon. He turned to the others. "I didn't notice it. Florence did. The second time she said, 'What are you calling me?' and he said, 'What?' She said, 'You keep calling me Farber.' And he looked absolutely thunderstruck."

"Just the same," said Davenheim, "it's not my unconscious that's bothering me. It's *his*."

"Farber's?" asked Drake, tamping out his cigarette with his stained fingers.

"The other one's," said Davenheim.

Trumbull said, "It's about time for the brandy anyway, Jeff. Do you want to grill our esteemed guest, or ought someone else do so?"

"I don't know that he needs to be grilled," said Avalon. "Perhaps he'll simply tell us what's occupying his unconscious when his conscious mind is being diverted."

"I don't know that I want to do that," said Davenheim grimly. "It's rather a delicate matter."

"You have my word," said Trumbull, "that everything said here is in strictest confidence. I'm sure Jeff has told you that already. And that includes our esteemed Henry. And, of course, you needn't go into full detail."

"I can't hide behind false names, though, can I?"

"Not if Farber is one of the true ones," said Gonzalo, grinning.

"Well, what the devil," sighed Davenheim. "Actually, it's not much of a story as stories go, and it may be nothing; nothing at all. I may be so *damned* wrong. But if I'm not wrong it's going to be embarrassing for the army, and expensive for the country. I could almost hope I was wrong, but I've committed myself so far that if I am wrong it may permanently—hamper my career. Yet I'm not so far away from retirement."

For a moment he seemed lost in thought, then he said fiercely, "No, I *want* to be right. However embarrassing, it's got to be stopped."

"Is it treason you're after?" asked Drake.

"No, not in the narrow sense of the word. I almost wish it were. There can be a colossal dignity about treason. A traitor is sometimes only the other side of the patriot coin. One man's traitor is another man's martyr. I'm not talking about the penny-ante handyman for hire. I'm talking about the man who thinks he is serving a higher cause than his country and wouldn't accept a penny for the risks he undergoes. We understand that quite well when it is the enemy's traitors we are dealing with. The men, for instance, whom Hitler considered—''

"It's not treason, then?" said Trumbull, a bit impatiently.

"No. Just corruption! Stinking, fetid corruption. A gang of men—soldiers, I'm sorry to say, officers, conceivably high officers—intent on bleeding Uncle Sam a bit."

"Why isn't that treason?" snapped Rubin. "It weakens us and spreads decay in the army. Soldiers who think so little of their country as to steal from it are scarcely going to think so much of it as to die for it."

"If it comes to that," said Avalon, "people put their emotions and actions in separate compartments. It's quite possible to steal from Uncle Sam today and die for him tomorrow and be perfectly sincere about it both times. Many a man who routinely cheats the national treasury out of half his proper income tax considers himself a loyal American patriot."

Rubin said, "Leave the income tax out of it. Considering what consumes most of federal spending, you can make a good case for maintaining that the true patriot is he who goes to jail rather than pay his taxes."

Davenheim said, "It's one thing not to pay your taxes out of principle, to admit it, and go to jail for it. It's another thing to duck your share of the fair load for no other reason than to see others carry their own burden and yours to boot. Both actions are equally illegal, but I have some respect for the former. In the case I'm talking about the only motivation is simple greed. It is quite possible that millions of dollars of the taxpayers' money are involved."

"Possible? Is that all?" asked Trumbull, his forehead wrinkling into a washboard.

"That's all. So far. I can't prove it and it's a difficult thing to track down without a damned good scent. If I push too hard and can't back my suspicions all the way, I'll be torn in half. Some big names might be involved—and might not."

"What's Farber got to do with it?" asked Gonzalo.

"So far we have two men, a sergeant and a private. The

sergeant is Farber; Robert J. Farber. The other is Orin Klotz. We've got nothing on them really."

"Nothing at all?" asked Avalon.

"Not really. As a result of the action of Farber and Klotz, thousands of dollars of army equipment have evaporated but we cannot show that their actions were illegal. They were covered in every case."

"You mean because higher-ups were involved?" Gonzalo smiled slowly. "Officers? With *brains?*"

"Unlikely as it seems," said Davenheim dryly. "That may be so. But I have no proof."

"Can't you question the two men you have?" said Gonzalo.

"I have," said Davenheim. "And with Farber I can get nothing. He is that most dangerous of men, the honest tool. I believe he was too stupid to know the significance of what he did, and that if he did know, he wouldn't have done it."

"Confront him with the truth," said Avalon.

"What is the truth?" asked Davenheim. "And I'm not ready to put my guesses on the table. If I tell what I know now, it will be dishonorable discharge for the two, at best, and the rest of the ring will pull in its horns for a breathing space and then start in again. No, I'd like to cover my hand until such time as I can get a lead, some lead I can be sufficiently sure of to run the risk I'm going to have to run."

"You mean a lead to someone higher up?" asked Rubin.

"Exactly."

"What about the other fellow?" asked Gonzalo.

Davenheim nodded. "He's the one. He knows. He's the brains of that pair. But I can't break his story. I've been over and over it with him and he's covered."

Halsted said, "If it's only a guess that there's something more to this than those two guys, why do you take it so seriously? Aren't the chances actually very good that you're wrong?"

"To other people it would seem so," said Davenheim. "And there's no way in which I could explain why I know I'm *not* wrong except by pleading experience. After all, Roger, an experienced mathematiciam can be quite certain that a particular conjecture is true and yet be unable to prove it by the strict rules of mathematical demonstration. Right?"

"I'm not sure that that's a good analogy," said Halsted.

"It seems a good one to me. I've talked to men who were guilty beyond a doubt and to men who were innocent beyond a doubt and the attitude of each under accusation is different and I can *sense* that difference. The trouble is that that sense I have is not admissible as evidence. Farber I can dismiss, but Klotz is just a shade too wary, just a shade too unconfused. He plays *games* with me and enjoys it, too, and that's one thing I can't possibly miss."

"If you insist that you can sense such things," said Halsted, dissatisfied, "there's no arguing about it, is there? You put it outside the rational."

"There's just no mistake in it," said Davenheim, unheeding, as though he were now caught up in the fury of his thoughts to the point where what Halsted said was just an outer sound that didn't impinge. "Klotz smiles just a little bit whenever I'm after him hotly. It's as though I'm a bull and he's a matador, and when I'm beginning to lunge at close quarters, he stands there rigidly with his cape flirting negligently to one side, daring me to gore him. And when I try, he's not there and the cape flips over my head."

"I'm afraid he's got you, Sam," said Avalon, shaking his head. "If you feel as though he's playing you for a fool, you've reached the point where you can't trust your judgment. Let someone else take over."

Davenheim shook his head. "No, if it's what I think it is, and I *know* it's what I think it is, I want to be the one to smash it."

"Look," said Trumbull. "I have a little experience in such things. Do you suppose Klotz can break the case wide open for you? He's only a private, and I suspect that even if there *is* some sort of conspiracy, he knows very little about it."

"All right. I'll accept that," said Davenheim. "I don't expect Klotz to hand me the moon. Yet he's got to know one other man, one man higher up. He's got to know some one fact, some one fact closer to the center than he himself is. It's that one man and that one fact I'm after. It's all I ask. And the thing that breaks me in two is that he's giving it away and I still don't get it."

"What do you mean, giving it away?" asked Trumbull.

"That's where the unconscious comes in. When he and I are sparring, he's entirely occupied with me, entirely engaged in stopping me, heading me off, stymying me, putting me behind the eight ball. It's a game he plays well, damn him. The last thing he's going to do is to give me the information I want, but it's in him just the same and when he's busy thinking of everything else but, that information bubbles out of him. Every time I'm close upon him and backing and maneuvering him into a corner—butting my horns against his damned cape just this far from his groin—he *sings*"

"He *what?*" exploded Gonzalo, and there was a general stir among the Black Widowers. Only Henry showed no trace of emotion as he refilled several of the coffeecups.

"He sings," said Davenheim. "Well, not quite—he hums. And it's always the same tune."

"What tune is that? Anything you know?"

"Of course I know it. Everyone knows it. It's 'Yankee Doodle.' "

Avalon said heavily, "Even President Grant, who had no ear for music, knew that one. He said he knew only two tunes. One was 'Yankee Doodle' and the other wasn't."

"And it's 'Yankee Doodle' that's giving the whole thing away?" asked Drake, with that look in his weary chemist's eyes that came when he began to suspect the rationality of another person.

"Somehow. He's masking the truth as cleverly as he can, but it emerges from his unconscious, just a bit; just the tip of the iceberg. And 'Yankee Doodle' is that tip. I don't get it. There's just not enough for me to grab hold of. But it's there! I'm sure of that."

"You mean there's a solution to your problem somewhere in 'Yankee Doodle'?" said Rubin.

"Yes!" said Davenheim emphatically. "I'm positive of that. The thing is he's not aware he's humming it. At one point I said, 'What's that?' and he was blank. I said, 'What are you humming?' and he just stared at me in what I could swear was honest amazement."

"As when you called Florence Farber," said Avalon.

Halsted shook his head. "I don't see where you can attach much importance to that. We all experience times when tunes run through our minds and we can't get rid of them for a while. I'm sure we're bound to hum them under our breath at times."

Davenheim said, "At *random* times, perhaps. But Klotz hums *only* 'Yankee Doodle' and only at the specific times when I'm pressing him. When things get tense in connection with my probing for the truth about the corruption conspiracy I am sure exists, that tune surfaces. It *must* have meaning."

"Yankee Doodle," said Rubin thoughtfully, half to himself. For a moment he looked at Henry, who was standing near the sideboard, a small vertical crease between his eyebrows. Henry caught Rubin's eye but did not respond.

There was a ruminating silence for a few moments and all the Black Widowers seemed to be, to one degree or another, unhappy. Finally, Trumbull said, "You may be all wrong, Sam. What you may be needing here is psychiatry. This guy Klotz may hum 'Yankee Doodle' at *all* moments of tension. All it may mean is that he heard his grandfather sing it when he was six years old or that his mother sang him to sleep with it."

Davenheim lifted his upper lip in mild derision. "Can you believe I didn't think of that? I had a dozen of his close friends in. Nobody had ever heard him hum anything!"

"They might be lying," said Gonzalo. "I wouldn't tell an officer anything if I could avoid it."

"They might never have noticed," said Avalon. "Few people are good observers."

"Maybe they lied, maybe they didn't know," said Davenheim, "but, taken at face value, their testimony, all of it, would make me think that the humming of 'Yankee Doodle' is specifically associated with my investigation and nothing else."

"Maybe it's just associated with army life. It's a march associated with the Revolutionary War," said Drake.

"Then why only with me, not with anyone else in the army?"

Rubin said, "Okay, let's pretend 'Yankee Doodle' means something in this connection. What can we lose? So let's consider how it goes. . . . For God's sake, Jeff, don't sing it."

Avalon, who had opened his mouth with the clear intention of singing, closed it with a snap. His ability to hold a true note rivaled that of an oyster and in his saner moments he knew it. He said, with a trace of hauteur, "I will recite the words!"

"Good," said Rubin, "but no singing."

Avalon, looking stern, struck an attitude and began declaiming in his most resonant baritone:

> "Yankee Doodle went to town
> A-riding on a pony.
> Stuck a feather in his cap
> And called it macaroni.
> Yankee Doodle, keep it up,
> Yankee Doodle dandy.
> Mind the music and the step
> And with the girls be handy."

Gonzalo said, "It's just a nonsense lyric."

"Nonsense, hell," said Rubin indignantly, and his straggly beard quivered. "It makes perfect sense. It's a satire on the country boy written by a city slicker. 'Doodle' is any primitive country instrument—a bagpipe, for instance—so a Yankee Doodle is a backwoods New Englander who's no more sophisticated than a bagpipe. He comes to town on his pony intent on cutting a fine figure, so he wears what he thinks are city clothes. He wears a feather in his hat and thinks he's a real dude. And in the late eighteenth century, that's what a 'macaroni' was, a city hepcat dressed in the latest style.

"The last four lines are the chorus and show the country boy stepping it up at a city dance. He is mockingly told to stamp away and be gallant to the ladies. The word 'dandy,' which first came into use about mideighteenth century, meant the same as 'macaroni.' "

Gonzalo said, "Okay, Manny, you win. It's not nonsense. But how does it help Sam's case?"

"I don't think it does," said Rubin. "Sorry, Sam, but Klotz sounds like a country boy making a fool of the city slicker and he can't help but think of the derisive song and how he's turning the tables on you."

Davenheim said, "I presume, Manny, that you think he must be a country boy because his name is Klotz. By that reasoning you must be a rube because your name is Rubin. Actually, Klotz was born and brought up in Philadelphia and I doubt that he's ever seen a farm. No country boy, he."

"All right," said Rubin, "then I might have been looking at the wrong end of the stick. *He's* the city slicker looking down on *you*, Sam."

"Because *I'm* a country boy? I was born in Stoneham, Massachusetts, and went through Harvard right up to my law degree. And he knows that, too. He has made enough round-about references to it in his matador moments."

Drake said, "Doesn't your Massachusetts birth and up-bringing make you a Yankee?"

"Not a Yankee Doodle," said Davenheim stubbornly.

"He might think so," said Drake.

Davenheim thought about that a while, then said, "Yes, I suppose he might. But if so, surely he would hum it openly, derisively. The point is, I think he's humming it uncon-sciously. It has a connection with something he's trying to hide, not something he's trying to show."

Halsted said, "Maybe he's looking forward to a future when he's going to be enriched by his crimes and when he'll be able to strut his way to town; when he can 'stick a feather in his cap' in other words."

Drake said, "Or maybe Klotz is thinking that his treatment of you is a feather in his cap."

Gonzalo said, "Maybe some particular word has signifi-cance. Suppose 'macaroni' means he's hooked up with the Mafia. Or suppose 'with the girls be handy' means that some Wac is involved. They still have Wacs in the army, don't they?"

It was at this point that Henry said, "I wonder, Mr. Avalon, if, as host, you will permit me to ask a few questions."

Avalon said, "Come on, Henry. You know you can at any time."

"Thank you, sir. Would the Colonel grant me the same permission?"

Davenheim looked surprised, but said, "Well, you're here, Henry, so you might as well."

Henry said, "Mr. Avalon recited eight lines of 'Yankee Doodle'—four lines of a verse followed by the four lines of the chorus. But verse and chorus have different tunes. Did Private Klotz hum all eight lines?"

Davenheim thought a moment. "No, of course not. He hummed—uh—" He closed his eyes, concentrated, and went "Dum-dum dum-dum dum-dum-dum, dum-dum dum-dum dum-du-u-um-dum. That's all. The first two lines."

"Of the verse?"

"That's right. 'Yankee Doodle went to town, A-riding on a pony.' "

"Always those two lines?"

"Yes, I think always."

Drake brushed some crumbs from the table. "Colonel, you say this humming took place when the questioning was particularly tense. Did you pay particular attention to exactly what was being discussed at those times?"

"Yes, of course, but I prefer not to go into detail."

"I understand, but perhaps you can tell me this. At those times, was it he himself who was under discussion or Sergeant Farber as well?"

"Generally," said Davenheim slowly, "the humming times came when he most emphatically protested innocence, but always on behalf of both. I'll give him that. He has never once tried to clear himself at the expense of the other. It was always that neither Farber nor he did thus-and-so or were responsible for this-and-that."

Henry said, "Colonel Davenheim, this is a long shot. If the answer is no, then I'll have nothing more to say. If, however, the answer is yes, it's just possible we may have something."

"What's the question, Henry?" asked Davenheim.

"At the same base where Sergeant Farber and Private Klotz are stationed, Colonel, does there happen to be a Captain Gooden or Gooding or anything resembling that in sound?"

Davenheim had, until then, been looking at Henry with grave amusement. Now that vanished in a flash. His mouth closed tight and his face whitened visibly. Then his chair scraped as he shoved it back and rose.

"Yes," he said strenuously. "Captain Charles Goodwin. How the *hell* could you possibly have known that?"

"In that case, he may be your man. I'd forget about Klotz and Farber, sir, if I were you, and concentrate on the captain. That might be the one step upward that you wanted. And the captain may prove an easier nut to crack than Private Klotz has been."

Davenheim seemed to find no way to speak further and Trumbull said, "I wish you'd explain, Henry."

"It's the 'Yankee Doodle,' as the Colonel expected. The point is, though, that Private Klotz *hummed* it. We have to consider what words he was thinking when he hummed."

Gonzalo said, "The Colonel said he hummed the lines that go 'Yankee Doodle went to town, A-riding on a pony.'"

Henry shook his head. "The original poem 'Yankee Doodle' had some dozen verses and the macaroni lines were not among them. They arose later, though they're now the most familiar. The original poem tells of the visit of a young farmboy to the camp of Washington's Continental Army and his naïveté is made fun of, so I believe Mr. Rubin's interpretation of the nature of the song to be correct."

Rubin said, "Henry's right. I remember now. Washington is even mentioned, but as *Captain* Washington. The farmboy wasn't even aware of the nature of military rank."

"Yes," said Henry. "I don't know all the verses and I imagine very few people do. Perhaps Private Klotz didn't, either. But anyone who knows the poem at all knows the first verse or, at any rate, the first two lines, and that's what Private Klotz may have been humming. The first line, for instance—and it's the farmboy speaking—is 'Father and I went down to camp.' You see?"

"No," said Davenheim, shaking his head. "Not quite."

"It occurred to me that whenever you pressed hard on Private Klotz and might say, 'Farber and you did thus-and-so,' and he answered, 'Farber and I did *not* do thus-and-so,' the humming would start. You said, Colonel, that it was at the moment of denial that it tended to come and that he always denied on behalf of both Farber and himself. So when he said 'Farber and I,' it would trigger the line 'Farber and I went down to camp.'" Henry sang it in a soft tenor voice.

"Farber and he were in an army camp," said Avalon, "but, good God, that's stretching for it."

"If it stood alone, sir, yes," said Henry. "But that's why I asked about a Captain Gooden in the camp. If he were a third member of the conspiracy, the push to hum the tune might be irresistible. The first verse, which is the only one I know—"

But here Rubin interrupted. Standing up, he roared:

> "Father and I went down to camp
> Along with Cap'n Good'n,
> And there we saw the men and boys
> As thick as hasty puddin'."

"That's right," said Henry calmly, "Farber and I went down to camp along with Captain Goodwin."

"By God," said Davenheim. "That must be it. If not, it's the most extraordinary coincidence. . . . And it can't be. Henry, you've put your finger on it."

"I hope so. More coffee, Colonel?" said Henry.

5

Quicker Than the Eye

If there's one type of puzzle story I particularly like, it's the one where you have to find an object that has been hidden—or any of the different variations on that theme.

It's a well-worn type of story dating from Edgar Allan Poe's classic "The Purloined Letter" and by now, you might think, that every trick of hiding, or of stealing, or of transferring will have been described. The most painstaking search, the most careful watch, reveals nothing and yet something can't have dropped out of the universe, can it?

It's delightful—it gives you a warm feeling all over to think of a way of doing it that you have never seen before. It is for the sake of that warm feeling that I include this story.

Thomas Trumbull, who worked for the government as a cryptologist, was clearly uneasy. His tanned and wrinkled face was set in a carved attitude of worry. He said, "He's a man from the department; my superior, in fact. It's damned important, but I don't want Henry to feel the pressure."

He was whispering and be couldn't resist the quick look over his shoulder at Henry, the waiter at the Black Widower monthly banquets. Henry, who was several years older than Trumbull, had a face that was unwrinkled, and, as he quickly set the table, he seemed tranquil and utterly unaware of the fact that five of the Black Widowers were huddled quietly at the opposite end of the room. Or, if not unaware, then certainly undisturbed.

Geoffrey Avalon, the tall patent lawyer, had, under the best of conditions, difficulty in keeping his voice low. Still, stirring his drink with a middle finger on the ice cube, he managed to impart sufficient hoarseness. "How can we prevent it, Tom? Henry is no fool."

"I'm not sure anyone from the federal administration qualifies as a guest, Tom," said Emmanuel Rubin in a swerving non sequitur. His sparse beard bristled truculently and his eyes flashed through the thick lenses of his glasses. "And I say that even though *you're* in the category. Eighty per cent of the tax money I pay to Washington is expended in ways of which I strongly disapprove."

"You've got the vote, haven't you?" said Trumbull testily.

"And a fat lot of good that does, when the manipulation—" began Rubin, quite forgetting to keep his voice low.

Oddly enough, it was Roger Halsted, the mathematics teacher, whose quiet voice had sufficient difficulty in controlling a junior high school class, who managed to stop Rubin in mid-roar. He did it by placing his hand firmly over the smaller man's mouth. He said, "You don't sound very happy about your boss coming here, Tom."

"I'm not," said Trumbull. "It's a difficult thing. The point is that I've gotten considerable credit on two different occasions over matters that were really Henry's insights. I've *had* to take the credit, damn it, since what we say here in this room is confidential. Now something has come up and they're turning to me, and I'm as stuck as the rest of them. I've had to invite Bob here without really explaining why."

James Drake, the organic chemist, coughed over his cigarette and fingered his walrus-head bolo-tie. "Have you been talking too much about our dinners, Tom?"

"I suppose it could be viewed in that way. What bothers me is Henry, though. He enjoys the game, I know, when it *is*

a game, but if there's real pressure and he won't—or can't—
under that pressure—''

"Then you'll look bad, eh, Tom?'' said Rubin with just a
touch, perhaps, of malice.

Avalon said frigidly, "I have said before and I will say it
again that what began as a friendly social get-together is
becoming a strain on us all. Can't we have *one* session with
just conversation?''

"I'm afraid not this one,'' said Trumbull. "All right,
here's my boss.—Now let's carry all the load we can and put
as little as possible on Henry.''

But it was only Mario Gonzalo walking noisily up the
stairs, uncharacteristically late, and resplendent in his long
hair, a crimson jacket, and subtly matching striped shirt, to
say nothing of a flowing scarf meticulously arranged to display the effect of casualness.

"Sorry I'm late, Henry—'' But the proper drink was in his
hand before he could say more. "Thanks, Henry. Sorry,
fellows, trouble with getting a taxi. That put me in a grim
mood and when the driver began to lecture me on the crimes
and misdemeanors of the mayor I argued with him.''

"Lord help us,'' said Drake.

"I always argue every tenth time I hear that kind of crap.
Then he managed to get lost, and I didn't notice and it took
us a long time to pull out.—I mean, he was giving me this
business about welfare recipients being a bunch of lazy,
free-loading troublemakers and how no decent person should
expect a handout but instead they should work for what they
get and earn every cent. So I said what about sick people and
old people and mothers with young children and he started
telling me what a hard life *he* had led and *he* had never gone
to anyone for a handout.

"Anyway, I got out and the fare came to $4.80, and it was
a good half dollar more than it should have been because of
getting lost, so I counted out four singles and then spent some
time getting the exact eighty cents change and I handed it to
him. He counted it over, looked surprised, and I said, just as
sweetly as I could, 'That's what you earned, driver. You
looking for a handout too?'''

Gonzalo burst out laughing, but no one joined him. Drake

said, "That's a dirty trick on the poor guy just because you egged him into arguing."

Avalon stared down austerely from his lean height and said, "You might have gotten beaten up, Mario, and I wouldn't blame him."

"That's a hell of an attitude you fellows are taking," said Gonzalo, aggrieved—and at that point Trumbull's boss did arrive.

Trumbull introduced the newcomer all round, looking uncommonly subdued as he did so. The guest's name was Robert Alford Bunsen and he was both heavy and large. His face was pink and his white hair was sleeked back from an old-fashioned part down the middle.

"What will you have, Mr. Bunsen?" said Avalon, with a small and courtly bend at the middle. He was the only one present who was taller than the newcomer.

Bunsen cleared his throat. "Glad to meet you all. No—no—I've had my alcoholic calories for today. Some diet drink." He snapped his fingers at Henry. "A diet cola, waiter. If you don't have that, a diet anything."

Gonzalo's eyes widened and Drake, whispering philosophically through the curling smoke of the cigarette stub he held between his tobacco-stained fingers, said, "Oh well, he's government."

"Still," muttered Gonzalo, "there's such a thing as courtesy. You don't snap your fingers. Henry isn't a peon."

"You're rude to taxi drivers," said Drake. "This guy's rude to waiters."

"That's a different thing," said Gonzalo vehemently, his voice rising. "That was a matter of principle."

Henry, who had shown no signs of resentment at being finger-snapped, had returned with a bottle of soft drink on a tray and had presented it solemnly for inspection.

"Sure, sure," said Bunsen, and Henry opened it and poured half its contents into an ice-filled glass and let the foam settle. Bunsen took it and Henry left the bottle.

The dinner was less comfortable than many in the past had been. The only one who seemed unsubdued over the fact that the guest was a high, if a not very well kmown, official of the government was Rubin. In fact, he seized the occasion to attack the government in the person of its surrogate by proclaiming loudly that diet drinks were one of the great causes of overweight in America.

"Because you drink a lot of them and the one calorie per bottle mounts up?" asked Halsted, with as much derision as he could pack into his colorless voice.

"They've got more than one calorie per bottle now that cyclamates have been elimimated on the basis of fallacious animal experiments," said Rubin hotly, "but that's not the point. Diet anything is bad psychologically. Anyone overweight who takes a diet drink is overcome with virtue. He has saved two hundred calories, so he celebrates by taking another pat of butter and consuming three hundred calories. The only way to lose weight is to stay hungry. The hunger is telling you that you're getting less calories than you're expending—"

Halsted, who knew very well that there was a certain softness in his abdominal region, muttered, "Oh well."

"But he's right, though," said Bunsen, attacking the veal Marengo with gusto. "The diet drinks don't do me any good, but I like the taste. And I approve of looking at matters from the psychological angle."

Gonzalo, frowning, showed no signs of listening. When Henry bent over him to fill his coffee cup, he said, "What do *you* think, Henry? I mean about the taxi driver. Wasn't I right?"

Henry said, "A gratuity is not quite a handout, Mr. Gonzalo. Personal service is customarily rewarded in a small way and to equate that with welfare is perhaps not quite just."

"You're just saying that because you—" began Gonzalo, and then he stopped abruptly.

Henry said, "Yes, I benefit in the same way as the taxi driver does, but despite that I believe my statement to be correct."

Gonzalo threw himself back in his chair and chafed visibly.

"Gentlemen," said Trumbull, tapping his empty water glass with a fork, as Henry poured the liqueur, "this is an interesting occasion. Mr. Bunsen, who is my superior at the department, has a small puzzle to present to us. Let's see what we can make of it." Again, he cast a quick glance at Henry, who had replaced the bottle on the sideboard and now stood placidly in the background.

Bunsen, wiping his mouth with his napkin and wheezing slightly, also cast an anxious glance at Henry, and Trumbull leaned over to say, "Henry is one of us, Bob."

Trumbull went on, "Bob Bunsen is going to present merely the bare bones, to keep from distorting your view of the matter with unnecessary knowledge to begin with. I will remain out of it myself since I know too much about the matter."

Halsted leaned over to whisper to Drake, "I think it won't look good for Tom in the department if this doesn't work."

Drake shrugged, and mouthed rather than said, "He brought it on himself."

Bunsen, having adjusted the position of the breadbasket unnecessarily (he had earlier prevented Henry from removing it), began. "I will give you those bare bones of a story. There's a man. Call him Smith. We want him, but not just him. He's of little account. Clever at what he does, but of little account. If we get him, we learn nothing of importance and we warn off men of greater importance. If, however, we can use him to lead us to the men of greater importance—"

"We all understand," interrupted Avalon.

Bunsen cleared his throat and made a new start. "Of course, we weren't sure about Smith to begin with. It seemed very likely, but we weren't sure. If he was indeed a link in the apparatus we were trying to break up, then we reasoned that he transferred the information at a restaurant he regularly frequented. Part of the reasoning was based on psychology, something I imagine Mr. Rubin would approve. Smith had the appearance and patina of a well-bred man about town who always did the correct social thing. On that basis, we—"

He paused to think, then he said, "No, I'm getting off the subject and it's more than you need. We laid a trap for him." For a moment he reddened as though in bashfulness and then he went on firmly, "*I* laid the trap and it was damned complicated. We managed to beat down his caution, never mind how, and we ended with Smith having in his hand something he had to transfer. It was a legitimate item and would be useful to them, but not too useful. It would be well worth the loss to us if we had gained what we hoped to gain."

Bunsen looked about him, clearing his throat, but no one made a sound. Henry, standing by the sideboard, seemed a quiet statue. Even the napkin he held did not move.

Bunsen said, "Smith walked into the restaurant with the object on his person. After he left the restaurant he did not have the object on his person. We know therefore that he transferred the object. What we don't know is the exact moment at which he transferred it, how, and to whom. We have not been able to locate the object anywhere. Now ask your questions, gentlemen."

Trumbull said, "Let's try this one at a time. Mario?"

Gonzalo thought a moment and then shrugged. Twiddling his brandy glass between thumb and forefinger, he said, "What did this object—as you call it—look like?"

"About an inch across and flat," said Bunsen. "It had a metallic shine so it was easy to see. It was too large to swallow easily; heavy enough to make a noise if it were dropped; too thick to place in a crack; too heavy to stick easily to anything; not iron so there could be no tricks with magnets. The object, as I still call it, was carefully designed to make the task of transferring, or hiding, difficult."

"But what did he do in the restaurant? He ate a meal, I suppose?" said Gonzalo.

"He ate a meal as he always did."

"Was it a fancy restaurant?"

"A fairly elaborate one. He ate there regularly."

"I mean, there's nothing phony about the restaurant?"

"Not as far as we know, although in general that is not enough to allow us to display a blind trust in it and, believe me, we don't."

"Who was with him at the meal?"

"No one." Bunsen shook his head gravely. "He ate alone. That was his custom. He signed the check when he was through, as he always did. He had an account in the restaurant, you see. Then he left, took a taxi, and after a while he was stopped and taken into custody. The object was no longer in his possession.''

"Wait, now," said Gonzalo, his eyes narrowing. "You say he signed the check. What was it he wrote? Would you know?''

"We know quite well. We have the check. He added a tip—quite the normal amount and we could find nothing wrong with that—and signed his name. That's all. Nothing more. He used the waiter's pencil and he returned that pencil. Nor did he pass along anything else, and the waiter did not escape scrutiny, I assure you.''

Gonzalo said, "I pass.''

Drake, stubbing out his cigarette, lifted a gray eyebrow as Trumbull's finger gestured at him. "I suppose Smith was kept under close surveillance while he was in the restaurant.''

"As close as though he were a coat and we were the lining. We had two men in that restaurant, each at a table near him. They were trained men and capable ones and their entire task was to note every movement he made. He could not scratch himself without being noticed. He couldn't fumble at a button, crook a finger, shift a leg, or raise a buttock without being noted.''

"Did he go to the men's room at any time?''

"No, he did not. If he had, we would have managed to follow.''

"Were you there yourself, Mr. Bunsen?''

"I? No, I'm no good for that kind of surveillance. I'm too noticeable. What's needed to keep a man in view is a shadow with a good, gray face and an overwhelming lack of distinction in form and feature. I'm too big, too broad; I stand out.''

Drake nodded. "Do you suppose Smith knew he was being watched?''

"He may have. People in his line of work don't last long if they don't assume at every moment that they might be watched. In fact, to be truthful, at one point I got a clear impression he felt he was watched. I was across the street at a window, with a pair of binoculars. I could see him come out from the corner entrance of the restaurant.

"The doorman held the taxi door open for him and Smith paused for just a minute. He looked about him as though trying to identify those who might be watching. And he smiled, a tight smile, not amusement, it seemed to me, as much as bravado. At that moment, I was sure we had lost. And, as it turned out, we had.''

"And you really are sure," said Drake, "that he had it on him when he walked into the restaurant and that he didn't have it on him when he left.''

"We really are sure. When he walked in, there was what amounted to a pickpocketing, an inspection, and a replacement. He had it; you can take that as given. When he left and took a taxi, that taxi driver was one of our men who came, when the doorman hailed him, in a completely natural manner. Smith got in with no hint of suspicion. We are positive about that. The driver, one of our best men, then—But never mind that. The point is that Smith found himself in a kind of minor trouble that had, apparently, nothing to do with us. He was arrested, taken to the police station, and searched. Later, when it became obvious that we couldn't find the object anywhere, he was searched more thoroughly. Eventually we used X rays.''

Drake said, "He might have left the object in the taxi.''

"I doubt he could have done that with our man driving, and in any case, the taxi was searched. See here," said Bunsen heavily, "there's no point in thinking we are incompetent in our business. When I say we watched, I mean that we watched with professional attention. When I say we searched, I mean we searched with professional thoroughness. You won't catch us on details.''

"All right," said Drake, nodding, "but you missed, didn't you? The object was there and then it wasn't there, so either we call upon the supernatural or we must admit that somewhere you failed. Somewhere you blinked when you were watching or skipped when you were searching. Right?''

Bunsen looked rather as though he had bitten into a lemon. "There's no way of avoiding that conclusion, I suppose.'' Then, belligerently, "But show me where.''

Drake shook his head, but Halsted intervened rapidly, his high forehead pink with excitement. "Now wait, the hand is quicker than the eye. The thing you're looking for was shiny and heavy, but did it have to stay that way? Smith might have pushed it into a lump of clay. Then he had something dull and shapeless which he could push against the bottom of the table or drop on the floor. It might still be there."

Bunsen said, "The hand is quicker than the eye when you have an audience that doesn't know what to watch for. We know all the tricks and we know what to expect. Smith couldn't have put the object into clay without our men knowing he was doing something. He couldn't have placed it under the table or on the floor without our men knowing he was doing something."

"Yes," said Halsted, "but in these quicker-than-the-eye things, a diversion is usually created. Your men were looking somewhere else."

"There was no diversion, and in any case the restaurant was searched quite thoroughly as soon as he left."

"You couldn't have searched it thoroughly," protested Halsted. "There were still people eating there. Did you make them all leave?"

"We searched his table, his area and eventually all the restaurant. We are quite certain that he did not leave the object behind anywhere. He did not leave anything behind anywhere."

Avalon had been sitting stiffly in his chair, his arms folded, his forehead creased in a portentous frown. His voice boomed out now. "Mr. Bunsen," he said, "I am not at all comfortable with this account of yours. I recognize the fact that you have told us very little and that neither places, names, occasions, nor identifications have been given.

"Nevertheless, you are telling me more than I want to know. Have you permission from your superiors to tell us this? Are you quite certain in your mind that each one of us is to be trusted? You might get into trouble as a result and that would be regrettable, but I must admit that that is not the point I am most concerned with at the moment. What *is* important is that I do not wish to become the object of questioning and investigation because you have seen fit to honor me with confidences I have not asked for."

Trumbull had vainly tried to break in and managed to say finally, "Come on, Jeff. Don't act like the rear end of a horse."

Bunsen raised a massive and pudgy hand. "That's all right, Tom. I see Mr. Avalon's point and, in a way, he's right. I *am* exceeding my authority and things *will* be sticky for me if some people decide they need a scapegoat. This little exercise of mine tonight, however, may get me off the hook if it works. To my way of thinking, it's worth the gamble. Tom assured me it would be."

"What you're saying," said Trumbull, forcing a smile, "is that if the department jumps on you, you'll jump on me."

"Yes," said Bunsen, "and I weigh a lot." He picked up a breadstick and munched on it. "One more point. Mr. Avalon asked if I were sure you could each be trusted. Aside from the fact that Tom assured me you could be—not that I consider it safe to trust to personal assurances from close friends—there has been a little bit of investigation. Nothing like a full-scale affair, you understand, but enough to give me some confidence."

It was at this point that Henry cleared his throat gently, and at once every face but that of Bunsen turned toward him. Bunsen turned only after he was aware of the shift of attention.

Trumbull said, "Have you got something, Henry?"

Bunsen turned a clearly astonished look in Trumbull's direction, but Trumbull said urgently, "Have you, Henry?"

"I only want to know," said Henry softly, "if I have been cleared also. I suspect I have not and that I should retire."

But Trumbull said, "For God's sake, nothing critical is being said."

Bunsen said, "Besides, the damage is done. Let him stay."

"It seems to me," said Henry, "that the damage is indeed done. Surely there is no longer any purpose to the investigation. The man you call Smith must know he is being watched. By the time you began to use X rays on him, he must have guessed that he had been set up for a kill.—Is he still in custody, by the way?"

"No, we had no grounds to keep him. He's released."

"Then the organization of which he is a part must undoubtedly know what has happened, and they will change their modus operandi. He will not be used further, perhaps; others involved will disappear. Things will be entirely rearranged."

Bunsen said impatiently, "Yes, yes. Nevertheless, knowledge is important in itself. If we find out exactly how he transferred the object, we will know something about a mode of operation we didn't know before. We will, at the least, get an insight into a system of thought.—It is *always* important to know."

Henry said, "I see."

Trumbull said, "Is that all you see, Henry? Do *you* have any ideas?"

Henry shook his head. "It may be, Mr. Trumbull, that what has happened is complex and subtle. That would not be for me."

"Bull, Henry," said Trumbull.

"But it might be for Mr. Rubin," said Henry gravely. "I believe he is anxious to speak."

"Darn right," said Rubin loudly, "because I'm annoyed. Now, Mr. Bunsen, you talk about watching carefully and searching thoroughly, but I think you'll agree with me when I say that it is very easy to overlook something which becomes obvious only after the fact. I can describe a way in which Smith could have transferred the object without any trouble and no matter how many people were watching him."

"I would love to hear that description," said Bunsen.

"Okay, then, I will describe exactly what might have happened. I don't say it *did* happen, but it *could* have happened. Let me begin by asking a question—" Rubin pushed his chair away from the table and, though he was short and small-boned, he seemed to tower.

"Mr. Bunsen," he said, "since your men watched everything, I presume they took note of the details of the meal he ordered. Was it lunch or dinner, by the way?"

"It was lunch and you are right. We did notice the details."

"Then isn't it a fact that he ordered a thick soup?"

Bunsen's eyebrows raised. "A score for you, Mr. Rubin. It was cream of mushroom soup. If you want the rest of the menu, it consisted of a roast beef sandwich with a side order of french fried potatoes, a piece of apple pie with a slice of cheese, and coffee."

"Well," muttered Drake, "we can't all be gourmets."

Rubin said, "Next, I would suggest that he finished only about half his soup."

Bunsen thought for a while, then smiled. It was the first time he had smiled that evening and he revealed white and even teeth that gave a clear indication that there was a handsome man beneath the layers of fat.

"You know," he said, "I wouldn't have thought you could ask me a single question of fact concerning that episode that I could not instantly have answered, but you've managed. I don't know, offhand, if he finished his soup or not, but I'm sure that detail is on record. But let's pretend you are right and he only finished half his soup. Go on."

"All right," said Rubin, "we begin. Smith walks into the restaurant with the object. Where does he have it, by the way?"

"Left pants pocket, when he walked in. We saw no signs whatever of his changing its position."

"Good," said Rubin. "He walks in, sits down at the table, orders his meal, reads his newspaper—was he reading a newspaper, Mr. Bunsen?"

"No," said Bunsen, "he wasn't reading anything; not even the menu. He knows the place and what it has to offer."

"Then once the first course was placed before him, he sneezed. A sneeze, after all is a diversion. Roger mentioned a diversion, but I guess he thought of someone rushing in with a gun, or a fire starting in the kitchen. But a sneeze is a diversion, too, and is natural enough to go unnoticed."

"It would not have gone unnoticed," said Bunsen calmly. "He didn't sneeze."

"Or coughed, or hiccuped, what's the difference?" said Rubin. "The point is that something happened that made it natural for him to pull out a handkerchief—from the left pants pocket, I'm sure—and put it to his mouth."

"He did no such thing," said Bunsen.

"When he took away his hand," said Rubin, overriding the other's remark, "the object that had been in the left pants pocket was in the mouth."

Bunsen said, "I don't think it would have been possible for him to place the object in his mouth without our seeing him do so, or keep it there without distorting his face noticeably, but go ahead—What next?"

"The soup is before him and he eats it. You certainly won't tell me he pushed it away untasted."

"No, I'm quite certain he didn't do that."

"Or that he drank it from the bowl."

Bunsen smiled. "No, I'm quite sure he didn't do that."

"Then there was only one thing he could do. He placed a tablespoon in the soup, brought it to his mouth, brought it back to the soup, brought it to his mouth, and so on. Correct?"

"I must agree with that."

"And on one of the occasions during which the tablespoon passed from mouth to bowl, the object was in it. It was placed in the soup and, since cream of mushroom soup is not transparent, it would not be seen there. He then drank no more of the soup and someone in the kitchen picked up the object." Rubin looked about at the others triumphantly.

There was a short silence. Bunsen said, "That is all you have to say, sir?"

"Don't you agree that's a possible modus operandi?"

"No, I don't." Bunsen sighed heavily. "Quite impossible. The hand is not quicker than the trained eye, and the object is large enough to be an uncomfortable fit in the tablespoon bowl.—Furthermore, you again underestimate our experience and our thoroughness. We had a man in the kitchen and no item came back from our man's table without being thoroughly examined. If the soup bowl came back with soup in it, you can be sure it was carefully emptied by a most careful man."

"How about the waiter?" interposed Avalon, forced into interest clearly against his will.

Bunsen said, "The waiter was not one of us. He was an old employee, and besides, he was watched too."

Rubin snorted and said, "You might have told us you had a man in the kitchen."

"I might have," said Bunsen, "but Tom told me it would be best to tell you as little as possible and let you think from scratch."

Avalon said, "If you had incorporated a tiny radio transmitter in the object—"

"Then we would have been characters in a James Bond movie. Unfortunately, we must allow for expertise on the other side as well. If we had tried any such thing, they would have tumbled to it. No, the trap had to be absolutely clean." Bunsen looked depressed. "I put a hell of a lot of time and effort into it." He looked about and the depression on his face deepened. "Well, Tom, are we through here?"

Trumbull said unhappily, "Wait a minute, Bob. Damn it, Henry—"

Bunsen said, "What do you want the waiter to do?"

Trumbull said, "Come on, Henry. Doesn't anything occur to you?"

Henry sighed gently. "Something did, quite a while back, but I was hoping it would be eliminated."

"Something quite plain and simple, Henry?" said Avalon.

"I'm afraid so, sir."

Avalon said, turning to Bunsen, "Henry is an honest man and lacks all trace of the devious mind. When we are through making fools of ourselves over complexities, he picks up the one straight thread we have overlooked."

Henry said thoughtfully, "Are you sure you wish me to speak, Mr. Bunsen?"

"Yes. Go on."

"Well then, when your Mr. Smith left the restaurant, I assume that your men inside did not follow him out."

"No, of course not. They had their own work inside. They had to make sure he had left nothing behind that was significant."

"And the man in the kitchen stayed there?"

"Yes."

"Well then, outside the restaurant, the taxi driver was your man; but it would seem fair to suppose that he had to keep his eye on the traffic so as to be able to be in a position where he could maneuver himself to the curb just in time to pick up Smith; no sooner, no later."

"And a very good job he did. In fact, when the doorman hailed him, he neatly cut out another cab." Bunsen chuckled softly.

"Was the doorman one of your men?" asked Henry.

"No, he was a regular employee of the restaurant."

"Did you have a man on the street at all?"

"If you mean actually standing on the street, no."

"Then surely there was a moment or two after Smith had left the restaurant, and before he had entered the taxi, when he was not being watched—if I may call it so—professionally."

Bunsen said with a trace of contempt, "You forget that I was across the street, at a window, with a pair of binoculars. I saw him quite well. I saw the taxi man pick him up. From the door of the restaurant to the door of the taxi took, I should say, not more than fifteen seconds, and I had him in view at every moment."

Rubin suddenly interrupted. "Even when you were distracted watching the taxi man maneuver to the curb?"

He was universally shushed, but Bunsen said, "Even then."

Henry said, "I don't forget that you were watching, Mr. Bunsen, but you have said you do not have the proper appearance for that kind of work. You do not watch, professionally."

"I have eyes," said Bunsen, and there was more than merely a trace of contempt now. "Or will you tell me the hand is quicker than the eye?"

"Sometimes even when the hand is quite slow, I think.—Mr. Bunsen, you arrived late and did not hear Mr. Gonzalo's tale. He had paid a taxi driver exactly the fare recorded on the meter, and so customary is it to pay more than that, that every one of us was shocked. Even I expressed disapproval. It is only when the completely customary is violated that the event is noticed. When it takes place, it is apt to be totally ignored."

Bunsen said, "Are you trying to tell me that something was wrong with the taxi driver? I tell you there wasn't."

"I am sure of that," said Henry earnestly. "Still, didn't you miss something that you took so entirely for granted that, even looking at it, you didn't see it?"

"I don't see what it could have been. I have an excellent memory, I assure you, and in the fifteen seconds that Smith went from restaurant to taxi he did nothing I did not note and nothing I do not remember."

Henry thought for a moment or two. "You know, Mr. Bunsen, it *must* have happened, and if you had seen it happen, you would surely have taken action. But you did *not* take action; you are still mystified."

"Then whatever it was," said Bunsen, "it did not happen."

"You mean, sir, that the doorman, a regular employee of

the restaurant, hailed a cab for Smith, who was a regular patron for whom he must have performed the same service many times, and that Smith, whom you described as a well-mannered man who always did the correct social thing, did *not* tip the doorman?''

"Of course he—'' began Bunsen, and then came to a dead halt.

And in the silence that followed, Henry said, ''And if he tipped him, then surely it was with an object taken from the left pants pocket, an object that, from your description, happened to look something like a coin.—Then he smiled, and *that* you saw.''

6

The Three Numbers

I'm always fascinated by puzzles involving numbers or words. In a way, this is a small tragedy, for I am very poor at solving such puzzles.

If you create a puzzle, however, then, of course, you know the solution. You might think there is no fun in knowing a solution from the beginning, but it becomes fun if you then invent a story in which the characters don't know the solution and have to work it out with something important hanging on the event.

This is a story involving a number puzzle and you have no idea how exciting it is to have your characters sweat it out.

When Tom Trumbull arrived—late, of course—to the Black Widowers' banquet, and called for his scotch and soda, he was met by James Drake, who was wearing a rather hangdog expression on his face.

Drake's head made a gentle gesture to one side.

Trumbull followed him, unpeeling his coat as he went, his tanned and furrowed face asking the question before his voice did. "What's up?" he said.

Drake held his cigarette to one side and let the smoke curl bluely upward. "Tom, I've brought a physicist as my guest."

"So?"

"Well, he has a problem and I think it's up your alley."

"A code?"

"Something like that. Numbers, anyway. I don't have all the details. I suppose we'll get those after the dinner. But that's not the point. Will you help me if it becomes necessary to hold down Jeff Avalon?"

Trumbull looked across the room to where Avalon was standing in staid conversation with the man who was clearly the guest of the evening since he was the only stranger present.

"What's wrong with Jeff?" said Trumbull. There didn't seem anything wrong with Avalon, who was standing straight and tall as always, looking as though he might splinter if he relaxed. His graying mustache and small beard were as neat and trim as ever and he wore that careful smile on his face that he insisted on using for strangers. "He looks all right."

Drake said, "You weren't here last time. Jeff has the idea that the Black Widowers is becoming too nearly a puzzle session each month."

"What's wrong with that?" asked Trumbull as he passed his hands over his tightly waved off-white hair to press down the slight disarray produced by the wind outside.

"Jeff thinks we ought to be a purely social organization. Convivial conversation and all that."

"We have that anyway."

"So when the puzzle comes up, help me sit on him if he gets grouchy. You have a loud voice and I don't."

"No problem. Have you talked to Manny?"

"Hell, no. He'd take up the other side to be contrary."

"You may be right.—Henry!" Trumbull waved his arm. "Henry, do me a favor. This scotch and soda won't be enough. It's cold outside and it took me a long time to get a taxi so—"

Henry smiled discreetly, his unlined face looking twenty years younger than his actual sixtyishness. "I had assumed that might be so, Mr. Trumbull. Your second is ready."

"Henry, you're a diamond of the first water"—which, to be sure, was a judgment concurred in by all the Black Widowers.

"I'll give you a demonstration," said Emmanuel Rubin. He had quarreled with the soup which, he maintained, had had just a shade too much leek to make it fit for human consumption, and the fact that he was in a clear minority of one rendered him all the more emphatic in his remaining views. "I'll show you that any language is really a complex of languages.—I'll write a word on each of these two pieces of paper. The same word. I'll give one to you, Mario—and one to you, sir."

The second went to Dr. Samuel Puntsch, who had, as was usually the case with guests of the Black Widowers, maintained a discreet silence during the prelimimaries.

Puntsch was a small, slim man, dressed in a funereal color scheme that would have done credit to Avalon. He looked at the paper and lifted his unobtrusive eyebrows.

Rubin said, "Now neither of you say anything. Just write down the number of the syllable that carries the stress. It's a four-syllable word, so write down either one, two, three, or four."

Mario Gonzalo, the Black Widowers' tame artist, had just completed the sketch of Dr. Puntsch, and he laid it to one side. He looked at the word on the paper before him, wrote a figure without hesitation, and passed it to Rubin. Puntsch did the same.

Rubin said, with indescribable satisfaction, "I'll spell the word. It's u-n-i-o-n-i-z-e-d, and Mario says it's accented on the first syllable."

"*Yoo*-nionized," said Mario. "Referring to an industry whose working force has been organized into a labor union."

Puntsch laughed. "Yes, I see. I called it un-*eye*-onized; referring to a substance that did not break down into ions in solution. I accent the second syllable."

"Exactly. The same word to the eye, but different to men in different fields. Roger and Jim would agree with Dr. Puntsch, I know, and Toni, Jeff, and Henry would probably agree with Mario. It's like that in a million different places. Fugue means different things to a psychiatrist and a musician. The phrase 'to press a suit' means one thing to a nineteenth-century lover and another to a twentieth-century tailor. No two people have exactly the same language."

Roger Halsted, the mathematics teacher, said with the slight hesitation that was almost a stammer but never quite, "There's enough overlap so that it doesn't really matter, does it?"

"Most of us can understand each other, yes," said Rubin querulously, "but there's less overlap than there ought to be. Every small segment of the culture develops its own vocabulary for the sake of forming an ingroup. There are a million verbal walls behind which fools cower, and it does more to create ill feeling—"

"That was Shaw's thesis in *Pygmalion*," growled Trumbull.

"No! You're quite wrong, Tom. Shaw thought it was the result of faulty education. I say it's *deliberate* and that this does more to create the proper atmosphere for world collapse than war does." And he tackled his roast beef with a fierce cut of his knife.

"Only Manny could go from unionized to the destruction of civilization in a dozen sentences," said Gonzalo philosophically, and passed his sketch to Henry for delivery to Puntsch.

Puntsch smiled a little shakily at it, for it emphasized his ears more than a purist might have thought consistent with good looks. Henry put it on the wall with the others.

It was perhaps inevitable that the discussion veer from the iniquities of private language to word puzzles and Halsted achieved a certain degree of silence over the dessert by demanding to know the English word whose pronunciation changed when it was capitalized. Then, when all had given up, Halsted said slowly, "I would say that 'polish' becomes 'Polish,' right?"

Avalon frowned portentously, his luxuriant eyebrows hunching over his eyes. "At least that isn't as offensive as the usual Polish jokes I can't avoid hearing sometimes."

Drake said, his small gray mustache twitching, "We'll try something a little more complicated after the coffee."

Avalon darted a suspicious glance in the direction of Puntsch and, with a look of melancholy on his face, watched Henry pour the coffee.

Henry said, "Brandy, sir?"

Puntsch looked up and said, "Why, yes, thank you. That was a very good meal, waiter."

"I am glad you think so," said Henry. "The Black Widowers are a special concern to this establishment."

Drake was striking his water glass with a spoon.

He said, trying to elevate his always fuzzily hoarse voice, "I've got Sam Puntsch here partly because he worked for the same firm I work for out in New Jersey, though not in the same division. He doesn't know a damn thing about organic chemistry; I know that because I heard him discuss the subject once. On the other hand, he's a pretty fair-to-middling physicist, I'm told. I've also got him here partly because he's got a problem and I told him to come down and entertain us with it, and I hope, Jeff, that you have no objections."

Geoffrey Avalon twirled his brandy glass gently between two fingers and said grimly, "There are no bylaws to this organization, Jim, so I'll go along with you and try to enjoy myself. But I must say I would like to relax on these evenings; though perhaps it's just the old brain calcifying."

"Well, don't worry, we'll let Tom be griller in chief."

Puntsch said, "If Mr. Avalon—"

Drake said at once, "Pay no attention to Mr. Avalon."

And Avalon himself said, "Oh, it's all right, Dr. Puntsch. The group is kind enough to let me pout on occasion."

Trumbull scowled and said, "Will you all let me get on with it? Dr. Puntsch—how do you justify your existence?"

"Justify it? I suppose you could say that trying to have our civilization last for longer than a generation is a sort of justification."

"What does this trying consist of?"

"An attempt to find a permanent, safe, and non-polluting energy source."

"What kind?"

"Fusion energy.—Are you going to ask me the details?"

Trumbull shook his head. "No, unless they're germane to the problem that's disturbing you."

"Only very tangentially; which is good." Puntsch's voice was reedy, and his words were meticulously pronounced as though he had at one time had ambitions to become a radio announcer. He said, "Actually, Mr. Rubin's point was a rather good one earlier in the evening. We all do have our private language, sometimes more so than is necessary, and I would not welcome the chance to have to go into great detail on the matter of fusion."

Gonzalo, who was wearing a costume in various complementing tones of red, and who dominated the table visually even more than was usually true, muttered, "I wish people would stop saying that Rubin is right."

"You want them to lie?" demanded Rubin, head thrown up at once and his sparse beard bristling.

"Shut up, you two," shouted Trumbull. "Dr. Puntsch, let me tell you what I know about fusion energy and you stop me if I'm too far off base.—It's a kind of nuclear energy produced when you force small atoms to combine into larger ones. You use heavy hydrogen out of the ocean, fuse it to helium, and produce energy that will last us for many millions of years."

"Yes, it's roughly as you say."

"But we don't have it yet, do we?"

"No, as of today, we don't have it."

"Why not, Doctor?"

"Ah, Mr. Trumbull, I take it you don't want a two-hour lecture."

"No, sir, how about a two-minute lecture?"

Puntsch laughed. "About two minutes is all anyone will sit still for. The trouble is we have to heat up our fuel to a minimum temperature of forty-five million degrees Centigrade, which is about eighty million Fahrenheit. Then we have to keep the fusion fuel—heavy hydrogen, as you say, plus tritium, which is a particularly heavy variety—at that temperature long enough for it to catch fire, so to speak, and we must keep it all in place with strong magnetic fields while this is happening.

"So far, we can't get the necessary temperature produced quickly enough, or hold the magnetic field in being long enough, for the fusion fuel to ignite. Delivering energy by laser may be another bet, but we need stronger lasers than we have so far, or stronger and better-designed magnetic fields than we now have. Once we manage it and *do* ignite the fuel, that will be an important breakthrough, but God knows there will remain plenty of engineering problems to solve before we can actually begin to run the Earth by fusion energy.''

Trumbull said, ''When do you think we'll get to that first breakthrough; when do you think we'll have ignition?''

''It's hard to say. American and Soviet physicists have been inching forward toward it for a quarter of a century. I think they've almost reached it. Five years more maybe. But there are imponderables. A lucky intuition might bring it this year. Unforeseen difficulties may carry us into the twenty-first century.''

Halsted broke in. ''Can we wait till the twenty-first century?''

''Wait?'' said Puntsch.

''You say you are trying to have civilization last more than a generation. That sounds as though you don't think we can wait for the twenty-first century.''

''I see. I wish I could be optimistic on this point, sir,'' said Puntsch gravely, ''but I can't. At the rate we're going, our petroleum will be pretty much used up by 2000. Going back to coal will present us with a lot of problems and leaning on breeder fission reactors will involve the getting rid of enormous quantities of radioactive wastes. I would certainly feel uncomfortable if we don't end up with working fusion reactors by, say, 2010.''

''*Après moi le déluge,*'' said Avalon.

Puntsch said with a trace of acerbity, ''The deluge may well come after your time, Mr. Avalon. Do you have any children?''

Avalon, who had two children and several grandchildren, looked uncomfortable and said, ''But fusion energy may stave off the deluge and I take it your feelings about the arrival of fusion are optimistic.''

''Yes, there I tend to be optimistic.''

Trumbull said, ''Well, let's get on with it. You're working

at Jim Drake's firm. I always thought of that as one of these drug supply houses."

"It's a hell of a lot more than that," said Drake, looking dolefully at what was left of a cigarette package as though wondering whether he ought to set fire to another one or rest for ten minutes.

Puntsch said, "Jim works in the organic chemistry section. I work on plasma physics."

Rubin said, "I was down there once, visiting Jim, and took a tour of the plant. I didn't see any Tokamaks."

"What's a Tokamak?" asked Gonzalo at once.

Puntsch said, "It's a device within which stable magnetic fields—pretty stable anyway—can be set up to confine the super-hot gas. No, we don't have any. We're not doing anything of the sort. We're more or less at the theoretical end of it. When we think up something that looks hopeful, we have arrangements with some of the large installations that will allow it to be tried out."

Gonzalo said, "What's in it for the firm?"

"We're allowed to do some basic research. There's always use for it. The finn produces fluorescent tubes of various sorts and anything we find about the behavior of hot gases—plasma, it's called—and magnetic fields may always help in the production of cheaper and better fluorescents. That's the practical justification of our work."

Trumbull said, "And have you come up with anything that looks hopeful? —In fusion, I mean, not in fluorescents."

Puntsch began a smile and let it wipe off slowly. "That's exactly it. I don't know."

Halsted placed his hand on the pink area of baldness in the forepart of his skull and said, "Is that the problem you've brought us?"

"Yes," said Puntsch.

"Well, then, Doctor, suppose you tell us about it."

Puntsch cleared his throat and pursed his lips for a moment, looking about at the men at the banquet table and leaning to one side in order to allow Henry to refill his coffee cup.

"Jim Drake," he said, "has explained that everything said in this room is confidential; that everyone"—his eye rested briefly on Henry—"is to be trusted. I'll speak freely, then. I have a colleague working at the firm. His name is Matthew Revsof and Drake knows him."

Drake nodded. "Met him at your house once."

Puntsch said, "Revsof is halfway between brilliance and madness, which is sometimes a good thing for a theoretical physicist. It means, though, that he's erratic and difficult to deal with at times. We've been good friends, mostly because our wives have gotten along together particularly well. It became one of those family things where the children on both sides use us almost interchangeably as parents, since we have houses in the same street.

"Revsof is now in the hospital. He's been there two months. I'll have to explain that it's a mental hospital and that he had a violent episode which put him into it and there's no point in going into the details of that. However, the hospital is in no hurry to let him go and that creates a problem.

"I went to visit him about a week after he had been hospitalized. He seemed perfectly normal, perfectly cheerful; I brought him up to date on some of the work going on in the department and he had no trouble following me. But then he wanted to speak to me privately. He insisted the nurse leave and that the door be closed.

"He swore me to secrecy and told me he knew exactly how to design a Tokamak in such a way as to produce a totally stable magnetic field that would contain a plasma of moderate densities indefinitely. He said something like this, 'I worked it out last month. That's why I've been put here. Naturally, the Soviets arranged it. The material is in my home safe; the diagrams, the theoretical analysis, everything.' "

Rubin, who had been listening with an indignant frown, interrupted. "Is that possible? Is he the kind of man who could do that? Was the work at the stage where such an advance—"

Puntsch smiled wearily. "How can I answer that? The history of science is full of revolutionary advances that required small insights that anyone might have had, but that, in fact, only one person did. I'll tell you this, though. When someone in a mental hospital tells you that he has something that has been eluding the cleverest physicists in the world for nearly thirty years, and that the Russians are after him, you don't have a very great tendency to believe it. All I tried to do was soothe him.

"But my efforts to do that just excited him. He told me he planned to have the credit for it; he wasn't going to have anyone stealing priority while he was in the hospital. I was to stand guard over the home safe and make sure that no one broke in. He was sure that Russian spies would try to arrange a break-in and he kept saying over and over again that I was the only one he could trust and as soon as he got out of the hospital he would announce the discovery and prepare a paper so that he could safeguard his priority. He said he would allow me coauthorship. Naturally, I agreed to everything just to keep him quiet and got the nurse back in as soon as I could."

Halsted said, "American and Soviet scientists are cooperating in fusion research, aren't they?"

"Yes, of course," said Puntsch. "The Tokamak itself is of Soviet origin. The business of Russian spies is just Revsof's overheated fantasy."

Rubin said, "Have you visited him since?"

"Quite a few times. He sticks to his story. —It bothers me. I don't believe him. I think he's mad. And yet something inside me says: What if he isn't? What if there's something in his home safe that the whole world would give its collective eyeteeth for?"

Halsted said, "When be gets out—"

Puntsch said, "It's not that easy. Any delay is risky. This is a field in which many minds are eagerly busy. On any particular day, someone else may make Revsof's discovery— assuming that Revsof has really made one—and he will then lose priority and credit, and a Nobel Prize for all I know. And, to take the broader view, the firm will lose a considerable amount of reflected credit and the chance at a substantial increase in its prosperity. Every employee of the firm will lose the chance of benefiting from what general prosperity increase the firm might have experienced. So you see, gentlemen, I have a personal stake in this, and so has Jim Drake, for that matter.

"But even beyond that— The world is in a race that it may not win. Even if we do get the answer to a stable magnetic field, there will be a great deal of engineering to work through, as I said before, and, at the very best, it will be years before fusion energy is really available to the world—years we might not be able to afford. In that case, it isn't safe to lose any time at all waiting for Revsof to get out."

Gonzalo said, "If he's getting out soon—"

"But he *isn't*. That's the worst of it," said Puntsch. "He may never come out. He's deteriorating."

Avalon said in his deep, solemn voice, "I take it, sir, that you have explained the advantages of prompt action to your friend."

"That I have," said Puntsch. "I've explained it as carefully as I could. I said we would open the safe before legal witnesses, and bring everything to him for his personal signature. We would leave the originals and take copies. I explained what he himself might possibly lose by delay. —All that happened was that he—well, in the end he attacked me. I've been asked not to visit him again till further notice."

Gonzalo said, "What about his wife? Does she know anything about this? You said she was a good friend of your wife's."

"So she is. She's a wonderful girl and she understands perfectly the difficulty of the situation. She agrees that the safe should be opened."

"Has *she* talked to her husband?" asked Gonzalo.

Puntsch hesitated. "Well, no. She hasn't been allowed to see him. He—he— This is ridiculous but I can't help it. He claims Barbara, his wife, is in the pay of the Soviet Union. Frankly, it was Barbara whom he—when he was put in the hospital—"

"All right," said Trumbull gruffly, "but can't you get Revsof declared incompetent and have the control of the safe transferred to his wife?"

"First, that's a complicated thing. Barbara would have to testify to a number of things she doesn't want to testify to. She—she loves the man."

Gonzalo said, "I don't want to sound ghoulish, but you said that Revsof was deteriorating. If he dies—"

"Deteriorating mentally, not physically. He's thirty-eight years old and could live forty more years and be mad every day of it."

"Eventually, won't his wife be forced to request he be declared incompetent?"

Puntsch said, "But when will that be? —And all this still isn't the problem I want to present. I had explained to Barbara exactly how I would go about it to protect Matt's priority. I would open the safe and Barbara would initial and date every piece of paper in it. I would photocopy it all and give her a notarized statement to the effect that I had done this and that I acknowledged all that I removed to be Revsof's work. The originals and the notarized statement would be returned to the safe and I would work with the copies.

"You see, she had told me at the very start that she had the combination. It was a matter of first overcoming my own feeling that I was betraying a trust, and secondly, overcoming her scruples. I didn't like it but I felt I was serving a higher cause and in the end Barbara agreed. We decided that if Revsof was ever sane enough to come home, he would agree we had done the right thing. And his priority *would* be protected."

Trumbull said, "I take it you opened the safe, then."

"No," said Puntsch, "I didn't. I tried the combination Barbara gave me and it didn't work. The safe is still closed."

Halsted said, "You could blow it open."

Puntsch said, "I can't bring myself to do that. It's one thing to be given the combination by the man's wife. It's another to—"

Halsted shook his head. "I mean, can't Mrs. Revsof ask that it be blown open?"

Puntsch said, "I don't think she would ask that. It would mean bringing in outsiders. It would be an act of violence against Revsof, in a way, and— Why doesn't the combination work? That's the problem."

Trumbull put his hands on the table and leaned forward. "Dr. Puntsch, are you asking us to answer that question? To tell you how to use the combination you have?"

"More or less."

"Do you have the combination with you?"

"You mean the actual slip of paper that has the combination written upon it? No. Barbara keeps that and I see her point. However, if you want it written down, that's no problem. I remember it well enough." He brought out a little notebook from his inner jacket pocket, tore off a sheet of paper, and wrote rapidly. "There it is!"

12 R 27 15

Trumbull glanced at it solemnly, then passed the paper to Halsted on his left. It made the rounds and came back to him.

Trumbull folded his hands and stared solemnly at the bit of paper. He said, "How do you know this is the combination to the safe?"

"Barbara says it is."

"Doesn't it seem unlikely to you, Dr. Puntsch, that the man you described would leave the combination lying about? With the combination available, he might as well have an unlocked safe. —This row of symbols may have nothing to do with the safe."

Puntsch sighed. "That's not the way of it. It isn't as though the safe ever had anything of intrinsic value in it. There's nothing of great intrinsic value in Revsof's house altogether, or in mine, for that matter. We're not rich and we're not very subject to burglary. Revsof got the safe about five years ago and had it installed because he thought he might keep papers there. He had this fetish about losing priority even then, but it wasn't till recently that it reached the point of paranoia. He did make a note of the combination for his own use so he wouldn't lock himself out.

"Barbara came across it one day and asked what it was and he said that it was the combination to his safe. She said, 'Well, don't leave it lying around,' and she put it in a little envelope in one of her own drawers, feeling he might need it someday. He never did, apparently, and I'm sure he must have forgotten all about it. But *she* didn't forget, and she says she is certain it has never been disturbed.''

Rubin said, ''He might have had the combination changed.''

''That would have meant a locksmith in the house. Barbara says she is certain it never happened.''

Trumbull said, ''Is that all there was written on the page? Just six numbers and a letter of the alphabet?''

''That's all.''

''What about the back of the sheet?''

''Nothing.''

Trumbull said, ''You understand, Dr. Puntsch, this isn't a code, and I'm not expert on combination locks. What does the lock look like?''

''Very ordinary. I'm sure Revsof could not afford a really fancy safe. There's a circle with numbers around it from 1 to 30 and a knob with a little pointer in the middle. Barbara has seen Matt at the safe and there's no great shakes to it. He turns the knob and pulls it open.''

''She's never done that herself?''

''No. She says she hasn't.''

''She can't tell you why the safe doesn't open when you use the combination?''

''No, she can't. —And yet it seems straightforward enough. Most of the combination locks I've dealt with—all of them, in fact—have knobs that you turn first in one direction, then in the other, then back in the first direction again. It seems clear to me that, according to the combination, I should turn the knob to the right till the pointer is at twelve, then left to twenty-seven, then right again to fifteen.''

Trumbull said thoughtfully, ''I can't see that it could mean anything else either.''

''But it doesn't work,'' said Puntsch. ''I turned twelve, twenty-seven, fifteen a dozen times. I did it carefully, making sure that the little pointer was centered on each line. I tried making extra turns; you know, right to twelve, then left one full turn and then to twenty-seven, then right one full turn and then to fifteen. I tried making one full turn in one direction and not in the other. I tried other tricks, jiggling the knob, pressing it. I tried everything.''

Gonzalo said, grinning, "Did you say 'Open sesame'?"

"It didn't occur to me to do so," said Puntsch, not grinning, "but if it had, I would have tried it. Barbara says she never noticed him do anything special, but of course, it could have been something unnoticeable and for that matter she didn't watch him closely. It wouldn't occur to her that she'd have to know someday."

Halsted said, "Let me look at that again." He stared at the combination solemnly. "This is only a copy, Dr. Puntsch. This can't be exactly the way it looked. It seems clear here but you might be copying it just as you thought it was. Isn't it possible that some of the numbers in the original might be equivocal so that you might mistake a seven for a one, for instance?"

"No, no," said Puntsch, shaking his head vigorously. "There's no chance of a mistake there. I assure you."

"What about the spaces?" said Halsted. "Was it spaced exactly like that?"

Puntsch reached for the paper and looked at it again. "Oh, I see what you mean. No, as a matter of fact, there were no spaces. I put them in because that was how I thought of it. Actually the original is a solid line of symbols with no particular spacing. It doesn't matter, though, does it? You can't divide it any other way. I'll write it down for you without spaces." He wrote a second time under the first and shoved it across the table to Halsted.

$$12R2715$$

He said, "You can't divide it any other way. You can't have a 271 or a 715. The numbers don't go higher than thirty."

"Well now," muttered Halsted, "never mind the numbers. What about the letter R?" He licked his lips, obviously enjoying the clear atmosphere of suspense that had now centered upon him. "Suppose we divide the combination this way":

$$12 \ R27 \ 15$$

He held it up for Puntsch to see, and then for the others. "In this division, it's the twenty-seven which would have the sign for 'right' so it's the two other numbers that turn left. In other words, the numbers are twelve, twenty-seven, and fifteen all right, but you turn left, right, left, instead of right, left, right."

Gonzalo protested. "Why put the R there?"

Halsted said, "All he needs is the minimum reminder. He knows what the combination is. If he reminds himself the middle number is right, he knows the other two are left."

Gonzalo said, "But that's no big deal. If he just puts down the three numbers, it's either left, right, left, or else it's right, left, right. If one doesn't work, he tries the other. Maybe the R stands for something else."

"I can't think what," said Puntsch gloomily.

Halsted said, "The symbol couldn't be something other than an R, could it, Dr. Puntsch?"

"Absolutely not," said Puntsch. "I'll admit I didn't think of associating the R with the second number, but that doesn't matter anyway. When the combination wouldn't work right, left, right, I was desperate enough not only to try it left, right, left; but right, right, right and left, left, left. In every case I tried it with and without complete turns in between. Nothing worked."

Gonzalo said, "Why not try all the combinations? There can only be so many."

Rubin said, "Figure out how many, Mario. The first number can be anything from one to thirty in either direction; so can the second; so can the third. The total number of possible combinations, if any direction is allowed for any number, is sixty times sixty times sixty, or over two hundred thousand."

"I think I'll blow it open before it comes to trying them all," said Puntsch in clear disgust.

Trumbull turned to Henry, who had been standing at the sideboard, an intent expression on his face. "Have you been following all this, Henry?"

Henry said, "Yes, sir, but I haven't actually seen the figures."

Trumbull said, "Do you mind, Dr. Puntsch? He's the best

man here, actually." He handed over the slip with the three numbers written in three different ways.

Henry studied them gravely and shook his head. "I'm sorry. I had had a thought, but I see I'm wrong."

"What was the thought?" asked Trumbull.

"It had occurred to me that the letter R might have been in the small form. I see it's a capital."

Puntsch looked astonished. "Wait, wait. Henry, does it matter?"

"It might, sir. We don't often think it does, but Mr. Halsted explained earlier in the evening that 'polish' becomes 'Polish,' changing pronunciation simply because of a capitalization."

Puntsch said slowly, "But, you know, it *is* a small letter in the original. It never occurred to me to produce it that way. I always use capitals when I print. How odd."

There was a faint smile on Henry's face. He said, "Would you write the combination with a small letter, sir."

Puntsch, flushing slightly, wrote:

12r2715

Henry looked at it and said, "As long as it is a small *r* after all, I can ask a further question. Are there any other differences between this and the original?"

"No," said Puntsch. Then, defensively, "No significant differences of any kind. The matter of the spacing and the capitalization hasn't changed anything, has it? Of course, the original isn't in my handwriting."

Henry said quietly, "Is it in anyone's handwriting, sir?"

"What?"

"I mean, is the original typewritten, Dr. Puntsch?"

Dr. Puntsch's flush deepened. "Yes, now that you ask, it *was* typewritten. That doesn't mean anything either. If there were a typewriter here I would typewrite it for you, though, of course, it might not be the same make of typewriter that typed out the original."

Henry said, "There is a typewriter in the office on this floor. Would you care to type it, Dr. Puntsch?"

"Certainly," said Puntsch defiantly. He was back in two

minutes, during which time not one word was said by anyone at the table. He presented the paper to Henry, with the typewritten series of numbers under the four lines of handwritten ones:

12r2715

Henry said, "Is this the way it looked now? The typewriter that did the original did not have a particularly unusual typeface?"

"No, it didn't. What I have typed looks just like the original."

Henry passed the paper to Trumbull, who looked at it and passed it on.

Henry said, "If you open the safe, you are very likely to find nothing of importance, I suppose."

"I suppose it too," snapped Puntsch. "I'm almost sure of it. It will be disappointing but much better than standing here wondering."

"In that case, sir," said Henry, "I would like to say that Mr. Rubin spoke of private languages early in the evening. The typewriter has a private language too. The standard typewriter uses the same symbol for the numeral one and the small form of the twelfth letter of the alphabet.

"If you had wanted to abbreviate 'left' and 'right' by the initial letters in handwriting, there would have been no problem, since neither form of the handwritten letter is confusing. If you had used a typewriter and abbreviated it in capitals it would have been clear. Using small letters, it is possible to read the combination as 12 right, 27, 15; or possibly 12, right 27, 15; or as left 2, right 27, left 5. The 1 in 12 and 15 is not the numeral 1 but the small version of the letter L and stands for left. Revsof knew what he was typing and it didn't confuse him. It could confuse others."

Puntsch looked at the symbols openmouthed. "How did I miss that?"

Henry said, "You spoke, earlier, of insights that anyone might make, but that only one actually does. It was Mr. Gonzalo who had the key."

"I?" said Gonzalo strenuously.

"Mr. Gonzalo wondered why there should be one letter," said Henry, "and it seemed to me he was right. Dr. Revsof would surely indicate the directions for all, or for none. Since one letter was indubitably present, I wondered if the other two night not be also."

7

The One and Only East

I don't like to cheat in presenting the views of my characters. Shakespeare has the Duke of Gloucester (later Richard III) openly announce himself to be a villain but, however dramatically necessary that might be, I disapprove. No one thinks of himself as a villain. Someone may seem a villain to us, but the villain himself can always find some specious argument (even if it's only "Everyone does it") that excuses himself to himself.

Consequently, I do my best to have all characters present their point of view as skillfully as possible, even characters whom I lack personal sympathy for. In this story, I do not agree in the slightest with Ralph Murdock's point of view, but so well do I have him argue that he beats down all objections by the Black Widowers. I found myself rather discomfited by that, but decided to accept it as a testimony to my literary/ intellectual honesty. I like being made to look skillful and honest and so I like the story for that reason.

Mario Gonzalo, host of the month's Black Widowers' banquet, was resplendent in his scarlet blazer but looked a little disconsolate nevertheless.

He said in a low voice to Geoffrey Avalon, the patent attorney, "He's sort of a deadhead, Jeff, but he's got an interesting problem. He's my landlady's cousin and we were talking about it and I thought, Well, hell, it could be interesting."

Avalon, on his first drink, bent his dark brows disapprovingly and said, "Is he a priest?"

"No," said Gonzalo, "not a Catholic priest. I think what you call him is 'elder.' He's a member of some small uptight sect. —Which reminds me that I had better ask Tom to go a little easy on his language."

Avalon's frown remained. "You know, Mario, if you invite a man solely on the basis of his problem, and without any personal knowledge of him whatever, you could be letting us in for a very sticky evening. —Does he drink?"

"I guess not," said Mario. "He asked for tomato juice."

"Does that mean *we* don't drink?" Avalon took an unaccustomedly vigorous sip.

"Of course we drink."

"You're the host, Mario—but I suspect the worst."

The guest, standing against the wall, was dressed in a somber black and wore a mournful expression which may have been merely the result of the natural downward slant of the outer corners of his eyes. His face almost glistened with a recent close shave and bore a pallor that might merely have been the contrast with his dark clothes. His name was Ralph Murdock.

Emmanuel Rubin, his spectacle-magnified eyes glaring and his sparse beard vibrating with the energy of his speech, had taken the measure of the man at once and had managed to maneuver the discussion into a sharp analysis of the nature of the Trinity almost before the meal had been fairly begun.

Murdock seemed unmoved, and his face remained as calm as that of Henry, the club waiter, who performed his functions as imperturbably as ever.

"The mistake," said Murdock, "usually made by those who want to discuss the mysteries in terms of ordinary logic is to suppose that the rules that originate from observation of the world of sense impression apply to the wider universe beyond. To some extent, they may, but how can we know where and how they do. not?''

Rubin said, ''That's an evasion.''

''It is not,'' said Murdock, ''and I'll give you an example within the world of sense impression. We obtain our common-sense notions of the behavior of objects from the observation of things of moderate size, moving at moderate speeds and existing at moderate temperatures. When Albert Einstein worked a scheme for a vast universe and enormous velocities, he ended with a picture that seemed against common sense; that is, against the observations we found it easy to make in everyday life.''

Rubin said, ''Yet Einstein deduced the relativistic universe from sense impressions and observations that anyone could make.''

''Provided,'' said Murdock smoothly, ''that instruments were used which were unknown to man some centuries earlier. The observations we can now make and the effects we can now produce would seem to mankind a few centuries ago like the result of wizardry, magic, or even, perhaps, revelation, if these things were made apparent without the proper introduction and education.''

''Then you think,'' said Rubin, ''that the revelation that has faced man with a Trinity now incomprehensible may make sense in a kind of super-relativity of the future?''

''Possibly,'' said Murdock, ''or possibly it makes sense in a kind of super-relativity that was reached by man long ago through the short-circuiting of mere reason and the use of more powerful instruments for gaining knowledge.''

With open delight, the others joined in the battle, everyone in opposition to Murdock, who seemed oblivious to the weight of the forces against him. With an unchanging expression of melancholy and with unmoved politeness, he answered them all without any sense of urgency or annoyance. It was all the more exciting in that it did not deal with matters that could be settled by reference to the club library.

Over the dessert, Trumbull, with a careful mildness of vocabulary that was belied by the ferocious wrinkling of his tanned face, said, ''Whatever you can say of reasoning, it has lengthened the average human life by some forty years in the last century. The forces beyond reason, whatever they may be, have been unable to lengthen it a minute.''

Murdock said, "That reason has its uses and seeming benefit no one can deny. It has enabled us to live long, but look round the world, sir, and tell me whether it has enabled us to live decently. And ask yourself further whether length without decency is so unmixed a blessing.''

By the time the brandy was served and the lances of all had been shivered against Murdock's calm verbal shield, it seemed almost anticlimactic to have Gonzalo strike his water glass with his spoon to mark the beginning of the post-dinner grilling.

Gonzalo said, "Gentlemen, we have had an unusually interesting dinner, I think''—and here he made a brief gesture at Avalon, who sat on his left, one it was well for Murdock not to have seen—''and it seems to me that our guest has already been put through his hurdles. He has acquitted himself well and I think even Manny has suspicious signs of egg on his face. —Don't say anything, Manny. —As host, I am going to end the grilling then and direct Mr. Murdock, if he will, to tell us his story.''

Murdock, who had ended the dinner with a large glass of milk, and who had refused Henry's offer of coffee and of brandy, said:

"It is kind of Mr. Gonzalo to invite me to this dinner and I must say I have been pleased with the courtesy extended me. I am grateful as well. It is not often I have a chance to discuss matters with unbelievers who are as ready to listen as yourselves. I doubt that I have convinced any of you, but it is by no means my mission to convince you—rather to offer you an opportunity to convince yourselves.

"My problem, or 'story' as Mr. Gonzalo has called it, has preyed on my mind these recent weeks. I have confided some of it, in a moment of agony of mind, to Sister Minerva, who is, by the reckoning of the world, a cousin of mine, but a sister by virtue of a common membership in our Church of the Disciples of Holiness. She, for reasons that seemed worthwhile to herself, mentioned it to her tenant, Mr. Gonzalo, and he sought me out and implored me to attend this meeting.

"He assured me that it was possible you might help me in

this problem that preys upon my mind. You may or you may not; that does not matter. The kindness you have already shown me is great enough to make failure in the other matter something of little consequence.

"Gentlemen, I am an elder of the Church of the Disciples of Holiness. It is a small church of no importance at all as the world counts importance, but the world's approval is not what we seek. Nor do we look for consolation in the thought that we alone will find salvation. We are perfectly ready to admit that all may find their way to the throne by any of an infinite number of paths. We find comfort only in that our own path seems to us to be a direct and comfortable one, a path that gives us peace—a commodity as rare in the world as it is desirable.

"I have been a member of the Church since the age of fifteen and have been instrumental in bringing into the fold several of my friends and relations.

"One whom I failed to interest was my Uncle Haskell.

"It would be easy for me to describe my Uncle Haskell as a sinner but that word is usually used to describe offenses against God, and I consider that to be a useless definition. God's mercy is infinite and His love is great enough to find offense in nothing that applies to Himself only. If the offense were against man that would be far graver, but here I can exonerate my Uncle Haskell by at least the amount by which I can exonerate mankind generally. One cannot live a moment without in some way harming, damaging or, at the very least, inconveniencing a fellow man, but I am sure my Uncle Haskell never intended such harm, damage, or inconvenience. He would have gone a mile out of his way to prevent this, if he knew what was happening and if prevention were possible.

"There remains the third class of damage—that of a man against himself—and it was here, I am afraid, that my Uncle Haskell was a sinner. He was a large man, with a Homeric sense of humor and gargantuan appetites. He ate and drank to excess, and womanized as well, yet whatever he did, he did with such gusto that one could be deluded into believing he gained pleasure from his way of life, and fall into the error of excusing him on the grounds that it was far better to enjoy life than to be a sour Puritan such as myself who finds a perverse pleasure in gloom.

"It was this, in fact, that was my Uncle Haskell's defense when I remonstrated with him on one occasion when what might have seemed to himself and to others to have been a glorious spree ended with himself in jail and possessing a mild concussion to boot.

"He said to me, 'What do you know of life, you such-and-such Puritan? You don't drink, you don't smoke, you don't swear, you don't—'

"Well, I will spare you the list of pleasures in which he found me lacking. You can, undoubtedly, imagine each one. It may seem sad to you, too, that I miss out on such routes to elevation of the spirit, but my Uncle Haskell, if he knew a dozen ladies of doubtful virtue, had never known the quiet heart-filling of love. He did not know the pleasurable serenity of quiet contemplation, of reasoned discourse, of communion with the great souls who have left their thoughts behind them. He knew my feelings in this respect but scorned them.

"He may have done so the more vehemently because he knew what he had lost. While I was in college—in the days when I first came to know my Uncle Haskell and to love him—he was writing a dissertation on Restoration England. At times he spoke as though he were planning to write a novel, at times a historical exposition. He had a home in Leonia, New Jersey, then—still had, I should say, for he had been born there, as had his ancestors and mine back to the Quaker days in colonial times. —Well, he lost it, along with everything else.

"Now, where was I? —Yes, in his Leonia home, he built up a library of material on Restoration England, in which he found, I honestly believe, more pleasure than in any of the sensualities that eventually claimed him.

"It was his addiction to gambling that did the real damage. It was the first of the passions he called pleasures that he took to extremes. It cost him his home and his library. It cost him his work, both that in which he made his living as an antique dealer, and that in which he found his joy as an amateur historian.

"His sprees, however rowdily joyful, left him in the hospital, the jail, or the gutter, and I was not always there to find and extricate him at once.

"What kept him going was the erratic nature of his chief vice, for occasionally he made some fortunate wager or turned up a lucky card and then, for a day or for a month, he would be well to do. At those times he was always generous. He never valued money for itself nor clung to it in the face of another's need—which would have been a worse vice than any he possessed—so that the good times never lasted long nor served as any base for the renewal of his former, worthier life.

"And, as it happened, toward the end of his life, he made the killing of a lifetime. I believe it is called a 'killing,' which is reasonable since the language of vice has a peculiar violence of its own. I do not pretend to understand how it was done, except that several horses, each unlikely to win, nevertheless won, and my Uncle Haskell so arranged his bets that each winning horse greatly multiplied what had already been multiplied.

"He was left, both by his standards and mine, a wealthy man, but he was dying and knew he would not have time to spend the money in his usual fashion. What occurred to him, then, was to leave the world in the company of a huge joke—a joke in which the humor rested in what he conceived to be my corruption, though I'm sure he didn't look upon it that way.

"He called me to his bedside and said to me something which, as nearly as I can remember, was this:

" 'Now, Ralph, my boy, don't lecture me. You see for yourself that I am virtuous now. Lying here, I can't do any of the terrible things you deplore—except perhaps to swear a little. I can only find time and occasion now to be as virtuous as you and my reward is that I am to die.

" 'But I don't mind, Ralph, because I've got more money now than I've had at one time for many years and I will be able to throw it away in a brand-new fashion. I am willing it to you, nephew.'

"I began to protest that I preferred his health and his true reform to his money, but he cut me off.

" 'No, Ralph, in your twisted way you have tried your best

for me and have helped me even though you disapproved of me so strongly and could have no hope of a reasonable return either in money or in conversion. On top of that, you're my only relative and you should get the money even if you had done nothing at all for me.'

"Again I tried to explain that I had helped him as a human being and not as a relative, and that I had not done so as a kind of business investment, but again he cut me off. He was having difficulty speaking and I did not wish to prolong matters unduly.

"He said, 'I will leave you fifty thousand dollars, free and clear. Matters will be so arranged that all legal expenses and all taxation will be taken care of. I have already discussed this with my lawyer. With your way of life, I don't know what you can possibly do with the money other than stare at it, but if that gives you pleasure, I'll leave you to it.'

"I said gently, 'Uncle Haskell, a great deal of good can be done with fifty thousand dollars and I will spend it in ways that the Disciples of Holiness will find fitting and useful. If this displeases you, then do not leave the money to me.'

"He laughed then, a feeble effort, and fumbled for my hand in a way that made it clear how weak he had grown. I had not seen him for a year and in that interval he had gone downhill at an incredible pace.

"The doctors said that a combination of diabetes and cancer, treated inadequately, had advanced too rapidly across the bastions of his pleasure-riddled body, heaven help him, and left him with nothing but the hope of a not too prolonged time of dying. It was on himself and the horse races that he had made a simultaneous killing.

"He clutched my hand weakly and said, 'No, do whatever you want with the money. Hire someone to sing psalms. Give it away, a penny at a time, to five million bums. That's your business; I don't care. But, Ralph, there's a catch to all this, a very amusing catch.'

" 'A catch? What kind of catch?' It was all I could think of to ask.

" 'Why, Ralph, my boy, I'm afraid you will have to gamble for the money.' He patted my hand and laughed again. 'It will be a good, straight gamble with the odds five to one against you.

" 'My lawyer,' he went on, 'has an envelope in which is located the name of a city—a nice, sealed envelope, which he won't open till you come to him with the name of a city. I will give you six cities to choose from and you will select one of these. One! If the city you select matches the one in the envelope, you get fifty thousand dollars. If it does not match, you get nothing, and the money goes to various charities. *My* kind of charities.'

" 'This is not a decent thing to do, Uncle,' I said, rather taken aback.

" 'Why not, Ralph? All you have to do is guess the city and you have a great deal of money. And if you guess wrong, you lose nothing. You can't ask better than that. My suggestion is that you number the cities from one to six, then roll a die and pick the city corresponding to the number you roll. A sporting chance, Ralph!'

"His eyes seemed to glitter, perhaps at the picture of myself rolling dice for money. I felt that sharply and I said, shaking my head, 'Uncle Haskell, it is useless to place this condition on me. I will not play games with the universe or abdicate the throne of conscience in order to allow chance to make my decisions for me. Either leave me the money, if that pleases you, or do not leave it, if *that* pleases you.'

"He said, 'Why do you think of it as playing games with the universe? Don't you accept what men call chance to be really God's will? You have said that often enough. Well then, if He thinks you worthy, you will get the money. Or don't you trust Him?'

"I said, 'God is not a man that He may be put to the test.'

"My Uncle Haskell was growing feebler. He withdrew his arm and let it rest passively on the blanket. He said in a while, 'Well, you'll have to. If you don't supply my lawyer with your choice within thirty days of my death, it will all go to my charities. Come, thirty days gives you enough time.'

"We all have our weaknesses, gentlemen, and I am not always free of pride. I could not allow myself to be forced to dance to my Uncle Haskell's piping merely in order to get the money. But then I thought that I could use the money—not for myself but for the Church—and perhaps I had no right to throw it away out of pride in my virtue, when so much would be lost in the process.

"But pride won. I said, 'I'm sorry, Uncle Haskell, but in that case, the money will have to go elsewhere. I will not gamble for it.'

"I rose to go but his hand motioned and I did not yet turn away. He said, 'All right, my miserable nephew. I want you to have the money, I really do; so if you lack sporting blood and can't take your honest chance with fate, I will give you one hint. If you penetrate it, you will know which city it is—beyond doubt, I think—and you will not be gambling when you hand in that name.'

"I did not really wish to prolong the discussion and yet I hated to abandon him and leave him desolate if I could avoid doing so. I said, 'What is this hint?'

"He said, 'You will find the answer in the one and only east—the one and only east.'

" 'The one and only east,' I repeated. 'Very well, Uncle Haskell, I will consider it. Now let us talk of other things.'

"I made as though to sit down again, but the nurse entered and said it was time for my Uncle Haskell to rest. And, indeed, I thought it was; he seemed worn to the last thread.

"He said, 'Saved a sermon, by the Almighty,' and laughed in a whisper.

"I said, 'Good-by, Uncle Haskell. I will come again.'

"When I reached the door he called out, 'Don't jump too soon, nephew. Think it over carefully. The one and only east.'

"That is the story, gentlemen. My uncle died twenty-seven days ago. Within three days, by this coming Monday, I must give my choice to the lawyer. I suspect I will not give that choice, for my Uncle Haskell's clue means nothing to me and I will not choose a city as a mere gamble. I will not."

There was a short silence after Murdock had finished his tale. James Drake puffed thoughtfully on his cigarette. Tom Trumbull scowled at his empty brandy glass. Roger Halsted doodled on his napkin. Geoffrey Avalon sat bolt upright and looked blank. Emmanuel Rubin shook his head slowly from side to side.

Gonzalo broke the silence uneasily, perhaps thinking it his duty to do so, as the host. He said, "Do you mind telling us the names of the six cities, Mr. Murdock?"

"Not at all, Mr. Gonzalo. Since you asked me to come here in order that I might possibly be helped—and since I agreed to come—I obviously seek help. With that in view, I must answer any honorable question. The names of the cities, as I received them from the lawyer on the day of my Uncle Haskell's death, are on this paper. You'll notice it is on the lawyer's stationery. It is the paper he gave me."

He passed it on to Gonzalo. Aside from the lawyer's letterhead, it contained only the typed list of six cities in alphabetical order:

> ANCHORAGE, ALASKA
> ATHENS, GEORGIA
> AUGUSTA, MAINE
> CANTON, OHIO
> EASTON, PENNSYLVANIA
> PERTH AMBOY, NEW JERSEY

Gonzalo passed it round. When he received it back he called, "Henry!" Then, to Murdock, "Our waiter is a member of the club. You have no objection to his seeing the list, I hope?"

"I have no objection to anyone seeing it," said Murdock.

Avalon cleared his throat. "Before we launch ourselves into speculation, Mr. Murdock, it is only fair to ask if you have given the matter some thought yourself."

Murdock's sorrowful face grew thoughtful. His lips pressed together and his eyes blinked. He said in a soft, almost shamefaced voice, "Gentlemen, I would like to tell you that I have resisted temptation completely, but the fact is I have not. I have thought at times and tried to convince myself that one city or another fits my Uncle Haskell's hint so that I can offer it to the lawyer on Monday with a clear conscience. On occasion I have settled on one or another of the cities on the list but each time it was merely a case of fooling myself, of compromising, of pretending I was not gambling when I was."

Rubin said, with a face innocently blank, "Have you prayed, Mr. Murdock? Have you sought divine guidance?"

For a moment it seemed as though Murdock's careful armor had been pierced, but only for a moment. After that slight pause he said, "If that were appropriate in this case, I would have seen a solution without prayer. In God's eyes, it is my needs that count and not my desires, and He knows my needs without my having to inform Him."

Rubin said, "Have you tried to approach the problem using the inferior weapon of reason?"

"I have, of course," said Murdock. "In a casual way. I have tried to resist being drawn into it too deeply. I mistrust myself, I fear."

Rubin said, "And have you come to any favorite conclusion? You've said that you have been unable to settle on any one city definitely, to the point where you would consider its choice as no longer representing a gamble—but do you lean in one direction or another?"

"I have leaned in one direction at one time and in another direction at another. I cannot honestly say that any one of the cities is my favorite. With your permission, I will not tell you the thoughts that have struck me since it is *your* help I seek and I would prefer you to reach your conclusions, or hypotheses, uninfluenced by my thoughts. If you miss anything I have thought of, I will tell you."

"Fair enough," said Gonzalo, smoothing down one collar of his blazer with an air of absent self-satisfaction. "I suppose we have to consider whether any of those cities is the one and only east."

Murdock said, "I would think so."

"In that case," said Gonzalo, "pardon me for mentioning the obvious, but the word 'east' occurs only in Easton. It is the one and only east."

"Oddly enough," said Murdock dryly, "I had not failed to notice that, Mr. Gonzalo. It strikes me as obvious enough to be ignored. My Uncle Haskell also said, 'Don't jump too soon.' "

"Ah," said Gonzalo, "but that might just be to throw you off. The real gambler has to know when to bluff and your uncle could well have been bluffing. If he had a real rotten kind of humor, it would have seemed fun to him to give you the answer, let it lie right there, and then scare you out of accepting it.''

Murdock said, ''That may be so, but that sort of thing would mean I would have to penetrate my Uncle Haskell's mind and see whether he was capable of a double double cross or something like that. It would be a gamble and I won't ganble. Either the hint, properly interpreted, makes the matter so plain that it is no longer a gamble, or it is worthless. In short, Easton may be the city, but if so, I will believe it only for some reason stronger than the mere occurrence of 'east' in its name.''

Halsted, leaning forward toward Murdock, said, ''I think no gambler worth his salt would set up a puzzle with so easy a solution as the connection between east and Easton. That's just misdirection. Let me point out something a little more reasonable, and a little more compelling. Of the six cities mentioned, I believe Augusta is easternmost. Certainly it is in the state of Maine, which is the easternmost of the fifty states. Augusta has to be the one and only east, and beyond any doubt.''

Drake shook his head violently. ''Quite wrong, Roger, quite wrong. It's just a common superstition that Maine is the easternmost state. Not since 1959. Once Alaska became the fiftieth state, *it* became the easternmost state.''

Halsted frowned. ''Westernmost, you mean, Jim.''

''Westernmost *and* easternmost. And northernmost too. Look, the 180° longitude line passes through the Aleutian Islands. The islands west of the line are in the Eastern Hemisphere. They are the *only* part of the fifty states that are in the Eastern Hemisphere and that makes Alaska the easternmost state, the one and only east.''

''What about Hawaii?'' asked Gonzalo.

''Hawaii does not reach the 180° mark. Even Midway Island, which lies to the west of the state, does not. You can look it up on the map if you wish, but I know I'm right.''

''It doesn't matter whether you're right or not,'' said Halsted hotly. ''Anchorage isn't on the other side of the 180° line, is it? So it's west, not east. In the case of Augusta, the *city* is the easternmost of the six mentioned.''

Murdock interrupted. "Gentlemen, it is not worth arguing the matter. I had thought of the eastern status of Maine but did not find it compelling enough to convert it into a bid. The fact that one can argue over the matter of Alaska versus Maine—and I admit that the Alaska angle had not occurred to me—removes either from the category of the one and only east."

Rubin said, "Besides, from the strictly geographic point, east and west are purely arbitrary terms. North and south are absolute since there is a fixed point on Earth that is the North Pole and another that is the South Pole. Of any two spots on Earth, the one closer to the North Pole is farther north, the other farther south, but of those same two spots, neither is farther east or farther west, for you can go from one to the other, or from the other to the one, by traveling either eastward or westward. There is no absolute eastern point or western point on Earth."

"Well then," said Trumball, "where does that get you, Manny?"

"To the psycholgical angle. What typifies east to us in the United States is the Atlantic Ocean. Our nation stretches from sea to shining sea and the only city on the list which is on the Atlantic Ocean is Perth Amboy. Augusta may be farther east geographically, but it is an inland town."

Trumbull said, "That's a bunch of nothing at all, Manny. The Atlantic Ocean symbolizes the east to us right now; but through most of the history of Western civilization it represented the west, the *far* west. It wasn't till after Columbus sailed westward that it became the east to the colonists of the New World. If you want something that's east in the Western tradition, and always has been east, it's China. The first Chinese city to be opened to Western trade was Canton and the American city of Canton was actually named for the Chinese city. Canton *has* to be the one and only east."

Avalon lifted his hand and said with majestic severity, "I don't see that at all, Tom. Even if Canton typifies the east by its recall of a Chinese city, why is that the one *and only* east? Why not Cairo, Illinois, or Memphis, Tennessee, each of which typifies the ancient Egyptian east?"

"Because those cities aren't on the list, Jeff."

"No, but Athens, Georgia, is, and if there is one city in all the world that is the one and only east, it is Athens, Greece— the source and home of all the humanistic values we hold dear today, the school of Hellas and of all the west—"

"Of all the *west*, you idiot," said Trumbull with sudden ferocity. "Athens was never considered the east either by itself or by others. The first great battle between east and west was Marathon in 490 B.C. and Athens represented the *west*."

Murdock interrupted. "Besides, my Uncle Haskell could scarcely have thought I would consider Athens unique, when it has purely secular value. Had he included Bethlehem, Pennsylvania, on his list, I might have chosen it at once with no sense of gamble. As it is, however, I can only thank you, gentlemen, for your efforts. The mere fact that you come to different conclusions and argue over them shows that each of you must be wrong. If one of you had the real answer it would be compelling enough to convince the others—and myself as well—at once. It may be, of course, that my Uncle Haskell deliberately gave me a meaningless clue for his own posthumous pleasure. If so, that does not, of course, in the least diminish my gratitude to you all for your hospitality, your company, and your efforts."

He would have risen to leave but Avalon, on his left, put a courteous but nonetheless authoritative hand on his shoulder. "One moment, Mr. Murdock, one member of our little band has not yet spoken. —Henry, have you nothing to add?"

Murdock looked surprised. "Your waiter?"

"A Black Widower, as we said earlier. Henry, can you shed any light on this puzzle?"

Henry said solemnly, "It may be that I can, gentlemen. I was impressed by Mr. Murdock's earlier argument that reason is sometimes inadequate to reach the truth. Nevertheless, suppose we start with reason. Not ours, however, but that of Mr. Murdock's uncle. I have no doubt that he deliberately chose cities that each represented the east in some ambiguous fashion, but where would he find in that list an unambiguous and compelling reference? Perhaps we would know the answer if we remembered his special interests—Mr. Murdock did say that at one time he was working on a book concerning

Restoration England. I believe that is the latter half of the seventeenth century."

"Charles II," said Rubin, "reigned from 1660 to 1685."

"I'm sure you are correct, Mr. Rubin," said Henry. "All the cities named are in the United States, so I wondered whether we might find something of interest in American history during the Restoration period."

"A number of colonies were founded in Charles II's reign," said Rubin.

"Was not Carolina one of them, sir?" asked Henry.

"Sure. Carolina was named for him, in fact. Charles is Carolus, in Latin."

"But later on Carolina proved unwieldy and was split into North Carolina and South Carolina."

"That's right. But what has that got to do with the list? There are no cities in it from either Carolina."

"True enough, but the thought reminded me that there is also a North Dakota and a South Dakota, and for that matter a West Virginia, but there is no American state that has East in its title. Of course, we might speak of East Texas or of East Kansas or East Tennessee but—"

"More likely to say 'eastern,' " muttered Halsted.

"Either way, sir, there would not be a one and only east, but—"

Gonzalo exploded in sudden excitement. "Wait a minute, Henry. I think I see what you're driving at. If we have the state of West Virginia—the one and only west—then we can consider Virginia to be East Virginia—the one and only east."

"No, you can't," said Trumbull, with a look of disgust on his face. "Virginia has been Virginia for three and a half centuries. Calling it East Virginia doesn't make it so."

"It would not matter if one did, Mr. Trumbull," said Henry, "since there is no Virginian city on the list. —But before abandoning that line of thought, however, I remembered that Mr. Murdock's uncle lived in New Jersey and that his ancestors had lived there since colonial times. Memories of my grade school education stirred, for half a century ago we were much more careful about studying colonial history than we are today.

"It seems to me, and I'm sure Mr. Rubin will correct me if I'm wrong, that at one time in its early history New Jersey was divided into two parts—East Jersey and West Jersey, the two being separately governed. This did not last a long time, a generation perhaps, and then the single state of New Jersey was reconstituted. East Jersey, however, is the only section of what are now the United States that had 'east' as a part of its official name as colony or state."

Murdock looked interested. His lips lifted in what was almost a smile. "The one and only east. It could be."

"There is more to it than that," said Henry. "Perth Amboy was, in its time, the capital of East Jersey."

Murdock's eyes opened wide. "Are you serious, Henry?"

"I am quite certain of this and I think it is the compelling factor. It was the capital of the one and only east in the list of colonies and states. I do not think you will lose the inheritance if you offer that name on Monday; nor do I think you will be gambling."

Rubin said, scowling, "I *said* Perth Amboy."

"For a non-compelling reason," said Drake. "How do you do it, Henry?"

Henry smiled slightly. "By abandoning reason for something more certain as Mr. Murdock suggested at the start."

"What are you talking about, Henry?" said Avalon. "You worked it out very nicely by a line of neat argument."

"After the fact, sir," said Henry. "While all of you were applying reason, I took the liberty of seeking authority and turned to the reference shelf we use to settle arguments. I looked up each city in Webster's Geographical Dictionary. Under Perth Amboy, it is clearly stated that it was once the capital of East Jersey."

He held out the book and Rubin snatched it from his hands, to check the matter for himself.

"It is easy to argue backward, gentlemen," said Henry.

8

The Cross of Lorraine

I've never considered myself as very adept at telling a love story, but in this case Eleanor Sullivan, then managing editor (now editor) of EQMM *(Ellery Queen's Mystery Magazine), was fond of the romantic aspect of the story. This was flattering to me and at once elevated the story in my esteem.*

Then, too, there are some things that are quite obvious once pointed out, and are absolutely opaque until then. The point of this story is one of those things. I happened to notice the peculiarity because I was actively looking for something to use in a story, but Eleanor said that an associate failed to see the object even when it stared him in the face. As a result, I think of this as perhaps the best of all the Black Widower stories.

Emmanuel Rubin did not, as a general rule, ever allow a look of relief to cross his face. Had one done so, it would have argued a prior feeling of uncertainty or apprehension, sensations he might feel but would certainly never admit to.

This time, however, the relief was unmistakable. It was monthly banquet time for the Black Widowers; Rubin was the host, and it was he who was supplying the guest; and here it was about twenty minutes after seven and only now—with but ten minutes left before the banquet was to start—only now did his guest arrive.

Rubin bounded toward him, careful, however, not to spill a drop of his second drink.

"Gentlemen," he said, clutching the arm of the newcomer, "my guest, the Amazing Larri—spelled L-A-R-R-I." And in a lowered voice, over the hum of pleased-to-meet-yous, "Where the hell were you?"

Larri muttered, "The subway train stalled." Then returned smiles and greetings.

"Pardon me," said Henry, the perennial—and nonpareil—waiter at the Black Widower banquets, "but there is not much time for the guest to have his drink before dinner begins. Would you state your preference, sir?"

"A good notion, that," said Larri, gratefully. "Thank you, waiter, and let me have a dry martini, but not too darned dry—a little damp, so to speak."

"Certainly, sir," said Henry.

Rubin said, "I've told you, Larri, that we members all have our *ex officio* doctorates, so now let me introduce them in nauseating detail. This tall gentleman with the neat mustache, black eyebrows, and straight back is Dr. Geoffrey Avalon. He's a lawyer and he never smiles. The last time he tried, he was fined for contempt of court."

Avalon smiled as broadly as he could and said, "You undoubtedly know Manny well enough, sir, not to take him seriously."

"Undoubtedly," said Larri. As he and Rubin stood together, they looked remarkably alike. Both were of a height—about five feet, five—both had active, inquisitive faces, both had straggly beards, though Larri's was longer and was accompanied by a fringe of hair down either side of his face as well.

Rubin said, "And here, dressed fit to kill anyone with a *real* taste for clothing, is our scribble expert, Dr. Mario Gonzalo, who will insist on producing a caricature of you in which he will claim to see a resemblance. Dr. Roger Halsted inflicts pain on junior-high students under the guise of teaching them what little he knows of mathematics. Dr. James

Drake is a superannuated chemist who once conned someone into granting him a Ph.D. And finally, Dr. Thomas Trumbull, who works for the government in an unnamed job as code expert and who spends most of his time hoping Congress doesn't find out.''

"Manny," said Trumbull wearily, "if it were possible to cast a retroactive blackball, I think you could count on five."

And Henry said, "Gentlemen, dinner is served."

It was one of those rare Black Widower occasions when the entrée was lobster, rarer now than ever because of the increase in prices.

Rubin, who as host bore the cost, shrugged it off. "I made a good paperback sale last month and we can call this a celebration."

"We can celebrate," said Avalon, "but lobster tends to kill conversation. The cracking of claws and shells, the extraction of meat, the dipping in melted butter, takes one's full concentration." And he grimaced with the effort he was putting into the compression of the nutcracker.

"In that case," said the Amazing Larri, "I shall have a monopoly on the conversation," and he grinned with satisfaction as a large platter of prime-rib roast was dexterously placed before him by Henry.

"Larri is allergic to seafood," said Rubin.

Conversation was indeed subdued as Avalon had predicted until the various lobsters had been clearly worsted in culinary battle, and then, finally, Halsted asked, "What makes you Amazing, Larri?"

"Stage name," said Larri. "I am a prestidigitator, an escapist *extraordinaire,* and the greatest living *exposeur.*"

Trumbull, who was sitting to Larri's right, formed ridges on his bronzed forehead. "What the devil do you mean by *exposeur?*"

Rubin beat a tattoo on his water glass at this point and said, "No grilling till we've had our coffee."

"For God's sake," said Trumbull, "I'm just asking the definition of a word."

"Host's decision is final," said Rubin.

Trumbull scowled blackly in Rubin's direction. "Then I'll

guess the answer. An *exposeur* is one who exposes fakes; people who, using trickery of one sort or another, pretend to produce effects they attribute to supernatural or paranatural forces.''

Larri thrust out his lower lip, raised his eyebrows, and nodded his head. ''Pretty good for a guess. I couldn't have put it better.''

Gonzalo said, ''You mean that whatever someone did by what he claimed was real magic, you could do by stage magic.''

''Exactly,'' said Larri. ''For instance, suppose that some mystic claimed he had the capacity to bend spoons by means of unknown forces. I can do the same by using natural force, this way.'' He lifted his spoon and, holding it by its two ends, he bent it half an inch out of true.

Trumbull said, ''That scarcely counts. Anyone can do it that way.''

''Ah,'' said Larri, ''but this spoon you saw me bend is not the amazing effect at all. That spoon you were watching merely served to trap and focus the ethereal rays that did the real work. Those rays acted to bend *your* spoon, Dr. Trumbull.''

Trumbull looked down and picked up his spoon, which was bent nearly at right angles. ''How did you do this?''

Larri shrugged. ''Would you believe ethereal forces?''

Drake laughed and, pushing his dismantled lobster toward the center of the table, lit a cigarette. He said, ''Larri did it a few minutes ago, with his hands, when you weren't looking.''

Larri seemed unperturbed by exposure. ''When Manny banged his glass, Dr. Trumbull, you looked away. I had rather hoped you all would.''

Drake said, ''I know better than to pay attention to Manny.''

''But,'' said Larri, ''if no one had seen me do it, would you have accepted the ethereal forces?''

''Not a chance,'' said Trumbull.

''Even if there had been no way in which you could explain the effect? Here, let me show you something. Suppose you wanted to flip a coin . . .''

He fell silent for a moment while Henry passed out the strawberry shortcake, pushed his own out of the way, and said, ''Suppose you wanted to flip a coin, without actually lifting it and turning it—this penny, for instance. There are a number of ways it could be done. The simplest would be simply to touch it quickly, because, as you all know, a finger is always slightly sticky, especially so at mealtime, so that the coin lifts up slightly as the finger is removed and can be made to flip over. It is tails now, you see. Touch it again and it is heads.''

Gonzalo said, ''No prestidigitation there, though. We see it flip.''

''Exactly,'' said Larri, ''and that's why I won't do it that way. Let's put something over it so that it can't be touched or flipped. Suppose we use a . . .'' He looked about the table for a moment and seized a salt shaker. ''Suppose we use this.''

He placed the salt shaker over the coin and said, ''Now it is showing heads? . . .''

''Hold on,'' said Gonzalo. ''How do we know it's showing heads? It could be tails and then, when you reveal it later, you'll say it flipped, when it was tails all along.''

''You're perfectly right,'' said Larri, ''and I'm glad you raised the point. Dr. Drake, you've got eyes that caught me before. Would you check this on behalf of the assembled company? I'll lift the salt shaker and you tell me what the coin shows.''

Drake looked and said, ''Heads!'' in his softly hoarse voice.

''You'll all take Dr. Drake's word, I hope, gentlemen? Please, watch me place the salt shaker back on the coin and make sure it doesn't flip in the process. . . .''

''It didn't,'' said Drake.

''Now to keep my fingers from slipping while performing this trick, I will put this paper napkin over the salt shaker.''

Larri molded the paper napkin neatly and carefully over the salt shaker, then said, ''But, in manipulating this napkin, I caused you all to divert your attention from the penny and you may think I have flipped it in the process.'' He lifted the salt shaker with the paper about it and said, ''Dr. Drake, will you check the coin again?''

Drake leaned toward it. ''Still heads,'' he said.

Very carefully and gently, Larri put back the salt shaker,

the paper napkin still molded about it, and said, "The coin remained as is?"

"Still heads," said Drake.

"In that case, I now perform the magic." Larri pushed down on the salt shaker, and the paper collapsed. There was nothing inside.

There was a moment of shock, and then Gonzalo said, "Where's the salt shaker?"

"In another plane of existence," said Larri airily.

"But you said you were going to flip the coin."

"I lied."

Avalon said, "There's no mystery. He had us all concentrating on the coin as a diversion tactic. When he picked up the salt shaker with the napkin around it to let Jim look at the coin, he just dropped the salt shaker into his hand and placed the empty, molded napkin over the coin."

"Did you see me do that, Dr. Avalon?" asked Larri.

"No. I was looking at the coin, too."

"Then you're just guessing," said Larri.

Rubin, who had not participated in the demonstration at all, but who had eaten his strawberry shortcake instead and now waited for the others to catch up, said, "The tendency is to argue these things out logically and that's impossible. Scientists and other rationalists are used to dealing with the universe, which fights fair. Faced with a mystic who does not, they find themselves maneuvered into believing nonsense and, in the end, making fools of themselves.

"Magicians, on the other hand," Rubin went on, "know what to watch for, are experienced enough not to be misdirected, and are not impressed by the apparently supernatural. That's why mystics generally won't perform if they know magicians are in the audience."

Coffee had been served and was being sipped at, and Henry was quietly preparing the brandy, when Rubin sounded the water glass and said, "Gentlemen, it is time for the official grilling, assuming you idiots have left anything to grill. Geoff, will you do the honors today?"

Avalon cleared his throat portentously and frowned down upon the Amazing Larri from under his dark and luxuriant eyebrows. Using his voice in the deepest of its naturally deep register, Avalon said, "It is customary to ask our guests to justify their existences, but if today's guest exposes phony mystics even now and then, I, for one, consider his existence justified and will pass on.

"The temptation is to ask you how you performed your little disappearing trick of a moment ago, but I quite understand that the ethics of your profession preclude your telling us. Even though everything said here is considered under the rose, and though nothing has ever leaked, I will refrain from such questions.

"Let me instead, then, ask after your failures. Sir, you describe yourself as an *exposeur*. Have there been any supposedly mystical demonstrations you have not been able to duplicate in prestidigitous manner and have not been able to account for by natural means?"

Larri said, "I have not attempted to explain all the effects I have ever encountered or heard of, but where I have studied an effect and made an attempt to duplicate it, I have succeeded in every case."

"No failures?"

"None!"

Avalon considered that, but as he prepared for the next question, Gonzalo broke in. His head was leaning on one palm, but the fingers of that hand were carefully disposed in such a way as not to disarray his hair. He said, "Now, wait, Larri, would it be right to suggest that you tackled only easy cases? The really puzzling cases you might have made no attempts on."

"You mean," said Larri, "that I shied away from anything that might spoil my perfect record or that might upset my belief in the rational order of the universe? If so, you're quite wrong, Dr. Gonzalo. Most reports of apparent mystical powers are dull and unimportant, are crude and patently false. I ignore those. The cases I do take on are precisely the puzzling ones that have attracted attention because of their unusual nature and their apparent divorce from the rational. So you see, the ones I take on are precisely those you suspect I avoid."

Gonzalo subsided and Avalon said, "Larri, the mere fact

that you can duplicate a trick by prestidigitation doesn't mean that it couldn't have been performed by the mystic through supernatural means. The fact that human beings can build machines that fly doesn't mean that birds are man-made machines.''

"Quite right," said Larri, "but mystics lay their claims to supernatural powers on the notion, either expressed or implicit, that there is no other way of producing the effect. If I show that the same effect *can* be produced by natural means, the burden of proof then shifts to them to show that the effect can be produced after the natural means I have used are made impossible. I don't know of any mystic who has accepted the conditions set by professional magicians to guard against trickery and who then succeeded.''

"And nothing has ever puzzled you? Not even the tricks other magicians have developed?''

"Oh yes, there are effects produced by some magicians that puzzle me in the sense that I don't know quite how they do it. I might duplicate it but perhaps using a different method. In any case, that's not the point. As long as an effect is produced by natural means, it doesn't matter whether I can reproduce it or not. I am not the best magician in the world. I am just a better magician than any mystic is.''

Halsted, his high forehead flushed with anxiety, and stuttering slightly in his eagerness to speak, said, "But then nothing would startle you? No disappearance like that you carried through on the salt shaker? . . .''

"You mean that one?" asked Larri, pointing. There was a salt shaker in the middle of the table, but no one had seen it placed there.

Halsted, thrown off a moment, recovered and said, "Have you ever been *startled* by any disappearance? I heard once that magicians have made elephants disappear.''

"Actually, making elephants disappear is childishly simple. I assure you there's nothing puzzling about disappearances in a magic act.'' And then a peculiar look crossed Larri's face, a flash of sadness and frustration. "Not in a magic act. Just . . .''

"Yes?" said Halsted. "Just what?''

"Just in real life," said Larri, smiling and attempting to toss off the remark lightheartedly.

"Just a minute," said Trumbull, "but we don't let that pass. If there has been a disappearance in real life you can't explain, we want to hear about it."

Larri shook his head, "No, no, Dr. Trumbull. It is not a mysterious disappearance or an inexplicable one. Nothing like that at all. I just lost—something, and can't find it and it—saddens me."

"The details," said Trumbull.

"It wouldn't be worth it," said Larri. "It's a—silly story and somewhat . . ." He fell into silence.

"Goddamn it," thundered Trumbull, "we all sit here and voluntarily refrain from asking anything that might result in your being tempted to violate your ethics. Would it violate the ethics of the magician's art for you to tell this story?"

"It's not that at all. . . ."

"Well, then, sir, I repeat what Geoff has told you. Everything said here is in confidence and the agreement surrounding these monthly dinners is that all questions must be answered. Manny?"

Rubin shrugged. "That's the way it is, Larri. If you don't want to answer the question, we'll have to declare the meeting at an end."

Larri sat back in his chair and looked depressed. "I can't very well allow that to happen, considering the fine hospitality I've been shown. I will tell you the story and you'll find there's nothing to it. I met a woman quite accidentally; I lost touch with her; I can't locate her. That's all there is."

"No," said Trumbull, "that's not all there is. Where and how did you meet her? Where and how did you lose touch with her? Why can't you find her again? We want to know the details."

Gonzalo said, "In fact, if you tell us the details, we may be able to help you."

Larri laughed sardonically, "I think not."

"You'd be surprised," said Gonzalo. "In the past . . ."

Avalon said, "Quiet, Mario. Don't make promises we might not be able to keep. Would you give us the details, sir? I assure you we'll do our best to help."

Larri smiled wearily. "I appreciate your offer, but you will see that there is nothing you can do sitting here."

He adjusted himself in his seat and said, "I was done with my performance in an upstate town—I'll give you the details when and if you insist, but for the moment they don't matter, except that this happened about a month ago. I had to get to another small town some hundred fifty miles away for a morning show and that meant a little transportation problem.

"My magic, unfortunately, is not the kind that can transport me a hundred fifty miles in a twinkling, or even conjure up a pair of seven-league boots. I did not have my car with me—just as well, for I don't like to travel the lesser roads at night when I am sleepy—and the net result was that I would have to take a bus that would make more stops than a telegram and would take nearly four hours to make the journey. I planned to catch some sleep while on wheels and make it serve a purpose anyway.

"But when things go wrong, they go wrong in battalions, so you can guess that I missed my bus and that the next one would not come along for two more hours. There was an enclosed station in which I could wait, one that was as dreary as you could imagine—with no reading matter except for some fly-blown posters on the wall—no place to buy a paper or a cup of coffee. I thought grimly that it was fortunate it wasn't raining, and settled down to drowse, when my luck changed.

"A woman walked in. I've never been married, gentlemen, and I've never even had what young people today call a 'meaningful relationship.' Some casual attachments, perhaps, but on the whole, though it seems trite to say so, I am married to my art and find it much more satisfying than women, generally.

"I had no reason to think that this woman was an improvement on others, but she had a pleasant appearance. She was something over thirty, and was just plump enough to have a warm, comfortable look about her, and she wasn't too tall.

"She looked about and said, smiling, 'Well, I've missed my bus, I see.'

"I smiled with her. I liked the way she said it. She didn't

fret or whine or act annoyed at the universe. It was a flat, good-humored statement of fact, and just hearing it cheered me up tremendously because actually I myself was in the mood to fret and whine and act annoyed. Now I could be as good-natured as she and say, 'Two of us, madam, so you don't even have the satisfaction of being unique.'

" 'So much the better,' she said, 'We can talk and pass the time that much faster.'

"I was astonished. She did not treat me as a potential rapist or as a possible thief. God knows I am not handsome or even particularly respectable in appearance, but it was as though she had casually penetrated to my inmost character and found it satisfactory. You have no idea how flattered I was. If I were ten times as sleepy as I was, I would have stayed up to talk to her.

"And we did talk. Inside of fifteen minutes, I knew I was having the pleasantest conversation in my life—in a crummy bus station at not much before midnight. I can't tell you all we talked about, but I can tell you what we *didn't* talk about. We didn't talk about magic.

"I can interest anyone by doing tricks, but then it isn't me they're interested in; it's the flying fingers and the patter they like. And while I'm willing to buy attention in that way, you don't know how pleasant it is to get the attention without purchase. She apparently just liked to listen to me, and I know I just liked to listen to her.

"Fortunately, my trip was not an all-out effort, so I didn't have my large trunk with the show-business advertising all over it, just two rather large valises. I told her nothing personal about myself, and asked nothing about her. I gathered briefly that she was heading for her brother's place; that he was right on the road; that she would have to wake him up because she had carelessly let herself be late—but she only told me that in order to say that she was glad it had happened. She would buy my company at the price of inconveniencing her brother. I liked that.

"We didn't talk politics or world affairs or religion or theater. We talked people—all the funny and odd and peculiar things we had observed about people. We laughed for two hours, during which not one other person came to join us. I had never had anything like that happen to me, had never felt so alive and happy, and when the bus finally came at 1:50 A.M., it was amazing how sorry I was. I didn't want the bus to come; I didn't want the night to end.

"When we got onto the bus, of course, it was no longer quite the same thing, even though it was sufficiently nonfull for us to find a double seat we could share. After all, we had been alone in the station and there we could talk loudly and laugh. On the bus we had to whisper; people were sleeping.

"Of course, it wasn't all bad. It was a nice feeling to have her so close to me; to be making contact. Despite the fact that I'm rather an old horse, I felt like a teen-ager. Enough like a teen-ager, in fact, to be embarrassed at being watched.

"Immediately across the way were a woman and her young son. He was about eight years old, I should judge, and *he* was awake. He kept watching me with his sharp little eyes. I could see those eyes fixed on us every time a street light shone into the bus and it was very inhibiting. I wished he were asleep but, of course, the excitement of being on a bus, perhaps, was keeping him awake.

"The motion of the bus, the occasional whisper, the feeling of being quite out of reality, the pressure of her body against mine—it was like confusing dream and fact, and the boundary between sleep and wakefulness just vanished. I didn't intend to sleep, and I started awake once or twice, but then finally, when I started awake one more time, it was clear that there had been a considerable period of sleep, and the seat next to me was empty."

Halsted said, "I take it she had gotten off."

"I didn't think she had disappeared into thin air," said Larri. "Naturally, I looked about. I couldn't call her name, because I didn't know her name. She wasn't in the rest room, because its door was swinging open.

"The little boy across the aisle spoke in a rapid high treble—in French. I can understand French reasonably well, but I didn't have to make any effort, because his mother was now awake and she translated. She spoke English quite well.

"She said, 'Pardon me, sir, but is it that you are looking for the woman that was with you?'

" 'Yes,' I said. 'Did you see where she got off?'

" 'Not I, sir. I was sleeping. But my son says that she descended at the place of the Cross of Lorraine.' "

" 'At the what?' "

"She repeated it, and so did the child, in French.

"She said, 'You must excuse my son, sir. He is a great hero-worshiper of President Charles de Gaule, and though he is young he knows the tale of the Free French forces in the war very well. He would not miss a sight like a Cross of Lorraine. If he said he saw it, he did.'

"I thanked them and then went forward to the bus driver and asked him, but at that time of night, the bus stops wherever a passenger would like to get off, or get on. He had made numerous stops and let numerous people on and off, and he didn't know for sure where he had stopped and whom he had left off. He was rather churlish, in fact."

Avalon cleared his throat. "He may have thought you were up to no good and was deliberately withholding information to protect the passenger."

"Maybe," said Larri despondently, "but what it amounted to was that I had lost her. When I came back to my seat, I found a little note tucked into the pocket of the jacket I had placed in the rack above. I managed to read it by a street light at the next stop, where the French mother and son got off. It said, 'Thank you so much for a delightful time. Gwendolyn.' "

Gonzalo said, "You have her first name, anyway."

Larri said, "I would appreciate having had her last name, her address, her telephone number. A firt name is useless."

"You know," said Rubin, "she may deliberately have withheld information because she wasn't interested in continuing the acquaintanceship. A romantic little interlude is one thing; a continuing danger is another. She may be a married woman."

"Or she may have been offended at your falling asleep," said Gonzalo.

"Maybe," said Larri. "But if I found her, I could apologize if she were offended, or I could reassure her if she feared me; or I might cultivate her friendship if she were neither offended nor afraid. Rather that than spend the rest of my life wondering."

"Have you done anything about it?" asked Gonzalo.

"Certainly," said Larri, sardonically. "If a magician is faced with a disappearing woman he must understand what has happened. I have gone over the bus route twice by car, looking for a Cross of Lorraine. If I had found it, I would have gone in and asked if anyone there knew a woman by the name of Gwendolyn. I'd have described her. I'd have gone to the local post office or the local police station, if necessary."

"But you have not found a Cross of Lorraine, I take it," said Trumbull.

"I have not."

Halsted said, "Mathematically speaking, it's a finite problem. You could try every post office along the whole route."

Larri sighed. "If I get desperate enough, I'll try. But, mathematically speaking, that would be so inelegant. Why can't I find the Cross of Lorraine?"

"The youngster might have made a mistake," said Trumbull.

"Not a chance," said Larri. "An adult, yes, but a child, riding a hobby? Never. Adults have accumulated enough irrationality to be very unreliable eyewitnesses. A bright eight-year-old is different. Don't try to pull any trick on a bright kid; he'll see through it.

"Just the same," he went on, "nowhere on the route is there a restaurant, a department store, or anything else with the name Cross of Lorraine. I think I've checked every set of yellow pages along the entire route."

"Now wait a while," said Avalon, "that's wrong. The child wouldn't have seen the words because they would have meant nothing to him. If he spoke and read only French, as I suppose he did, he would know the phrase as *Croix de Lorraine*. The English would have never caught his eyes. He must have seen the symbol, the cross with the two horizontal bars, like this." He reached out and Henry obligingly handed him a menu.

Avalon turned it over and on the blank back drew the following:

$$\ddagger$$

"Actually," he said, "it is more properly called the Patriarchal Cross or the Archiepiscopal Cross, since it symbolized the high office of patriarchs and archbishops by doubling the bars. You will not be surprised to hear that the Papal Cross has three bars. The Patriarchal Cross was used as a symbol by Godfrey of Bouillon, who was one of the leaders of the First

Crusade, and since he was Duke of Lorraine, it came to be called the Cross of Lorraine. As we all know, it was adopted as the emblem of the Free French during the Hitlerian War." He coughed slightly and tried to look modest.

Larri said, a little impatiently, "I understand about the symbol, Dr. Avalon, and I didn't expect the youngster to note words. I think you'll agree, though, that any establishment calling itself the Cross of Lorraine would surely display the symbol along with the name. I looked for the name in the yellow pages, but for the symbol on the road."

"And you didn't find it?" said Gonzalo.

"As I've already said, I didn't. I was desperate enough to consider things I didn't think the kid could possibly have seen at night. I thought, who knows how sharp young eyes are and how readily they may see something that represents an overriding interest. So I looked at signs in windows, at street signs—even at graffiti, damn it."

"If it were a graffito," said Trumbull, "then, of course, it could have been erased between the time the child saw it, and the time you came to look for it."

"I'm not sure of that," said Rubin. "It's my experience that graffiti are never erased. We've got some on the outside of our apartment house. . . ."

"That's New York," said Trumbull. "In smaller towns, there's less tolerance for these evidences of anarchy."

"Hold on," said Gonzalo. "What makes you think graffiti are necessarily signs of anarchy? As a matter of fact . . ."

"Gentlemen! Gentlemen!" And as always, when Avalon's voice was raised to its full baritone splendor, a silence fell. "We are not here to argue the merits and demerits of graffiti. The question is: How can we find this woman who disappeared? Larri has found no restaurant or other establishment with the name of Cross of Lorraine; he has found no evidence of the symbol along the route taken. Can we help?"

Drake held up his hand and squinted through the curling smoke of his cigarette. "Hold on, there's no problem. Have you ever seen a Russian Orthodox Church? Do you know what its cross is like?" He made quick marks on the back of the menu and shoved it toward the center of the table. "Here. . . ."

He said, "The kid, being hipped on the Free French, would take a quick look at that and see it as the Cross of Lorraine. So what you have to do, Larri, is look for some Russian Orthodox Church en route. I doubt that there would be more than one."

Larri thought about it, but did not seem overjoyed. "The cross with that second bar set at an angle would be on the top of the spire, wouldn't it?"

"I imagine so."

"And it wouldn't be floodlighted, would it? How would the child be able to see it at four o'clock in the morning?"

Drake stubbed out his cigarette. "Well, now, churches usually have bulletin board affairs near the entrance. I don't know, there could have been a Russian Orthodox cross on the . . ."

"I would have seen it," said Larri firmly.

"Could it have been a Red Cross?" asked Gonzalo feebly. "You know, there might be a Red Cross headquarters along the route."

"The Red Cross," said Rubin, "is a Greek Cross with all four amns equal. I don't see how that could possibly be mistaken for a Cross of Lorraine by a Free French enthusiast. Look at it. . . ."

+

Halsted said, "The logical thing, I suppose, is that you simply missed it, Larri. If you insist that, as a magician, you're such a trained observer that you *couldn't* have missed it, which sounds impossible to me, then maybe it was a symbol on something movable—on a truck in a driveway, for instance—and it moved on after sunrise."

"The boy made it quite clear that it was at the *place* of the Cross of Lorraine," said Larri. "I suppose even an eight-year-old can tell the difference between a place and a movable object."

"He spoke French. Maybe you mistranslated."

"I'm not that bad at the language," said Larri, "and his mother translated and French is her native tongue."

"But English isn't. *She* might have gotten it wrong. The kid might have said something else. He might not even have said the Cross of Lorraine."

Avalon raised his hand for silence and said, "One moment, gentlemen, I see Henry, our esteemed waiter, smiling. What is it, Henry?"

Henry, from his place at the sideboard, said, "I'm afraid that I am amused at your doubting the child's evidence. It is quite certain, in my opinion, that he did see the Cross of Lorraine."

There was a moment's silence and Larri said, "How can you tell that, Henry?"

"By not being oversubtle, sir."

Avalon's voice boomed out. "I knew it. We're being too complicated. Henry, how is it possible to gain greater simplicity?"

"Why, Mr. Avalon, the incident took place at night. Instead of looking at all signs, all places, all varieties of cross, why not begin by asking ourselves what very few things *can* be easily seen on a highway at night?"

"A Cross of Lorraine?" asked Gonzalo incredulously.

"Certainly," said Henry, "among other things. Especially if we don't call it a Cross of Lorraine. What the youngster saw as a Cross of Lorraine, out of his special interest, we would see as something else so clearly that its relationship to the Cross of Lorraine would be invisible. What has been happening just now has been precisely what happened earlier with Mr. Larri's trick with the coin and salt shaker. We concentrated on the coin and didn't watch the salt shaker, and now we concentrate on the Cross of Lorraine and don't look for the alternative."

Trumbull said, "Henry, if you don't stop talking in riddles, you're fired. What the hell is the Cross of Lorraine, if it isn't the Cross of Lorraine?"

Henry said gravely, "What is this?" and carefully he drew on the back of the menu . . .

Trumbull said, "A Cross of Lorraine—tilted."

"No, sir, you would never have thought so, if we hadn't been talking about the Cross. Those are English letters and a very common symbol on highways if you add something to it. . . . . He wrote quickly and the tilted Cross became:

EXⳭON

"The one thing," said Henry, "that is designed to be seen, without trouble, day or night, on any highway is a gas-station sign. The child saw the Cross of Lorraine in this one, but Mr. Larri, retracing the route, sees only a double X, since he reads the entire word as Exxon. All signs showing this name, whether on the highway, in advertisements, or on credit cards, show the name in this fashion."

Now Larri caught fire. "You mean, Henry, that if I go into the Exxon stations en route and ask for Gwendolyn . . ."

"The proprietor of one of them is likely to be her brother, and there would not be more than five or six at most to inquire at."

"Good God, Henry," said Larri, "you're a magician."

"Merely simpleminded," said Henry, "though perhaps in the nonpejorative sense."

9

The Next Day

I wrote this story in an automobile. I had had a mild coronary two months before. and dear Janet was full of an exaggerated fear for my survival. We were in rustic surroundings for several days and drove out to see a waterfail. Janet and some friends got out of the car to walk about and this was judged too strenuous for me. So I sat in the car with a pad and paper and wrote a story.

I have often wondered how small an ambiguity I could use as a kernel about which to build a Black Widower story. I have, in this story, I think the smallest possible ambiguity, but I think it works just the same. What's more, I rarely tell a story about writers and editors because my own experience in this direction is so enormously atypical that it offers me no guidance at all. For all these reasons, I am including this story.

Emmanuel Rubin's glasses always gave the illusion of magnifying his eyes with particular intensity when he was aroused. He said, in an intense whisper, "You brought an *editor* as your guest?"

144

James Drake's train from New Jersey had arrived late and he had, in consequence, almost committed tbe solecism of being late to his own hostship over the monthly banquet of the Black Widowers. He was in an uncharacteristically snappish mood therefore and said, "Why not?"

He flicked the ash from his cigarette and added, "If we can have writers for guests, and even as members, Zeus help us, why not editors?"

Rubin, a writer, of course, said haughtily, "I wouldn't expect a chemist to understand." He looked briefly in the direction of the guest, who was tall and spare, with longish red-blond hair and with the kind of abbreviated mustache and beard that gave him a Robin Hood air.

Drake said, "I may be a chemist to you, Manny and to all the world besides, but I'm a writer to him." Drake tried to look modest, and failed signally. "I'm doing a book."

"You?" said Rubi."

"Why not? I can spell and, judging by your career, that's the only requirement."

"If your guest thinks it is, he has about the mental equipment needed for an editor. What's his name again?"

"Stephen Bentham."

"And what firm is he with?"

Drake stubbed out his cigarette. "Southby Publications."

"A *shlock* outfit," said Rubin, with contempt. "They're a sex-and-sensation house. What do they want with you?"

Drake said, "I'm doing a book on recombinant DNA, which is a sensational subject these days—not that you know anything about it."

Mario Gonzalo had just entered, brushing at his brown velvet jacket to remove the city fly-ash. He said, "Come on, Jim, all the papers are full of it. That's the stuff they're going to make new disease germs with and depopulate the world."

Rubin said, "If Mario's heard about it, Jim, you'll have to admit I have, too—and everyone else in the world has."

"Good. Then my book is what the world needs," said Drake.

Gonzalo said, "The world needs it about as much as it needs air pollution. I've seen two books on the subject advertised already.

"Ha," said Drake, "they're talking about the controversy, the politics. I'm going to talk about the chemistry."

"Then it will never sell," said Rubin.

It was at this point that Henry, that paragon of waiters, without whom no Black Widowers banquet could endure, announced softly to Drake that the gentlemen might seat themselves.

Geoffrey Avalon drifted toward Henry, having now had the pleasure of a sedate conversation with the guest—with whom he had talked eye to eye, something which, from his 74 inches of height, he could not often do.

"I detect a fishy aroma, Henry," he said. "What has been planned for this evening?"

"A bouillabaisse, sir," said Henry. "An excellent one, I believe."

Avalon nodded gravely, and Roger Halsted, smiling, said, "Even an average bouillabaisse is excellent, and with Henry's encomium, I stand ready to be delighted."

Avalon said, "I hope, Mr. Bentham, that you have no objection?"

"I can't say I've ever eaten it." Bentham spoke in a distinct, but not exaggerated, English accent, "but I'm prepared to have a go at it. A French dish, I believe."

"Marseillaise in origin," said Halsted, looking as though he were coming very close to licking his chops, "but universal in appeal. Where's Tom, by the way?"

"Right here," came an exasperated voice from the steps. "Damn taxi driver. Thanks, Henry." Thomas Trumbull, his tanned forehead creased and furrowed into fifty lines of anger, gratefully took the scotch and soda. "You haven't started eating, have you?"

"Just about," said Gonzalo, "and if you hadn't arrived, Roger would have had your share of the bouillabaisse, so it would have been a silver lining for someone. What was with the taxicab?"

Trumbull seated himself, took another invigorating sip of his drink, buttered a roll, and said, "I told the idiot to take me to the Milano and the next thing I knew I was at some dive movie on West Eighty-sixth Street called the Milano. We had to make our way through four extra miles of Manhattan streets to get here. He claimed he had never heard of the Milano Restaurant, but he did know that flea dive. It cost me three bucks extra in taxi fare."

Rubin said, "You're pretty far gone, Tom, if you couldn't tell he was going northwest when you wanted to go southeast."

"You don't think I was watching the streets, do you?" growled Trumbull. "I was lost in thought."

Avalon said austerely, "You can't rely on the local wisdom of the New York taxi driver. You ought to have said explicitly, 'Fifth Avenue and Thirteenth Street.' "

"Thanks a lot," said Trumbull. "I shall instantly turn the clock back and say it."

"I presume there'll be a next time, Tom, and that you're capable of learning from experience," said Avalon, and received a scowl for his pains.

After the bouillabaisse arrived, there was a lull in the conversation for a while as the banqueters concentrated on the evisceration of mussels and the cracking of lobster shells.

It was Drake who broke it. He said, "If we consider recombinant DNA . . ."

"We aren't," said Rubin, spearing a scallop neatly.

". . . then what it amounts to is that the whole argument is about benefits that no one can demonstrate and dangers that no one can really pinpoint. There are only blue-sky probabilities on either side, and the debaters make up for their lack of hard knowledge by raising their voices. What I propose to do is to go into the chemistry and genetics of the matter and try to work out the real chances and significance of specific genetic change. Without that, both sides are just searching in a dark room for a black cat that isn't there."

Avalon said, "And all this for the general public?"

"Certainly."

"Isn't that rather heavy going for the general public?"

"It isn't for the comic-book audience, but I think I can manage the *Scientific American* to *Natural History* range. Tell them, Bentham," said Drake, with perhaps a trace of smugness, "you've seen the sample chapters."

Bentham, who had tackled the bouillabaisse with a certain tentativeness but had grown steadily more enthusiastic, said, "I can only judge by myself, to be sure, but I suspect that since I follow the line of argument, the average college man ought to.''

"That still limits your audience," said Gonzalo.

Bentham said, "We can't say that. It's a very hot subject and, properly promoted . . ."

"A Southby specialty," muttered Rubin.

"It could catch on," Bentham said. "People who don't really understand might nevertheless buy it to be in fashion; and who knows, they might read it and get *something* out of it.''

Drake tapped his water glass as Henry doled out the brandy. Drake said, "If everyone is sufficiently defishified and if Henry will remove the towels and finger bowls, I think we may start to grill our guest, Mr. Stephen Bentham. Tom, will you do the honors?"

"Glad to," said Trumbull. "Mr. Bentham, it is our custom, ordinarily, to inquire as to how a guest may justify his existence. In this case, I suppose we can allow the fact that you are involved with the production of a book by our esteemed colleague, Dr. Drake, to speak for you. We will therefore pass on to more mundane questions. You seem young. How old are you?"

"Twenty-eight."

"I have the feeling you have not been long in the United States. Am I right?"

"I've been living and working here for about five months now, but I have been here on brief visits before. Three times."

"I see. And what are your qualifications for your post; as editor, that is?"

"Not overwhelming." Bentham smiled suddenly, an oddly charming and rueful smile. "I have done some editing with Fearn and Russell in London. Rather happy with them—low-key concern, you know, but then, British publishing generally is low-key."

"Why throw that over to take a job with an American firm where the pressures are bound to be greater? They are greater, I assume."

"Very much so," again the rueful smile, "but there's no

mystery as to why I came. The explanation is so simple that it embarrasses me to advance it. In a word—money. I was offered three times my British salary, and all moving expenses paid.''

Halsted intervened suddenly. "Are you a married man, Mr. Bentham?''

"No, Mr. Halsted. Quite single, though not necessarily celibate. However, single men can use money, too.''

Rubin said, "If you don't mind, Tom, I would like to add the reverse of the question you asked. I can see why you've joined Southby Publications. Money is a potent argument. But why the hell did that *schlock* concern hire you? You're young, without much experience, and they're not the kind of firm to hire promising young men out of benevolence. Yet they triple your salary and pay moving expenses. What have you got on them?''

Bentham said, "I met Mr. Southby on one of my earlier trips and I think he was rather taken with me.'' His fair skin turned a noticeable pink. "I suspect it was my accent and my appearance. Perhaps it seemed to him I would lend an air of scholarship to the firm.''

"A touch of class,'' murmured Avalon, and Bentham turned pinker still.

Trumbull resumed the questioning, "Manny calls Southby Publications a *shlock* concern. Do you agree with that?''

Bentham hesitated. "I don't know. What does the expression mean?''

Rubin said, "Cheap, worthless books, sold by high-pressure campaigns hinting at sex and sensationalism.''

Bentham remained silent.

Drake said, "Go ahead, Bentham. Anything you say here will never go beyond these walls. The club observes complete confidentiality.''

"It isn't that, Jim,'' said Bentham, "but if I were to agree, it might wound your feelings. You're an author of ours.''

Drake lit another cigarette. "That wouldn't bother me. You're hired to give the firm a touch of class and you'll do my book as another touch of class.''

Bentham says, "I grant you that I don't think much of some of the books on the list, but Dr. Drake is right. Mr.

Southby doesn't object to good books if he thinks they will sell. He is personally pleased with what he has seen of Dr. Drake's book; even enthusiastic. Perhaps the firm's character can be improved.''

Avalon said, "I would like to put in my oar, Tom, if you don't mind. Mr. Bentham, I am not a psychologist, or a tracer of men's thoughts through their expressions. I am just a humble patent attorney. However, it seems to me that you have looked distinctly uneasy each time you mentioned your employer. Are you sure that there is nothing you are keeping from Dr. Drake that he ought to know? I want an unequivocal answer.''

"No,'' said Bentham quickly, "there is nothing wrong with Dr. Drake's book. Provided he completes the book and that the whole is of the quality of the parts we have seen, we will publish and then promote it adequately. There are no hidden reservations to that statement.''

Gonzalo said, "Then what are you uneasy about? Or is Geoff all wrong about your feelings in the first place?'' He was gazing complacently at the caricature of Bentham he had produced for the guest gallery that lined the walls of the meeting room. He had not missed the Robin Hood resemblance and had even lightly sketched in a feathered hat in green, of the type one associated with the Merry Men.

Bentham said, in sudden anger, "You could say I'm uneasy, considering that I'm about to be bloody well slung out on my can.''

"Fired?'' said Gonzalo, on a rising note.

"That's the rough one-syllable version of what I have just said.''

"Why?'' said Drake, in sudden concern.

"I've lost a manuscript,'' said Bentham. "Not yours, Dr. Drake.''

Gonzalo said, "In the mails?''

"No. Through malice, according to Southby. Actually, I did every ruddy thing I could do to get it back. I don't know *what* was in that man's mind.''

"Southby's?''

"No, the author's. Joshua Fairfield's his name.''

"Never heard of him,'' said Rubin.

Trumbull said, "Suppose you tell us what happened, Mr. Bentham."

Bentham said, "It's a grim, stupid thing. I don't want to cast a pall over a very pleasant evening."

Trumbull said, "Sorry, Mr. Bentham, but I think Jim warned you that answering our questions was the price of the meal. Please tell us exactly what happened."

Bentham said, "I suppose the most exciting thing that can happen in a publishing house is to have something good come in over the transom; something good that has not passed through the hands of a reputable agent and is not by a recognized author; something that has reached you by mail, written by someone whom no one has ever heard of.

"Aside from the sheer pleasure of the unexpected windfall, there is the possibility that you have a new author who can be milked for years to come, provided the product is not that of a one-book author—which is not an unheard-of phenomenon."

Rubin began, "Margaret Mitchell . . ." and stopped when Trumbull, who sat next to him, elbowed him ungently.

"Anyway," said Bentham, jarred only momentarily by the interruption, "Southby thought he had one. One of the readers brought it to him in excitement, as well he might, for readers don't often get anything that's above the written-in-crayon-on-lined-paper level.

"He should have gone to an editor—not necessarily me—with the manuscript, but he chose to go directly to Southby. I presume he felt there might be a deal of credit for the discovery and he didn't want Southby to be unaware of the discoverer. I can't say I blame him.

"In any case, Southby was infatuated with the manuscript, called an editorial conference, said he was accepting the book and had notified the author. He explained, quite enthusiastically, that it was to get the full Southby treatment. . . ."

Rubin said indignantly, "Up to and including cooking the best-seller lists. Tom, if you give me the elbow again, I'll break it off."

Bentham said, "I dare say you're right, Mr. Rubin, but this book deserved all it could get—potentially. Southby said he thought it needed work and he gave it to me to edit. That struck me as a remarkable sign of confidence and I was rather gung-ho on the matter. I saw quick promotions on the horizon if I could manage to carry it off. The other editors didn't seem to mind, though. One of them said to me, 'It's your butt that's in the sling if this doesn't work, because Southby's never wrong.' "

Avalon said gravely, "It sometimes happens that when the boss makes a mistake, the underling tabbed to reverse the mistake is fired if he fails."

Bentham nodded. "The thought occurred to me, eventually, but it excited me further. The scent of dangers sharpens the desire to be in at the kill, you know.

"You can see, then, I went over the manuscript in a painstaking manner. I went through it once at moderate speed to get a sense of the whole and was not displeased. Southby's description of it was not, on the whole, wrong. It had a good pace and was rich in detail. A long family saga—a rough and domineering father, a smooth and insinuating mother in a rather subtle battle over the sons, their wives, and their children. The plot was interlocking, never halting, and there was enough sex to be suitable for Southby, but the sex *worked*. It fit the story.

"I turned in a favorable report of my own on the book, indicating its chief flaws, and how I proposed to handle them. It came back with a large 'very good' on it, so I got to work. It had to be tightened up. The last thing any beginner, however talented, learns is to tighten. Some scenes were misplaced or misemphasized, and that had to be corrected.

"I am not myself a great writer and could never be, but I've studied writing that *is* great sufficiently closely to be able to amend and improve what is already written well, even if, from a cold start, I could not produce anything nearly as good. It took me some six weeks of intense work to complete the job. I knew that my head was on the line and I was not about to lose the war for lack of a horseshoe nail.

"It wasn't till after I had done a thorough piece of work that I called in the author, Joshua Fairfield. I thought it better that way. Had I called him in en route, so to speak, there would have been bound to be acrimonious arguments over the changes, and much time would be wasted on trivial points. If he could see the revisions as a whole, I felt he would be satisfied. Any minor disagreements could be easily settled.

"Or so I reasoned, and perhaps I had need of a little experience myself. The author arrived and we met, actually, for the first time. I can't say I particularly liked his looks. He was about my age but he had a rather somber cast of countenance, small, dark eyes—almost beady—and poor teeth.

"I went through the amenities. We shook hands. I told him how pleased we all were with the book; how well it was going to do; the promotion we would give it; and so on.

"I then said, rather casually, in order to emphasize the minor nature of the changes—compared to what was not changed, you know—that I had taken the liberty of introducing some small emendations here and there. At that, he sat upright and his small eyes bulged. He seized the manuscript, which was on the table before us, shook some of it out of one of the boxes, riffled through the pages where I had made the necessary changes in a fine-point pencil, done quite lightly to allow of further changes, and *shrieked*.

"He really did. He screamed that I had written something on every page and that he would have to get the whole thing retyped and that the bill would go straight to me. Then he seized the boxes and was gone. I couldn't stop him. I swear to you, I couldn't move, I was that thunderstruck.

"But not panicky, either. The manuscript was photocopied and I had made copious notes of the changes I had made. Since he was under contract—or so I assumed—we could publish over his objections. He might proceed to sue us, but I don't think he could have won, and the publicity, I couldn't help but think, would simply sell more books.

"The trouble is that when I went to see Southby to tell him what had happened, it turned out there was no contract and everything came apart. It seemed that Southby and Fairfield were haggling over the advance. I suppose I might have been more diplomatic when I heard this. It was *not* a good idea to ask Southby if, in view of the advertising budget being planned, it made much sense to haggle over a matter of two thousand dollars in the advance."

Rubin grunted. "Well, now you know something about Southby."

"I know he didn't like to have it made to look as though it were his fault. He ordered me to get that manuscript back and he made it pretty clear that I was in for it if I did not.

"It proved difficult from the start. I tried Fairfield at his apartment, I tried him on the phone. It took me three days and then he finally answered the phone. I managed to keep him on the phone. I told him he could have the advance he wanted. I told him that every change was negotiable and that we could go over the book line by line—which was exactly what I had tried desperately to avoid in the first place—and I warned him that no publisher would take it precisely as it was.

"He said, with a rather snide and unpleasant snicker, that that was not so, that another publisher *would* take it exactly as was. He had still not turned it over to that other publisher, but he hinted that he might.

"I took that as a bluff and didn't let it rattle me. I just told him quietly that no firm could guarantee a best seller as Southby could, reminded him of some of our other books . . ."

Rubin said, "Sure. Trash like *Dish for the Gods*"

Avalon said, "Let him speak, Manny."

"Well," said Bentham, "we were on the phone for over an hour and he finally put it to me straight. Would I publish it as written? I said, just as straight, that we could negotiate every change, but that there would have to be some—for his own good.

"He remained truculent and nasty, but he gave in, just like that. He said he would deliver it the next day and I said enthusiastically—and trying to hide my relief—that that was top hole, and that he was to go to it, the sooner the better, and I would send a messenger if he'd like. He said, no, he didn't want any stinking messenger, and hung up."

Halsted said, "Happy ending."

"No, because he never delivered the manuscript. We waited a week and then Southby finally got him on the phone and all he got out of Fairfield were snarls to the effect that his paid monkey, Bentham, could keep his stinking sarcasm and shove it and we would get no manuscript from him on any terms, or words to that effect.

"That's where it stands. Needless to say, I was *not* sarcastic. I was perfectly reasonable and diplomatic at all times. I was firm on the key point of revision, but not offensively so. In fact, he had agreed to deliver it the next day. As far as Southby was concerned, however, I had lost the manuscript through my malicious treatment of the man, and he's out of his mind with rage.''

Drake said, ''But he hasn't fired you yet, Bentham. And if he hasn't, maybe he won't.''

''No, because he still has hopes. I told him that Fairfield was probably bluffing and was probably psychotic, but he's not listening to me these last few days.

''In fact, I may soon be sliding along the street with Southby's bootmarks clearly imprinted on my rear end. This is all the more certain since he must realize that none of this would have happened if he had not played silly haggling games over pin money. He would certainly have had the man under contract otherwise. Firing me will be the evidence he needs for all the world, and most of all for himself, to see that I was to blame and not he.''

Halsted said, ''But it would be difficult for you to work for Southby after this anyway, wouldn't it? You'd be better off somewhere else.''

Bentham said, ''Unquestionably—but in my own time and at my own resignation. After all, the editorial field is not exactly wide open now, and I might have difficulty finding a new position, and with an as-yet thin reserve of savings, that prospect does not fill me with delight. Southby might well try to see to it that my chances were even less than normal.''

Rubin said, ''You mean, he would try to blacklist you? I wouldn't put it past him.''

Bentham's gloom showed him to be in full agreement. He said, ''Still, what's worst is that with my editing we would have had a good book there. It would be something we could be proud of. Southby and Fairfield could make a fortune and I could make a reputation that would move me on to a much better position elsewhere. And the world would have a whacking good first novel with the promise of better things to come.

''Fairfield has the makings of a great novelist, blast his soul, and I have my editorial pride and wanted to be part of that greatness. And I was *not* sarcastic and he *did* give in. He *did* say he'd deliver it the next day. Why in the devil's name didn't he? That's what bothers me. Why didn't he?"

There was a rather dank pause. Avalon finally said, "There may be an explanation for this. There have been first-class men of genius who have been monsters of villainy in their private lives. Richard Wagner was one; Jean-Jacques Rousseau was another. If this man, Fairfield, is bluffing, and I rather guess he is, too, then he may simply have judged Southby to be a kindred soul and he feels that you will be fired. It's what he would do in Southby's place. Then, when you are gone, he will show up with the manuscript."

"But why?" said Bentham.

"No puzzle there, I think," said Avalon. "In the first place, you dared tamper with his manuscript and he feels you must be punished. In the second, once you are gone he can be reasonably certain that Southby, after all this, will publish his manuscript as written."

"Then why did he say he would deliver it the next day?"

Avalon bent his formidable eyebrows together for a moment and said, "I suppose he felt you would tell Southby, ebulliently, that the thing was in the bag—as you did—and that Southby's anger, sharply intensified by falsely raised hopes, would explode and make certain your rapid firing."

"And all that stuff about my sarcasm would then just be designed to further infuriate Southby?"

"I should think so. Yes."

Bentham thought about it. "That's a pretty dismal picture you've painted. Between Fairfield and Southby there's no escape."

Avalon looked uneasy. "I'm sorry, Mr. Bentham, but that's the way it looks to me."

Bentham said, "I can't believe it, though. I spoke to the man for an hour or more on the phone. He did not *sound* vindictive. Stubborn and nasty, yes, but not personally vindictive."

Avalon said, "I hate to be the insistent advocate of a solution personally abhorrent to me, but surely you were not looking for vindictiveness and would not be expected to see it if it were not absolutely in plain view."

Bentham said desperately, "But there's more. I have read his book and you have not. I believe no one, however skillful, can write a book alien to his own philosophy and . . ."

"That's nonsense," said Rubin. "I can write a piece of fiction hewing to any philosophy you please. I could write one from the Nazi point of view if I were of a mind to, which I'm not."

"You couldn't," said Bentham. "Please don't interpret that as a challenge, but you couldn't. In Fairfield's book there were a variety of motivations, but none was out of the kind of motiveless malignity some people attribute to Iago. There was no unreasoning anger arising over trivial causes."

"But that's the very point," said Avalon. "It seems a trivial cause to you but you don't see through this man's eyes. Changing his novel in even a minor way is to him unforgivable and he'll hound you down over it."

Trumbull said in a troubled voice, "I hate to join in this gallows fiesta, Mr. Bentham, but Geoff sounds as though he might be right."

"Ah," said Rubin suddenly, "but I don't think he is."

Bentham turned in his direction eagerly. "You mean you don't think Fairfield is out to get me?"

Rubin said, "No. He's mad at you, surely, but not to the point of wanting to cut his own throat. What we've got to do is look at this thing carefully with writer psychology in mind. No, Mr. Bentham, I don't mean trying to see a writer's personality in his writing, which I still say can't be done for any really good writer. I mean something that holds for *any* beginning writer.

"I grant that a beginner might feel psychotic enough to fly into a fury at any changes imposed on his golden prose, but even that pales into nothing compared to another need—that of getting into print.

"Remember, this guy was haggling with Southby over a few thousand dollars in advance money, and what was that to him? We sneer at Southby for sticking at a small sum when millions might be in view. Isn't it queerer that the author should do so and risk not only millions, but publication altogether? Is it conceivable that a beginner who must have worked on his book for years would even dream of chancing failure to publish by haggling over the advance?''

Avalon said, ''If he were tbe semipsychotic individual whom Mr. Bentham has described, why not?''

Rubin said, ''Isn't it much more likely that he *already* had another publisher on the string, and that he tried Southby only because of the firm's reputation for turning out best sellers? His quarrel over the advance was his effort to make the two firms bid against each other in an auction they didn't know was taking place. Then, when Bentham tried to make changes, he turned back to the other publisher, who perhaps was willing to make fewer changes, or even none.''

Bentham said, ''Do you mean, Mr. Rubin, that Fairfield originally went to some publisher—call him X? X read the manuscript, suggested a revision, and Fairfield took it back, presumably to revise, but brought it to us instead. When we offered a lower advance and suggested greater revision, he took it back to X?''

''Yes, and you marked up his copy,'' said Rubin. ''I think that annoyed him more than the revision itself had. It meant he had to have the copy retyped *in toto* before submitting it. Even erasing the pencil marks would leave some marks, and he might be a little shy of letting X know he was playing tricks with the manuscript.

''After all, you got him on the phone three days after he had stormed out and he already had another publisher on the hook. After three *days?*''

Bentham said, ''That's why I assumed he was bluffing.''

''And risk publication? No, Publisher X exists, all right.''

Trumbull said, ''I must be going crazy, but I've switched sides. You've convinced me, Manny.''

Bentham said, ''Even if you're right, Mr. Rubin, I'm still in a hopeless position.''

''Not if you can prove this Fairfield was playing games. Once Southby sees that, he'll be furious with the author, not with you. Then you can bide your time and resign at such time as suits yourself.''

Bentham said, ''But for that I would have to know who Publisher X is, and I don't. And without that, he simply won't believe the story. Why should he?''

Rubin said, "Are you sure Fairfield didn't mention the publisher?"

"I'm sure."

Halsted said, with a mild stutter, "How would you know? You've only been in the country a few months and may not know all the publishers."

"There are hundreds in New York and surrounding areas and I certainly don't know them all," said Bentham. "I know the larger ones, though. Surely X would be among the larger ones."

Rubin said, "I should think so. No hint at all?"

"If there was, it whizzed by me."

Rubin said, "Think. Go over the conversation in your mind."

Bentham closed his eyes and sat quietly. No one else made a noise except Drake, whose bolo-tie tip clinked against his water glass when he reached forward to stub out a cigarette.

Bentham opened his eyes and said, "It's no use. There's nothing there."

Drake looked leftward toward the sideboard where Henry was standing. "This is a serious situation, Henry. Do you have any suggestions?"

"Only the publisher's name, sir."

Bentham looked around in astonishment, "What?"

Trumbull said hastily, "Henry is one of us, Mr. Bentham. What are you talking about, Henry? How can you know?"

"I believe the author, Mr. Fairfield, mentioned it in his phone conversation with Mr. Bentham."

Bentham said, on the edge of anger, "He did *not!*"

Henry's unlined face showed no emotion. "I beg your pardon, sir, I do not mean to offend you, but you inadvertently omitted an important part of the story. It was rather like Mr. Trumbull's misadventure in the cab when he left out an important part of the direction. Or like Dr. Drake's point that those who argue about recombinant DNA do so without adequate knowledge of the fundamentals."

Gonzalo said, "You mean we're looking in a dark room for a black cat that *is* there?"

"Yes, sir. If Mr. Bentham had told his story otherwise, the whereabouts of the black cat would be obvious."

"In what way could I have told the story otherwise?" demanded Bentham.

"You told the story with indirect quotations throughout, sir, and thus we never got the exact words anyone used."

"For a very good reason," said Bentham. "I don't remember the exact words. I'm not a recording device."

"Yet sometimes in indirect quotation, a person is reported as saying something he could not possibly have said in direct quotation."

"I assure you," said Bentham coldly, "my account was accurate."

"I'm sure it is, within its limitations, sir. But if there is a Publisher X, why did Mr. Fairfield promise to deliver the manuscript the next day?"

Bentham said, "Oh God, I forgot about that. Are we back to motiveless malignity?"

"No, sir. I would suggest he didn't say that."

"Yes, he did, Henry," said Bentham. "I'm unshakable in that."

"Do you wish to put his remark into direct quotations and maintain that he said, 'I will deliver the manuscript the next day.'?"

Bentham said, "Oh I take your meaning. 'The next day' *is* a paraphrase, of course. He said, 'I will deliver the manuscript tomorrow.' What's the difference?"

Henry said, "And then you agreed enthusiastically, urged him to do so at once, and offered to place a messenger at his service. You don't think that sounded like sarcasm, sir?"

"*No.* He said, 'I will deliver the manuscript tomorrow' and I was enthusiastic. Where's the sarcasm?"

"To Morrow," said Henry carefully, pronouncing it as two words.

"Good God," said Bentham blankly.

Rubin brought his fist down on the table, "Damn! William Morrow & Company," he said, "one of New York's larger publishing houses."

"Yes, sir," said Henry. "I looked it up in the telephone book, to make certain, immediately after Mr. Bentham's account of the phone conversation. It is at 105 Madison Avenue, about a mile from here."

Gonzalo said, "There you are, Mr. Bentham. Just tell your boss that it's with William Morrow & Company and that the author had it in to them first."

"And he can then fire me for stupidity. Which I deserve."

"Not a chance," said Gonzalo. "Don't tell him the literal truth. Tell him that as a result of your own clever detective work you uncovered the facts of the case through a confidential source you cannot reveal."

Henry said, "After all, sir, confidentiality is the policy of the Black Widowers."

10

What Time Is It?

This is another murder mystery, which alone makes it special for me. No, not because I revel in murder—quite the reverse— but just because I have the miserable feeling that whenever I avoid some type of writing some among my readers decide it's because I just can't do it. It is with a certain pleasure, then, that I occasionally show them that I can do it. The reason I don't usually do it is because I usually don't want to.

Besides, although all my mystery stories are clever (well, that's my opinion), I must admit that there are degrees of cleverness and that some are more clever than others. Well, this is one I consider particularly clever. You may not agree with me, of course, but it's my own estimate that decides the quantity of fun I get out of writing a story, so I have to go by what I think.

The monthly banquet of the Black Widowers had proceeded its usually noisy course and then, over the coffee, there had fallen an unaccustomed quiet.

Geoffrey Avalon sipped at his coffee thoughtfully and said, "It's the little things—the little things. I know a couple who

162

might have been happily married forever. He was a lay reader at an Episcopalian Church and she was an unreformed atheist, and they never gave each other a cross look over that. But he liked dinner at six and she liked it at seven, and that split them apart."

Emmanuel Rubin looked up owlishly from his part of the table, eyes unblinking behind thick lenses, and said, "What's 'big' and what's 'little,' Geoff? Every difference is a little difference if you're not involved. There's nothing like a difference in the time sense to reduce you to quivering rage."

Mario Gonzalo looked complacently at the high polish on his shoes and said, "Ogden Nash once wrote that some people like to sleep with the window closed and some with the window open and each other is whom they marry."

Since it was rather unusual that at any Black Widowers banquet three successive comments should be made without an explosive contradiction, it didn't really surprise anyone when Thomas Trumbull furrowed his brows and said, "That's a lot of horsehair. When a marriage breaks up, the trivial reason is never the reason."

Avalon said mildly, "I know the couple, Tom. It's my brother and sister-in-law—or ex-sister-in-law."

"I'm not arguing that they don't say they've split over a triviality, or even that they don't believe it," said Trumbull. "I just say there's something deeper. If a couple are sexually compatible, if there are no money problems, if there is no grave difference in beliefs or attitudes, then they'll stick together. If any of these things fail, then the marriage sours and the couple begin to chafe at trivialities. The trivialities then get blamed—but that's not so."

Roger Halsted, who had been chasing the last of the apple pie about his plate, now cleansed his mouth of its slight stickiness with a sip of black coffee and said, "How do you intend to prove your statement, Tom?"

"It doesn't require proof," said Trumbull, scowling. "It stands to reason."

"Only in your view," said Halsted, warmly, his high forehead flushing pinkly, as it always did when he was moved. "I once broke up with a young woman I was crazy about because she kept saying 'Isn't it a riot?' in and out of season. I swear she had no other flaw."

"You'd be perjuring yourself unconsciously," said Trumbull. "Listen, Jim, call a vote."

James Drake, host for the evening, stubbed out his cigarette and looked amused. His small eyes, nested in finely wrinkled skin, darted around the table and said, "You'll lose, Tom."

"I don't care if I win or lose," said Trumbull, "I just want to see how many jackasses there are at the table."

"The usual number, I suppose," said Drake. "All those who agree with Tom raise their hands."

Trumbull's arm shot up and was the only one to do so.

"I'm not surprised," he said, after a brief look, left and right. "How about you, Henry? Are you voting?"

Henry, the unparalleled waiter at all the Black Widower banquets, smiled paternally, "Actually, I was not, Mr. Trumbull, but if I had voted, I would have taken the liberty of disagreeing with you." He was passing about the table, distributing the brandy.

"You, too, Brutus?" said Trumbull.

Rubin finished his coffee and put the cup down with a clatter. "What the devil, all differences are trivial. Forms of life that are incredibly different superficially are all but identical on the biochemical level. There seems a world of difference between the worm and the earth it burrows in, but, considering the atoms that make it up, both of them . . ."

Trumbull said, "Don't wax poetical, Manny, or, if you must, wax it in your garage and not here. I suspect jackassery is universal but, just to make sure, I'll ask our guest if he is voting."

Drake said, "Let's make that part of the grilling then. It's time. And you can do the grilling, Tom."

The guest was Barry Levine, a small man, dark-haired, dark-eyed, slim, and nattily dressed. He was not exactly handsome, but he had a cheerful expression that was a good substitute. Gonzalo had already sketched his caricature, exaggerating the good cheer into inanity, and Henry had placed it on the wall to join the rest.

Trumbull said, "Mr. Levine, it is our custom at these

gatherings of ours to ask our guest, to begin with, to justify his existence. I shall dispense with that since I will assume that your reason for existence at the moment is to back me up, if you can, in my statement—self-evident, to my way of thinking—that trivialities are trivial.''

Levine smiled and said, in a slightly nasal voice, "Trivialities on the human level, or are we talking about earthworms?"

"We are talking about humans, if we omit Manny."

"In that case, I join the jackassery, since, in my occupation, I am concerned almost exclusively with trivia."

"And your occupation, please?"

"I'm the kind of lawyer, Mr. Trumbull, who makes his living by arguing with witnesses and with other lawyers in front of a judge and jury. And that immerses me in triviality.''

Trumbull growled, "You consider justice a triviality, do you?"

"I do not," said Levine, with equanimity, "but that is not with what we are directly concerned in the courtroom. In the courtroom, we play games. We attempt to make favorable testimony admissible and unfavorable testimony inadmissible. We play with the rules of questioning and cross-examination. We try to manipulate the choosing of favorable jurors, and then we manipulate the thoughts and emotions of the jurors we do get. We try to play on the prejudices and tendencies of the judge as we know them to be at the start or as we discover them to be in the course of the trial. We try to block the opposition attorney or, if that is not possible, to maneuver him into overplaying his hand. We do all this with the trivia and minutiae of precedence and rationale.''

Trumbull's tone did not soften. "And where in all this litany of judicial recreation does justice come in?"

Levine said, "Centuries of experience with our Anglo-American system of jurisprudence has convinced us that in the long run and on the whole, justice is served. In the short run, and in a given specific case, however, if may very well not be. This can't be helped. To change the rules of the game to prevent injustice in a particular case may, and probably will, insure a greater level of injustice on the whole—though once in a while an overall change for the better can be carried through.''

"In other words," interposed Rubin, "you despair of universal justice even as a goal of the legal profession?"

"As an attainable goal, yes," said Levine. "In heaven, there may be perfect justice; on Earth, never."

Trumbull said, "I take it, then, that if you are engaged in a particular case, you are not the least interested in justice?"

Levine's eyebrows shot upward. "Where have I said that? Of course I am interested in justice. The immediate service to justice is seeing to it that my client gets the best and most efficient defense that I can give him, not merely because he deserves it, but also because American jurisprudence demands it, and because *he* is deprived of it at *your* peril, for you may be next.

"Nor is it relevant whether he is guilty or innocent, for he is legally innocent in every case until he is proven guilty according to law, rigorously applied. Whether the accused is morally or ethically innocent is a much more difficult question, and one with which I am not primarily concerned. I am secondarily concerned with it, of course, and try as I might, there will be times when I cannot do my full duty as a lawyer out of a feeling of revulsion toward my client. It is then my duty to advise him to obtain another lawyer.

"Still, if I were to secure the acquittal of a man I considered a scoundrel, the pain would not be as intense as that of failing to secure the acquittal of a man who, in my opinion, was wrongfully accused. Since I can rarely feel certain whether a man is wrongfully accused or is a scoundrel past redemption, it benefits both justice and my conscience to work for everyone as hard as I can, within the bounds of ethical legal behavior."

Gonzalo said, "Have you ever secured the acquittal of someone you considered a scoundrel?"

"On a few occasions. The fault there lay almost always in mistakes made by the prosecution—their illegal collection of evidence, or their slovenly preparation of the case. Nor would I waste pity on them. They have the full machinery of the law on their side and the boundless public purse. If we allow them to convict a scoundrel with less than the most legal of evidence and the tightest of cases simply because we are anxious to see a scoundrel punished, then where will you and I find safety? We, too, may seem scoundrels through force of circumstance or of prejudice."

Gonzalo said, "And have you ever failed to secure the acquittal of someone you considered wrongfully accused?"

Here Levine's face seemed to crumple. The fierce joy with which he defended his profession was gone and his lower lip seemed to quiver for a moment. "As a matter of fact," he said, softly, "I am engaged in a case right now in which my client may well be convicted despite the fact that I consider him wrongfully accused."

Drake chuckled and said, "I told you they'd get that out of you eventually, Barry!" He raised his voice to address the others generally. "I told him not to worry about confidentiality; that everything here was *sub rosa*. And I also told him it was just possible we might be able to help him."

Avalon stiffened and said in his most stately baritone, "Do you know any of the details of the case, Jim?"

"No, I don't."

"Then how do you know we can help?"

"I called it a possibility."

Avalon shook his head. "I expect that from Mario's enthusiasm, but not from you, Jim."

Drake raised his hand. "Don't lecture, Geoff. It doesn't become you."

Levine interposed. "Don't quarrel, gentlemen. I'll be pleased to accept any help you can offer, and if you can't, I will be no worse off. Naturally, I want to impress on you the fact that even though confidentiality may be the rule here, it is particularly important in this case. I rely on that."

"You may," said Avalon stiffly.

Trumbull said, "All right, now. Let's stop this dance and get down to it. Would you give us the details of the case you're speaking of, Mr. Levine?"

"I will give you the relevant data. My client is named Johnson, which is a name that I would very likely have chosen if I were inventing fictitious names, but it is a real name. There is a chance that you might have heard of this case, but I rather think you haven't, for it is not a local case and, if you don't mind, I will not mention the city in which it occurred, for that is not relevant.

"Johnson, my client, was in debt to a loan shark, whom he knew—that is, with whom he had enough of a personal relationship to be able to undertake a personal plea for an extension of time.

"He went to the hotel room that the loan shark used as his office—a sleazy room in a sleazy hotel that fit his sleazy business. The shark knew Johnson well enough to be willing to see him, and even to affect a kind of spurious *bonhomie*, but would not grant the extension. This meant that when Johnson went into default he would, at the very least, be beaten up; that his business would be vandalized; that his family, perhaps, would be victimized.

"He was desperate—and I am, of course, telling you Johnson's story as he told it to me—but the shark explained quite coolly that if Johnson were let off then others would expect the same leniency. On the other hand, if Johnson were made an example of, it would nerve others to pay promptly and perhaps deter some from incurring debts they could not repay. It was particularly galling to Johnson, apparently, that the loan shark waxed virtuous over the necessity of protecting would-be debtors from themselves."

Rubin said dryly, "I dare say, Mr. Levine, that if a loan shark were as articulate as you are, he could make out as good a case for his profession as you could for yours."

Levine said, after a momentary pause, "I would not be surprised. In fact, before you bother to point it out, I may as well say that, given the reputation of lawyers with the public, people hearing the defenses of both professions might vote in favor of loan sharks as the more admirable of the two. I can't help that, but I still think that if you're in trouble you had better try a lawyer before you try a loan shark.

"To continue, Johnson was not at all impressed by the shark's rationale for trying to extract blood from a stone, then pulverizing the stone for failure to bleed. He broke down into a rage, screaming out threats he could not fulfill. In brief, he threatened to kill the shark."

Trumbull said, "Since you're telling us Johnson's story, I assume he admitted making the threat."

"Yes, he did," said Levine. "I told him at the start, as I tell all my clients, that I could not efficiently help him unless he told me the full truth, even to confessing to a crime. Even after such a confession, I would still be compelled to defend him, and to fight, at worst, for the least punishment to which he might be entitled and, at best, for acquittal on any of several conceivable grounds.

"He believed me, I think, and did not hesitate to tell me of the threat; nor did he attempt to palliate or qualify it. That impressed me, and I am under the strong impression that he has been telling me the truth. I am old enough in my profession and have suffered the protestations of enough liars to feel confident of the truth when I hear it. And, as it happens, there is evidence supporting this part of the story, though Johnson did not know that at the time and so did not tell the truth merely because he knew it would be useless to lie."

Trumbull said, "What was the evidence?"

Levine said, "The hotel rooms are not soundproofed and Johnson was shrieking at the top of his voice. A maid heard just about every word and so did a fellow in an adjoining room who was trying to take a nap and who called down to the front desk to complain."

Trumbull said, "That just means an argument was going on. What evidence is there that it was Johnson who was shrieking?"

"Oh ample," said Levine. "The desk clerk also knows Johnson, and Johnson had stopped at the desk and asked if the shark were in. The desk clerk called him and sent Johnson up—and he saw Johnson come down later—and the news of the death threat arrived at the desk between those two periods of time.

"Nevertheless, the threat was meaningless. It served, in fact, merely to bleed off Johnson's rage and to deflate him. He left almost immediately afterward. I am quite certain that Johnson was incapable of killing."

Rubin stirred restlessly. He said, "That's nonsense. Anyone is capable of killing, given a moment of sufficient rage or terror and a weapon at hand. I presume that after Johnson left, the loan shark was found dead with his skull battered in; with a baseball bat, with blood and hair on it, lying on the bed; and you're going to tell us that you're sure Johnson didn't do it."

Johnson held up his glass for what he indicated with his

fingers was to be a touch more brandy, smiled his thanks to
Henry, and said, "I have read some of your murder mysteries, Mr. Rubin, and I've enjoyed them. I'm sure that in your
mysteries such a situation could occur and you'd find ways of
demonstrating the suspect to be innocent. This, however, is
not a Rubin mystery. The loan shark was quite alive when
Johnson left."

Rubin said, "According to Johnson, of course."

"And unimpeachable witnesses. The man who called down
said there was someone being murdered in the next room, and
the desk clerk sent up the security man at once, for he feared
it was his friend being murdered. The security man was well
armed, and though he is not an intellectual type, he is perfectly competent to serve as a witness. He knocked and called
out his identity, whereupon the door opened and revealed the
loan shark, whom the security man knew, quite alive—and
alone. Johnson had already left, deflated and de-energized.

"The man at the desk, Brancusi is his name, saw Johnson
leave a few seconds after the security man had taken the
elevator up. They apparently passed each other in adjoining
elevators. Brancusi called out, but Johnson merely lifted his
hand and hurried out. He looked white and ill, Brancusi says.
That was about a quarter after three, according to Brancusi—
and according to Johnson, as well.

"As for the loan shark, he came down shortly after four
and sat in the bar for an hour or more. The bartender, who
knew him, testified to that and can satisfactorily enumerate
the drinks he had. At about a quarter after five he left the bar
and, presumably, went upstairs."

Avalon said, "Did he drink enough to have become
intoxicated?"

"Not according to the bartender. He was well within his
usual limit and showed no signs of being drunk."

"Did he talk to anyone in particular?"

"Only to the bartender. And according to the bartender, he
left the bar alone."

Gonzalo said, "That doesn't mean anything. He might
have met someone in the lobby. Did anyone see him go into
the elevator alone?"

"Not as far as we know," said Levine. "Brancusi didn't

happen to notice, and no one else has admitted to seeing him, or has come forward to volunteer the information. For that matter, he may have met someone in the elevator or in the corridor outside his room. We don't know, and have no evidence to show he wasn't alone when he went into his room shortly after a quarter after five.

"Nevertheless, this two-hour period between a quarter after three and a quarter after five is highly significant. The security guard who encountered the loan shark immediately after Johnson had left at a quarter after three, found the shark composed and rather amused at the fuss. Just a small argument, he said; nothing important. Then, too, the barman insists that the loan shark's conversation and attitude throughout his time in the bar was normal and unremarkable. He made no reference to threats or arguments."

Halsted said, "Would you have expected him to?"

"Perhaps not," said Levine, "but it is still significant. After all, he knew Johnson. He knew the man to be both physically and emotionally a weakling. He had no fear of being attacked by him, or any doubt that he could easily handle him if he did attack.

"After all, he had agreed to see him without taking the precaution of having a bodyguard present, even though he knew Johnson would be desperate. He was not even temporarily disturbed by Johnson's outburst and shrugged it off to the guard. During that entire two-hour interval he acted as though he considered my client harmless and I would certainly make that point to the jury."

Avalon shook his head. "Maybe so, but if your story is going to have any point at all, the loan shark, you will tell us, met with a violent death. And if so, the man who made the threat is going to be suspected of the murder. Even if the loan shark was certain that Johnson was harmless, that means nothing. The loan shark may simply have made an egregious error."

Levine sighed. "The shark did die. He returned to his room at a quarter after five or a minute or two later and, I suspect, found a burglar in action. The loan shark had a goodish supply of cash in the room—necessary for his business—and the hotel was not immune to burglaries. The loan shark grappled with the intruder and was killed before half past five.''

Trumbull said, ''And the evidence?''

''The man in the adjoining room who had been trying to take a nap two hours before had seethed sufficiently to have been unable to fall asleep until about five and then, having finally dropped off, he was roused again by loud noises. He called down to the desk in a rage, and informed Brancusi that this time he had called the police directly.''

Gonzalo said, ''Did he hear the same voice he had heard before?''

''I doubt that any voice identification he would try to make would stand up in court,'' said Levine. ''However, he didn't claim to have heard voices. Only the noises of furniture banging, glass breaking, and so on.

''Brancusi sent up the security guard who, getting no answer to his knock and call this time, used his passkey at just about half past five and found the loan shark strangled, the room in wild disorder, and the window open. The window opened on a neighboring roof two stories lower. An experienced cat burglar could have made it down without trouble and might well have been unobserved.

''The police arrived soon after, at about twenty to six.''

Trumbull said, ''The police, I take it, do not buy the theory that the murder was committed by a burglar.''

''No. They could detect no signs on the wall or roof outside the window to indicate the recent passage of a burglar. Instead, having discovered upon inquiry of the earlier incident from the man who had called them, they scorn the possibility of coincidence and feel that Johnson made his way to the room a second time, attacked and strangled the loan shark, knocking the furniture about in the process, then opened the window to make it look as though an intruder had done the job, hastened out of the door, missing the security man by moments, and passing him on the elevator again.''

Trumbull said, ''Don't you believe that's possible?''

''Oh anything's *possible*,'' said Levine, coolly, ''but it is not the job of the prosecutor to show it's possible. He has to show it's actually so beyond a reasonable doubt. The fact that the police saw nothing on the walls or roof is of no significance whatever. They may not have looked hard enough. A negative never impresses either judge or jury—and shouldn't. And threats at a quarter after three have nothing to do with an act at twenty after five or so unless the man who made the threat at the former time can be firmly placed on the scene at the later time.''

Gonzalo was balancing his chair on its back legs with his hands gripping the table. ''So what's the problem?''

''The problem is, Mr. Gonzalo,'' said Levine, ''that Johnson *was* placed on the scene of the crime at about the time of the killing.''

Gonzalo brought his chair forward with a clatter. ''With good evidence?''

''The best,'' said Levine. ''He admits it. Here is what happened: In the two hours after he had left the loan shark, Johnson hurriedly scraped up every bit of money he had, borrowed small sums from several friends, made a visit to a pawnshop, and had raised something like a third of what he owed. He then came back to the hotel hoping for as long an extension as possible through payment of this part sum. He had little hope of success, but he had to try.

''He arrived at the hotel at about a quarter to six, after the murder had been committed, and he noted a police squad car at the curb outside the hotel. Except for noticing its existence, he paid it little attention. He had only one thing on his mind.

''He headed straight for the elevator, which happened to be at the lobby with its door open. As he stepped out of it at the loan shark's floor, he saw a policeman at the door of the room he was heading for. Almost instinctively, he ducked back into the elevator and pushed the lobby button. He was the only man in the elevator and there were no calls to higher floors. The elevator moved downward, stopping at no floors. When he reached the lobby, he hastened out, went home, and stayed there till the police came for him.''

A curl of cigarette smoke hung above Drake's head. He said, ''I suppose they learned of the earlier threat and took him in for questioning.''

''Right,'' said Levine.

''But they can't make Johnson testify against himself, so how do they show he was on the spot at the time of the murder?''

"For one thing, Brancusi saw him when he was heading for the elevator. Brancusi called out to head him off and prevent him from running into the police. Johnson didn't hear him and the elevator doors closed behind him before Brancusi could do anything else. Brancusi insists, however, that Johnson was back down again in two minutes or so and hastened out. And he is prepared to swear that Johnson left at precisely ten minutes to six.

Drake said, "Is Brancusi really sure of that?"

"Absolutely. His shift was over at six o'clock and he was furious at the fact that the murder had not taken place an hour later, when he would have been off duty. As it was, he was sure he would be needed for questioning and might be kept for hours. He was therefore unusually aware of the time. There was an electric clock on the wall to one side of his desk, a nice large one with clear figures that was new and had been recently installed. It was accurate to the second and he is absolutely certain it said ten to six."

Avalon cleared his throat. "In that case, Mr. Levine, Brancusi backs up Johnson's story and places your client at the scene not at the time of the murder but afterward."

Levine said, "Here is where the trivialities come in. Brancusi is a bad witness. He has a small stutter, which makes him sound unsure of himself; he has one drooping eyelid, which makes him look hangdog and suspicious; and he has distinct trouble in looking you in the eye. The jury will be ready to believe him a liar.

"Second, Brancusi is a friend of Johnson's, has known him from childhood, and is still a drinking buddy of the man. That gives him a motive for lying, and the prosecution is sure to make the most of that.

"Finally, Brancusi may not want to testify at all. He served six months in jail for a minor offense quite a number of years ago. He has lived a reasonably exemplary life since and naturally doesn't want that earlier incident to be made public. For one thing, it could cost him his job."

Rubin said, "Could the prosecution bring up the matter? It's irrelevant, isn't it?"

"Quite irrelevant, but if the prosecution takes the attitude that it serves to cast a doubt on the reliability of Brancusi as a witness, they might slip it past the judge."

Rubin said, "In that case, if you put neither Johnson nor Brancusi on the stand, the prosecution would still be stuck with the task of proving that Johnson was at the scene at the right time. They can't call Johnson themselves, and they won't call Brancusi to give his evidence because they then can't cross-examine him and bring out that jail term."

Levine sighed. "There's another witness. The man is an accountant named William Sandow. He had stopped at the hotel lobby to buy a small container of breath fresheners, and while he was at the newsstand, he saw Johnson pass him, hurrying out of the hotel. Later in the evening, he read about the murder, and called the police to volunteer the information. His description of the man he saw was a good one and, eventually, he made a positive identification out of a lineup.

"Sandow said that what drew his attention to the man who passed him was the look of horror and anguish on his face. Of course, he can't use terms like that on the witness stand, but the prosecution can get him to make factual statements to the effect that Johnson was sweating and trembling, and this would give him the air of an escaping murderer."

Rubin said, "No, it doesn't. Lots of things could make a man sweat and tremble, and Johnson had good reason to do so short of murder. Besides, Sandow just bears out the story of Brancusi and Johnson."

Levine shook his head. "No, he doesn't. Sandow says he happened to catch a glimpse of the time as Johnson passed him and swears it was exactly half past five, which is just after the murder was committed but *before* the police arrived. If true, that ruins Johnson's story and makes the assumption that he committed the murder a very tempting one."

Rubin said, "Brancusi backs Johnson. It's one man's word against another. You can't convict on that."

"You can," said Levine, "if the jury believes one man and not the other. If Brancusi is bound to make a bad impression, Sandow is bound to make a good one. He is open-faced, clean-cut, has a pleasant voice, and exudes efficiency and honesty. The mere fact that he is an accountant gives him an impression of exactness. And whereas Brancusi is a friend of Johnson and therefore suspect, Sandow is a complete outsider with no reason to lie.''

Rubin said, ''How sure are you of that? He was very ready to volunteer information and get involved. Does he have some secret grudge against Johnson? Or some connection with the loan shark?''

Levine shrugged his shoulders. ''There are such things as public-spirited citizens, even today. The fact that he came forward will be in his favor with the jury. Naturally, my office has investigated Sandow's background. We've turned up nothing we can use against him—at least so far.''

There was a short silence around the table, and then finally Rubin said, ''Honest people make mistakes, too. Sandow says he just happened to catch a glimpse of the time. Just how did that happen? He just happened to glance at his wristwatch? Why? Brancusi had a good reason to watch the clock. What was Sandow's?''

''He does not claim to have looked at his watch. He caught a glimpse of the same wall clock that Brancusi looked at. Presumably both Brancusi and Sandow were looking at the same clock at the same moment. The same clock couldn't very well tell half past five to one person and ten to six to another at the same time. Clearly, one person is lying or mistaken, and the jury will believe Sandow.''

Rubin said, ''Brancusi was staring at the clock. Sandow just caught a glimpse. He may have caught the wrong glimpse.''

Levine said, ''I have considered stressing that point, but I am not sure I ought to. Sandow's statement that he just happened to catch a glimpse sounds honest, somehow. The mere fact that he doesn't claim to see more than he saw, that he doesn't make an undue effort to strengthen his evidence, makes him ring true. And he's an accountant. He says he's used to figures, that he can't help noticing and remembering them. The prosecution will surely have him say that on the stand, and the jury will surely accept that.

''On the other hand, Mr. Rubin, if I try to balance Sandow's cool certainty by having Brancusi become very, very definite and emotional about how certain he is it was ten to six, then he will carry all the less conviction for he will impress the jury as someone who is desperately trying to support a lie.

And if it looks as though he is making a good impression, the prosecution will make a major effort to bring out his previous prison record."

Halsted broke in with sudden animation. "Say, could Sandow see the clock from where he says he was standing at the newsstand?"

Levine said, "A good point. We checked that out at once and the answer is: Yes, he could. Easily."

There was another silence around the table, a rather long one.

Trumbull finally said, "Let's put it as briefly as we can. You are convinced that Johnson is innocent and that Brancusi is telling the truth. You are also convinced that Sandow is either lying or mistaken, but you can't think of any reason he might be or any way of showing he is. And the jury is going to believe Sandow and convict Johnson."

Levine said, "That's about it."

Rubin said, "Of course, juries are unpredictable."

"Yes, indeed," said Levine, "but if that's my only hope, it isn't much of one. I would like better."

Avalon's fingers were drumming noiselessly on the tablecloth. He said, "I'm a patent lawyer myself, and I have just about no courtroom experience. Still, all you need do is cast a reasonable doubt. Can't you point out that a man's liberty rests on a mere glimpse of a clock?"

"I can, and will try just as hard as I can short of pushing the prosecution into attempting to uncover Brancusi's prison record. I would like something better than that, too."

From the sideboard, Henry's voice sounded suddenly. "If you'll excuse me, Mr. Levine—I assume that the clock in question, the one to which both Mr. Brancusi and Mr. Sandow referred, is a digital clock."

Levine frowned. "Yes, it is. I didn't say it was, did I? How did you know?" His momentary confusion cleared, and he smiled. "Well, of course. No mystery. I said it was a new clock, and these days digital clocks are becoming so popular that it is reasonable to suppose that any new clock would be digital."

"I'm sure that is so," said Henry, "but that was not the reason for my conclusion. You said a few moments ago that

Mr. Sandow was an accountant and that accountants couldn't help but notice and remember figures. Of course you don't notice and remember figures on an ordinary dial clock—you remember the position of the hands. On a dial clock it is just as easy to tell time when the hour numbers are replaced with dots or with nothing at all.''

"Well, then?" said Levine.

"Almost any grown person of reasonable intelligence can tell time at a glance in that way. Accountants have no special advantage. A digital clock is different."

Levine said, "Since it was a digital clock, then accountants *do* have a special advantage. You're not helping me, Henry."

Henry said, "I think I am. You have been unconsciously misleading us, Mr. Levine, by giving the time in the old-fashioned way appropriate to a dial clock. You speak of a quarter after three and a quarter to six and so on. Digital clocks specifically show such times to be three-fifteen and five forty-five. As digital clocks become more and more universal, times will be spoken of in this way exclusively, I imagine."

Levine seemed a little impatient. "How does this change anything, Henry?"

Henry said, "Your statement was that Brancusi was certain that the time at the crucial moment was ten to six, while Sandow was certain it was half past five. If this were so, and if a dial clock were involved, the position of the hands at the two times would be widely different and neither could make a mistake. A deliberate lie by one or the other would have to be involved.

"On the other hand, if it is a digital clock, Brancusi claims he read five-fifty and Sandow claims he read five-thirty, you see."

Levine said, "Ah, and you think that Sandow misread the figure five for a three. No good; it could be maintained with equal justice that Brancusi mistook the three for a five in his annoyance over the fact that the end of his shift was approaching."

Henry said, "It is not a question of a mistake that anyone could make. It is a mistake that an accountant particularly might make. There are fifty cents to half a dollar but thirty minutes to half an hour, and an accountant above all is apt to think of figures in terms of money. To an accountant five-fifty is most likely to mean five and a half dollars. A quick glimpse at a digital clock reading five-fifty might trigger the response five and a half in an accountant's mind, and he will later swear he had seen the time as half past five.''

Avalon looked astonished. "You really think Mr. Sandow could have made that mistake, Henry?"

But it was Levine who answered jubilantly, "Of course! It's the only way of explaining how two people could read the same clock at the same time and honestly come up with two different answers. Besides, *there's* the reasonable doubt. Suppose I set up a screen on which I can flash numbers on the pretext that I have to test Sandow's eyesight and memory of numbers, and ask him to detect and identify numbers flashed only briefly on the screen. If I show him five-fifty with a dollar sign before it, he will be bound to say, 'five and a half dollars.' ''

Gonzalo said, "He might say 'five-fifty' or something like that."

"If he does, I'll ask him if he means five hundred and fifty dollars or five and a half dollars—after all, does he or does he not see the decimal point?—and he will be sure to say five and a half dollars. He will then repeat that with five-fifty written in other printing styles and with the dollar sign left out. Finally, when I flash the image of a digital clock reading five-fifty and ask whether that is five and a half or ten to six, he won't even have to answer. The jury will get the point."

Levine rose to shake Henry's hand. "Thank you, Henry. I said that cases depend on trivialities, but I never dreamed that this one would rest on something as trivial as the difference between a digital clock and a dial clock."

"But," said Henry, "on that piece of trivia depends the freedom of a man who is presumably wrongfully accused of murder, and that is no triviality at all."

11

Middle Name

The Black Widowers club is stag (no women admitted) only because the real-life club on which it is modeled is stag.

This involves me in a paradox. On the one hand, I am a feminist and fight strongly against sexism in all its aspects What's more, I get tremendous enjoyment out of being in the company of women.

And yet—once in the company of women, no amount of philosophic and intellectual determination to the contrary can keep me from treating them as sex objects. Furthermore, I must admit that when I am in the womb of one of my stag club meetings and am surrounded by men only, there is a certain ease and relaxation that engulfs me.

Sure, I feel guilty and that's why every once in a while I am forced to take up the matter of sexism in a Black Widower story. This one temporarily exorcized some of the guilt, for which I am grateful to it.

Roger Halsted looked a bit doleful and said, ''I almost didn't get here tonight.''

Geoffrey Avalon looked down at him from his straight-backed seventy-four inches and said, "Automobile accident?"

"Nothing so dramatic," said Halsted. "Alice was in one of her feminist moods this afternoon and objected rather strenuously to the fact that the Black Widowers Society is a stag organization."

"But she's known that from the start, hasn't she?" asked Avalon.

"Of course, and it's graveled her from the start, too," said Halsted. "Sometimes it's worse than other times, that's all. And today, well, she may have seen something on TV, read something in the newspapers, had a talk with a friend, or whatever. Anyway, she was upset, and the trouble is, I rather sympathize with her."

Emmanuel Rubin walked over from the other end of the room, where he had been exchanging insults with Mario Gonzalo, host at this month's Black Widowers banquet.

Rubin said, "Are you talking about your wife, Roger?"

"Yes, as a matter of fact."

"I could tell by the troubled look on your face. Bad form. Black Widowers don't have wives."

"Yes?" said Halsted sharply. "Have you told that to Jane?"

"I mean during the banquets, and you know that's what I mean."

"I've heard you mention Jane at the banquets and, besides, my own discussion is germane to the banquets. I would hate to have to give them up."

"Who can make you?" demanded Rubin scornfully, his scanty beard bristling.

Halsted said, "My own conscience, for one thing. And it's not worth breaking up a marriage over."

"Why should it break up a marriage?" said Rubin. "Even if we grant equality for women—political, economic, and social—why should that prevent me from spending one evening a month with friends of my own choosing who just happen to be male?"

Avalon said, "You know better than that, Manny. They don't just happen to be male. They are forbidden by the rules of the club to be anything but male."

"And anything but intelligent," said Rubin, "and anything but compatible. If any one of us takes a dislike to anyone proposed for membership, however trivial or even nonexistent the cause of that dislike might be, that potential member can be blackballed. Just one of us can do it, regardless of the wishes of the rest, and we don't have to explain either."

"Manny," said Avalon, "you're not usually so obtuse. A woman can't be blackballed, because she can't even be *proposed* for membership. Don't you see the difference? Whichever one of us is host for the evening can bring any guest he wishes, even one who would be instantly blackballed if he were proposed for membership. But the guest must be male. No woman can be brought. Don't you see the difference?"

"Exactly," said Halsted. "If it were a black that we ruled out, or a Jew, or an Irishman, that would be bigotry and not one of us could live with it. But since it's only women, we don't seem to mind. What moral blindness!"

"Well, then," said Rubin, "are you two suggesting that we permit women to join the society?"

"No," said Avalon and Halsted in quick and emphatic simultaniety.

"Then what are we arguing about?"

Halsted said, "I'm just pointing out that we ought to recognize the immorality of it."

"You mean as long as we know something is immoral, we are free to be immoral."

"Of course I don't," said Halsted. "I happen to think that hypocrisy aggravates any sin. Nothing is so male chauvinist as to say, 'I'm not a male chauvinist, but . . .' as I've heard Manny say."

Mario Gonzalo joined them and said with clear self-satisfaction, "I don't say, 'I'm not a male chauvinist, but . . .' I *am* a male chauvinist. I expect a woman to take care of me."

"That's just an admission you can't take care of yourself," said Rubin, "which is something I've always suspected, Mario."

Gonzalo looked over his shoulder hurriedly in the direction of his guest and then said, in a low voice, "Listen, keep talking feminism during the dinner, off and on. It's a stroke of luck you've started on your own.''

"Why?" said Avalon in a voice that had not been hushed since its invention. "What dire plot are you . . ."

"Shh," said Gonzalo. "I want to draw out my guest. He's got something eating him he won't talk about. That's why I brought him. It could be interesting.''

"Do you know what it is?" asked Halsted.

"Only in a general way . . ." said Gonzalo.

Henry, whose elegant service at the banquets ennobled the occasion, interrupted in his soft way. "If you don't mind, Mr. Gonzalo, dinner is served.''

Gonzalo placed his guest immediately to his right and said, "Has everyone met Mr. Washburn now?''

There was a general murmur of agreement. Lionel Washburn was an almost classically handsome individual with a head of thick, dark hair cut neatly, with black-rimmed glasses, white shirt, dark-blue suit, and shiny black shoes. He looked dressed up without being uncomfortable. He did not yet seem to have passed his thirtieth birthday.

He said to Gonzalo somberly, "Is there some argument about whether the organization is to be stag, Mario? I heard . . ."

"No argument," said Gonzalo quickly. "It *is* stag. I invited *you*. I didn't suggest you bring a girlfriend.''

"I don't have one," said Washburn, biting off each word. Then, more normally, "How long have you been stag?''

"From the start, but it's Jim's story. Jim, my guest would like to hear how the society got its start—if you don't mind, that is.''

James Drake smiled and held his cigarette to one side so that he could see the other's face clearly. "I don't mind, though I'm sure the others are pretty sick of it. Still—any objections?''

Thomas Trumbull, who was cutting into his rack of lamb, said, "Plenty of objections, but you go ahead and I'll attend to the inner man. Henry, if you can scare up an extra helping of mint sauce, I would be infinitely appreciative. And Jim, I would suggest you get our personal Book of Genesis printed up and handed out at the start of each banquet to the guest. The rest of us can then be spared. Thank you, Henry.''

Drake said, ''Now that we have Tom out of the way, I'll go on. About thirty years ago, I married, but then we all make mistakes, don't we? I believe I was fascinated at the time, though I don't remember why. My friends, however, were not fascinated.''

Avalon drew in his breath in a long, rumbling sniff. ''*We* remember why.''

''I'm sure you do,'' agreed Drake good-humoredly. ''As a result, I found myself outcast. My friends fell away and I couldn't endure *her* friends or, after a time, her. It occurred to Ralph Ottur, then—He lives in California now, I'm sorry to say—to start a club for the sole purpose of seeing me without my wife. Naturally, this would only work if the club were stag. So there you are. We called it the Black Widowers because black widow spiders are quite apt to devour their mates, and we were determined to survive.''

Washburn said, ''And does your wife know the nature of the origin of the club?''

''She's not my wife,'' said Drake. ''Anymore, that is. I divorced her after seven years.''

''And were you all members at the start?''

Drake shook his head. ''Jeff, Tom, and I are charter members. The others joined later. Some members have died or now live too far away to attend.''

''But the reason for the men-only character of the club is gone. Why do you . . .''

''Because we want to,'' said Gonzalo quickly. ''Because I like women in their place and I know exactly where that place is and here isn't it.''

''That's a disgusting statement,'' said Halsted, with the slight stutter that came when he grew emotional.

Gonzalo said coolly, ''You've got to say that because you're married and you're afraid that if you don't keep in practice, you'll let something chauvinistic, so-called, slip in front of your wife and then you'll be in trouble. I'm not married so I'm a free man. My girlfriends know where I stand, and if they don't like it, they can leave.''

Avalon said, "There's an uncomfortable Don Juanism about that statement. Don't you care if they leave?"

"Sometimes," admitted Gonzalo, "but I'd care a lot more if they stayed and argued with me. And there are always others."

"Disgusting," said Halsted again.

"The truth usually is," said Gonzalo. "Why don't all you highly moral feminists tell me why you don't want women at these meetings and see if you can make the reason nonchauvinist?"

There was an uncomfortable silence about the table, and Gonzalo said, "Henry, you're a Black Widower, too, and I'm not letting you escape. Would you like to see women at these meetings?"

Henry's face crinkled into a pleasant smile. "No, Mr. Gonzalo, I would not."

"Aha," said Gonzalo. "Now, you're an honest man, Henry, unlike these Black Hypocriticers you wait on. Tell me why not."

Henry said, "Like you, Mr. Gonzalo, I am not married, but I'm afraid I lack your variegated experience with young women."

"What's that got to do with it?"

Henry said, "I was merely explaining the situation in case my theory on the subject should prove to be childishly foolish to other, more experienced men. It seems to me that most men during their childhood have had their mothers as their chief authority figures. Even when the father is held up as a mysterious and ogreish dispenser of punishments, it is, in fact, the mother whose outcries, yanks, pushes, and slaps perpetually stand in the way of what we want to do. And we never recover."

Rubin said, in a voice of deep, masculine disdain, "Come, Henry, are you trying to say that men are afraid of women?"

Henry said, "I believe many are. Certainly, many feel a sense of relief and freedom when in the company of men only and feel particularly free when women are not allowed to intrude. This society originated as a haven from women under the guise of being one from a particular woman. That particular woman is gone but the haven is still needed and still persists.''

Avalon said, ''Well, that is at least not an example of outright chauvinism.''

''And totally untrue,'' said Rubin, his eyes flashing behind the thick lenses that covered them. ''How many here are afraid of women?''

It was Washburn who intervened at this point. With his handsome face contorted into a mask of fury, he brought his fist down with a smash that rattled the dishes and caused Henry to pause in his task of pouring the coffee.

Washburn said, ''You don't expect anyone to admit it, do you? Your waiter is correct, but he doesn't go far enough. Of course, we're afraid of women. Why shouldn't we be? They're man-eaters, cannibals, harpies. They're bound by no rules, no canons of sportsmanship. They're the ruin of men and of all that is decent and human. I don't care if I never see another one in my life.''

He paused, drew a deep breath, then passed a hand over his forehead, which had dampened with perspiration and said, ''Pardon me, gentlemen, I did not mean to lose my temper.''

Trumbull said, ''But why . . .'' and stopped at Gonzalo's raised hand.

Gonzalo was grinning in triumph. ''Later, Tom. It's almost grilling time and I'll choose you as inquisitor and you can ask your question.''

And, indeed, it was not long before Gonzalo began the ritualistic tapping of the water glass as the brandy was being distributed. He said, ''It's up to you, Tom.''

Trumbull frowned ferociously under his white and crisply waved hair and said, ''I will assume, Mr. Washburn, that Mario has explained to you that the payment, for what we hope you will agree is a fine dinner and at least partly edifying conversation, is a grilling. To our questions, you will be expected to answer fully and truthfully, even when that may be embarrassing. I must assure you that nothing said here ever leaves these four walls.

''With that preamble, let me say this. I am not a judge of

masculine pulchritude, Mr. Washburn, but it seems to me that women would judge you to be handsome.''

Washburn flushed and said, ''I would not try to account for women's tastes. Still it is true that I have found that I can, on occasion, attract women.''

''That's a very modest way of putting it,'' said Trumbull. ''Does the converse hold as well? Do women attract you?''

For a moment, Washburn looked puzzled. Then he frowned and said, ''Are you asking me if I am gay?''

Trumbull shrugged and said in a level voice, ''In these times, it is a permissible question, and it is even permissible to answer in an open affirmative, if that should happen to be the case. I ask out of no personal interest, I assure you, but merely out of curiosity over your earlier angry remarks about women as a group.''

Washburn relaxed. ''I see your point. No, I'm interested in women. Far too interested. And it was not the sex as a whole that I was really berating. I was striking out at one! One woman! And myself!''

Trumbull hesitated. ''The logical thing,'' he said, ''would be to question you, Mr. Washburn, concerning this woman who so distresses you. Yet I hesitate. On the one hand, it is a peculiarly private matter, which I do not wish to probe and, on the other, if you don't mind my saying so, the details are likely to be peculiarly uninteresting. I suppose every one of us in our time . . .''

Avalon interrupted. ''If *you* don't mind, Tom, you are displaying an uncommon combination of delicacy and insensitivity. I am prepared, with your permission, to take over the grilling.''

''If you think you can do so, Jeff, within the bounds of good taste,'' said Trumbull huffily.

Avalon lifted his dense eyebrows to maximum and said, ''I think highly of you, Tom, and yet have never considered you an arbiter of good taste. Mr. Washburn, I have no wish to probe wounds unnecessarily, but let me guess. Your outburst came during a discussion of the pros and cons of feminism. May we take it, then, that your unhappy experience, whatever it was, involved feminism?''

Washburn nodded and said, ''It sure as hell did.''

"Good! Now it may be superfluous to ask this, but was whatever it was that happened something that has happened to many others? Putting aside the great pain it may have caused you and the unique unhappiness you may consider you have felt, would you in your calmer moments think that it might be the common lot of male humanity?"

Washburn seemed lost in thought, and Avalon went on as gently as he could. "After all, millions have been jilted, millions have been sold out, millions have been betrayed by their lovers and their friends."

"What happened to me," said Washburn, between remarkably white and even teeth, "has in a way happened to very many, as you suggest. I recognize that. To lose the woman one loves is not so rare. To be laughed at and humiliated," he swallowed, "may be the lot of many. But in one respect, I have been ill used particularly. In one respect."

Avalon nodded. "Very good. I won't ask you any leading questions. Just tell us about that one respect."

Washburn bent his glance down to his brandy snifter and spoke in a hurried tone of voice. "I fell in love. It wasn't the first time. She was—she was not the most beautiful woman I have ever known—nor the pleasantest. In fact, we did not get along. Her company was always a maddening bumpy ride in a springless cart down a rough road. But, oh God, I couldn't help myself. I still can't seem to. Don't ask me to analyze it. All I can say is that I was caught, tangled, trapped, and I wanted her. And I couldn't get her.

"She acted as though she hated me. She acted as though she wanted me to want her, just so she could show the world I couldn't have her.

"She was a feminist. Her nerve endings stuck out six inches beyond her skin on that subject. She was successful. She was a magazine illustrator at the top of her field and commanded high fees. It wasn't enough, though. To make it right for her, I had to fail.

"And there was no way I could argue effectively with her. She won every time. Of course, she was an intellectual and I'm not—though I like to think I'm intelligent. . . ."

Rubin said, "Intelligence is the diamond and intellectualism only the facets. I've known many a beautifully faceted rhinestone. What do you do for a living?''

Washburn said, ''I'm a stockbroker.''

"Do you do well? I mean, as well as your feminist?''

Washburn flushed. ''Yes. And I've inherited a rather sizable trust fund. She seemed to resent that.''

"Let me guess,'' said Rubin dryly. ''You make more money with less brains because you're a man. You get farther with less deserving because you're a man. You probably even inherited the trust fund because you were a man. Your sister would have gotten less.''

"That's about it,'' said Washburn. ''She said the way I dressed, the way I held myself, everything about me was designed to show my masculine wealth and power. She said I might as well wear a neon sign saying, 'I can buy women.' ''

Trumbull said, ''Did you ever try to defend yourself?''

"Sure,'' said Washburn, ''and that meant a fight. I asked her why, if she thought she should be considered as a human being and as an intellectual, without being penalized for her sex, she insisted on emphasizing her sex? Why didn't she remove her makeup and meet the world with an unpainted face as men did? Why didn't she wear less revealing clothes, and accentuate her breasts and hips less? I said she might as well wear a neon sign saying, 'I sell for a high price.' ''

"She must have loved that,'' muttered Rubin.

"You bet she didn't,'' said Washburn grimly. ''She said a masculine society forced that on her in self-defense, and she wouldn't give up the only weapon they granted her. I said she needed no weapon with me. I said I would marry her without enticement or allure, straight out of the shower with wet hair and a pimple on her shoulder if she had one. And she said, 'To do what? To cook your dinner and clean your house for you?' And I said, 'I have a housekeeper for that.' And she said, 'Of course; another woman.' ''

Halsted said, ''What good would it have done you to marry her? You would have fought like that every day. It would have been a purgatory. Why not just walk away from that?''

"Why not?'' said Washburn. ''Sure, why not? Why not just kick the heroin habit? Why not just stop breathing if the air gets polluted? How do I know why not? It's not the sort of thing you can reason out. Maybe—maybe—if I had the chance, I could win her over.''

"You wouldn't have," said Rubin flatly. "She's a ballbuster, and she'd stay one.''

Halsted said, "That's a stupid phrase, Manny. It's part of the routine bigotry of the chauvinist. A man is ambitious; a woman is unscrupulous. A man is firm; a woman is stubborn. A man is witty; a woman is bitchy. A man is competitive; a woman is abrasive. A man is a hard-driving leader; a woman is a ballbuster.''

Rubin said, "Call it what you want. Say she's a lily of the valley if you want. I say her ambition and occupation would have been to make our friend here wish he had never been born, and she would have succeeded.''

Turning to Washburn, he said, "I assume from your early outburst, your failure with her was complete. If so, I congratulate you, and if I knew of a way to help you succeed, I would refuse to give it to you.''

Washburn shook his head. "No fear. She's married someone else—a dumb creep—and the last I've heard she *is* cooking and cleaning house.''

"Did she give up her career?" said Avalon in astonishment.

"No," said Washburn, "but she does the other, too. What I'll never understand is why *him*.''

Trumbull said, "There's no accounting for the nature of attraction. Maybe this other fellow makes her laugh. Maybe he dominates her without bothering to argue the point. Maybe she likes the way he smells. How can you tell? How do you account for the way she attracts you? Nothing you've said makes her attractive to me.''

"If she liked him better," said Washburn, fuming, "why not say so, for whatever reason—or for no reason? Why make it look like a straightforward test? Why humiliate me?''

"Test?" said Rubin. "What test?''

"That's what I referred to when I said earlier that in one way I had been particularly ill used. She said she would see if I were the kind of man she could live with. She dared me to give her a one-syllable middle name to represent what every schoolchild knew—and yet didn't know. She implied that she was giving the other fellow the same test. I knew about him and I didn't worry about him. My God, he was a stupid advertising copy writer who shambled about in turtleneck sweaters and drank beer."

Avalon said, "Surely, you couldn't believe a woman would choose one man over another according to whether he could solve a puzzle. That happens in fairytales perhaps; otherwise, not."

Washburn said, "I see that *now*. She married him, though. She said he had the answer. That idiot passed, she said, and I failed. Not getting her was bad enough, but she arranged to make me lose in a battle of wits to someone I despised—or at least she *said* I had lost. It wasn't a *test*. It was nonsense. Suppose you chose a middle name with one syllable—John, Charles, Ray, George—any one of them. Who's to say the answer is right or wrong, except her?

"If she were going to marry him anyway, she might have done that without going out of her way to make me look foolish in my own eyes."

Halsted said, "What if the question were a legitimate one? What if he had gotten the correct answer and you hadn't? Would that make you feel better?"

"I suppose so," said Washburn, "but the more I think of it, the more certain I am that it's a fake."

"Let's see now," said Halsted thoughtfully. "We need a one-syllable middle name that every schoolboy knows—and yet doesn't know."

"Schoolchild," growled Washburn. "Schoolboy is chauvinistic."

Gonzalo said, "Go ahead, Roger. You teach school. What does every schoolchild know—and yet not know?"

"In my class at the junior high school," said Halsted, gloomily, "every schoolchild knows he ought to know algebra, and what he doesn't know is algebra. If algebra were a one-syllable middle name that would be the answer."

Drake said, "Let's be systematic. Only people have middle names in the usual meaning of the word, so we can start with that. If we find a person whom every schoolchild knows— and yet doesn't know, then that person will have a middle name and that middle name will be the answer."

"And if you think that," said Washburn, "where does it

get you? For one thing, how is it possible to know something or someone—and yet not know? And if it *were* possible, then it's quite impossible that this should be true of only one person. How would you pick out the correct person? No, that witch was playing games."

"Actually," said Avalon, "middle names are, on the whole, uncommon. Nowadays, everyone gets one, but they were much against the rule in the past, it seems to me. Think of some famous people—George Washington, Abraham Lincoln, Napoleon Bonaparte, William Shakespeare—no middle names in the lot. The Greeks had only one name—Socrates, Plato, Demosthenes, Creon. It limits the field somewhat."

Halsted said, "There's Robert Louis Stevenson, Franklin Delano Roosevelt, Gustavus Adolphus Vasa."

"Who's Gustavus Adolphus Vasa?" asked Gonzalo.

"A King of Sweden in the early 1600s," said Halsted.

Gonzalo said, "I suppose every Swedish schoolchild would know him, but we should stick to the knowledge of American schoolchildren."

"I agree," said Avalon.

Rubin said thoughtfully, "The Romans had three names as a matter of course. Julius Caesar was really Gaius Julius Caesar. His assassin, Cassius, was Gaius Cassius Longinus. Every American schoolchild would know the names Julius Caesar and Cassius from Shakespeare's play *Julius Caesar*, which every American schoolchild is put through. Yet he wouldn't know the names Gaius Julius Caesar and Gaius Cassius Longinus. He would think Julius was a first name and Cassius was a last name, but each would be a middle name. That would be the sort of thing we're after."

Avalon said, "Many cultures use patronymics as routine middle names. Every Russian has one. Peter I of Russia, or Peter the Great, as he's usually known, was really Peter Alexeievich Romanov. Every schoolchild knows Peter the Great and yet doesn't know his middle name, or even that he has one."

Rubin said, "There are other possibilities. Some middle names are treated as first names even for Americans. President Grover Cleveland was really Stephen Grover Cleveland. He dropped his first name and used his middle name, so every schoolchild knows Grover Cleveland and doesn't know Stephen Grover Cleveland. The same is true for Thomas Woodrow Wilson and John Calvin Coolidge.

"Then again, some middle names are lost in pen names. Mark Twain was really Samuel Langhorne Clemens, and Lewis Carroll was really Charles Lutwidge Dodgson. Every schoolchild knows Mark Twain and Lewis Carroll but probably doesn't know Langhorne and Lutwidge."

Washburn said impatiently, "Pardon me, gentlemen, but what good is all this? How does it help with the problem? You can rattle off a million middle names, but which one did that female *want?*"

Avalon said solemnly, "We are merely outlining the dimensions of the problem, Mr. Washburn."

"And doing it all wrong," said Gonzalo. "Look, every middle name I've heard from Julius to Lutwidge has more than one syllable. Why not think of a one-syllable middle name and work backward? If we want to consider American Presidents, we can start with the letter 's.' You can't be more one-syllable than a single letter. Well, it was Harry S Truman; and the S was just S and stood for nothing. Every schoolchild has heard of Harry S Truman, but how many of them know S doesn't stand for anything?"

Drake said, "For that matter, every schoolchild knows Jimmy Carter; but his name really is James Earl Carter, Jr. The schoolchildren don't know about Earl, and that's one-syllable."

Washburn said, "You still have a million answers, and you don't have *one.*"

Trumbull suddenly roared out angrily, "Damn it to hell, gentlemen, you're leaving out the third and crucial clue. I'm sitting here waiting for one of you to realize this fact, and you just run around in solemn pedantic circles."

"What third clue, Tom?" asked Avalon quietly.

"You need a one-syllable middle name; that's one. You need that rigmarole about schoolchildren; that's two. And you have the fact that the woman said that the puzzle was intended to indicate whether Washburn was a man she could live with. *That's* three. It means that the puzzle must somehow involve male chauvinism, since the woman is an ardent feminist. The implication is that a male chauvinist, such as she firmly believes Washburn to be, would not get the answer.''

Rubin said, ''Good Lord, Tom, you've made sense. What next? Don't tell me you've worked out the answer, too.''

Trumbull shook his head. ''Not exactly, but I suggest we confine ourselves to women's names. A feminist would argue that many women have played important roles in history but that male chauvinism tends to blot them out. Therefore every schoolchild *should* know them, but doesn't.''

Halsted said, ''No, Tom. That's not the clue. It's not something every schoolchild *should* know but doesn't. It's something every schoolchild *knows* and doesn't. That's different.''

''Besides,'' said Rubin, ''even if we confine ourselves to women, we have no clear route to the answer. If we stick to historic feminists, for instance, we have Susan Brownell Anthony, Carrie Chapman Catt, Helen Gurley Brown, Gloria Steinem, Betty Friedan—who's got a one-syllable middle name?''

Drake said, ''It needn't be a feminist.'' His little eyes seemed to peer thoughtfully into the middle distance. ''It might just be a woman who contributed to history—like the one who wrote *Uncle Tom's Cabin* and helped cause the Civil War, as Lincoln said.''

''Harriet Beecher Stowe,'' said Rubin impatiently, ''and Beecher has two syllables.''

''Yes,'' said Drake, ''but I merely mentioned it as an example. What about the woman who wrote 'The Battle Hymn of the Republic,' Julia Ward Howe? How many syllables in Ward?''

Avalon said, ''How is that something every schoolchild knows and yet doesn't know?''

Drake said, ''Every schoolchild knows, 'Mine eyes have seen the glory of the coming of the Lord' and yet doesn't know the author, because she's a woman. At least that's what a feminist might claim.''

There was a confused outcry of objections, and Avalon's deep voice suddenly rose into an overtopping bellow, ''How about *Little Women*, which was written by Louisa May Alcott? Which would the answer be: Ward or May?''

Washburn suddenly cut in sharply, "Neither one."

Drake said, "Why not? How do you know?"

Washburn said, "Because she sent me what she said was the answer when she wrote to say she was married. And it isn't either Ward or May."

Rubin said indignantly, "You've withheld information, sir."

"No, I haven't," said Washburn. "I didn't have that information when I tried to get the answer, and now that I have it, I still don't see *why*. I think she just chose an answer at random as a continuing part of her intention of making me feel like an idiot.

"Nor will I give you the solution *now,* since you'll be able to dream up a reason once you have the name, and that's not good. The point is to be able to get a solution and reason it out without knowing the answer in advance—though she *did* hand me a feminine name. I'll give Mr. Trumbull that much."

Gonzalo said, "If we can reason out the name she gave and tell you what it is and why, will you feel better?"

Washburn said gloomily, "I think so. At least I might imagine it was a fair test and that I might have had her if I were brighter, and she wasn't just laughing at me. But can anyone tell me what the middle name is?"

He looked about the table and met six thoughtful stares.

Gonzalo said, "Do *you* have any ideas on the subject, Henry?"

The waiter, who was removing the brandy glasses, said, quietly, "Unless the middle name in question is Ann, Mr. Gonzalo, I'm afraid I am helpless."

Washburn let out an incoherent cry, pushed back his chair with a loud scraping noise, and jumped up.

"But it *is* Ann," he cried out. "How did you come to decide on that? Was it a guess or do you have a reason?"

He had reached out almost as though he were going to seize Henry by his shoulders and shake the answers out of him, but controlled himself with obvious difficulty.

Henry said, "The gentlemen of the Black Widowers supplied the pieces, sir. I needed only to put them together. Mr. Rubin said that a middle name might be hidden by a pseudonym, as in the case of Mark Twain. Mr. Trumbull pointed out that feminism was involved. It seemed to me quite possible that at times in history someone who was a woman might hide under a male pseudonym, and I pondered over whether there were such a case in connection with something every schoolchild would know.

"Surely, one book that schoolchildren have notoriously been required to read for decade after decade has been *Silas Marner*. Every schoolchild knows it, and the further fact that it was written by George Eliot. It seemed to me, though, that that was a pseudonym. I checked it in the encyclopedia on the reference shelf, while the discussion raged, and I found that Eliot's real name is Mary Ann Evans."

Washburn said, eyes big with wonder, "Then it *was* a fair question. I'm glad of *that*. But do you mean that the jerk she married figured it out?"

Henry said, "He may well have. I think it would be best for you, sir, to believe that he did."

12

Sixty Million Trillion Combinations

I love to feel ingenious. Suppose you have sixty million trillion possible combinations of letters and from that enormous number you have to choose exactly one. Can you do it?

Unfortunately, I don't remember any longer exactly how long it took me to think up the gimmick to this story, but I suspect that, like all such things, it came to me in a flash.

People ask me, "Where do you get your ideas?" A young man (an aspiring writer) called me from South Dakota last night, thinking that perhaps I had a magic formula I could give him. I said I didn't. I just thought and thought. The thing is that the thinking goes on unconsciously while I am doing other things and then, apparently out of nowhere, it comes up with something and surfaces

Then I feel ingenious and love the story.

Since it was Thomas Trumbull who was going to act as host for the Black Widowers that month, he did not, as was his wont, arrive at the last minute, gasping for his preprandial drink.

There he was, having arrived in early dignity, conferring

with Henry, that peerless waiter, on the details of the menu for the evening, and greeting each of the others as he arrived.

Mario Gonzalo, who arrived last, took off his light overcoat with care, shook it gently, as though to remove the dust of the taxicab, and hung it up in the cloakroom. He came back, rubbing his hands, and said, "There's an autumn chill in the air. I think summer's over."

"Good riddance," called out Emmanuel Rubin, from where he stood conversing with Geoffrey Avalon and James Drake.

"I'm not complaining," called back Gonzalo. Then, to Trumbull, "Hasn't your guest arrived yet?"

Trumbull said distinctly, as though tired of explaining, "I have not brought a guest."

"Oh?" said Gonzalo, blankly. There was nothing absolutely irregular about that. The rules of the Black Widowers did not require a guest, although not to have one was most unusual. "Well, I guess that's all right."

"It's more than all right," said Geoffrey Avalon, who had just drifted in their direction, gazing down from his straight-backed height of seventy-four inches. His thick graying eyebrows hunched over his eyes and he said, "At least that guarantees us one meeting in which we can talk aimlessly and relax."

Gonzalo said, "I don't know about that. I'm used to the problems that come up. I don't think any of us will feel comfortable without one. Besides, what about Henry?"

He looked at Henry as he spoke and Henry allowed a discreet smile to cross his unlined, sixtyish face. "Please don't be concerned, Mr. Gonzalo. It will be my pleasure to serve the meal and attend the conversation even if there is nothing of moment to puzzle us."

"Well," said Trumbull, scowling, his crisply waved hair startlingly white over his tanned face, "you won't have that pleasure, Henry. I'm the one with the problem and I hope someone can solve it: *you* at least, Henry."

Avalon's lips tightened, "Now by Beelzebub's brazen bottom, Tom, you might have given us *one* old-fashioned—"

Trumbull shrugged and turned away, and Roger Halsted said to Avalon in his soft voice, "What's that Beelzebub bit? Where'd you pick that up?"

Avalon looked pleased. "Oh, well, Manny is writing some

sort of adventure yarn set in Elizabeth's England—Elizabeth I of course—and it seems—''

Rubin, having heard the magic sound of his name, approached and said, "It's a sea story."

Halsted said, "Are you tired of mysteries?''

"It's a mystery also," said Rubin, his eyes flashing behind the thick lenses of his glasses. "What makes you think you can't have a mystery angle to *any* kind of story?"

"In any case," said Avalon, "Manny has one character forever swearing alliteratively and never the same twice and he needs a few more resounding oaths. Beelzebub's brazen bottom is good, I think."

"Or Mammon's munificent mammaries," said Halsted.

Trumbull said, violently, "There you are! If I don't come up with some problem that will occupy us in worthwhile fashion and engage our Henry's superlative mind, the whole evening would degenerate into stupid triplets—by Tutankhamen's tin trumpet."

"It gets you after a while," grinned Rubin, unabashed.

"Well, get off it," said Trumbull. "Is dinner ready, Henry?"

"Yes it is, Mr. Trumbull."

"All right, then. If you idiots keep this alliteration up for more than two minutes, I'm walking out, host or no host."

The table seemed empty with only six about it, and conversation seemed a bit subdued with no guest to sparkle before.

Gonzalo, who sat next to Trumbull, said, "I ought to draw a cartoon of you for our collection since you're your own guest, so to speak." He looked up complacently at the long list of guest-caricatures that lined the wall in rank and file. "We're going to run out of space in a couple of years."

"Then don't bother with me," said Trumbull, sourly, "and we can always make space by burning those foolish scrawls."

"Scrawls!" Gonzalo seemed to debate within himself briefly concerning the possibility of taking offense. Then he compromised by saying, "You seem to be in a foul mood, Tom."

"I seem so because I am. I'm in the situation of the Chaldean wise men facing Nebuchadnezzar."

Avalon leaned over from across the table. "Are you talking about the Book of Daniel, Tom?"

"That's where it is, isn't it?"

Gonzalo said, "Pardon me, but I didn't have my Bible lesson yesterday. What are these wise men?"

"Tell him, Jeff," said Trumbull. "Pontificating is your job."

Avalon said, "It's not pontificating to tell a simple tale. If you would rather—"

Gonzalo said, "I'd rather you did, Jeff. You do it much more authoritatively."

"Well," said Avalon, "it's Rubin, not I, who was once a boy preacher, but I'll do my poor best.—The second chapter of the Book of Daniel tells that Nebuchadnezzar was once troubled by a bad dream and he sent for his Chaldean wise men for an interpretation. The wise men offered to do so at once as soon as they heard the dream but Nebuchadnezzar couldn't remember the dream, only that he had been disturbed by it. He reasoned, however, that if wise men could interpret a dream, they could work out the dream, too, so he ordered them to tell him both the dream *and* the interpretation. When they couldn't do this, he very reasonably—by the standards of Oriental potentates—ordered them all killed. Fortunately for them Daniel, a captive Jew in Babylon, could do the job."

Gonzalo said, "And that's your situation, too, Tom?"

"In a way. I have a problem that involves a cryptogram—but I don't have the cryptogram. I have to work out the cryptogram."

"Or you'll be killed?" asked Rubin.

"No. If I fail, I won't be killed, but it won't do me any good, either."

Gonzalo said, "No wonder you didn't feel it necessary to bring a guest. Tell us all about it."

"Before the brandy?" said Avalon, scandalized.

"Tom's host," said Gonzalo, defensively. "If he wants to tell us now—"

"I don't," said Trumbull. "We'll wait for the brandy as we always do, and I'll be my own griller, if you don't mind."

When Henry was pouring the brandy, Trumbull rang his spoon against his water glass and said, "Gentlemen, I will dispense with the opening question by admitting openly that I cannot justify my existence. Without pretending to go on by question-and-answer, I will simply state the problem. You are free to ask questions, but for God's sake, don't get me off on any wild-goose chases. This is serious."

Avalon said, "Go ahead, Tom. We will do our best to listen."

Trumbull said, with a certain weariness, "It involves a fellow named Pochik. I've got to tell you a little about him in order to let you understand the problem but, as is usual in these cases, I hope you don't mind if I tell you nothing that isn't relevant.

"In the first place he's from Eastern Europe, from someplace in Slovenia, I think, and he came here at about fourteen. He taught himself English, went to night school and to University Extension, working every step of the way. He worked as a waiter for ten years, while he was taking his various courses, and you know what that means.—Sorry, Henry."

Henry said, tranquilly, "It is not necessarily a pleasant occupation. Not everyone waits on the Black Widowers, Mr. Trumbull."

"Thank you, Henry. That's very diplomatic of you. —However, he wouldn't have made it, if it weren't plain from the start that he was a mathematical wizard. He was the kind of young man that no mathematics professor in his right mind wouldn't have moved heaven and earth to keep in school. He was their claim to a mark in the history books—that they had taught Pochik. Do you understand?"

Avalon said, "We understand, Tom."

Trumbull said, "At least, that's what they tell me. He's working for the government now, which is where I come in. They tell me he's something else. They tell me he's in a class by himself. They tell me he can do things no one else can. They tell me they've got to have him. I don't even know what he's working on, but they've got to have him."

Rubin said, "Well, they've got him, haven't they? He hasn't been kidnapped and hijacked back across the Iron Curtain, has he?"

"No, no," said Trumbull, "nothing like that. It's a lot

more irritating. Look, apparently a great mathematician can be an idiot in every other respect.''

''Literally an idiot?'' asked Avalon. ''Usually idiots savants have remarkable memories and can play remarkable tricks in computation, but that is far from being any kind of mathematician, let alone a great one.''

''No, nothing like that, either.'' Trumbull was perspiring and paused to mop at his forehead. ''I mean he's childish. He's not really learned in anything but mathematics and that's all right. Mathematics is what we want out of him. The trouble is that he feels backward; he feels stupid. Damn it, he feels inferior, and when he feels *too* inferior, he stops working and hides in his room.''

Gonzalo said, ''So what's the problem? Everyone just has to keep telling him how great he is all the time.''

''He's dealing with other mathematicians and they're almost as crazy as he is. One of them, Sandino, hates being second best and every once in a while he gets Pochik into a screaming fit. He's got a sense of humor, this Sandino, and he likes to call out to Pochik, 'Hey, waiter, bring the check.' Pochik can't ever learn to take it.''

Drake said, ''Read this Sandino the riot act. Tell him you'll dismember him if he tries anything like that again.''

''They did,'' said Trumbull, ''or at least as far as they quite dared to. They don't want to lose Sandino either. In any case, the horseplay stopped but something much worse happened.—You see there's something called, if I've got it right, 'Goldbach's conjecture.' ''

Roger Halsted galvanized into a position of sharp interest at once. ''Sure,'' he said. ''Very famous.''

''You know about it?'' said Trumbull.

Halsted stiffened. ''I may just teach algebra to junior high school students, but yes, I know about Goldbach's conjecture. Teaching a junior high school student doesn't *make* me a junior—''

''All right. I apologize. It was stupid of me,'' said Trumbull. ''And since you're a mathematician, you can be temperamental too. Anyway, can you explain Goldbach's conjecture? —Because I'm not sure I can.''

''Actually,'' said Halsted, ''it's very simple. Back in 1742,

I think, a Russian mathematician, Christian Goldbach, stated that he believed every even number greater than 2 could be written as the sum of two primes, where a prime is any number that can't be divided evenly by any other number but itself and 1. For instance, $4 = 2 + 2$; $6 = 3 + 3$; $8 = 3 + 5$; $10 = 3 + 7$; $12 = 5 + 7$; and so on, as far as you want to go."

Gonzalo said, "So what's the big deal?"

"Goldbach wasn't able to prove it. And in the two hundred and something years since his time, neither has anyone else. The greatest mathematicians haven't been able to show that it's true."

Gonzalo said, "So?"

Halsted said patiently, "Every even number that has ever been checked always works out to be the sum of two primes. They've gone awfully high and mathematicians are convinced the conjecture is true—but no one can *prove* it."

Gonzalo said, "If they can't find any exceptions, doesn't *that* prove it?"

"No, because there are always numbers higher than the highest we've checked, and besides we don't know all the prime numbers and can't, and the higher we go, then the harder it is to tell whether a particular number is prime or not. What is needed is a *general* proof that tells us we don't have to look for exceptions because there just aren't any. It bothers mathematicians that a problem can be stated so simply and seems to work out, too, and yet that it can't be proved."

Trumbull had been nodding his head. "All right, Roger, all right. We get it. But tell me, does it *matter?* Does it really matter to anyone who isn't a mathematician whether Goldbach's conjecture is true or not; whether there are any exceptions or not?"

"No," said Halsted. "Not to anyone who isn't a mathematician; but to anyone who is and who manages either to prove or disprove Goldbach's conjecture, there is an immediate and permanent niche in the mathematical hall of fame."

Trumbull shrugged. "There you are. What Pochik's really doing is of great importance. I'm not sure whether it's for the Department of Defense, the Department of Energy, NASA, or what, but it's vital. What *he's* interested in, however, is

Goldbach's conjecture, and for that he's been using a computer."

"To try higher numbers?" asked Gonzalo.

Halsted said promptly, "No, that would do no good. These days, though, you can use computers on some pretty recalcitrant problems. It doesn't yield an elegant solution, but it is a solution. If you can reduce a problem to a finite number of possible situations—say, a million—you can program a computer to try every one of them. If every one of them checks out as it's supposed to, then you have your proof. They recently solved the four-color mapping problem that way; a problem as well known and as recalcitrant as Goldbach's conjecture."

"Good," said Trumbull, "then that's what Pochik's been doing. Apparently, he had worked out the solution to a particular lemma. Now what's a lemma?"

Halsted said, "It's a partway solution. If you're climbing a mountain peak and you set up stations at various levels, the lemmas are analogous to those stations and the solution to the mountain peak."

"If he solves the lemma, will he solve the conjecture?"

"Not necessarily," said Halsted, "any more than you'll climb the mountain if you reach a particular station on the slopes. But if you *don't* solve the lemma, you're not likely to solve the problem, at least not from that direction."

"All right, then," said Trumbull, sitting back. "Well, Sandino came up with the lemma first and sent it in for publication."

Drake was bent over the table, listening closely. He said, "Tough luck for Pochik."

Trumbull said, "Except that Pochik says it wasn't luck. He claims Sandino doesn't have the brains for it and couldn't have taken the steps he did independently; that it is asking too much of coincidence."

Drake said, "That's a serious charge. Has Pochik got any evidence?"

"No, of course not. The only way that Sandino could have stolen it from Pochik would have been to tap the computer for Pochik's data and Pochik himself says Sandino couldn't have done that."

"Why not?" said Avalon.

"Because," said Trumbull, "Pochik used a code word. The code word has to be used to alert the computer to a particular person's questioning. Without that code word, everything that went in *with* the code word is safely locked away."

Avalon said, "It could be that Sandino learned the code word."

"Pochik says that is impossible," said Trumbull. "He was afraid of theft, particularly with respect to Sandino, and he never wrote down the code word, never used it except when he was alone in the room. What's more, he used one that was fourteen letters long, he says. Millions of trillions of possibilities, he says. No one could have guessed it, he says."

Rubin said, "What does Sandino say?"

"He says he worked it out himself. He rejects the claim of theft as the ravings of a madman. Frankly, one could argue that he's right."

Drake said, "Well, let's consider. Sandino is a good mathematician and he's innocent till proven guilty. Pochik has nothing to support his claim and Pochik actually denies that Sandino could possibly have gotten the code word, which is the only way the theft could possibly have taken place. I think Pochik has to be wrong and Sandino right."

Trumbull said, "I *said* one could argue that Sandino's right, but the point is that Pochik won't work. He's sulking in his room and reading poetry and he says he will never work again. He says Sandino has robbed him of his immortality and life means nothing to him without it."

Gonzalo said, "If you need this guy so badly can you talk Sandino into letting him have his lemma?"

"Sandino won't make the sacrifice and we can't make him unless we have reason to think that fraud was involved. If we get any evidence to that effect we can lean on him hard enough to squash him flat.—But now listen, I think it's possible Sandino *did* steal it."

Avalon said, "How?"

"By getting the code word. If I knew what the code word was, I'm sure I could figure out a logical way in which Sandino could have found it out or guessed it. Pochik, however, simply won't let me have the code word. He shrieked at me when I asked. I explained why, but he said it was impossible. He said Sandino did it some other way—but there is no other way."

Avalon said, "Pochik wants an interpretation but he won't tell you the dream, and you have to figure out the dream first and then get the interpretation."

"Exactly! Like the Chaldean wise men."

"What are you going to do?"

"I'm going to try to do what Sandino must have done. I'm going to try to figure out what the fourteen-letter code word was and present it to Pochik. If I'm right, then it will be clear that what I could do, Sandino could do, and that the lemma was very likely stolen."

There was a silence around the table and then Gonzalo said, "Do you think you can do it, Tom?"

"I don't think so. That's why I've brought the problem here. I want us all to try. I told Pochik I would call him before 10:30 P.M. tonight"—Trumbull looked at his watch—"with the code word just to show him it *could* be broken. I presume he's waiting at the phone."

Avalon said, "And if we don't get it?"

"Then we have no reasonable way of supposing the lemma was stolen and no really ethical way of trying to force it away from Sandino. But at least we'll be no worse off."

Avalon said, "Then you go first. You've clearly been thinking about it longer than we have, and it's your line of work."

Trumbull cleared his throat. "All right. My reasoning is that if Pochik doesn't write the thing down, then he's got to remember it. There are some people with trick memories and such a talent is fairly common among mathematicians. However, even great mathematicians don't always have the ability to remember long strings of disjointed symbols and, upon questioning of his coworkers, it would seem quite certain that Pochik's memory is an ordinary one. He can't rely on being able to remember the code unless it's easy to remember.

"That would limit it to some common phrase or some regular progression that you couldn't possibly forget. Suppose it were ALBERT EINSTEIN, for instance. That's fourteen letters and there would be no fear of forgetting it. Or SIR ISAAC NEWTON, or ABCDEFGHIJKLMN, or, for that matter, NMLKJIHGFEDCBA. If Pochik tried something like this, it could be that Sandino tried various obvious combinations and one of them worked.''

Drake said, ''If that's true, then we haven't a prayer of solving the problem. Sandino might have tried any number of different possibilities over a period of months. One of them finally worked. If he got it by hit-and-miss over a long time, we have no chance in getting the right one in an hour and a half, without even trying any of them on the computer.''

''There's that, of course,'' said Trumbull, ''and it may well be that Sandino had been working on the problem for months. Sandino pulled the waiter routine on Pochik last June, and Pochik, out of his mind, screamed at him that he would show him when his proof was ready. Sandino may have put this together with Pochik's frequent use of the computer and gotten to work. He may have had months, at that.''

''Did Pochik say something on that occasion that gave the code word away?'' asked Avalon.

''Pochik swears all he said was 'I'll show you when the proof is ready,' but who knows? Would Pochik remember his own exact words when he was beside himself?''

Halsted said, ''I'm surprised that Pochik didn't try to beat up this Sandino.''

Trumbull said, ''You wouldn't be surprised if you knew them. Sandino is built like a football player and Pochik weighs 110 pounds with his clothes on.''

Gonzalo said, suddenly, ''What's this guy's first name?''

Trumbull said, ''Vladimir.''

Gonzalo paused a while, with all eyes upon him, and then he said, ''I knew it. VLADIMIR POCHIK has fourteen letters. He used his own name.''

Rubin said, ''Ridiculous. It would be the first combination anyone would try.''

''Sure, the purloined letter bit. It would be so obvious that no one would think to use it. Ask him.''

Trumbull shook his head. ''No. I can't believe he'd use that.''

Rubin said, thoughtfully, "Did you say he was sitting in his room reading poetry?"

"Yes."

"Is that a passion of his? Poetry? I thought you said that outside mathematics he was not particularly educated."

Trumbull said, sarcastically, "You don't have to be a Ph.D. to read poetry."

Avalon said, mournfully, "You would have to be an idiot to read modern poetry."

"That's a point," said Rubin. "Does Pochik read contemporary poetry?"

Trumbull said, "It never occurred to me to ask. When I visited him, he was reading from a book of Wordsworth's poetry, but that's all I can say."

"That's enough," said Rubin. "If he likes Wordsworth then he doesn't like contemporary poetry. No one can read that fuddy-duddy for fun and like the stuff they turn out these days."

"So? What difference does it make?" asked Trumbull.

"The older poetry with its rhyme and rhythm is easy to remember and it could make for code words. The code word could be a fourteen-letter passage from one of Wordsworth's poems, possibly a common one: LONELY AS A CLOUD has fourteen letters. Or any fourteen-letter combinations from such lines as 'The child is father of the man' or 'trailing clouds of glory' or 'Milton! thou shouldst be living at this hour.'—Or maybe from some other poet of the type."

Avalon said, "Even if we restrict ourselves to passages from the classic and romantic poets, that's a huge field to guess from."

Drake said, "I repeat. It's an impossible task. We don't have the time to try them all. And we can't tell one from another without trying."

Halsted said, "It's even more impossible than you think, Jim. I don't think the code word was in English words."

Trumbull said, frowning, "You mean he used his native language?"

"No, I mean he used a random collection of letters. You say that Pochik said the code word was unbreakable because there were millions of trillions of possibilities in a fourteen-letter combination. Well, suppose that the first letter could be any of the twenty-six, and the second letter could be any of the twenty-six, and the third letter, and so on. In that case the total number of combinations would be 26 × 26 × 26, and so on. You would have to get the product of fourteen 26's multiplied together and the result would be''—he took out his pocket calculator and manipulated it for a while—"about 64 million trillion different possibilities.

"Now, if you used an English phrase or a phrase in any reasonable European language, most of the letter combinations simply don't occur. You're not going to have an HGF or a QXZ or an LLLLC. If we include only *possible* letter combinations in words then we might have trillions of possibilities, probably less, but certainly not millions of trillions. Pochik, being a mathematician, wouldn't say millions of trillions unless he meant exactly that, so I expect the code word is a random set of letters.''

Trumbull said, "He doesn't have the kind of memory—"

Halsted said, "Even a normal memory will handle fourteen random letters if you stick to it long enough."

Gonzalo said, "Wait awhile. If there are only so many combinations, you could use a computer. The computer could try every possible combination and stop at the one that unlocks it.''

Halsted said, "You don't realize how big a number like 64 million trillion really is, Mario. Suppose you arranged to have the computer test a billion different combinations every second. It would take two thousand solid years of work, day and night, to test all the possible combinations."

Gonzalo said, "But you wouldn't have to test them all. The right one might come up in the first two hours. Maybe the code was AAAAAAAAAAAAAA and it happened to be the first one the computer tried."

"Very unlikely," said Halsted. "He wouldn't use a solid-A code anymore than he would use his own name. Besides Sandino is enough of a mathematician not to start a computer attempt he would know could take a hundred lifetimes.''

Rubin said, thoughtfully, "If he did use a random code I bet it wasn't truly random."

Avalon said, "How do you mean, Manny?"

"I mean if he doesn't have a superlative memory and he didn't write it down, how could he go over and over it in his mind in order to memorize it? Just repeat fourteen random letters to yourself and see if you can be confident of repeating them again in the exact order immediately afterward. And even if he *had* worked out a random collection of letters and managed to memorize it, it's clear he had very little self-confidence in anything except mathematical reasoning. Could he face the possibility of not being able to retrieve his own information because he had forgotten the code?"

"He could start all over," said Trumbull.

"With a new random code? And forget that, too?" said Rubin. "No. Even if the code word seems random, I'll bet Pochik has some foolproof way of remembering it, and if we can figure out the foolproof way, we'd have the answer. In fact, if Pochik would give us the code word, we'd see how he memorized it and then see how Sandino broke the code."

Trumbull said, "And if Nebuchadnezzar would only have remembered the dream, the wise men could have interpreted it. Pochik won't give us the code word, and if we work it with hindsight, we'll never be sufficiently sure Sandino cracked it without hindsight.—All right, we'll have to give it up."

"It may not be necessary to give it up," said Henry, suddenly. "I think—"

All turned to Henry, expectantly. "Yes, Henry," said Avalon.

"I have a wild guess. It may be all wrong. Perhaps it might be possible to call up Mr. Pochik, Mr. Trumbull, and ask him if the code word is WEALTMDITEBIAT," said Henry.

Trumbull said, *"What?"*

Halsted said, his eyebrows high, "That's some wild guess, all right. Why that?"

Gonzalo said, "It makes no sense."

No one could recall ever having seen Henry blush, but he was distinctly red now. He said, "If I may be excused. I don't wish to explain my reasoning until the combination is tried. If I am wrong, I would appear too foolish.—And, on second thought, I don't urge it be tried."

Trumbull said, "No, we have nothing to lose. Could you write down that letter combination, Henry?"

"I have already done so, sir."

Trumbull looked at it, walked over to the phone in the corner of the room, and dialled. He waited for four rings, which could be clearly heard in the breath-holding silence of the room. There was then a click, and a sharp, high-pitched "Hello?"

Trumbull said, "Dr. Pochik? Listen. I'm going to read some letters to you—No, Dr. Pochik, I'm not saying I've worked out the code. This is an exper— It's an experiment sir. We may be wrong—No, I can't say how—Listen, W, E, A, L—Oh, good God." He placed his hand over the mouthpiece. "The man is having a fit."

"Because it's right or because it's wrong?" asked Rubin.

"I don't know." Trumbull put the phone back to his ear. "Dr. Pochik, are you there?—Dr. Pochik?—The rest is"—he consulted the paper—"T, M, D, I, T, E, B, I, A, T." He listened. "Yes, sir, I think Sandino cracked it, too, the same way we did. We'll have a meeting with you and Dr. Sandino, and we'll settle everything. Yes—please, Dr. Pochik, we will do our best."

Trumbull hung up, heaved an enormous sigh, then said, "Sandino is going to think Jupiter fell on him.—All right, Henry, but if you don't tell us how you got that, you won't have to wait for Jupiter. I will kill you personally."

"No need, Mr. Trumbull," said Henry. "I will tell you at once. I merely listened to all of you. Mr. Halsted pointed out it would have to be some random collection of letters. Mr. Rubin said, backing my own feeling in the matter, that there had to be some system of remembering in that case. Mr. Avalon, early in the evening was playing the game of alliterative oaths, which pointed up the importance of initial letters. You yourself mentioned Mr. Pochik's liking for old-fashioned poetry like that of Wordsworth.

"It occurred to me then that fourteen was the number of lines in a sonnet, and if we took the initial letters of each line of some sonnet we would have an apparently random collection of fourteen letters that could not be forgotten as long as the sonnet was memorized or could, at worst, be looked up.

"The question was: which sonnet? It was very likely to be a well-known one, and Wordsworth had written some that

were. In fact, Mr. Rubin mentioned the first line of one of
them: 'Milton! thou shouldst be living at this hour.' That
made me think of Milton, and it came to me that it *had* to be
his sonnet 'On His Blindness' which as it happens, *I* know by
heart. Please note the first letters of the successive lines. It
goes:

> "When I consider how my light is spent
> Ere half my days, in this dark world and wide,
> And that one talent which is death to hide,
> Lodged with me useless, though my soul more bent
> To serve therewith my Maker, and present
> My true account, lest he returning chide;
> 'Doth God exact day-labor, light denied?'
> I fondly ask; But Patience, to prevent
> That murmur, soon replies, 'God doth not need
> Either man's work or his own gifts; who best
> Bear his mild yoke, they serve him best. His state
> Is kingly. Thousands at his bidding speed
> And post o'er land and ocean without rest: . . .' "

Henry paused and said softly, "I think it is the most
beautiful sonnet in the language, Shakespeare's not excepted,
but that was not the reason I felt it must hold the answer. It
was that Dr. Pochik had been a waiter and was conscious of
it, and I am one, which is why I have memorized the sonnet.
A foolish fancy, no doubt but the last line, which I have not
quoted, and which is perhaps among the most famous lines
Milton ever constructed—"

"Go ahead, Henry," said Rubin. "Say it!"

"Thank you, sir," said Henry, and then he said, solemnly,

" 'They also serve who only stand and wait.' "

13

The Good Samaritan

Two stories ago, I mentioned the matter of the stag nature of the Black Widowers (I might mention also that I routinely suggest the entrance of women into membership at occasional meetings of the real club and I am promptly wiped out—but lest I sound as though I'm trying to get credit for virtue, I will admit that I never resign my membership in anger at being rebuffed.)

Nevertheless, I felt that on one occasion, at least, there ought to be a real fight over the matter in my fictional club, even if I never have the guts to reduce it to that in my real-life club. So I wrote "The Good Samaritan" and had a great deal of pleasure in watching Manny Rubin's reaction to the whole thing.

The Black Widowers had learned by hard experience that when Mario Gonzalo took his turn as host of the monthly banquet, they had to expect the unusual. They had reached the point where they steeled themselves, quite automatically, for disaster. When his guest arrived there was a lightening of spirit if it turned out he had the usual quota of heads and could speak at least broken English.

When the last of the Black Widowers arrived, therefore, and when Henry's efficient setting of the table was nearly complete, Geoffrey Avalon, standing, as always, straight and tall, sounded almost lighthearted as he said, "I see that your guest has not arrived yet, Mario."

Gonzalo, whose crimson velvet jacket and lightly striped blue pants reduced everything else in the room to monochrome said, "Well—"

Avalon said, "What's more, a quick count of the settings placed at the table by our inestimable Henry shows that six people and no more are to be seated. And since all six of us are here, I can only conclude that you have not brought a guest."

"Thank Anacreon," said Emmanuel Rubin, raising his drink, "or whatever spirit it is that presides over convivial banquets of kindred souls."

Thomas Trumbull scowled and brushed back his crisply waved white hair with one hand. "What are you doing, Mario? Saving money?"

"Well—" said Gonzalo again, staring at his own drink with a totally spurious concentration.

Roger Halsted said, "I don't know that this is so good. I like the grilling sessions."

"It won't hurt us," said Avalon, in his deepest voice, "to have a quiet conversation once in a while. If we can't amuse each other without a guest, then the Black Widowers are not what once they were and we should prepare, sorrowing, for oblivion. Shall we offer Mario a vote of thanks for his unwonted discretion?"

"Well—" said Gonzalo a third time.

James Drake interposed, stubbing out a cigarette and clearing his throat. "It seems to me, gentlemen, that Mario is trying to say something and is amazingly bashful about it. If he has something he hesitates to say, I fear we are not going to like it. May I suggest we all keep quiet and let him talk."

"Well—" said Gonzalo, and stopped. This time, though, there was a prolonged and anxious silence.

"Well—" said Gonzalo again, "I *do* have a guest," and once more he stopped.

Rubin said, "Then where the hell is he?"

"Downstairs in the main dining room—ordering dinner—at my expense, of course."

Gonzalo received five blank stares. Then Trumbull said, "May I ask what dunderheaded reason you can possibly advance for that?"

"Aside," said Rubin, "from being a congenital dunderhead?"

Gonzalo put his drink down, took a deep breath, and said, firmly, "Because I thought she would be more comfortable down there."

Rubin managed to get out an "And why—" before the significance of the pronoun became plain. He seized the lapels of Gonzalo's jacket, "Did you say *'she'*?"

Gonzalo caught at the other's wrists. "Hands off, Manny. If you want to talk, use your lips not your hands. Yes, I said 'she.' "

Henry, his sixtyish, unlined face showing a little concern, raised his voice a diplomatic notch and said, "Gentlemen! Dinner is served!"

Rubin, having released Gonzalo, waved imperiously at Henry and said, "Sorry, Henry, there may be no banquet. —Mario, you damned jackass, *no woman can attend these meetings"*

There was, in fact, a general uproar. While no one quite achieved the anger and decibels of Rubin, Gonzalo found himself at bay with the five others around him in a semicircle. Their individual comments were lost in the general explosion of anger.

Gonzalo, waving his arms madly, leaped onto a chair and shouted, "Let me speak!" over and over until out of exhaustion, it seemed, the opposition died off into a low growl.

Gonzalo said, "She is not our guest at the banquet. She's just a woman with a problem, an old woman, and it won't do us any harm if we see her *after* dinner."

There was no immediate response and Gonzalo said, "She needn't sit at the table. She can sit in the doorway."

Rubin said, "Mario, if she comes in here, I go, and if I go, damn it, I may not come back ever."

Gonzalo said, "Are you saying you'll break up the Black Widowers rather than listen to an old woman in trouble?"

Rubin said, "I'm saying rules are *rules!*"

Halsted, looking deeply troubled, said, "Listen, Manny, maybe we ought to do this. The rules weren't delivered to us from Mount Siani."

"You, too?" said Rubin, savagely. "Look, it doesn't matter what any of you say. In a matter as fundamental as this, one blackball is enough, and I cast it. Either she goes or I go and, by God, you'll never see me again. In view of that, is there anyone who wants to waste his breath?"

Henry, who still stood at the head of the table, waiting with markedly less than his usual imperturbability for the company to seat itself, said, "May I have a word, Mr. Rubin?"

Rubin said, "Sorry, Henry, no one sits down till this is settled."

Gonzalo said, "Stay out, Henry. I'll fight my own battles."

It was at this point that Henry departed from his role as the epitome of all Olympian waiters and advanced on the group. His voice was firm as he said, "Mr. Rubin, I wish to take responsibility for this. Several days ago, Mr. Gonzalo phoned me to ask if I would be so kind as to listen to a woman he knew who had the kind of problem he thought I might be helpful with. I asked him if it was something close to his heart. He said that the woman was a relative of someone who was very likely to give him a commission for an important piece of work—"

"Money!" sneered Rubin.

"Professional opportunity," snapped Gonzalo. "If you can understand that. And sympathy for a fellow human being, if you can understand *that*."

Henry held up his hand. *"Please,* gentlemen! I told Mr. Gonzalo I could not help him but urged him, if he had not already arranged a guest, to bring the woman. I suggested that there might be no objection if she did not actually attend the banquet itself."

Rubin said, "And why couldn't you help her otherwise?"

Henry said, "Gentlemen, I lay no claims to superior insight. I do not compare myself, as Mr. Gonzalo occasionally does on my behalf, to Sherlock Holmes. It is only after you gentlemen have discussed a problem and eliminated what is extraneous that I seem to see what remains. Therefore—''

Drake said, ''Well, look, Manny, I'm the oldest member here, and the original reason for the prohibition. We might partially waive it just this once.''

''No,'' said Rubin, flatly.

Henry said, ''Mr. Rubin, it is often stated at these banquets that I am a member of the Black Widowers. If so, I wish to take the responsibility. I urged Mr. Gonzalo to do this and I spoke to the woman concerned and assured her that she would be welcomed to our deliberations after dinner. It was an impulsive act based on my estimate of the characters of the gentlemen of the club.

''If the woman is now sent away, Mr. Rubin, you understand that my position here will be an impossible one and I will be forced to resign my position as waiter at these banquets. I would have no choice.''

Almost imperceptibly the atmosphere had changed while Henry spoke and now it was Rubin who was standing at bay. He stared at the semicircle that now surrounded him and said, rather gratingly, ''I appreciate your services to the club, Henry, and I do not wish to place you in a dishonorable position. Therefore, on the stipulation that this is not to set a precedent and reminding you that you must not do this again, I will withdraw my blackball.''

The banquet was the least comfortable in the history of the Black Widowers. Conversation was desultory and dull and Rubin maintained a stony silence throughout.

There was no need to clatter the water glass during the serving of the coffee, since there was no babble of conversation to override. Gonzalo simply said, ''I'll go down and see if she's ready. Her name, by the way, is Mrs. Barbara Lindemann.''

Rubin looked up and said, ''Make sure she's had her coffee, or tea, or whatever, downstairs. She can't have anything up here.''

Avalon looked disapproving, "The dictates of courtesy, my dear Manny—"

"She'll have all she wants downstairs at Mario's expense. Up here, we'll listen to her. What more can she want?"

Gonzalo brought her up and led her to an armchair that Henry had obtained from the restaurant office and that he had placed well away from the table.

She was a rather thin woman, with blunt good-natured features, well-dressed and with her white hair carefully set. She carried a black purse that looked new and she clutched it tightly. She glanced timidly at the faces of the Black Widowers and said, "Good evening."

There was a low chorused rumble in return and she said, "I apologize for coming here with my ridiculous story. Mr. Gonzalo explained that my appearance here is out of the ordinary and I have thought over my dinner that I should not disturb you. I will go if you like, and thank you for the dinner and for letting me come up here."

She made as though to rise and Avalon, looking remarkably shamefaced, said, "Madame, you are entirely welcome here and we would like very much to hear what you have to say. We cannot promise that we will be able to help you, but we can try. I'm sure that we all feel the same way about this. Don't you agree, Manny?"

Rubin shot a dark look at Avalon through his thick-lensed glasses. His sparse beard bristled and his chin lifted but he said in a remarkably mild tone, "Entirely, ma'am."

There was a short pause, and then Gonzalo said, "It's our custom, Mrs. Lindemann, to question our guests and under the circumstances, I wonder if you would mind having Henry handle that. He is our waiter, but he is a member of our group."

Henry stood motionless for a moment, then said, "I fear, Mr. Gonzalo, that—"

Gonzalo said, "You have yourself claimed the privilege of membership earlier this evening, Henry. Privilege carries with it responsibility. Put down the brandy bottle, Henry, and sit down. Anyone who wants brandy can take his own. Here, Henry, take my seat." Gonzalo rose resolutely and walked to the sideboard.

Henry sat down.

Henry said mildly to Mrs. Lindemann, "Madame, would you be willing to pretend you are on the witness stand?"

The woman looked about and her look of uneasiness dissolved into a little laugh. "I never have been and I'm not sure I know how to behave on one. I hope you won't mind if I'm nervous."

"We won't, but you needn't be. This will be very informal and we are anxious only to help you. The members of the club have a tendency to speak loudly and excitably at times, but if they do, that is merely their way and means nothing. —First, please tell us your name."

She said, with an anxious formality, "My name is Barbara Lindemann. Mrs. Barbara Lindemann."

"And do you have any particular line of work?"

"No, sir, I am retired. I am sixty-seven years old as you can probably tell by looking at me.—and a widow. I was once a schoolteacher at a junior high school."

Halsted stirred and said, "That's my profession, Mrs. Lindemann. What subject did you teach?"

"Mostly I taught American history."

Henry said, "Now from what Mr. Gonzalo has told me you suffered an unpleasant experience here in New York and—"

"No, pardon me," interposed Mrs. Lindemann, "it was, on the whole, a very pleasant experience. If that weren't so, I would be only too glad to forget all about it."

"Yes, of course," said Henry, "but I am under the impression that you *have* forgotten some key points and would like to remember them."

"Yes," she said, earnestly. "I am so ashamed at not remembering. It must make me appear senile, but it was a very *unusual* and *frightening* thing in a way—at least parts of it were—and I suppose that's my excuse."

Henry said, "I think it would be best, then, if you tell us what happened to you in as much detail as you can and, if it will not bother you, some of us may ask questions as you go along."

"It won't bother me, I assure you," said Mrs. Lindemann. "I'll welcome it as a sign of interest."

She said, "I arrived in New York City nine days ago. I was going to visit my niece, among other things, but I didn't want to stay with her. That would have been uncomfortable for her and confining for me, so I took a hotel room.

"I got to the hotel at about 6 P.M. on Wednesday and after a small dinner, which was very pleasant, although the prices were simply awful, I phoned my niece and arranged to see her the next day when her husband would be at work and the children at school. That would give us some time to ourselves and then in the evening we could have a family outing.

"Of course, I didn't intend to hang about their necks the entire two weeks I was to be in New York. I fully intended to do things on my own. In fact, that first evening after dinner, I had nothing particular to do and I certainly didn't want to sit in my room and watch television. So I thought—well, all of Manhattan is just outside, Barbara, and you've read about it all your life and seen it in the movies and now's your chance to see it in real life.

"I thought I'd just step out and wander about on my own and look at the elaborate buildings and the bright lights and the people hurrying past. I just wanted to get a *feel* of the city, before I started taking organized tours. I've done that in other cities in these recent years when I've been travelling and I've always so enjoyed it."

Trumbull said, "You weren't afraid of getting lost, I suppose."

"Oh, *no*," said Mrs. Lindemann, earnestly. "I have an excellent sense of direction and even if I were caught up in my sight-seeing and didn't notice where I had gone, I had a map of Manhattan and the streets are all in a rectangular grid and numbered—not like Boston, London, or Paris, and I was never lost in those cities. Besides, I could always get in a taxi and give the driver the name of my hotel. In fact, I am sure anyone would give me directions if I asked."

Rubin emerged from his slough of despond to deliver himself of a ringing, "In Manhattan? Hah!"

"Why, certainly," said Mrs. Lindemann, with mild reproof. "I've always heard that Manhattanites are unfriendly, but I have not found it so. I have been the recipient of many kindnesses—not the least of which is the manner in which you gentlemen have welcomed me even though I am quite a stranger to you."

Rubin found it necessary to stare intently at his fingernails.

Mrs. Lindemann said, "In any case, I did go off on my little excursion and stayed out much longer than I had planned. Everything was so colorful and busy and the weather was so mild and pleasant. Eventually, I realized I was terribly tired and I had reached a rather quiet street and was ready to go back. I reached in one of the outer pockets of my purse for my map—"

Halsted interrupted. "I take it, Mrs. Lindemann, you were alone on this excursion."

"Oh, yes," said Mrs. Lindemann, "I always travel alone since my husband died. To have a companion mems a perpetual state of compromise as to when to arise, what to eat, where to go. No, no, I want to be my own woman."

"I didn't quite mean that, Mrs. Lindemann," said Halsted. "I mean to ask whether you were alone on this particular outing in a strange city—at night—with a purse."

"Yes, sir. I'm afraid so."

Halsted said, "Had no one told you that the streets of New York aren't always safe at night—particularly, excuse me, for older women with purses who look, as you do, gentle and harmless?"

"Oh, dear, of *course* I've been told that. I've been told that of every city I've visited. My own town has districts that aren't safe. I've always felt, though, that all life is a gamble, that a no-risk situation is an impossible dream, and I wasn't going to deprive myself of pleasant experiences because of fear. And I've gone about in all sorts of places without harm."

Trumbull said, "Until that first evening in Manhattan, I take it."

Mrs. Lindemann's lips tightened and she said, "Until then. It was an experience I remember only in flashes, so to speak. I suppose that because I was so tired, and then so frightened, and the surroundings were so new to me, much of what happened somehow didn't register properly. Little things seem to have vanished forever. That's the problem." She bit her lips and looked as though she was battling to hold back the tears.

Henry said softly, "Could you tell us what you remember?"

"Well," she said, clearing her throat and clutching at her purse, "as I said, the street was a quiet one. There were cars moving past, but no pedestrians, and I wasn't sure where I was. I was reaching for the map and looking about for a street sign when a young man seemed to appear from nowhere and called out, 'Got a dollar lady?' He couldn't have been more than fifteen years old—just a boy.

"Well, I would have been perfectly willing to let him have a dollar if I thought he needed it, but really, he seemed perfectly fit and reasonably prosperous and I didn't think it would be advisable to display my wallet, so I said, 'I'm afraid I don't, young man.'

"Of course, he didn't believe me. He came closer and said, 'Sure you do, lady. Here, let me help you look,' and he reached for my purse. Well, I wasn't going to let him have it, of course—"

Trumbull said, firmly, "No 'of course' about it, Mrs. Lindemann. If it ever happens again, you surrender your purse at once. You can't save it in any case, and the hood-lums will think nothing of using force, and there is nothing in the purse that can possibly be worth your life."

Mrs. Lindemann sighed. "I suppose you're right, but at the time I just wasn't thinking clearly. I held on to my purse as a reflex action, I suppose, and that's when I start failing to remember. I recall engaging in a tug-of-war and I seem to recall other young men approaching. I don't know how many but I seemed surrounded.

"Then I heard a shout and some very bad language and the loud noise of feet. There was nothing more for a while except that my purse was gone. Then there was an anxious voice, low and polite, 'Are you hurt, madam?'

"I said, 'I don't think so, but my purse is gone.' I looked about vaguely. I think I was under the impression it had fallen to the street.

"There was an older young man holding my elbow respect-fully. He might have been twenty-five. He said, 'They got that, ma'am, I'd better get you out of here before they come back for some more fun. They'll probably have knives and I don't.'

"He was hurrying me away. I didn't see him clearly in the dark but he was tall and wore a sweater. He said, 'I live close by, ma'am. It's either get to my place or we'll have a battle.' I *think* I was aware of other young men in the distance, but that may have been a delusion.

"I went with the new young man quite docilely. He seemed earnest and polite and I've gotten too old to feel that I am in danger of—uh—*personal* harm. Besides, I was so confused and light-headed that I lacked any will to resist.

"The next thing I remember is being at his apartment door. I remember that it was apartment 4-F. I suppose that remains in my mind because it was such a familiar combination during World War II. Then I was inside his apartment and sitting in an upholstered armchair. It was a rather run-down apartment, I noticed, but I don't remember getting to it at all.

"The man who had rescued me had put a glass into my hand and I sipped at it. It was some kind of wine, I think. I did not particularly like the taste, but it warmed me and it seemed to make me less dizzy—rather than more dizzy, as one would suppose.

"The man seemed anxious about my possibly being hurt, but I reassured him. I said if he would just help me get a taxi I would get back to my hotel. He said I had better rest a while.

"He offered to call the police to report the incident, but I was adamant against that. That's one of the things I remember *very* clearly. I knew the police could not recover my purse and I did *not* want to become a newspaper item.

"I think I must have explained that I was from out of town because he lectured me, quite gently, on the dangers of walking on the streets of Manhattan.—I've heard so much on the subject in the last week. You should hear my niece go on and on about it.

"I remember other bits of the conversation. He wanted to know whether I'd lost much cash and I said, well, about thirty or forty dollars, but that I had traveller's checks which could, of course, be replaced. I think I had to spend some time reassuring him that I knew how to do that, and that I knew how to report my missing credit card. I had only had one in my purse.

"Finally, I asked him his name so that I could speak to him properly and he laughed and said, 'Oh, first names will do for that.' He told me his and I told him mine. And I said, 'Isn't it astonishing how it all fits together, your name, and your address, and what you said back there.' I explained and he laughed and said he would never have thought of that.—So you see I knew his address.

"Then we went downstairs and it was quite late by then, at least by the clock, though, of course, it wasn't really very late by my insides. He made sure the streets were clear, then made me wait in the vestibule while he went out to get a cab. He told me he had paid the driver to take me wherever I wanted to go and then before I could stop him he put a twenty-dollar bill in my hand because he said I mustn't be left with no money at all.

"I tried to object, but he said he loved New York, and since I had been so mistreated on my first evening there by New Yorkers, it had to be made up for by New Yorkers. So I took it—because I knew I would pay it back.

"The driver took me back to the hotel and he didn't try to collect any money. He even tried to give me change because he said the young man had given him a five-dollar bill but I was pleased with his honesty and I wouldn't take the change.

"So you see although the incident began very painfully, there was the extreme kindness of the Good Samaritan young man and of the taxi driver. It was as though an act of unkindness was introduced into my life in order that I might experience other acts of kindness that would more than re-dress the balance—And I *still* experience them; yours, I mean.

"Of course, it was quite obvious that the young man was not well off and I strongly suspected that the twenty-five dollars he had expended on me was far more than he could afford to throw away. Nor did he ask my last name or what my hotel was. It was as though he knew I would pay it back without having to be reminded. Naturally, I would.

"You see, I'm quite well-to-do really, and it's not just a

matter of paying it back. The Bible says that if you cast your bread upon the waters it will be returned tenfold, so I think it's only fair that if he put out twenty-five dollars, he ought to get two hundred fifty back and I can afford it.

"I got back to my room and slept so soundly after all that; it was quite refreshing. The next morning, I arranged my affairs with respect to the credit card and the traveller's checks and then I called my niece and spent the day with her.

"I told her what had happened, but just the bare essentials. After all, I had to explain why I had no bag and why I was temporarily short of cash. She went on and *on* about it. I bought a new purse—this one—and it wasn't till the end of the day when I was in bed again that I realized that I had not made it my business to repay the young man *first thing*. Being with family had just preoccupied me. And then the real tragedy struck me."

Mrs. Lindemann stopped and tried to keep her face from crumpling but failed. She began to weep quietly and to reach desperately into her bag for a handkerchief.

Henry said softly, "Would you care to rest awhile, Mrs. Lindemann?"

Rubin said, just as softly, "Would you like a cup of tea, Mrs. Lindemann, or some brandy?" Then he glared about as though daring anyone to say a word.

Mrs. Lindemann said, "No, I'm all right. I apologize for behaving so, but I found I had forgotten. I don't remember the young man's address, *not at all*, though I must have known it that night because I talked about it. I don't remember his first name! I stayed awake all night trying to remember, and that just made it worse. I went out the next day to try to retrace my steps, but everything looked so different by day—and by night, I was afraid to try.

"What must the young man think of me? He's never heard from me. I took his money and just vanished with it. I am worse than those terrible young hoodlums who snatched my purse. I had never been kind to *them*. They owed *me* no gratitude."

Gonzalo said, "It's not your fault that you can't remember. You had a rough time."

"Yes, but *he* doesn't know I can't remember. He thinks

I'm an ungrateful thief. Finally, I told my nephew about my trouble and he was just thinking of employing Mr. Gonzalo for something and he felt that Mr. Gonzalo might have the kind of worldly wisdom that might help. Mr. Gonzalo said he would try, and in the end—here I am. But now that I've heard myself tell the story I realize how hopeless it all sounds."

Trumbull sighed. "Mrs. Lindemann, please don't be offended at what I am about to ask, but we must eliminate some factors. Are you sure it all really happened?"

Mrs. Lindemann looked surprised, "Well, of *course* it really happened. My purse was *gone!*"

"No," said Henry, "what Mr. Trumbull means I think is that after the mugging, you somehow got back to the hotel and then had a sleep that may have been filled with nightmares so that what you remember now is partly fact and partly dream—which would account for the imperfect memory."

"No," said Mrs. Lindemann firmly, "I remember what I do remember perfectly. It was not a dream."

"In that case," said Trumbull, shrugging, "we have very little to go on."

Rubin said, "Never mind, Tom. We're not giving up. If we choose the right name for your rescuer, Mrs. Lindemann, would you recognize it, even though you can't remember it now?"

"I hope so," said Mrs. Lindemann, "but I don't know. I've tried looking in a phone directory to see different first names, but none seemed familiar. I don't think it could have been a very common name."

Rubin said, "Then it couldn't have been Sam?"

"Oh, I'm certain that's not it."

"Why Sam, Manny?" asked Gonzalo.

"Well, the fellow was a Good Samaritan. Mrs. Lindemann called him that herself. Sam for Samaritan. His number and street may have represented the chapter and verse in the Bible where the tale of the Good Samaritan begins. You said his name and address fitted each other and that's the only clue we have."

"Wait," put in Avalon eagerly, "the first name might have been the much less common one of Luke. That's the gospel in which the parable is to be found."

"I'm afraid," said Mrs. Lindemann, "that doesn't sound right, either. Besides, I'm not *that* well acquainted with the Bible. I couldn't identify the chapter and verse of the parable."

Halsted said, "Let's not get off on impossible tangents. Mrs. Lindemann taught American history in school so it's very likely that what struck her applied to American history. For instance, suppose the address were 1812 Madison Avenue and the young man's name was James. James Madison was President during the War of 1812."

"Or 1492 Columbus Avenue," said Gonzalo, "and the young man was named Christopher."

"Or 1775 Lexington Avenue and the name Paul for Paul Revere," said Trumbull.

"Or 1623 Amsterdam Avenue and the name Peter," said Avalon, "for Peter Minuit, or 1609 Hudson Avenue and the name Henry. In fact, there are many named streets in lower Manhattan. We can never pick an appropriate one unless Mrs. Lindemann remembers."

Mrs. Lindemann clasped her hands tightly together. "Oh, dear, oh, *dear,* nothing sounds familiar."

Rubin said, "Of course not, if we're going to guess at random. Mrs. Lindemann, I assume you are at a midtown hotel."

"I'm at the New York Hilton. Is that midtown?"

"Yes. Sixth Avenue and Fifty-third Street. The chances are you could not have walked more than a mile, probably less, before you grew tired. Therefore, let's stick to midtown. Hudson Avenue is much too far south and places like 1492 Columbus or 1812 Madison are much too far north. It would have to be midtown, probably West Side—and I can't think of anything."

Drake said, through a haze of cigarette smoke, "You're forgetting one item. Mrs. Lindemann said it wasn't just the name and address that fit but what the young man said back there; that is, at the site of the rescue. What did he say back there?"

"It's all so hazy," said Mrs. Lindemann.

"You said he called out roughly at the muggers. Can you repeat what he said?"

Mrs. Lindemann colored. "I could repeat *some* of what he said, but I don't think I want to. The young man apologized for it afterward. He said that unless he used bad language the hoodlums would not have been impressed and would not have scattered. Besides, I know I couldn't have referred to *that* at all."

Drake said thoughtfully, "That bites the dust then. Have you thought of advertising? You know, 'Will the young man who aided a woman in distress—' and so on."

"I've thought of it," said Mrs. Lindemann, "but that would be *so* dreadful. He might not see it and so many imposters might arrive to make a claim.—Really, this is so dreadful."

Avalon, looking distressed, turned to Henry and said, "Well, Henry, does anything occur to you?"

Henry said, "I'm not certain.—Mrs. Lindemann, you said that by the time you took the taxi it was late by the clock but not by your insides. Does that mean you arrived from the West Coast by plane so that your perception of time was three hours earlier than the clock?"

"Yes, I did," said Mrs. Lindemann.

"Perhaps from Portland, or not too far from there?" asked Henry.

"Why, yes, from just outside Portland. Had I mentioned that?"

"No, you hadn't," interposed Trumbull. "How did you know, Henry?"

"Because it occurred to me, sir," said Henry, "that the young man's name was Eugene, which is the name of a town only about a hundred miles south of Portland."

Mrs. Lindemann rose, eyes staring. "My goodness! The name *was* Eugene! But that's marvellous. How could you possibly tell?"

Henry said, "Mr. Rubin pointed out the address had to be in midtown Manhattan on the West Side. Dr. Drake pointed out your reference to what the young man had said at the scene of the rescue and I recalled that one thing you reported him to have said besides the bad language you did *not* describe specifically was that you had better get to his place or there'd be a battle.

"Mr. Halsted pointed out that the address ought to have some significance in American history and so I thought it might be 54 West Fortieth Street, since there is the well-known election slogan of '54-40 or fight,' the election of 1844, I believe. It would be particularly meaningful to Mrs. Lindemann if she were from the Northwest since it pertained to our dispute with Great Britain over the Oregon Territory. When she said she was indeed from near Portland, Oregon, I guessed that the rescuer's name might be Eugene."

Mrs. Lindemann sat down, "To my dying day, I will never forget this. That *is* the address. How could I have forgotten it when you worked it out so neatly from what little I did remember."

And then she grew excited. She said, "But it's not too late. I must go there *at once*. I must pay him or shove an envelope under his door or something."

Rubin said, "Will you recognize the house if you see it?"

"Oh, yes," said Mrs. Lindemann. "I'm sure of that. And it's apartment 4-F. I remembered that. If I knew his last name, I would call, but, no, I want to *see* him and explain."

Rubin said mildly, "You certainly can't go yourself, Mrs. Lindemann. Not into that neighborhood at this time of night after what you've been through. Some of us will have to go with you. At the very least, I will."

Mrs. Lindemann said, "I very much dislike inconveniencing you, Mr. Rubin."

"Under the circumstances, Mrs. Lindemann," said Rubin, "I consider it my duty."

Henry said, "I believe we will all accompany you, Mrs. Lindemann. I know the Black Widowers."

14

Can You Prove It?

Another thing I don't like to do in my mysteries (there seem to be so many things I don't like to do) is to write an Iron Curtain story. For one thing, I don't like to picture good and evil as associated with different nationalities. There are many decent people and a few sourballs in every group of human beings, no matter how you slice them. I admit that back in the 1930s and 1940s I had difficulty feeling charitable toward Germans—any Germans—but even then I avoided placing German villains in my early stories

Then, too, at the present time, Soviet-American enmity poses such a threat to the world generally that I hesitate to add the tiniest trifle to that enmity.

And yet, enmity exists between nations, and that can serve as the necessary basis for a mystery. So here is an Iron Curtain story that I'm proud of because I did it my way. The country is not named and the man on the other side is clearly a decent individual.

Henry, the smoothly functioning waiter at the monthly Black Widowers banquet, filled the water glass of the evening's guest as though knowing in advance that that guest was reaching into his shirt pocket for a small vial of pills.

The guest looked up. "Thank you, waiter—though the pills are small enough to go down au jus, so to speak."

He looked about the table and sighed. "Advancing age! In our modern times we are not allowed to grow old ad lib. Doctors follow the faltering mechanism in detail and insist on applying the grease. My blood pressure is a touch high and I have an occasional extrasystole, so I take a pretty little orange pill four times a day."

Geoffrey Avalon, who sat immediately across the table, smiled with the self-conscious superiority of a man moderately stricken in years who kept himself in good shape with a vigorous system of calisthenics, and said, "How old are you, Mr. Smith?"

"Fifty-seven. With proper care, my doctor assures me I will live out a normal lifetime."

Emmanuel Rubin's eyes flashed in magnified form behind his thick spectacles as he said, "I doubt there's an American who reaches middle age these days who doesn't become accustomed to a regimen of pills of one kind or another. I take zinc and vitamin E and a few other things."

James Drake nodded and said in his soft voice as he peered through his cigarette smoke, "I have a special weekly pillbox arrangement to keep the day's dosages correct. That way you can check on whether you've taken the second pill of a particular kind. If it's in the Friday compartment still—assuming the day is Friday—you haven't taken it."

Smith said, "I take only this one kind of pill, which simplifies things. I bought a week's supply three years ago—twenty-eight of them—on my doctor's prescription. I was frankly skeptical, but they helped me tremendously and I persuaded my doctor to prescribe them for me in bottles of a thousand. Every Sunday morning, I put twenty-eight into my original vial, which I carry with me everywhere and at all times and which I still use. I know at all times how much I should have—right now, I should have four left, having just taken the twenty-fourth of the week, and I do. In three years, I've missed a pill only twice."

"I," said Rubin, loftily, "have not yet reached that pitch of senility that requires any mnemonic devices at all."

"No?" asked Mario Gonzalo, spearing his last bit of baba au rhum. "What pitch of senility *have* you reached?"

Roger Halsted, who was hosting the banquet that night, forestalled Rubin's rejoinder by saying, hastily, "There's an interesting point to be made here. As increasing numbers of people pump themselves full of chemicals, there must be fewer and fewer people with untampered tissue chemistry."

"None at all," growled Thomas Trumbull. "The food we eat is loaded with additives. The water we drink has purifying chemicals. The air we breathe is half pollution of one sort or another. If you could analyze an individual's blood carefully enough, you could probably tell where he lived, what he eats, what medicines he takes."

Smith nodded. His short hair exposed prominent ears, something Gonzalo had taken full advantage of in preparing his caricature of the evening's guest. Now Smith rubbed one of them thoughtfully, and said, "Maybe you could file everyone's detailed blood pattern in some computer bank. Then if all else fails, your blood would be your identification. The pattern would be entered into the computer which would compare it with all those in its memory files and, within a minute, words would flash across a screen saying, 'The man you have here is John Smith of Fairfield, Connecticut,' and I would stand up and bow."

Trumbull said, "If you could stand up and bow, you could stand up and identify yourself. Why bother with a blood pattern?"

"Oh, yes?" said Smith, grimly.

Halsted said, "Listen, let's not get involved in this. Henry is distributing the brandy and it's past time for the grilling. Jeff, will you assume the task?"

"I will be glad to," said Avalon in his most solemn tone.

Bending his fierce and graying eyebrows over his eyes, Avalon said, with incongruous mildness, "And just how do you justify your existence, Mr. Smith?"

"Well," said Smith, cheerfully, "I inherited a going business. I did well with it, sold it profitably, invested wisely, and now live in early retirement in a posh place in Fairfield—a widower with two grown children, each on his own. I toil not, neither do I spin and, like the lilies of the field, my justification is my beauty and the way it illuminates the landscape.'' A grin of self-mockery crossed his pleasantly ugly face.

Avalon said, indulgently, ''I suppose we can pass that. Beauty is in the eye of the beholder. Your name is John Smith?''

''And I can prove it,'' said Smith quickly. ''Name your poison. I have my card, a driver's license, a variety of credit cards, some personal letters addressed to me, a library card, and so on.''

''I am perfectly willing to accept your word, sir, but it occurs to me that with a name like John Smith you must frequently encounter some signs of cynical disbelief—from hotel clerks, for instance. Do you have a middle initial?''

''No, sir, I am the real thing. My parents felt that any modification of the grand cliché would spoil the grandeur. I won't deny that there haven't been times when I've longed to say my name was Eustace Bartholomew Wasservogel, but the feeling passes. Of the Smiths I am, and of that tribe—variety, John—I remain.''

Avalon cleared his throat portentously and said, ''And yet, Mr. Smith, I feel you have reason to feel annoyance at your name. You reacted to Tom's suggestion that you could merely announce your name and make the blood identification unnecessary with a clear tone of annoyance. Have you had some special occasion of late when you failed to identify yourself?''

Trumbull said, ''Let me guess that you did. Your eagerness to demonstrate your ability to prove your identity would show that some past failure to do so rankles.''

Smith stared around the table in astonishment, ''Good God, does it show that much?''

Halsted said, ''No, John, it doesn't, but this group has developed a sixth sense about mysteries. I told you when you accepted my invitation that if you were hiding a skeleton in your closet, they'd have it out of you.''

''And I told you, Roger,'' said Smith, ''that I had no mystery about me.''

"And the matter of inability to prove identity?" said Rubin.

"Was a nightmare rather than a mystery," said Smith, "and it is something I've been asked not to talk about."

Avalon said, "Anything mentioned within the four walls of a Black Widowers banquet represents privileged communication. Feel free."

"I can't." Smith paused, then said, "Look, I don't know what it's all about. I think I was mistaken for someone once when I was visiting Europe and after I got out of the nightmare, I was visited by someone from the—by someone, and asked not to talk about it. Though come to think of it, there *is* a mystery of a sort."

"Ah," said Avalon, "and what might that be?"

"I don't really know how I got out of the nightmare," said Smith.

Gonzalo, looking pleased and animated, said, "Tell us what happened and I'll bet we tell you how you got out of it."

"I can't very well—" began Smith.

Trumbull's frowning face, having attempted to wither Gonzalo, turned to Smith. "I understand such things, Mr. Smith," he said. "Suppose you omit the name of the country involved and the exact dates and any other such identifiable paraphernalia. Just tell it as a story out of the Arabian Nights—if the nightmare will stand up without the dangerous detail."

Smith said, "I think it will, but seriously, gentlemen, if the matter does involve national security—and I can imagine ways in which it might—how can I be sure you are all to be trusted?"

Halsted said, "If you trust me, John, I'll vouch for the rest of the Black Widowers—including, of course, Henry, our esteemed waiter."

Henry, standing at the sideboard, smiled gently.

Smith was visibly tempted. "I don't say I wouldn't like to get this off my chest—"

"If you choose not to," said Halsted, "I'm afraid the banquet ends. The terms of the invitation were that you were to answer all questions truthfully."

Smith laughed. "You also said I would not be asked

anything designed to humiliate me or to put me in a disgraceful light—but have it your way.''

"I was visiting Europe last year," said Smith, "and I'll put the location and date no closer than that. I was a recent widower, a little lost without my wife, and rather determined to pick up the threads of life once again. I had not been much of a traveller before my retirement and I was anxious to make up for that.

"I travelled alone and I was a tourist. Nothing more than that. I want to stress that in all truthfulness. I was not serving any organ of the government—and that's true of *any* government, not just my own—either officially or unofficially. Nor was I there to gather information for any private organization. I was a tourist and nothing more and so steeped in innocence that I suppose it was too much to expect that I not get into trouble.

"I could not speak the language of the country but that didn't bother me. I can't speak any language but English and I have the usual provincial American attitude that that's enough. There would always be *someone*, anywhere I might be, who would speak and understand English.—And as a matter of fact, that always proved to be correct.

"The hotel I stayed at was reasonably comfortable in appearance, though there was so foreign an aura about it that I knew I would not feel at home—but then I didn't expect to feel at home. I couldn't even pronounce its name, though that didn't bother me.

"I only stayed long enough to deposit my luggage and then it was ho, for the great foreign spaces where I could get to know the people.

"The man at the desk—the concierge, or whatever he might be called—spoke an odd version of English that, with a little thought, could be understood. I got a list of tourist attractions from him, some recommended restaurants, a stylized map of the city (not in English, so I doubted it would do me much good), and some general assertions as to how safe the city was and how friendly the inhabitants.

"I imagine Europeans are always eager to impress that on Americans, who are known to live dangerously. In the nineteenth century they thought every America city lay under imminent threat of Indian massacre; in the first half of the twentieth century, every one was full of Chicago gangsters; and now they are all full of indiscriminate muggers. So I wandered off into the city cheerfully.''

"Alone? Without knowing the language?'' said Avalon, with manifest disapproval. "What time was it?''

"The shades of evening were being drawn downward by a cosmic hand and you're right in the implication, Mr. Avalon. Cities are never as safe as their boosters claim, and I found that out. But I started off cheerfully enough. The world was full of poetry and I was enjoying myself.

"There were signs of all kinds on buildings and in store windows that were beginning to be lit up in defense against the night. Since I could read none of them, I was spared their deadly prosiness.

"The people *were* friendly. I would smile and they would smile in return. Many said something—I presume in greeting—and I would smile again and nod and wave. It was a beautiful, mild evening and I was absolutely euphoric.

"I don't know how long I was walking or how far I had gone before I was quite convinced that I was lost, but even that didn't bother me. I stepped into a tavern to ask my way to the restaurant where I had determined to go and whose name I had painstakingly memorized. I called out the name of the restaurant, and pointed vaguely in various directions and shrugged my shoulders and tried to indicate that I had lost my way. Several gathered around and one of them asked in adequate English if I was an American. I said I was and he translated that jubilantly to the others, who seemed delighted.

"He said, 'We don't see many Americans here.' They then fell to studying my clothes and the cut of my hair and asking where I was from and trying to pronounce 'Fairfield' and offering to stand me drinks. I sang 'The Star-Spangled Banner' because they seemed to expect it and it was a real love feast. I did have a drink on an empty stomach and after that things got even love-feastier.

"They told me the restaurant I asked for was very expensive, and not very good, and that I should eat right there and they would order for me and it would be on the house. It was hands across the sea and building bridges, you know, and I doubt if I had ever been happier since before Regina had died. I had another drink or two.

"And then after that my memory stops until I found myself out in the street again. It was quite dark, much cooler. There were almost no people about, I had no idea where I was, and every idea that I had a splitting headache.

"I sat down in a doorway and knew, even before I felt for it, that my wallet was gone. So was my wristwatch, my pens—In fact, my trousers pockets were empty and so were my jacket pockets. I had been Mickey Finned and rolled by my dear friends across the sea and they had probably taken me by car to a distant part of the city and dumped me.

"The money taken was not terribly vital. My main supply was safely back in the hotel. Still I had no money at the moment, I didn't know where I was, I didn't remember the name of the hotel, I felt woozy, sick, and in pain—and I needed help.

"I looked for a policeman or for anyone in anything that looked like a uniform. If I had found a street cleaner, or a bus conductor, he could direct me or, better, take me to a police station.

"I found a policeman. Actually, it wasn't difficult. They are, I imagine, numerous and deliberately visible in that particular city. And I was then taken to a police station—in the equivalent of a paddy wagon, I think. My memory has its hazy spots.

"When I begin to remember a bit more clearly, I was sitting on a bench in what I guessed to be the police station. No one was paying much attention to me and my headache was a little better.

"A rather short man with a large mustache entered, engaged in conversation with a man behind a massive desk, then approached me. He seemed rather indifferent, but to my relief he spoke English and quite well, too, though he had a disconcertingly British accent.

"I followed him into a rather dingy room, gray and depressing, and there the questioning began. It was the questioning that was the nightmare, though the questioner remained unfailingly, if distantly, polite. He told me his name but I don't remember it. I honestly don't. It began with a *V*, so I'll just call him 'Vee' if I have to.

"He said, 'You say your name is John Smith.'

" 'Yes.'

"He didn't exactly smile. He said, 'It is a very common name in the United States and, I understand, is frequently assumed by those who wish to avoid investigation.'

" 'It is frequently assumed *because* it is common,' I said, 'and since it is common, why shouldn't I be one of the hundreds of thousands who bear it?'

" 'You have identification?'

" 'I've been robbed. I've come in to complain—'

"Vee raised his hand and made hushing noises through his mustache. 'Your complaint has been recorded, but I have nothing to do with the people here. They merely made sure you were not wounded and then sent for me. They have not searched you or questioned you. It is not their job. Now—do you have identification?'

"Wearily, and quietly, I told him what had happened.

" 'Then,' he said, 'you have nothing with which to support your statement that you are John Smith of Fairfield, Connecticut?'

" 'Who else should I be?'

" 'That we would like to find out. You say you were mistreated in a tavern. Its location, please.'

" 'I don't know.'

" 'Its name?'

" 'I don't know.'

" 'What were you doing there?'

" 'I told you. I was merely walking through the city—'

" 'Alone?'

" 'Yes, alone. I told you.'

" 'Your starting point?'

" 'My hotel.'

" 'And you have identification there?'

" 'Certainly. My passport is there and all my belongings.'

" 'The name of the hotel?'

"I winced at that. Even to myself my answer would seem too much to accept. 'I can't recall,' I said in a low voice.

" 'Its location?'

" 'I don't know.'

"Vee sighed. He looked at me in a nearsighted way and I thought his eyes seemed sad, but perhaps it was only myopia.

"He said, 'The basic question is: What is your name? We must have some identification or this becomes a serious matter. Let me explain your position to you, Mr. Blank. Nothing compels me to do so, but I am not in love with every aspect of my work and I shall sleep better if I make sure you understand that you are in great danger.'

"My heart began to race. I am not young. I am not a hero. I am not brave. I said, 'But why? I am a wronged person. I have been drugged and robbed. I came voluntarily to the police, sick and lost, looking for help—'

"Again, Vee held up his hand, 'Quietly! Quietly! Some speak a little English here and it is better we keep this between ourselves for now. Things may be as you have described, or they may not. You are an American national. My government has cause to fear Americans. That, at least, is our official position. We are expecting an American agent of great ability to penetrate our borders on a most dangerous mission.

" 'That means that any strange American—any American encountered under suspicious circumstances—has, for a week now, been referred instantly to my department. Your circumstances were suspicious to begin with and have grown far more suspicious now that I have questioned you.'

"I stared at him in horror. 'Do you think *I*'m a spy? If I were, would I come to the police like this?'

" 'You may not be *the* spy, but you may still be *a* spy. There are people who will think so at once. Even I view it as a possibility.'

" 'But *no* kind of *spy* would come to the police—'

" 'Please! It will do you good to listen. You may be a distraction. If you play chess, you will know what I mean when I say you may be a sacrifice. You are sent in to confuse and distract us, occupying our time and efforts, while the real work is done elsewhere.'

"I said, 'But it hasn't worked, if that's what I'm supposed to be. You're not confused and distracted. No one could be fooled by anything as silly as this. It's not a reasonable sacrifice and so it's no sacrifice at all. It's nothing but the truth I've been telling you.'

"Vee sighed. 'Then what's your name?'

" 'John Smith. Ask me a million times and it will stay my name.'

" 'But you can't prove it.—See here,' he said, 'you have two alternatives. One is to convince me in some reasonable way that you are telling the truth. Mere statements, however eloquent, are insufficient. There must be evidence. Have you nothing with your name on it? Nothing material you can show me?'

" 'I told you,' I said, despairingly. 'I've been robbed.'

" 'Failing that,' he said, as though he hadn't heard my remark, 'it will be assumed you are here to fulfill some function for your country that will not be to the interest of my country, and you will be interrogated with that in mind. It will not be my job, I am glad to say, but those who interrogate will be most thorough and most patient. I wish it were not so, but where national security is at stake—'

"I was in utter panic. I said, stuttering, 'But I can't tell what I don't know, no matter how you interrogate.'

" 'If so, they will finally be convinced, but you will not be well off by then. And you will be imprisoned, for it will not then be politic to let you go free in your condition. If your country succeeds in what it may be attempting, there will be anger in this country and you will surely be the victim of that and will receive a long sentence. Your country will not be able to intercede for you. It will not even try.'

"I screamed. 'That is unjust! That is unjust!'

" 'Life *is* unjust,' said Vee, sadly. 'Your own President Kennedy said that.'

" 'But what am I to do?' I babbled.

"He said, 'Convince me your story is true. Show me something! Remember something! Prove your name is John Smith. Take me to the tavern; better yet to the hotel. Present me with your passport. Give me anything, however small, as a beginning, and I will have sufficient faith in you to try for the rest—at some risk to myself, I might add.'

" 'I appreciate that, but I cannot. I am helpless. I cannot.' I was babbling. All I could think of was that I was facing torture and an extended prison term for the crime of having been drugged and robbed. It was more than I could bear and I fainted. I'm sorry. It is not a heroic action, but I told you I wasn't a hero.''

Halsted said, ''You don't know what they had put in your drink in the tavern. You were half-poisoned. You weren't yourself.''

''It's kind of you to say so, but the prospect of torture and imprisonment for nothing was not something I could have faced with stoicism on my best day.

''The next memory I have is that of lying on a bed with a vague feeling of having been manhandled. I think some of my clothing may have been removed.

''Vee was watching me with the same expression of sadness on his face. He said, 'I'm sorry. Would you care for some brandy?'

''I remembered. The nightmare was back. I shook my head. All I wanted was to convince him of my utter innocence somehow. I said, 'Listen! You *must* believe me. Every word I have told you is true! I—'

''He placed his hand on my shoulder and shook it. 'Stop! I believe you!'

''I stared at him stupidly, 'What!'

''He said, 'I believe you. For one thing, no one who was sent on a task such as yours might have been, could have portrayed utter terror so convincingly, in my opinion. But that is only my opinion. It would not have convinced my superiors and I could not have acted on it. However, no one could be as stupid as you have now proved to be without having been sufficiently stupid to step into a strange tavern so confidingly and to have forgotten the name of your hotel.'

'' 'But I don't understand.'

'' 'Enough! I have wasted enough time. I should, properly, now leave you to the police, but I do not wish to abandon you just yet. For the tavern and the thieves within, I can do nothing now. Perhaps another time after another complaint. Let us, however, find your hotel.—Tell me anything you remember—the décor—the position of the registration desk— the hair color of the man behind it—were there flowers?

Come, come, Mr. Smith, what kind of street was it on? Were there shops? Was there a doorman? Anything?'

"I wondered if it were a scheme to trap me into something, but I saw no alternative but to try to answer the questions. I tried to picture everything as it had been when I had walked into the hotel for the first time less than twelve hours before. I did my best to describe and he hurried me on impatiently, asking questions faster than I could answer.

"He then looked at the hurried notes he had taken and whispered them to another official of some sort, who was on the spot without my having seen him enter—a hotel expert, perhaps. The newcomer nodded his head wisely and whispered back.

"Vee said, 'Very well, then. We think we know what hotel it was, so let us go. The faster I locate your passport, the better all around.'

"Off we went in an official car. I sat there, fearful and apprehensive, fearing that it was a device to break my spirit by offering me hope only to smash it by taking me to prison instead. God knows my spirit needed no breaking.—Or what if they took me to a hotel, and it was the wrong one, would they then listen to anything at all that I had to say?

"We did speed to a hotel, however. I shrugged helplessly when Vee asked if it was *the* hotel. How could I tell in pitch-darkness? And I feared committing myself to what would turn out to be a mistake.

"But it *was* the correct hotel. The night man behind the desk didn't know me, of course, but there was the record of a room for a John Smith of Fairfield. We went up there and behold—my luggage, my passport, my papers. Quite enough.

"Vee shook hands with me and said, in a low voice, 'A word of advice, Mr. Smith. Get out of the country quickly. I shall make my report and exonerate you, but if things go wrong in some ways, someone may decide you should be picked up again. You will be better off beyond the borders.'

"I thanked him and never took anyone's advice so eagerly in all my life. I checked out of the hotel, grabbed a taxi to the nearest station, and I don't think I breathed till I crossed the border.

"To this day, I don't know what it was all about—whether

the United States really had an espionage project under way in that country at that time or whether, if we did, we succeeded or failed. As I said, some official asked me to keep quiet about the whole thing, so I suppose the suspicions of Vee's government were more or less justified.

"In any case, I never plan to go back to that particular country."

Avalon said, "You were fortunate, Mr. Smith. I see what you mean when you said you were puzzled by the ending. Vee, as you call him, did make a sudden about-face, didn't he?"

"I don't think so," interposed Gonzalo. "I think he was sympathetic to you all along, Mr. Smith. When you passed out, he called some superior, convinced him you were just a poor jerk in trouble, and then let you go."

"It might be," said Drake, "that it was your fainting that convinced him. If you were actually an agent, you would know the dangers you ran, and you would be more or less steeled for them. In fact, he said so, didn't he? He said you couldn't fake fear so convincingly and you therefore had to be what you said you were—or something like that."

Rubin said, "If you've told the story accurately, Mr. Smith, I would think that Vee is out of sympathy with the regime or he wouldn't have urged you to get out of the country as he did. I should think he stands a good chance of being purged, or has been since that time."

Trumbull said, "I hate to agree with you, Manny, but I do. My guess is that Vee's failure to hang on to Smith may have been the last straw."

"That doesn't make me feel very good," muttered Smith.

Roger Halsted pushed his coffee cup out of the way and placed his elbows on the table. He said earnestly, "I've heard the bare bones of the story before and I've thought about it and think there's more to it than that. Besides, if all five of you agree on something, that must be wrong."

He turned to Smith. "You told me, John, that this Vee was a young man."

"Well, he struck me as being in his early thirties."

"All right, then," said Halsted, "if a youngish man is in the secret police, it must be out of conviction and he must plan to rise in the ranks. He isn't going to run ridiculous risks for some nonentity. If he were an old man, he might remember an earlier regime and might be out of sympathy with the new government, but—''

Gonzalo said, "How do you know this Vee wasn't a double agent? Maybe that's why our government doesn't want Smith to be talking about the matter."

"If Vee were a double agent," said Halsted, "then, considering his position in the government intelligence there, he would be enormously valuable to us. All the more reason that he wouldn't risk anything for the sake of a nonentity. I suspect that there's more than sympathy involved. He must have thought of something that authenticated John's story."

"Sometimes I think that's it," said Smith, morosely. "I keep thinking of his remark after I came out of my faint to the effect that I was too stupid to be guilty. He never did explain that remark."

"Wait a minute," said Rubin. "After you came out of your faint, you said you seemed to be in disarray. While you were out, they inspected your clothes closely, realized they were American make—"

"What would that prove?" demanded Gonzalo, scornfully. "An American spy is as likely to wear American clothes as an American jerk is.—No offense, Mr. Smith."

"None taken," said Smith. "Besides, I had bought the clothes I was then wearing in Paris."

Gonzalo said, "I guess you didn't ask him why he thought you were stupid."

Smith snorted. "You mean did I say to him, 'Hey, wise guy, who're you calling stupid?' No, I didn't say that, or anything like it. I just held my breath."

Avalon said, "The comments on your stupidity, Mr. Smith, need not be taken to heart. You have said several times that you were not yourself at any time during that difficult time. After being drugged, you might well have *seemed* stupid. In any case, I don't see that we'll ever know the inwardness of Vee's change of mind. It would be sufficient to accept it and not question the favors of fortune. It is enough that you emerged safely from the lion's mouth."

"Well, wait," said Gonzalo. "We haven't asked Henry for his opinion yet."

Smith said, with astonishment, "The waiter?" Then, in a lower voice, "I didn't realize he was listening. Does he understand this is all confidential?"

Gonzalo said, "He's a member of the club and the best man here.—Henry, can you understand Vee's change of heart?"

Henry hesitated. "I do not wish to offend Mr. Smith. I would not care to call him stupid, but I can see why this foreign official, Vee, thought so."

There was a general stir about the table. Smith said, stiffly, "What do you mean, Henry?"

"You say the events of the nightmare took place some time last year."

"That's right," said Smith.

"And you say your pockets were rifled. Were they completely emptied?"

"Of course," said Smith.

"But that is clearly impossible. You've said you still carry the original vial of pills, and that you have carried it everywhere and at all times, so that I suppose you had it with you when you travelled abroad and that you had it with you when you entered the tavern—and therefore still had it with you when you left the tavern."

Smith said, "Well, yes, you're right. It was in my shirt pocket as always. Either they missed it or decided they didn't want it."

"You didn't say anything about that in the course of the tale you have just told us."

"It never occurred to me."

"Nor did you tell Vee about them, I suppose?" said Henry.

"Look here," said Smith, angrily, "I didn't think of them. But even if I did, I wouldn't voluntarily bring up the matter. They would use it to place a trumped-up charge of carrying dope against me and in that way justify an imprisonment."

"You'd be right, if you thought of the pills only, sir," said Henry.

"What else is there to think of?"

"The container," said Henry, mildly. "The pills were

available only by prescription and you told us it was the original vial. May we see it, Mr. Smith?"

Smith withdrew it from his shirt pocket, glanced at it and said, vehemently, "Hell!"

"Exactly," said Henry. "On the label placed on the vial by the pharmacist, there should be printed the pharmacist's name and address, probably in Fairfield, and *your* name should be typed in as well, together with directions for use."

"You're right."

"And after you had denied having any identification on you, even in the face of torture, Vee looked through your pockets while you were unconscious, and found exactly what he had been asking you to give him."

"No wonder he thought I was stupid," said Smith, shaking his head. "I *was* stupid. Now I *really* feel rotten."

"And yet," said Henry, "you have an explanation of something that has puzzled you for a year, and that should make you feel good."

15

The Redhead

I dreamed this one. Yes, I did. At least I dreamed the solution. There's no point in going into the details of the dream, but the important thing is this: At the end when I discovered the answer to what (in the dream) was puzzling me, I said (in the dream), "What a terrific idea for a Black Widower story."

Then when I woke up I remembered the dream, the solution, and what I had said, and as soon as I could, I wrote the story.

While I never suffer unduly in the process of getting an idea for a story, the quicker and more easily it comes, the better. I wish I could dream all my stories, but even if I can't, one successful dream is one better than none.

Mario Gonzalo, host of that evening's meeting of the Black Widowers, had evidently decided to introduce his guest with éclat. At least he rattled his glass with a spoon and, when all had broken off their preprandial conversations and looked up from their cocktails, Mario made his introduction. He had even waited for Thomas Trumbull's as-usual late arrival before doing so.

"Gentlemen," he said, "this is my guest, John Anderssen— that's an *s-s-e-n* at the end. You can discover anything you want about him in this evening's grilling. One thing, however, I must tell you now because I know that this bunch of asexual loudmouths will never discover it on their own. John has a wife who is, absolutely, the most gorgeous specimen of femininity the world has ever seen. And I say this as an artist with an artist's eye."

Anderssen reddened and looked uncomfortable. He was a blond young man, perhaps thirty, with a small mustache and a fair complexion. He was about five-ten in height and had rather chiseled features that came together to form a handsome face.

Geoffrey Avalon, looking down from his stiff-backed seventy-four inches, said, "I must congratulate you, Mr. Anderssen, although you need not take seriously Mario's characterization of ourselves as asexual. I'm sure that each of us is quite capable of appreciating a beautiful woman. I, myself, although I might be considered to be past the first flush of hot-blooded youth, can—"

Trumbull said, "Spare us, Jeff, spare us. If you are going to give an embarrassing account of your prowess, you are better off being interrupted. From my point of view, the next best thing to having the young woman in our midst—if our customs allowed it—would be to see her photograph. I imagine, Mr. Anderssen, you carry a photo of your fair wife in your wallet. Would you consent to let us look at it?"

"No," said Anderssen, emphatically. Then, blushing furiously, he said, "I don't mean you can't look at it. I mean I don't have a photograph of her with me. I'm sorry." But he said it challengingly, and was clearly not sorry.

Gonzalo, unabashed, said, "Well, that's your loss, my friends. You should see her hair. It's gloriously red, a live red that just about glows in the dark. And natural, totally natural— and no freckles."

"Well," said Anderssen in half a mutter, "she stays out of the sun.—Her hair *is* her best feature."

Emmanuel Rubin, who had been standing on the outskirts, looking rather dour, said in a low voice, "And temper to match, I suppose."

Anderssen turned to him, and said, with an edge of bitterness, "She has a temper." He did not elaborate.

Rubin said, "I don't suppose there's a more durable myth than the one that redheads are hot-tempered. The redness of the hair is that of fire, and the principles of sympathetic magic lead people to suppose that the personality should match the hair."

James Drake, who shared, with Avalon, the dubious privilege of being the oldest of the Widowers, sighed reminiscently, and said, "I've known some very hot-blooded redheads."

"Sure you have," said Rubin. "So has everyone. It's a self-fulfilling assumption. Redheaded children, especially girls, are forgiven for being nasty and ill-behaved. Parents sigh fatuously and mutter that it goes with the hair, and the one with red hair in the family explains how Great-Uncle Joe would mop up the floor with anyone in the barroom who said anything that was less than a grovelling compliment. Boys usually grow up and have the stuffing knocked out of them by non-redheaded peers and that teaches them manners, but girls don't. And, if they're beautiful besides, they grow up knowing they can indulge their impoliteness to the hilt. An occasional judicious kick in the fanny would do them worlds of good."

Rubin carefully did not look at Anderssen in the course of his comment and Anderssen said nothing at all.

Henry, the indispensable waiter at all the Black Widower functions, said quietly, "Gentlemen, you may be seated."

The chef at the Milano had clearly decided to be Russian for the evening, and an excellent hot borscht was followed by an even more delightful beef Stroganoff on a bed of rice. Rubin, who usually endured the food with an expression of stoic disapproval, on principle, allowed a smile to play over his sparsely bearded face on this occasion, and helped himself lavishly to the dark pumpernickel.

As for Roger Halsted, whose affection for a good meal was legendary, he quietly negotiated a second helping with Henry.

The guest, John Anderssen, ate heartily, and participated eagerly in the conversation which, through a logical association, perhaps, dealt largely with the shooting down of the Korean jetliner by the Soviets. Anderssen pointed out that the ship had been widely referred to as "Flight 007," which was the number on the fuselage, during the first couple of weeks. Then someone must have remembered that 007 was the code number of James Bond, so when the Soviets insisted the liner had been a spy plane, it became "Flight 7" in the news media, and the "00" disappeared as though it had never been.

He also maintained vigorously that the jetliner, having gone off course almost immediately after leaving Alaska, should not have been left uninformed of the fact. He was shouting, red-faced, that failure to do so, when the Soviet Union was known to be on the hair trigger with respect to American reconnaissance planes and to Reagan's "evil empire" rhetoric, was indefensible.

He paid no attention, in fact, to his dessert, a honey-drenched baklava; left his coffee half-finished; and totally ignored Henry's soft request that he make his wishes known with respect to the brandy.

He was actually pounding the table when Gonzalo rattled his spoon against his water glass. Avalon was forced to raise his baritone voice to a commanding, "Mr. Anderssen, *if* you please—"

Anderssen subsided, looking vaguely confused, as though he were, with difficulty, remembering where he was.

Gonzalo said, "It's time for the grilling, and Jeff, since you seem to have the commanding presence needed in case John, here, gets excited, suppose you do the honors."

Avalon cleared his throat, gazed at Anderssen solemnly for a few moments, then said, "Mr. Anderssen, how do you justify your existence?"

Anderssen said, "What?"

"You exist, sir. Why?"

"Oh," said Anderssen, still collecting himself. Then, in a low harsh voice, he said, "To expiate my sins in an earlier existence, I should think."

Drake, who was at the moment accepting a refresher from Henry, muttered, "So are we all.—Don't you think so, Henry?"

And Henry's sixtyish unlined face remained expressionless as he said, very softly, "A Black Widowers banquet is surely a reward for virtue rather than an expiation for sins."

Drake lifted his glass, "A palpable hit, Henry."

Trumbull growled, "Let's cut out the private conversations."

Avalon raised his hand. "Gentlemen! As you all know, I do not entirely approve of our custom of grilling a guest in the hope of searching out problems that might interest us. Nevertheless, I wish to call your attention to a peculiar phenomenon. We have here a young man—young, certainly, by the standards of old mustaches such as ourselves—well-proportioned, of excellent appearance, seeming to exude good health and an air of success in life, though we have not yet ascertained what the nature of his work is—"

"He's in good health and is doing well at his work," put in Gonzalo.

"I am glad to hear it," said Avalon, gravely. "In addition, he is married to a young and beautiful woman, so that one can't help but wonder why he should feel life to be such a burden as to lead him to believe that he exists only in order to expiate past sins. Consider, too, that during the meal just concluded, Mr. Anderssen was animated and vivacious, not in the least abashed by our older and wiser heads. I believe he shouted down even Manny, who is not one to be shouted down with impunity—"

"Anderssen was making a good point," said Rubin, indignantly.

"I think he was, too," said Avalon, "but what I wish to stress is that he is voluble, articulate, and not backward at expressing his views. Yet during the cocktail period, when the conversation dealt with his wife, he seemed to speak most reluctantly. From this, I infer that the source of Mr. Anderssen's unhappiness may be Mrs. Anderssen.—Is that so, Mr. Anderssen?"

Anderssen seemed stricken and remained silent.

Gonzalo said, "John, I explained the terms. You must answer."

Anderssen said, "I'm not sure how to answer."

Avalon said, "Let me be indirect. After all, sir, there is no intention to humiliate you. And please be aware that nothing said in this room is ever repeated by any of us elsewhere. That includes our esteemed waiter, Henry. Please feel that you can speak freely.—Mr. Anderssen, how long have you been married?"

"Two years. Actually, closer to two and a half."

"Any children, sir?"

"Not yet. We hope to have some one day."

"For that hope to exist, the marriage must not be foundering. I take it you are not contemplating divorce."

"Certainly not."

"I take it then that you love your wife?"

"Yes. And before you ask, I am quite satisfied she loves me."

"There is, of course, a certain problem in being married to a beautiful woman," said Avalon. "Men *will* flock about beauty. Are you plagued by jealousy, sir?"

"No," said Anderssen. "I've no cause for it. Helen—that's my wife—has no great interest in men—"

"Ah," said Halsted, as though a great light had dawned.

"Except for myself," said Anderssen, indignantly. "She's not in the least bit asexual. Besides," he went on, "Mario exaggerates. She does have this luxuriant head of remarkable red hair, but aside from that she is not really spectacular. Her looks, I would say, are average—though I must rely now on your assurance that all said here is confidential. I would not want *that* assessment to be repeated. Her figure is good, and *I* find her beautiful, but there are no men caught helplessly in her toils, and I am not plagued by jealousy."

"What about her temper?" put in Drake, suddenly. "That's been mentioned and you've admitted she had one. I presume there's lots of fighting and dish throwing?"

"Some fights, sure," said Anderssen, "but no more than is par for the course. And no dish throwing. As Mr. Avalon has pointed out, I'm articulate, and so is she, and we're both pretty good at shouting, but after we work off our steam, we can be just as good at kissing and hugging."

"Then am I to take it, sir, that your wife is *not* the source of your troubles?" said Avalon.

Anderssen fell silent again.

"I must ask you to answer, Mr. Anderssen," said Avalon.

Anderssen said, "She *is* the problem. Just now, anyway. But it's too silly to talk about."

Rubin sat up at that and said, "On the contrary. Till now, I felt that Jeff was just wasting our time over the kind of domestic irritations that we attend these dinners, in part, to escape. But if there's something *silly* involved, then we want to hear it."

"If you must know," said Anderssen. "Helen says she's a witch."

"Oh?" said Rubin. "Has she always claimed this, or just recently?"

"Always. We joke about it. She would say she put me under enchantment to get me to marry her, and that she would cast spells and get me a promotion or a raise. Sometimes, when she is furious, she'll say, 'Well, don't blame me if you blotch out in pimples just because you're going to be that stupid and mean.' That sort of thing."

Rubin said, "It sounds harmless to me. She probably *did* put you under enchantment. You fell in love with her and any woman of reasonable intelligence and looks can make a young man fall in love with her if she works hard enough being charming. You can call that enchantment if you wish."

"But I *do* get the promotions and raises."

"Surely that could be because you deserve them. Do you get the pimples, too?"

Anderssen smiled. "Well, I managed to trip and sprain an ankle and, of course, she said she had changed the spell because she didn't want to spoil my pretty face."

Halsted laughed and said, "You don't really act disturbed at this, Mr. Anderssen. After all, this sort of playacting by a young and vivacious woman isn't unusual. Personally, I find it charming. Why don't you?"

Anderssen said, "Because she pulled it on me once too often. She did something that I can't understand." He threw himself back in his chair and stared sombrely at the table in front of him.

Trumbull bent to one side as though to look into Anderssen's eyes and said, "You mean you think she really is a witch?"

"I don't know what to think. I just can't explain what she did."

Avalon said, forcibly, "Mr. Anderssen, I must ask you to explain just what it was that Mrs. Anderssen did. Would you do that, sir?"

"Well," said Anderssen, "maybe I should. If I talk about it, maybe I can forget it.—But I don't think so."

He brooded a bit and the Widowers waited patiently.

Finally, he said, "It was just about a month ago—the sixteenth. We were going out for dinner, just the two of us. We do that once in a while, and we like to try new places. We were trying a new place this time, the door to which was reached by passing through the lobby of a small midtown hotel. It was an unpretentious restaurant, but we had had good reports of it.—The trouble started in the lobby.

"I don't remember exactly what set it off. In fact, I don't even remember what it was all about, really. What happened afterward pushed it out of my mind. What it amounted to was that we had a—a disagreement. In less than a minute, we would have been inside the restaurant and studying the menu, and instead, we were standing to one side of the lobby, under a plastic potted plant of some sort. I can remember the sharply pointed leaves touching my hand disagreeably when I waved it to make a point. The registration desk was across the way, between the door to the restaurant and the door to the street. The scene is still painted in my mind.

"Helen was saying, 'If that's your attitude, we don't have to have dinner together.'

"I swear to all of you, I don't remember what my attitude was, but we're both of us highly vocal, and we were both of us furious, I admit. The whole thing was highly embarrassing. It was one of those times when you and someone else—usually your wife or girlfriend, I suppose—are shouting at each other in whispers. The words are being squeezed out between clenched teeth, and every once in a while one of you says, 'For Heaven's sake, people are staring,' and the other says, 'Then shut up and listen to reason,' and the first one says, 'You're the one who isn't listening,' and it just keeps on and on."

Anderssen shook his head at the memory. "It was the most intense argument we had ever had up to that time, or since, and yet I can't remember what it was about. Unbelievable!

"Then she suddenly said, 'Well, then, I'm going home. Good-bye.' I said, 'Don't you dare humiliate me by leaving me in public.' And she said, 'You can't stop me.' And I said, 'Don't tempt me, or I *will* stop you.' And she said, 'Just try,' and dashed into the restaurant.

"That caught me by surprise. I had thought she would try to get past me to the door to the street—and I was ready to seize her wrist and hang on. It would have been better to let her go than to make a scene, I suppose, but I was past reason. In any case, she fooled me, and made a dash for the restaurant.

"I was stunned for a moment—two moments—and then I hurried in after her. I may have been twenty seconds behind her.—Let me describe the restaurant. It was not a large one, and it had the deliberate decor of a living room. In fact, the restaurant is called The Living Room.—Are any of you acquainted with it?"

There was a blank murmur about the table, but Henry, who had cleared the dishes with his usual unobtrusive efficiency and was standing by the sideboard, said, "Yes, sir. It is, as you say, a small but well-run restaurant."

"It had about a dozen tables," Anderssen proceeded, "the largest of which would hold six. There were windows with drapes, but not real windows. They had city views painted on them. There was a fireplace in the wall opposite the entrance door with artificial logs in it, and a couch facing it. The couch was real and, I suppose, could be used by people who were waiting for the rest of their party to arrive. At least, there was one man sitting on the left end of the couch. He had his back to me, and was reading a magazine that be held rather high and close to his head as though he were near-sighted. I judged from its typography that it was *Time*—"

Avalon put in suddenly, "You seem to be a good observer and you are going into minutiae. Is this important that you've just told us?"

"No," said Anderssen, "I suppose not, but I am trying to impress on you that I was not hysterical and that I was entirely myself and saw everything there was to see quite clearly. When I came in, about half the tables were taken, with two to four people at each. There may have been fifteen to twenty people present. There were no waitresses on the scene at the moment and the cashier was stationed just outside the restaurant, to one side of the door in a rather unobtrusive recess, so it really did look like a living room."

Drake stubbed out his cigarette. "It sounds like an idyllic place. What was present there that disturbed you?"

"Nothing was present that disturbed me. That's the point. It was what was absent there. Helen wasn't there.—Look, she had gone in. I saw her go in. I am *not* mistaken. There was no other door on that side of the lobby. There was no crowd within which she might have been lost to view for a moment. My vision was entirely unobstructed and she went in and did not come out. I followed in her tracks and entered, at the most, twenty seconds after her—maybe less, but not more. And she was not there. I could tell that at a glance."

Trumbull growled. "You can't tell anything at a glance. A glance will fool you."

"Not in this case," said Anderssen. "Mario mentioned Helen's hair. There's just nothing like it. At least I've seen nothing like it. There may have been, at most, ten women there and not one had red hair. Even if one of them had been a redhead, I doubt she would have been a redhead in quite the fluorescent and lavishly spectacular way that Helen was. Take my word for it. I looked right—left, and there was no Helen. She had disappeared."

"Gone out to the street by another entrance, I suppose," said Halsted.

Anderssen shook his head. "There was no entrance to the street. I checked with the cashier afterward, and with the fellow at the registration desk. I've gone back there since to order lunch and managed to look over the place. There isn't any entrance to the outside. What's more, the windows are fakes and they're solid something-or-other. They don't open. There are ventilation ducts, of course, but they're not big enough for a rabbit to crawl through."

Avalon said, "Even though the windows are fake, you mentioned drapes. She might have been standing behind one of them."

"No," said Anderssen, "the drapes hug the wall. There would have been an obvious bump if she were behind one. What's more, they only came down to the bottom of the window and there are two feet of bare wall beneath them. She would have been visible to mid-thigh if she were standing behind one.''

"What about the ladies' room?'' inquired Rubin. ''You know, so strong is the taboo against violating the one-sex nature of these things, we tend to forget the one we don't use is even there.''

"Well, I didn't,'' said Anderssen, with clear exasperation. ''I looked around for it, didn't see any indication, and when I asked later, it turned out that both rest rooms were in the lobby. A waitress did show up while I was looking around and I said to her in, I suppose, a rather distracted voice, 'Did a redheaded woman just come in here?'

"The waitress looked at me in a rather alarmed way, and mumbled, 'I didn't see anyone,' and hastened to deliver her tray load to one of the tables.

"I hesitated because I was conscious of my embarrassing position, but I saw no way out. I raised my voice and said, 'Has anyone here seen a redheaded woman come in just a moment ago?' There was dead silence. Everyone looked up at me, staring stupidly. Even the man on the couch turned his head to look at me and he shook his head at me in a clear negative. The others didn't even do that much, but their vacant stares were clear enough indication that they hadn't seen her.

"Then it occurred to me that the waitress must have emerged from the kitchen. For a minute, I was sure that Helen was hiding there and I felt triumphant. Regardless of the fact that my actions might induce some of the staff to call hotel security, or the police, even, I marched firmly through a pair of swinging doors into the kitchen. There was the chef there, a couple of assistants, and another waitress. No Helen. There was one small further door which might have been a private lavatory for the kitchen staff, and I had gone too far to back down. I walked over and flung the door open. It *was* a lavatory, and it was empty. By then the chef and his assistants were shouting at me, and I said, 'Sorry,' and left quickly. I didn't see any closets there large enough to hold a human being.

"I stepped back into the restaurant. Everyone was still

looking at me, and I could do nothing but return to the lobby. It was as though the instant Helen had passed through the doorway into the restaurant, she had vanished."

Anderssen sat back, spread his hands in blank despair. "Just vanished."

Drake said, "What did you do?"

Anderssen said, "I went out and talked to the cashier. She had been away from her station for a few moments and she hadn't even seen me go in, let alone Helen. She told me about the rest rooms and that there was no exit to the street.

"Then I went to talk to the room clerk, which demoralized me further. He was busy and I had to wait. I wanted to yell, 'This is a matter of life and death,' but I was beginning to think I would be carried off to an asylum if I didn't behave in a totally proper way. And when I spoke to him, the room clerk turned out to be a total zero, though what could I really have expected from him?"

"And then what did you do?" asked Drake.

"I waited in the lobby for about half an hour. I thought Helen might show up again; that she had been playing some practical joke and that she would return. Well, no Helen. I could only spend my time fantasizing, as I waited, of calling the police, of hiring a private detective, of personally scouring the city, but you know—What do I tell the police? That my wife has been missing for an hour? That my wife vanished under my eyes? And I don't know any private detectives. For that matter, I don't know how to scour a city. So, after the most miserable half hour of my whole life, I did the only thing there was to do. I hailed a taxi and went home."

Avalon said, solemnly, "I trust, Mr. Anderssen, that you are not going to tell us your wife has been missing ever since."

Gonzalo said, "She can't be, Jeff. I saw her two days ago."

Anderssen said, "She was waiting for me when I got home. For a minute, a wave of intense thankfulness swept over me. It had been a terrible taxi ride. All I could think of was that she would have to be missing twenty-four hours before I could call the police and how would I live through the twenty-four hours? And what would the police be able to do?

"So I just grabbed her and held on to her. I was on the point of weeping, I was so glad to see her. And then, of course, I pushed her away and said, 'Where the hell have you been?'

"She said, coolly, 'I told you I was going home.'

"I said, 'But you ran into the restaurant.'

"She said, 'And then I went home. You don't suppose I needed a broomstick, do you? That's quite old-fashioned. I just—*pfft*—and I was home.' She made a sweeping motion of her right hand.

"I was furious. I had gotten completely over my relief. I said, 'Do you know what you've put me through? Can you imagine how I felt? I rushed in like a damn fool and tried to find you and then I just stood around.—I almost went to the police.'

"She grew calmer and icier and said, 'Well, it serves you right for what you did. Besides, I *told* you I was going home. There was no need for you to do anything at all but go home, too. Here I am. Just because you refuse to believe I have the power is no reason for you to begin scolding me, when I did exactly what I told you I would do.'

"I said, 'Come on, now. You didn't *pfft* here. Where were you in the restaurant? How did you get here?'

"I could get no answer from her on that. Nor have I been able to since. It's ruining my life. I *resent* her having put me through an hour of hell. I *resent* her making a fool of me."

Avalon said, "Is the marriage breaking up as a result? Surely, you need not allow one incident—"

"No, it's not breaking up. In fact, she's been sweet as apple pie ever since that evening. She hasn't pulled a single witch trick, but it bothers the dickens out of me. I brood about it. I *dream* about it. It's given her a kind of—superiority—"

Rubin said, "She's got the upper hand now, you mean."

"Yes," said Anderssen, violently. "She's made a fool of me and gotten away with it. I *know* she's not a witch. I *know* there are no such things as witches. But I don't know how she did it, and I've got this sneaking suspicion she's liable to do it again, and it keeps me—it keeps me—*under*."

Anderssen then shook his head and said, in a more composed way, "It's such a silly thing, but it's poisoning my life."

Again there was silence about the table, and then Avalon said, "Mr. Anderssen, we of the Black Widowers are firm disbelievers in the supernatural. Are you telling us the truth about the incident?"

Anderssen said, fiercely, "I assure you I have told you the truth. If you have a Bible here, I'll swear on it. Or, which is better as far as I am concerned, I'll give you my word as an honest man that everything I've told you is as completely true as my memory and my human fallibility will allow."

Avalon nodded. "I accept your word without reservation."

Gonzalo said, in an aggrieved way, "You might have told me, John. As I said, I saw Helen two days ago, and nothing seemed wrong to me. I had no idea—Maybe it's not too late for us to help."

"How?" said Anderssen. "How could you help?"

Gonzalo said, "We might discuss the matter. Some of us may have some ideas."

Rubin said, "I have one, and, I think, a very logical one. I begin by agreeing with Anderssen and everyone else here that there is no witchcraft and that, therefore, Mrs. Anderssen is no witch. I think she went into the restaurant and somehow managed to evade her husband's eyes. Then when he was busy in the kitchen or at the registration desk, she left the restaurant and the hotel quickly, took a taxi, went home, and then waited for him. Now she won't admit what it is she has done in order to stay one-up in this needless marriage combat. My own feeling is that a marriage is useless if—"

"Never mind the homilies," said Anderssen, the shortness of his temper fuse showing. "Of *course* that's what happened. I don't need you to explain it to me. But you skip over the hard part. You say she went into the restaurant and 'somehow managed to evade her husband's eyes.' Would you please tell me just how she managed that trick?"

"Very well," said Rubin. "I will. You came in, looked right and left, and were at once certain she wasn't there. Why? Because you were looking for an unmistakable redhead. —Have you ever heard of a wig, Mr. Anderssen?"

"A *wig?* You mean she put on a *wig?*"

"Why not? If she appeared to have brown hair, your eyes would pass right over her. In fact, I suspect that her red hair is so much the most important thing you see in her that if she were wearing a brown wig and had taken a seat at one of the tables, you could have been staring right at her face without recognizing it."

Anderssen said, "I insist I would have recognized her even so, but that point is of no importance. The important thing is that Helen has never owned a wig. For her to use one is unthinkable. She is as aware of her red hair as everyone else is, and she is vain about it, and wouldn't dream of hiding it. Such vanity is natural. I'm sure everyone here is vain about his intelligence."

Rubin said, "I grant you. Intelligence is something to be vain about. Yet, if it served some purpose that seemed important to me, I would pretend to be an idiot for a few minutes, or even considerably longer. I think your wife would have been willing to slip on a brown wig just long enough to escape your eye. Vanity is never an absolute in anyone who isn't an outright fool."

Anderssen said, "I know her better than you do, and I say she wouldn't wear a wig. Besides, I told you this was a month ago. It was the height of summer and it was a hot evening. All Helen was wearing was a summer dress with only summer underwear beneath, and she had a light shawl to put on against the air conditioning. She was holding a small pocketbook, just large enough to contain some money and her makeup. There was nowhere she could have hidden a wig. She had no wig with her. Why should she have brought one with her, anyway? I can't and won't believe that she was deliberately planning to have a fight, and to trick me in this way in order to achieve a long-term upper hand. She's a creature of impulse, I tell you, and is incapable of making plans of that kind. I *know* her."

Trumbull said, "Conceding her vanity and impulsiveness, what about her dignity? Would she have been willing to duck under one of the tables and let the tablecloth hide her?"

"The tablecloths did not come down to the ground. I would have seen her.—I tell you I've gone back to the restaurant and studied it in cold blood. There is *nowhere* she could have hidden. I was even desperate enough to wonder if she could have worked her way up the chimney, but the fireplace isn't real and isn't attached to one.''

Drake said, "Anyone have any other ideas? I don't.''

There was silence.

Drake turned half about in his chair. "Do you have anything to volunteer, Henry?''

Henry said, with a small smile, "Well, Dr. Drake, I have a certain reluctance to spoil Mrs. Anderssen's fun.''

"Spoil her fun?'' said Anderssen in astonishment. "Are you telling me, waiter, that you know what happened?''

Henry said, "I know what might easily have happened, sir, that would account for the disappearance without the need for any sort of witchcraft and I assume, therefore, that that was, indeed, what happened.''

"What was it, then?''

"Let me be certain I understand one point. When you asked the people in the restaurant if they had seen a red-headed woman enter, the man on the couch turned around and shook his head in the negative. Is that right?''

"Yes, he did. I remember it well. He was the only one who really responded.''

"But you said the fireplace was at the wall opposite the door into the restaurant and that the couch faced it, so that the man had his back to you. He had to turn around to look at you. That means his back was also to the door, and he was reading a magazine. Of all the people there, he was least likely to see someone enter the door, yet he was the one person to take the trouble to indicate he had seen no one. Why should he have?''

"What has all that got to do with it, waiter?'' said Anderssen.

"Call him Henry,'' muttered Gonzalo.

Henry said, "I would suggest that Mrs. Anderssen hurried in and took her seat on the couch, an ordinary and perfectly natural action that would have attracted no attention from a group of people engaged in dining and in conversation, even despite her red hair.''

"But I would have seen her as soon as I came in,'' said Anderssen. "The back of the couch only reaches a person's shoulders and Helen is a tall woman. Her hair would have blazed out at me.''

"On a chair," said Henry, "it is difficult to do anything but sit. On a couch, however, one can lie down."

Anderssen said, "There was a man already sitting on the couch."

"Even so," said Henry. "Your wife, acting on impulse, as you say she is apt to do, reclined. Suppose you were on a couch, and an attractive redhead, with a fine figure, dressed in a skimpy summer costume, suddenly stretched out and placed her head in your lap; and that, as she did so, she raised her finger imploringly to her mouth, pleading for silence. It seems to me there would be very few men who wouldn't oblige a lady under those circumstances."

Anderssen's lips tightened, "Well—"

"You said the man was holding his magazine high, as though he were nearsighted, but might that not be because he was holding it high enough to avoid the woman's head in his lap? And then, in his eagerness to oblige a lady, would he not turn his head and unnecessarily emphasize that he hadn't seen her?"

Anderssen rose. "Right! I'll go home right now and have it out with her."

"If I may suggest, sir," said Henry, "I would not do that."

"I sure will. Why not?"

"In the interest of family harmony, it might be well if you would let her have her victory. I imagine she rather regrets it and is not likely to repeat it. You said she has been very well behaved this last month. Isn't it enough that you know in your heart how it was done so that you needn't feel defeated yourself? It would be her victory without your defeat and you would have the best of both worlds."

Slowly, Anderssen sat down and, amid a light patter of applause from the Black Widowers, said, "You may be right, Henry."

"I think I am," said Henry.

PART II

UNION CLUB MYSTERIES

16

He Wasn't There

In 1980, after I had been writing Black Widower stories for eight years, Gallery magazine (a so-called "girlie" magazine) asked if I would write a short mystery for them in each issue. After I had made it plain that I would not write erotica, I accepted the task. These stories are something like the Black Widower stories, but they are shorter and feature a narrator called Griswold. I have now done forty-six of these Union Club mysteries and I present twelve of them here.

In the case of this first one I offer, the idea wasn't mine. It was suggested to me by Martin Gardner, that wonderful science writer. Generally, ideas that are offered to me are not useful; they are the product of another's mind and don't fit the bent of mine. Gardner's mind, however (and I hope he'll forgive my presumption), is sufficiently like mine for the idea to pass smoothly out of his and into mine. I thank him.

The mood at the Union Club was one of isolation that night as the four of us sat in the library. It was fairly late and we had it to ourselves.

Jennings must have felt that sense of removal from the rest

of the world, for he said dreamily, "If we just stayed here, I wonder if anyone would ever come looking for us."

"Our wives would miss us after a week or two," I said encouragingly. "The dragnet would be thrown out."

"Listen," said Baranov. "You can't rely on dragnets. Back in 1930, a certain Judge Crater stepped out onto the streets of New York and was never seen again. In fifty years, not a clue."

"Nowadays," I said, "with social security numbers, credit cards and computers, it's not that easy to disappear."

"Yes?" said Baranov. "How about James Hoffa?"

"I mean, deliberately," I said. "While still alive."

From the depth of his armchair, Griswold stirred and rumbled slowly to life. "In some way," he said, "it's easier to disappear now, I suppose. With today's increasingly heterogeneous society, its increasingly self-centered people, who's to care if one person, more or less, slips quietly through the mechanical motions of minimal social involvement? I knew a man once the Department was aching to find who simply wasn't there."

Jennings said quickly, "What Department?" but Griswold never answers questions like that.

I wonder [said Griswold] if you ever give thought to the careful putting together of small bricks of evidence into a careful edifice that isolates the foreign agent and neutralizes him. He doesn't have to be taken into custody and shot at sunrise. We have to know who and where he or she is. After that, he is no longer a danger. In fact, he becomes a positive help to us, particularly if the agent doesn't know he is known, for then we can see to it that he gets false information. He becomes *our* conduit and not theirs.

But it's not easy; or, at least, not always easy. There was one foreign agent who flickered always just beyond our focus of vision. Some of us called him Out-of-Focus.

And yet, little by little, we narrowed the search until we were convinced his center of operations was in a particular run-down building. We had his office located, in other words.

With infinite caution, we tried to track him down further without startling him into a change of base, which would mean having to redo all the weary work. We found threads of his existence at the local food stores, for instance, at the newsstands, at the post office, but we could never get a clear description or positive evidence that he was our man.

He remained Out-of-Focus.

We located the name he was using. It was William Smith and that gave us an idea.

Suppose a lawyer were looking for a William Smith who was a legatee for a sizable sum of money. In that case, neighbors would be delighted to help. If someone you know is likely to get a windfall, you *want* to help if only because that might induce gratitude and bring about the possibility of a loan. Smith himself might instinctively stand still for one moment if the possibility of money dangled before him, and even though he would know he was not the legatee, he might not question the search.

A real lawyer, amply briefed by ourselves, moved in to face William Smith—and he wasn't there. He hadn't been seen for days and no one had any information. Only the superintendent of the small building seemed curious. After all, there was the question of the next month's rent, one might suppose.

The disappearance, though frustrating—he always seemed one step ahead of us—at least gave us a chance to institute a legitimate police search. Nothing dramatic: just a missing person's case. A local detective, rather bored, asked to see the apartment. The super let him in.

Two rooms, a kitchenette, a toilet. That was it. And it told us nothing useful about the occupant, except that he might have been a writer—and the super told us that much.

The days passed and no trace of William Smith could be picked up. He was no longer merely Out-of-Focus, he was clean gone, and we all had the rotten feeling he would be forever gone, like Judge Crater, and that he would be more dangerous than ever until we managed to get on the track again.

Then the boss did what he should have done in the first place.

He sent me to look about the apartment.

I was always good at presenting a rather bumbling appearance, even in my younger days. A useful thing, too, because it sets people off their guard. I was sure the super would talk the more freely for feeling sorry for me when I looked about the apartment helplessly.

He made no move to leave after he let me in, and of course I did not ask him to leave. He said, "Still looking for him, huh?"

"Yeah," I said. "I've got to fill out a report."

"His family must be plenty worried. You know he got a legacy or something, and I guess they want the money even if they don't want him."

I said, "I suppose," and kept on looking around.

One room was a library, not a big one, either the room or the library. The books were mostly reference and science books, so I suppose Smith could be considered a science writer—he had to have some cover. They weren't brand-new; some of them looked used. There was also one upholstered couch, one wooden rocking chair, and one end table in the room. That was all except for the bookcases.

The other room also had several bookcases, including one that contained an Encyclopaedia Britannica. It had a large desk, an upholstered armchair, several filing cabinets, an electric typewriter on a typewriting stand with a small swivel chair in front of it, a globe, and the minor paraphernalia of the writer's trade, such as reams of paper; also pens, paper clips, carbon paper, paperweights, envelopes, stamps and so on.

He was a very neat fellow. Everything was in the bookcases or in the filing cabinets or in the desk drawers or on top of the desk. Except for the items of furniture I've mentioned, there was nothing on the floor. Nor were there photographs of any kind and the walls were bare of anything framed.

There had been no useful fingerprints.

I said to the super, "You didn't take anything out, did you?" After all, he had a key.

"Who, me? With the police around? You crazy?"

I said, "You sure you can't describe the guy?"

"You guys asked me a million times. I tried, but he ain't much to look at. You know—just like a million other people."

I grunted. A successful agent has to look like a million

other people or he's useless. They had taken the super to the local police station and had him look at endless pictures to locate someone who looked *like* William Smith and he ended by picking six pictures, and not one of the six looked anything like the other five. Smith remained Out-of-Focus.

There were two closets in the workroom. Clothes, of course. Nothing unusual.

I wandered into the bathroom. The usual toiletries, more or less used.

In the kitchenette, a sparse collection of comestibles in jars and cans. Some cutlery and pans and a can opener. None of it looked very used.

The super shrugged and said, "I suppose he ate out mostly. That's what I told the other guys."

"But you don't know where?"

He shrugged again, "I mind my own business. In this neighborhood, you got to."

"The guys at the station say you claim you talked to him sometimes."

"Well, you know, like when I come to collect the rent, or fix the shower when it leaks. Like that."

"What kind of stuff does he write."

"I don't know. Nothing *I* read, I can tell you that." He sniggered.

I said, "I don't see any books around with his name on them."

He said, "He said once he wrote for the magazines a lot. Maybe he don't write books. I don't think he used his own name, either. I think he said that once."

"What magazines did he write for?"

"I don't know."

"What name did he use?"

"I don't know that either. He never told me and I didn't ask. No business of mine."

"His typing ever bother the neighbors?"

"Nobody ain't never complained. Listen, in this house you could beat up on your old lady at three in the morning and set her to screaming like a banshee, and no one would complain."

"Did *you* ever hear the typing?"

"You mean in my apartment? Nah. I'm two floors down."

"I mean, in the hall?"

"Sure. Once in a while. Very light. An old building like this got good walls."

"Ever see him type?"

"Sure. I'd come to fix something and I'd hear the type-writer going, tap, tap. Like I said, lightly. He'd let me in and then he'd sit down again, and go back to typing. Probably didn't make much money out of it or he wouldn't live here." He sniggered again.

I grunted and left. There were three other neighbors on the floor. None could describe the missing man; all insisted they knew nothing about him. One thought she could hear the typing sometimes, but she never paid any attention. "We keep ourselves *to* ourselves, mister," she said.

They surely did. There was no use pursuing the case any further.

For one thing, we didn't have to. Smith was now clearly *in* focus. Without his knowing it, we knew where he was and who he was and from that point on Smith was useless to the opposition and very useful to us—until such time as the opposition realized his cover had been broken. At that time we took him neatly into custody before they could arrange a fatal accident for him.

But if you don't mind, I'll go freshen my drink.

Griswold made as though to rise, but Jennings pulled his own chair in front of Griswold's and said, "You'll simply have to die of thirst unless you tell us first where and who he was."

Griswold drew his white eyebrows together in an annoyed frown. "You mean it isn't obvious?—There was *no* William Smith. He was a decoy designed to deflect the Department's attention if they ever got too close, and it almost worked. Thanks to one forgotten detail, however, it was clear to me that no one ever used that apartment for writing of any kind, and since the super claimed he had actually seen Smith typing, the conclusion was that it was the super himself who was maintaining the deception and that he was our man. That's all. Simplicity itself."

"No, it isn't," said Baranov. "How could you tell the apartment was never used for writing?"

"It lacked the essential. You can write without a library and without reference books. You can write without a desk. You can write without a typewriter. You don't even have to have ordinary paper. You can write on the back of envelopes or on shopping bags or in the margins of newspapers.

"But, gentlemen, any writer will tell you that there is one object that no writer can possibly do without, and that object was not in the apartment. I told you everything that was in the apartment and I didn't mention that object."

"But what was it?" I demanded.

Griswold's white mustache bristled. "A wastepaper basket! How can a professional writer do without that?"

17

Hide and Seek

A sizable number of my Union Club mysteries are spy stories Griswold himself has been involved with some unnamed Department, and it may sound to some not-very-experienced readers as though I must have some inside knowledge of the world of secret agents

Not so at all. I know nothing about it. I am totally ignorant. I make it all up. I keep waiting for people to write to me and tell me that I've got it all wrong and I will then apologize and say that I'm just writing puzzle stories. So far, though, I haven't been beaten over the head in the matter.

And I like this story because, in my imagination, it describes exactly how staunchly upright, Sunday-school-and-apple-pie agents might act.

"I see," said Baranov, peering slyly in the direction of Griswold, "where two agents have been convicted of searching a place without a warrant."

He paused and neither Jennings nor I said anything. Griswold was at right angles to us, facing tbe fireplace in which a log smoldered, for it was a rather chilly fall evening. For a wonder, he wasn't asleep, for his scotch and soda moved slowly to his lips and then away again. But he said nothing.

Baranov tried again. "This sort of thing makes it hard for law-enforcement agencies to do their work; especially if they must work in secrecy and in the interest of national security."

Another pause. Jennings said in a slightly higher voice, "On the other hand, you can't let law-enforcement agents break the law they are sworn to defend. That puts the liberties of the people in direct jeopardy."

At that point, Griswold swiveled his chair, faced the three of us with his eyebrows hunched over his china-blue eyes and his white mustache twitching. He said, "You're trying to get a reaction out of me and you're wasting your time. It is not so much a question of law as of prudence. They could have done what they did with impunity, if they had been given a direct mandate by those who were entitled to judge when something was a matter of national security. They did not obtain the proper authority, and not merely a search warrant.—Let me tell you. What can hold back an organization far more than just legal constraints is its own set of mind—which can be foolish. For instance—"

He took another delicate sip at his scotch and soda and then went on.

For instance [said Griswold] back in the days when the agency was run by you-know-who, there wasn't an agent who dared lift his voice against any ukase, however ridiculous. After all, senators threw themselves over mud puddles so the chief could use them to avoid getting his shoes muddy, and presidents cowered in the corner when he frowned.

You could tell an agent a mile away by their chief-imposed uniforms. No one else had shirts so white, so glossy, so buttoned-down, or ties so narrow and so neatly centered, or suits so subdued, or waistlines so carefully flat, or hair so short and so neatly parted, or was scented in so masculine a fashion, or seemed so much younger and callower than his years. Well, they might just possibly have been mistaken for Mormon missionaries, but for nothing else.

And of course, they were all in a state of constant terror. It was not so much that they might make a mistake. That might be forgiven. The real fear was that they might make the agency, and the chief, look foolish. For that it was evisceration the first time. There was no forgiveness and the agents knew it.

Naturally, I could never make it with the agency in any official capacity. I wouldn't shave my mustache, which was dark in those days but almost as impressive as it is now, and I wouldn't wear the uniform, and worst of all, I once chose to look over the head of the chief, which was easy to do, and to pretend I didn't see him. He might forget anything else, but he never forgot a slur on his height, however indirect.

It didn't matter. I made out. When things got tough there was many an agency official who came to me for help.

Jack Winslow came to me once, I remember, with an ingratiating smile on his face and some telltale beads of sweat on his forehead, despite the rule that no agent must perspire. Jack Winslow was his real name, by the way, which helped him a lot at the agency. The only better name would have been Jack Armstrong.

He said, "Listen, Griswold, the damndest thing happened today and I'd appreciate it if you would let me have your thoughts on it."

"Tell me what happened," I said, "and I'll tell you if I have any thoughts about it. And I won't tell the chief you asked me."

He thanked me very sincerely for that, but, of course, there was no way I could tell the chief if I wanted to. We were not on speaking terms—which suited me fine.

There's no point in telling you Winslow's story in full detail because he's an awfully tedious fellow. Still is, I understand, though he's retired now. I'll give you the essentials in brief.

The agency had gotten on to the fringes of an operation it was important to stop. They had located a pawn in the game. They could pick him up any time they wanted to, but it would have done them no good. He wouldn't know enough and he could be too easily replaced. If he were left at large, however, he might be used as a wedge that could pry out something far more useful than himself. It was tedious and delicate work, and sometimes this sort of thing was fumbled and no

agent was ever allowed to enjoy that fumble—so Winslow
was in a difficult position.

The goal at this particular time was to spot a relay: the
passage of something important from one person to another.
Two items of information were desired: the manner of the
surreptitious passage, because that could be an important clue
to the system of thought being used by these people; and the
identity of the pick-up, that is, the one who received the item,
for the pick-up was likely, but not certain, to be more important than the transmitter.

The pawn had been maneuvered into accepting something
to put through the relay. It was something that was legiti-
mately important; though not as important as the others had
been led to believe. Still, they were not fools and had to be
fed *something* in order to make them bite. It was important
enough, at any rate, to make the agents prefer not to lose it
without having gained something at least equally important.

The real coup was the shape of the object to be transferred.
Somehow the opposition had been persuaded to order their
pawn to pick up a package which, while not heavy, was six
feet long and about four inches wide. It looked like a pack-
aged fishing rod and there was no way in which it could be
disguised or made to look inconspicuous. Winslow was proud
of this and wouldn't tell me how the trick had been turned,
but I didn't care. I knew that, as a general rule, the people we
fight against are as vulnerable as we are.

There were five agents at various places and in various
forms watching the progress of the pawn or, rather, of the
very conspicuous package. They didn't stay close; they couldn't
have, or they would have been easily spotted by their white
shirts and beautiful gray fedoras in a neighborhood in which
neither was ever seen on the inhabitants.

The pawn walked into a crummy restaurant in this slummish
neighborhood. He had to maneuver the package to get it
through the door, and Winslow held his breath lest he break
it, but he got it into the restaurant in one piece. He stayed
there about five minutes—four minutes, twenty-three seconds,
Winslow told me, since he had stupidly been watching his
watch instead of the restaurant—and then he came out. He

didn't have the package with him, or anything that could possibly have held it.

They expected that. Somehow, though, they expected that it would come out in the hands of someone else, or in *some* fashion, and it never did. After two hours, Winslow got very uneasy. Could they have frightened off the pick-up by being insufficiently clandestine in their surveillance? They couldn't help that as long as they wore their uniform, but that wouldn't protect them against the chief's wrath.

Worse yet, could they have allowed the package—six feet long, four inches wide—to be slipped out under their noses somehow? If so, their careers were finished.

Finally, Winslow could stand no more. In desperation, he ordered his men into the restaurant, and then came the final blow.

"It wasn't there," said Winslow desperately. "It wasn't such a damned big place and the package just wasn't there. As soon as I could see that was the situation, I came here. I remembered you lived only a mile away and hoped you might be in." He looked decidedly grateful I *was* in.

I said, "I suppose I can trust your agents to find it if it's there. Something six feet long isn't exactly a diamond or a piece of microfilm."

"It's not there."

"Could it have been dismembered, taken apart, hidden in parts, or, for that matter, taken out in parts?"

"No, it would then be broken, useless. It had to be intact.—I'm not telling you what it is, mind you."

"I'm not asking and you probably don't know yourself. —Did you look over the people in the restaurant?"

"Certainly. They were the type who were completely un-cooperative, who turn sullen and resentful at the least sign of the law. But there's no way something like that could be hidden on anyone's person."

"By the way," I said, "do you have a search warrant?"

Winslow reddened a bit. "We have a sort of catchall search warrant for safety violations. Never mind about that."

I'm sure it wouldn't have held up in court, but in those days such things weren't questioned.

I said, "Maybe it was taken upstairs."

"There is no upstairs. It's a crummy little one-story greasy-spoon restaurant, between two tenements."

"Well then," I said, "there must be an entrance into one of the adjoining tenements, or both."

"Not a chance. Solid wall, both ways."

"Cellar?"

"We looked through it. A junkyard with some food staples. What we wanted wasn't there."

"Entrances into the adjoining tenements through the cellar?"

"No. Damn it, Griswold, give us some credit for brains."

"Kitchen?"

"Plenty of cockroaches; nothing of what we wanted."

"Egress from the kitchen?"

"There was a door to a back alley, where they put out the garbage—such garbage as they didn't serve—but we had a man there and I assure you he's reliable. People came out long enough to dump garbage and then went back in.—And before you ask, he looked through the garbage cans, something that didn't require much detail work, since an intact sixfoot package would—"

"Stick out like a sore thumb. Rest rooms?"

"I looked through it carefully myself. Personally. Two stalls. I looked in both of them and both were empty, thank goodness. I even checked the urinals, so help me, just in case they were loose and you could slip a six-foot package into the wall behind them. There was a small window, caked with dust and old paint. No way of opening it and the glass was unbroken."

I said, "If the pawn took it in and didn't take it out, then it must still be in the restaurant."

"But it isn't. I swear."

"Then if it isn't there, it must have been sneaked out—a six-foot package with five agents watching."

Winslow winced. "That couldn't be."

"One or the other," I said.

But Winslow looked so miserable, I relented. I said, "Stop suffering, Winslow. I'll save your hide. I know where it is."

And it was where I knew it was. And I *did* save his hide.

Griswold just sat there smiling at us fatuously. Then he

leaned back in his chair as though he were about to close his eyes.

I said, "Come on, Griswold. This time you've gone too far. You couldn't possibly know where it was. I defy you to explain yourself."

"Defy? Defy? Good God, man, it was so easy. I told you what agents were like and what their chief had trained them to be. They might dash fearlessly into enemy fire, they might fearlessly search a place quite illegally. But not one of the chief's men would think of doing anything that was downright unmannerly and crude. They would poke about everywhere but one place—a place they probably didn't even let themselves realize existed."

"What are you talking about?" said I.

"With regard to the rest rooms, Winslow said, 'I looked through *it* carefully myself.' *It*. Singular! It was the men's room, because it had urinals. He mentioned them. Well, a restaurant can't possibly have a men's room without having one for women, too. Our culture demands that symmetry. —But what respectable agent would dream of walking into a ladies' room, even in a slum restaurant?"

"You mean the pawn hid it there?"

"Sure. I imagine he listened to make sure it was empty, then he opened it and propped it up against one corner. Any woman entering that crummy rest room would have neither leisure nor desire to investigate the package, or do anything but go in and get out. Even if the room were not empty, it could be done so quickly, the woman inside would have had no time to scream.—In any case, that's where Winslow and his men found the package when they forced themselves to look."

"But why would he put it there?"

"As it turned out on another occasion, the pick-up was a woman. So why not?"

18

Dollars and Cents

Considering the state of the world today, a great many thrillers deal with terrorism. Again, I am at a disadvantage, since I don't want to be too grisly. (It makes me wonder why I am so intent on writing mysteries—but then when I was in high school I passed through a phase when I wanted to be a surgeon, and if I didn't have that on record, I would refuse to believe it. Anyway, I didn't become a surgeon.)

But here is a terrorist plot and, as you can guess, nobody gets hurt. At least, I demonstrate that I can do it—after a fashion.

"My own feeling," said Jennings, as we sat in the somewhat brooding and melancholy atmosphere of the Union Club library, "is that in order to cut down on terrorist activity, it would be best to bring down an absolute curtain of silence over it."

"You mean," I said sarcastically, "like not letting anyone know that the President has been shot, in case he's shot."

"No," said Jennings, "that's not what I mean at all. I mean you don't release the name of the would-be assassin, or anything about him, or show any pictures, or talk about him. He becomes a nonperson and so does anyone who's involved in terrorist activity. What's more, you cut down on all television coverage particularly, except for the bare announcement of what is happening."

Baranov said, "I take it you are trying to imply that terrorists do it for the publicity involved. Take away the publicity and there's no point in doing it."

"To a certain extent, yes," said Jennings. "Let's say there's some movement for independence for Fairfield, Connecticut. A Fairfield Liberation Committee is established by five nuts. They call themselves the FLC and begin a campaign of tire slashing in Hartford, sending letters to the newspapers taking credit for it. As the tire slashings continue and as the media give it full exposure, not only does this make the five nuts feel powerful and important, but the publicity actually gets lots of weak-minded people to thinking that there may be something to the notion of making Fairfield independent. On the other hand, if the tire slashings are investigated under cover of a strict news blackout—"

"It just isn't possible," I said, "for two reasons. First, the people whose tires are slashed are going to talk, and rumors will get around that will be worse than the truth. Second, once the principle is established that you can set up a news blackout over something like that, you can do it over anything you conceive as dangerous for people to know, and that means *anything*.—Never in the United States, I hope. Sooner the occasional terrorism."

"Besides," boomed out Griswold's voice suddenly, "there comes a time when the blackout may break down. How do you keep it secret when you have to evacuate a hotel in the evening rush hour and must send out every fire engine in the area."

He had both eyes open, the blue of them blazing at us, and he sat erect. It was the widest-awake I'd seen him in years.

"Something you were involved in, Griswold?" I asked.

It began [said Griswold] when a reporter at one of the New York newspapers received a neatly typed, unsigned note, delivered through the mail, to the effect that a dummy bomb had been deposited in a particular room in a particular hotel. The number of the room was given.

The reporter wondered what to do about it, decided it was some sort of gag being pulled on him by one of the jokers about the place, then, after a while, decided he couldn't take the chance. He fished the crumpled letter out of the wastebasket and took it to the police. It meant running the risk of making a fool of himself, but he felt he had no choice.

The police were not in the least sympathetic. They thought it was a gag being pulled on the reporter, too, but *they* had no choice. They sent a member of the bomb squad to the hotel and he was gotten into the room in question. Fortunately, the occupant was not there at the time. Under the eyes of a disapproving hotel official, and feeling very much the jerk, the policeman searched the room rather perfunctorily and, in no time at all, found a box on the shelf in the closet where the extra blankets were stored. On the outside it said in straggly capital letters: BOMB. On the inside was excelsior. Nothing else.

They checked the box for fingerprints, of course. Nothing. The letter was covered by the reporter's fingerprints. It still seemed like a gag of some sort, but more serious than it had been considered at first. The reporter was instructed to bring any further letter to the police forthwith and to try not to handle it. He took to opening his letters while wearing kid gloves.

It turned out to be a useful precaution, because three days later he received another letter. It named another hotel and gave the room number again. He brought it in at once and a member of the bomb squad was sent out. A box filled with bits of cardboard was found in the bathroom, wedged behind the toilet seat. It also said: BOMB.

No fingerprints anywhere.

The police had informed all the general newspapers of the city of what had happened, had asked for no publicity to avert panic, and had urged them all to watch for the letters.

A good thing, too, for the third letter came to a different reporter on a different paper. Same as the others except that this time there was an additional paragraph, which said, "I trust you understand all this is practice. One of these days, it will be the real thing. In that case, of course, I will not give you the room number.''

By that time, the police called me in and showed me the letters.

I said, "What has the lab found out?"

My friend on the force, a police lieutenant named Cassidy, said, "It's an electric typewriter, undoubtedly an IBM product, and the fake bomber is a man of education and an accomplished typist. No fingerprints. Nothing distinctive about either paper or envelope, or about the fake bombs for that matter. The postmark indicates the letters were posted from different places, but all in Manhattan.''

"That doesn't seem particularly helpful.''

Cassidy curled his lip. "It sure doesn't. Do you know how many IBM electric typewriters there are in Manhattan? And how many good typists with some education there are? If he sends enough letters, though, we'll be able to gather more information, I hope.''

I could see nothing further to do, either. I may be extraordinarily good at understanding the trifles that escape others, uncanny even—but it is only everyone else who considers me a miracle man. I make no such claims on my own behalf. Still, I stayed in close touch for the duration of the case.

Additional letters did come and they did contain more information, at least as to motive. The mysterious bomber began to express himself more freely. He was apparently sick and tired of our money-mad society and wanted a return to a purer, more spiritual day. Just how this would be effected by his antics, he didn't say.

I said to Cassidy, "He clearly doesn't have any trouble getting into hotel rooms, but then there's no reason why he should.''

"Oh," said Cassidy, "skeleton keys?''

"Simpler," I said. "Every room is cleaned every day. The cleaning women occasionally wander off on some errand while cleaning and leave doors open, especially if the room is between occupants and there are no personal items in it to be stolen. In fact, I have seen hotel-room doors open and cleaning women nowhere in sight, even when there is luggage and clothing in clear view. No one stops anyone from wandering about hotel corridors so all our bomber has to do is to find an open door.''

The word went out to every hotel in New York that cleaning women were on no account to leave room doors open. Some of the hotels instructed the women to keep an eye out for small boxes and to call anything that seemed suspicious to the attention of the management.

One box turned up and reached police headquarters before the letter announcing it arrived. The letter was delayed in the mail, which is not really surprising.

''I hope,'' said Cassidy dolefully, ''that when it's the real thing, he doesn't announce it by mail. It will never come in time to give us a chance.''

The precautions about leaving doors open slowed up the bomber. The letters were fewer, but they didn't stop altogether. Increasing difficulty seemed to make him more irritable. He denounced the banks and financiers generally. The police psychologists tried to work up a personality profile of the letter writer from what he said. Banks were asked whether anyone had been refused a loan who had reacted to that refusal with unusual bitterness or with threats. Continued analysis of the postmarks on the letters seemed to pinpoint some neighborhoods in preference to others as the bomber's home ground.

Cassidy said, ''If he keeps it up long enough, we'll get him.''

''But one of these days,'' I said, ''it will be the real thing and very likely before we've managed to squeeze him out of the several million who live or work in Manhattan.''

''This may go on quite awhile, though. He may be in no position to make or get a bomb. All this fake-bomb stuff is a way of blowing off steam and when he's blown off enough, he'll stop.''

''That would be nice,'' I said, ''but these days I imagine anyone can manage to get an explosive device or learn to make one, If he tries long enough.''

And then one day, a police officer came hurriedly to Cassidy. He said, ''A guy claiming to be the fake bomber was on the phone.''

Cassidy started to his feet, but the officer said, ''He's off

the phone. We couldn't hold him. He says he'll call again.
—And he says it's the real thing, now."

He called a half-dozen times, at intervals, from different
public coin telephones. The bomb, he said, was placed. The
real bomb. He named the hotel—only the newest in Manhattan. And he named the time for which it was set: 5 P.M. that
day—only the peak of the rush hour.

"You have time to evacuate the hotel," he said in a hoarse
whisper. "I don't want anyone to die. I just want to strike at
property to teach a lesson to those who place property before
humanity."

It was a little after 2 P.M. when he finally gave us the place
and time. There was time to do the job, but considering not
only the evacuation, but the cordoning-off of the area, and the
gathering of fire engines, there would be an incredible tie-up
of Manhattan traffic.

Cassidy, on the phone, did his best. "Look," he said in as
ingratiating a manner as he could manage. "You're an ideal-
ist. You're a man of honor. You want no one hurt. Suppose
we don't manage to get everyone out. Suppose we leave a
child behind despite all we can do. Would you want that on
your conscience? Just let us have the room number. Do that
and I will guarantee you a fair hearing on your grievances."

The bomber wasn't buying that. He said, "I'll call back."

Fifteen interminable minutes later, during which the police
and the bomb squad were making for the spot, we got the
call.

"All right," he said. "Dollars and cents. That's all people
think about. Dollars and cents. If you're too dumb to understand that, then I'm not responsible. *You* are." He hung up.

Cassidy stared at the dead phone. "What the devil did he
mean by that?"

But I had heard the conversation on the conference-call
tie-in and said urgently, "Hold off on the evacuation just a
few minutes. The bomb squad is on the scene by now. Get in
touch with them. I think I've got the room number, and they
may be able to handle the bomb on the spot."

I was right. The bomb, a simple but real one, was easily
dismantled without disturbing anyone in the hotel. We didn't

get the bomber, but he's never tried again. He'd apparently had enough, and since no one was hurt—

Griswold's words trailed off into a soft snore, and Jennings called out, "Don't go to sleep, damn it. Where did you get the room number from? What was the clue?"

I followed my usual practice of stamping on Griswold's nearer foot, but he was prepared for me this time and kicked my ankle rather sharply.

He said, "I *told* you the clue. The bomber said 'dollars and cents' and said if we were too dumb to understand that, *we* were responsible."

"That's a *clue?*" said Baranov. "That's just his standard complaint about the money-mad society."

"It could be that, too, but I felt it to be the clue. I told you the man was an expert typist, and a typist tends to think of words in terms of typewriter keys."

I said, "I'm an expert typist, and the phrase means nothing to me."

"I'm not surprised about that," said Griswold rather nastily. "But if you type 'dollars and cents,' and are pressed for time, you are quite likely to type the symbols '$&c't '" and he made the signs in the air.

"You can do that by tapping three typewriter keys on the IBM electrics with the shift key depressed. If you *don't* depress the shift key, those same keys give you the number 476. Try it and see. So I thought we might gamble on Room 476, and that was it."

19

The Sign

I had to write these Union Club mysteries one a month, with the inexorability of a pendulum ticking off the seconds. Sometimes it meant that I had a hard time coming up with a sensible ending. What I did in such cases was to think of something that I had never dealt with in any of my mysteries and worry it like a dog chewing a rubber bone till something happened.

"I never did a zodiac story," I would say to myself. "Zodiac . . . zodiac . . .zodiac . . . ." Then I came up with the following story and was very pleased, for I was off the hook.—But only for another month.

Baranov said, "According to the forecast in the daily paper, today was a good day for taking financial risks, so I bet a friend of mine fifty cents it wouldn't rain this afternoon and you saw what happened. It poured! The question is: should I sue the forecaster?"

I said with infinite disdain (for I had carefully carried an umbrella), "By forecast, I presume you mean the astrological column?"

"Do you suppose I meant the weather forecast?" said Baranov tartly. "Of course I meant the astrologer. Who else would tell me to take financial risks?"

"The weatherman," said Jennings, "said 'partly cloudy.' He didn't predict rain, either."

I refused to be lured off the track. "Asking a stupid question isn't as bad as falling for stupid mysticism. Since when has astrology impressed you as a substitute for financial acumen?"

"Reading the column is an amusement," said Baranov stiffly, "and I can afford fifty cents."

"The question is whether you can afford intellectual decay. I think not," I said.

In his high-backed armchair in the library of the Union Club where we all sat, Griswold was comfortably asleep to the tune of a faint snoring. But now he attracted our attention when he scraped the sole of his shoe on the floor, as he shifted position without spilling the drink he held in his hand.

I said softly, "You know the way he's always reminded of a story by anything we say. I'll bet if we wake him up and talk about astrology, he won't be able to think of a thing."

Baranov said eagerly, "I'll take that bet. Fifty cents. I want to make it back."

At this point, Griswold's drink moved toward his lips. He sipped daintily, his eyes still closed. He said, "As it happens, I do have an astrological story to tell, so hand over the half-dollar."

The last was addressed to me, and Griswold opened his eyes now to reinforce the remark.

I said, "You'll have to tell the story first."

The most delicate job a spy can have [said Griswold] is recruiting. How do you persuade someone else to betray his country without revealing your own position?

For that matter, the problem is a difficult one for the person being recruited. There have been cases of perfectly loyal government employees—whether civilian or armed service—who allowed recruiting efforts to go on because they honestly didn't understand what was happening, or because they thought the other fellow was joking.

By the time they do report—if they do—there may be people in government intelligence who have grown suspicious of them, and their careers may therefore be inhibited or ruined without their having ever really done anything out of the way.

In fact, I have known cases where the recruiting agent deliberately spread suspicion against his victim in order to enrage the poor person against the government for falsely suspecting him. The person in question is then actually recruited.

The man I am going to tell you about, whom I shall refer to as Davis, avoided the obvious pitfalls.

He carefully reported the first sign of recruitment to his superior, whom we shall call Lindstrom, at a time when, in fact, what had occurred might well have been only idle conversation. It was, however, during those years when Senator McCarthy had inflamed American public opinion and had reduced men in public office to near hysteria.

Davis was, however, a man of integrity. Though he reported the incident, he refused to give the name of the army officer who was involved. His reasoning was that it might indeed have been an innocent conversation and that, in the heat of the times, his testimony could serve to destroy a man unjustly.

That put Lindstrom in a delicate position. He himself might be victimized if things went wrong. Nevertheless, he was a man of integrity too, so he accepted Davis's reserve, assured him he would bear witness to his loyalty in reporting, and in writing (carefully worded, you may be sure) ordered him to play along until he was certain that the person involved was really disloyal and then to give his name.

Davis was worth recruiting, you understand. It was before the days when computers became omnipresent, and Davis was one of the very few who had his finger on the statistical records of the government. He knew where all the dossiers were, and he had access to them. He could conjure up more rapidly than one would believe possible, considering that he had no computer to help him, the intimate details of any one of millions of people.

It would make, of course, an unparalleled instrument for blackmail, if Davis could be persuaded in that direction, but

Davis—a single man who could afford to be single-minded—had thought for only one thing, his hobby.

He was an astrologer. No, not the kind you think. He didn't prepare horoscopes or make predictions. He had a strictly scientific interest. He was trying to see whether, in truth, one could correlate the signs of the zodiac with personal characteristics or with events. He was studying all the people in Leo, all the people in Capricorn and so on, and trying to find out if a disproportionate number of Leos were athletes, or whether Capricornians were prone to be scientists and so on.

I don't think he ever found out anything useful, but it was his obsession. In his department, the standing joke was that he might not know someone's name, but he surely knew his sign.

Eventually, he was convinced that the recruitment was seriously meant, and he grew increasingly indignant. He told Lindstrom that the traitor would be coming to his apartment to work out the final matters, and that he (Davis) would come to Lindstrom at midnight with the full details.

But Davis was not an experienced operator. The recruiter had divined the fact that Davis might be reporting to the authorities and took the most direct action to stop him.

When Davis didn't keep his midnight appointment, Lindstrom went to Davis's apartment and found him there—knifed.

He did not find him quite dead, however. Davis's eyes opened and he stared glassily at Lindstrom. Davis was lying across a small table and trying feebly to reach toward some file cards resting nearby. There were four of them, all somewhat bloodstained.

Davis mumbled, "Should have known—misfit—only sign doesn't fit the name." Then he died.

The next day, at noon, I got a phone call from Lindstrom, begging me to come see him at once! I was reluctant to do so because it would mean missing the first game of the World Series on my brand-new television set, but Lindstrom grew so panicky I had no choice.

When I arrived, Lindstrom was in conference with a young first lieutenant, who looked even more dreadfully disturbed than Lindstrom did. The entire department must have been in turmoil that day. As soon as I came, though, Lindstrom sent the lieutenant away, saying absently after him, "And happy birthday."

He waited till the lieutenant was gone, then opened the door, made sure the corridor was empty and returned.

I said sardonically, "Are you sure this place isn't bugged?"

"I've checked it," he said quite seriously. Then he told me what had happened.

"Too bad," I said.

"Worse than that," he said. "Here's a man who knew of a traitor right in our department and I didn't force the information out of him at once. Now I've lost the man, *and* the traitor and McCarthy will have my head for it."

"Will he find out?" I asked.

"Of course. There must be at least one person in this department who reports to him regularly."

"Do you have any leads?"

"Not really. The four cards on the table were Davis's own cards, the kind he uses to file and cross-file human characteristics against astrological signs.—That's his obsession. Let me explain!" And he did.

I said, "What were the four cards doing there?"

"Perhaps nothing. They were four officers in this department, and I don't know what he was doing with them. Still, he was reaching toward them as though he wanted to take one or point to one and he talked about someone being a misfit, with a sign that didn't fit his name."

"He didn't say his name?"

"No. He was dying, almost dead. His last thought was of his obsession: his damned astrological signs."

"Then you don't know which of the four it is."

"That's right. And as long as we don't know, all four will be under suspicion. That will mean ruined careers if McCarthy zeroes in on it; and for at least three of them, possibly all four, it would be an incredible injustice.—Listen, do you know the astrological signs?"

"Yes, certainly. Aries the Ram, Taurus the Bull, Gemini the Twins, Cancer the Crab, Leo the Lion, Virgo the Virgin, Libra the Scales, Scorpio the Scorpion, Sagittarius the Archer, Capricorn the Goat, Aquarius the Water Bearer and Pisces the

Fish. Twelve of them, in that order. Aries governs the month beginning March 21, and the rest follow, month by month.''

"All right," said Lindstrom, "and the English names are all direct translations of the Latin. I checked that. So Davis's remark about the sign not fitting the name doesn't refer to that. The only alternative is that the name of the sign doesn't fit the name of the officer. The cards had each the name of an officer and, among other personal data, the sign he was born under.''

"Any obvious misfits?''

"No, the four names happen, by a miserable chance, to be utterly common; Joseph Brown, John Jones, Thomas Smith and William Clark; and not one of the names, first, last, or in combination, seems to either fit, or not fit, the person's sign in any way.''

"Does each have a different sign?''

"Yes.''

"And what do you want me to do?''

Lindstrom looked at me out of a face twisted in misery. "Help me. I have the cards. They've been checked for fingerprints and only Davis's have been found. Look them over and see if you can see anything in them that will make sense to you in the light of Davis's final remark.''

I said, "I may have the answer now. That first lieutenant who was here when I came in— You wouldn't talk until you were sure he was gone. You even looked out in the hall to make sure he wasn't hanging about near the door. Was his one of the names on the list?''

"Yes, as a matter of fact. He's Lieutenant Tom Smith.''

"Then I think he's your man. Judging by his face, he was in a bad way. Call him in, with a witness, and tackle him hard, and I'm sure he'll break.''

He *did* break. We had the traitor; and three innocent men (four, counting Lindstrom) were saved.

Griswold looked smug and self-satisfied, and I said, "Griswold, you've made that up. There's no way you could have gotten the answer on the information you had.''

Griswold looked at me haughtily. "No way *you* could have. I said I was called in the first day of the World Series.

That meant early October. Count the astrological signs from Aries, which governs the month beginning March 21, and you'll find that six months afterward comes Libra, which governs the month beginning September 22. Lindstrom wished the lieutenant a happy birthday, so he was born in early October under the sign of Libra.''

"So?'' I said with a sarcastic inflection.

"So Davis said 'the sign doesn't fit *the* name,' not '*his* name.' It wasn't the *man's* name being referred to. The signs are all part of the zodiac and, in Greek, 'zodiac' means 'circle of animals.' You don't have to know Greek to see that the beginning 'zo' is in 'zoo' and 'zoology.' Well, look at the list of signs: ram, bull, crab, lion, scorpion, goat and fish—seven animals. If you remember that human beings are part of the animal kingdom, there are four more: a pair of twins, a virgin, an archer, and a water bearer. Eleven animals altogether. One and only one sign is not an animal, or even alive. It is the *only* sign that doesn't fit the name of zodiac. Since the four names were all officers in the department and I met one officer, who looked miserable and who was a Libra, I thought that *if* he was one of the four, he was also the supposed misfit, and the murderer. Well, he *was* one of the four, and he *was* the murderer.''

So I paid Baranov the half-dollar, and the bum took it.

20

Getting the Combination

I ought to go through my mysteries and count up all the times I've had my characters choose a particular combination out of a number of alternatives. It just fascinates me and I'm not very good at it in real life.

Intelligence tests frequently stick you with a series of numbers and ask you to reason out what the next number ought to be. This is Mensa stuff (and Mensa is an organization of high-IQ people). To be sure, I'm a member of Mensa—the International Vice-President, in fact (a purely honorary position) —but I still have trouble with it.

In any case, I suppose all my Mensa readers will solve the following puzzle immediately—but I don't care.

Baranov arrived when the rest of us were already at the Union Club. He sat down with a triumphant air. "Is Griswold asleep?"

I looked in Griswold's direction and shrugged. "As asleep as he ever is."

"Well, forget him. Remember the time when he told us about solving a mystery by knowing that there was no number under a thousand which, when spelled out, contains the letter 'a'?"

Jennings and I both nodded.

"That got me to thinking. Look, there is an infinite array of numbers. Suppose you spell them out—the whole infinite array—"

"Can't be done," said Jennings. "How can you spell out every one of an infinite number?"

"In imagination," said Baranov impatiently. "Now arrange them all—the whole infinite set of them—in alphabetical order. Which number is first in line?"

Jennings said, "How can you tell unless you look at all the numbers? And how can you look at all of an infinite number?"

"Because there's a pattern to number names," said Baranov. "There may be an infinite set of numbers, but there are only a small number of ways in which their names are formed. The number first in line, alphabetically, is 'eight.' Nothing comes ahead of it. There's no number in the entire infinite array that starts with 'a,' 'b,' 'c,' or 'd,' and how do you like that?"

"What about 'billion'?" I said.

Baranov sneered at me elaborately. "That's not a number name. If you write the number 'one' followed by nine zeroes, that's not 'billion' starting with 'b'; that's 'one billion' starting with 'o.' "

And at this point, Griswold, without seeming to interrupt his soft snore, said, "And what's the last number in line?"

I thought rapidly and was the first to answer. " 'Two.' There are no numbers starting with any letter after 't,' and nothing past the 'w' in second place. The other 'tw's,' like 'twelve' and 'twenty' have an 'e' in third place and come ahead of 'two.'"

I felt that to be an excellent analysis considering that I did it so rapidly, but Griswold's eyes opened and he looked at me with infinite contempt. "You get *zero*," he said. "Let me tell you a story."

I have a friend [said Griswold] who likes to play with numbers. He's not a mathematician and has no talent for mathematics, any more than I have. Still, playing with numbers is fun even if you have no talent for it.

This friend of mine—his name is Archie Bates—used his hobby, in part, as a defense against boredom.

All of us, I suppose, have been trapped in an audience with a speaker delivering a particularly boring address, or with an orchestra playing some piece that does not grip us, or with a play turning out to be unexpectedly maladroit.

What do you do in such a case?

You might fall asleep, but that could be fraught with embarrassment if you are with others before whom you don't want to seem a clod. You might think deep thoughts, but suppose none come to mind?

Well, then, you might do as Bates would and play with numbers. He would count the chandeliers, or the lights, or the ornamental repetitions on the walls and ceilings and ring all the permutations upon the matter that he could. He found it (he frequently told me) the perfect antidote to boredom.

Or he would work up odd sequences of numbers according to some system and ask people to work out the system and predict the next number. He was never profound, you understand, but he was sometimes amusing. For instance, he once presented me with the series of Arabic digits, 8, 5, 4, 9, 7, 6, 3, 2, 0. He pointed out that every digit was included except 1, and asked me where 1 rightfully belonged.

It took me a while to realize he had placed the digits in alphabetical order, if each was spelled out, and that meant 1 belonged between 9 and 7. That was how I could so easily improve on Baranov's puzzle.

It was also possible for Bates's hobby to bring about discomfort and embarrassment, and at one time it did so. —Which brings up an important fact.

Most of the little cases I have presented you with are examples of high crimes: murder, espionage and so on. It is possible, however, to puzzle over something very small and insignificant—and even so that might annoy you and occupy your mind every bit as much as murder might. And, given friendship or interest, I have no objection to being of service in such cases, however minute in importance they might seem to outsiders.

Mrs. Bates called me one day in some agitation and asked me if I would be so kind as to come over at once. She had a problem and thought I might be able to help her. She doubted that anyone else could.

I am not proof against that kind of invitation.

When I arrived, she took me into Bates's study and showed me a safe. It was moderately large, strongly and sturdily made, and had a combination lock that included four dials, each with all the digits from 0 to 9. If each dial were turned so that the central row of the three that were exposed read some appropriate number, one to which the safe was keyed, the door would open. Otherwise it would not.

I said, "What is the problem, Mrs. Bates?"

Mrs. Bates said, "Archie got this safe last week. Why he wants it is more than I know, unless it amuses him to play with the combination. We have no valuables that wouldn't be better off in a bank vault, and we have no secrets that must be hidden away. But there it is."

"Well?"

"He has all our family records inside. I have to make out a check for something I should have made out a check for a month ago, but forgot. I have to get the check into the mail, and postmarked by midnight, or we will be involved in serious complications. The trouble is that I don't know the exact amount, or even the name and address of the people I must make it out to. Not offhand. For that matter, the checkbook is in the safe, too."

"Why is everything in the safe?"

"Because he's safe-happy, that's why. He's got the safe and he has to use it. It's *so* embarrassing."

"You've forgotten the combination, I suppose?"

"I never knew it. He never told me. I can't even call the company that made the safe, because Archie set up the combination himself."

"Why don't you telephone Archie?"

"I would, if I knew where he was. He's in Baltimore, but I don't know where. He usually writes up his itinerary and gives it to me, but this time, I think he just shoveled it into the safe along with everything else."

"But what can I do, Mrs. Bates? I don't know the combination."

She said, "There's a hint. On the floor, right next to the

safe, was a slip of paper. He must have dropped it and didn't notice that he had. On it is one of those series of numbers he plays with. You know the way he does that!"

"Yes, I do."

"Here it is, then."

She handed me a slip of paper on which seven numbers were written in a vertical column: 1, 2, 6, 12, 60, 420 and 840. Underneath the 840 was an asterisk and I knew that it was Bates's habit to use an asterisk to indicate the number that was to be guessed.

"What I think," said Mrs. Bates, "is that the next number in the series is the combination to the safe. He was probably working out one of his series—you know the way he is—and that gave him the idea of making the next number, whatever it is, the combination. The trouble is I don't know the next number. If you start with 1, you must multiply it by 2 to get 2, and that by 3 to get 6, then 2 again to get 12, then 5, then 7, then 2 again. I don't know what you're supposed to multiply 840 by."

I smiled a little and said, "It doesn't matter, Mrs. Bates. Just multiply 840 by each number from 2 to 9, and then try each product. It will take you only a few minutes. In fact, if you start with 0000 and try each number in order up to 9999, you will surely open the door eventually. If you try only one combination each second, you will go through the entire list in 2 3/4 hours and will probably open the door within an hour and a half. Then you can make out the check. This combination system is not a very good one, you see."

Mrs. Bates looked exasperated. "Oh yes, it is. Archie explained that to me. In this make, he said, if you set any combination *except* the right one, and try to open the door, the little number things freeze and can't be moved again until they are unfrozen with a special magnetic key. Archie says that without the key the safe has to be blown open with an explosive."

I said, "And your husband has the key with him, wherever he is, I suppose."

She nodded. "That's right, so I have to figure out the correct combination right off. I just don't have the nerve to make a guess and try. If I'm wrong, then I have to call a locksmith. And even if a locksmith is willing to come right over and blow it open and I make out the check—which I should have done a mouth ago—the safe will be destroyed. I guess Archie would just about kill me.''

''But then what do you expect *me* to do?''

She sighed. ''But isn't it obvious? You're always telling Archie about all the clever ways in which you solve crimes when the police and FBI are stuck, so can't you just look at the series of numbers and tell me what the combination is?''

''But suppose I'm wrong. I may be clever but I'm not a superman,'' I said, for as you gentlemen all know, if I have a fault at all, it is the possession of a certain excess of diffidence and modesty.

''I'm certain you're not,'' said Mrs. Bates coolly. ''If *you* freeze it, however, Archie will have to take it out on you and what do you care?''

I wasn't at all sure that it was safe for me not to care. Bates is a large man with a hair-trigger temper. I doubted that he would actually strike his wife, though he would surely storm at her and berate her mercilessly. I was not at all sure, however, that he might not grant me less consideration, and black my eye for me.

I will admit, however, that Mrs. Bates's apparent certainty that I was not a superman rankled. *I* might say so, but I saw no reason for having *her* take the privilege. So I merely adjusted the four dials to the appropriate number, turned the handle and opened the door for her.

Then, with a rather chilly bow, I said, ''Your husband will have no occasion for anger with either of us now,'' and left.

Griswold snorted grimly at the conclusion of the tale and sipped gently at his scotch and soda. ''I suspect you all saw the proper combination long before I completed the story.''

''Not I,'' I said. ''What is the combination, and how did you get it?''

Griswold snorted again. ''Look at those numbers,'' he said. ''The larger ones look easy to divide evenly in a number of different ways. The first number, 1, can, of course, be divided only by 1 itself. The second number, 2, can be divided by 1 and 2. The third number, 6, can be divided

evenly by 1, 2 and 3. In fact, it is the smallest number that can
be divided by 1, 2 and 3, as you can easily check for yourself.

"It can be divided by 6," I pointed out.

"Irrelevant," said Griswold. "I am speaking of the consecutive digits, beginning with 1, that will serve as divisors.
The fourth number, 12, is the smallest number that can be
divided by each of the first four digits, 1, 2, 3 and 4. It can
also be divided by 6 and 12, but that is irrelevant.

"You see that the fifth number is 60. It can be divided
evenly by 1, 2, 3, 4 and 5; and, as it happens, by 6 also. It is
the smallest number that can be divided by each of the first
six digits. The next number is divided evenly by all the digits
from 1 through 7, and the final number 840, by all the digits
from 1 through 8.

"The next number, which would be the combination, should
therefore be the smallest number that can be divided by all the
digits from 1 through 9. If you multiply 840 by 3, the product
is divisible by 9 and stays divisible by all the smaller digits.
Since 840 multiplied by 3 is 2520, that is the combination.
The number 2520 is the smallest number divisible by all the
digits, 1 through 9, and, as a matter of fact, it happens to be
divisible by 10 as well.—And there you are!"

21

The Library Book

When I was young, my family could not afford to buy books. Consequently, they managed to get me a library card when I was six years old and for about twenty years or so I visited the library regularly.

After that I found I had a respectable income and could afford to buy books. Now my abode is simply littered with books in every room to the point where one of my big problems is to decide which books to give away and whom to give them to.

And yet, somehow I miss the old days. There was something so delightful about going to the library. The anticipation of wandering through the stacks was so exciting. So was walking home with one book under each arm and a third open in my hands (I've never figured out how I avoided being run over while crossing a street.) Anyway, this story is, in a way, a tribute to the old days

I looked about at the other three at the Union Club library (Griswold had smoothed his white mustache, taken up his scotch and soda and settled back in his tall armchair) and said rather triumphantly, "I've got a word processor now and, by golly, I can use it."

Jennings said, "One of those typewriter keyboards with a television screen attached?"

"That's right," I said. "You type your material onto a screen, edit it there—adding, subtracting, changing—then print it up, letter-perfect, at the rate of 400-plus words per minute."

"No question," said Baranov, "that if the computer revolution can penetrate your stick-in-the-mud way of life, it is well on the way to changing the whole world."

"And irrevocably," I said. "The odd part of it, too, is that there's no one man to whom we can assign the blame. We know all about James Watt and the steam engine, or Michael Faraday and the electric generator, or the Wright Brothers and the airplane, but to whom do we attribute this new advance?"

"There's William Shockley and the transistor," said Jennings.

"Or Vannevar Bush and the beginnings of electronic computers," I said, "but that's not satisfactory. It's the microchip that's putting the computer onto the assembly line and into the home, and who made that possible?"

It was only then that I was aware that for once Griswold had not closed his eyes but was staring at us, as clearly wide awake as if he were a human being. "I, for one," he said.

"You, for one, what?" I demanded.

"I, for one, am responsible for the microchip," he said haughtily.

It was back in the early 1960's [said Griswold] when I received a rather distraught phone call from the wife of an old friend of mine, who, the morning's obituaries told me, had died the day before.

Oswald Simpson was his name. We had been college classmates and had been rather close. He was extraordinarily bright, was a mathematician, and after he graduated went on to work with Norbert Wiener at M.I.T. He entered computer technology at its beginnings.

I never quite lost touch with him, even though, as I need not tell you, my interests and his did not coincide at all. However, there is a kinship in basic intelligence, however differently it might express itself from individual to individual. This I *do* have to tell you three, as otherwise you would have no way of telling.

Simpson had suffered from rheumatic fever as a child and his heart was damaged. It was a shock, but no real surprise to me, therefore, when he died at the age of forty-three. His wife, however, made it clear that there was something more to his death than mere mortality and I therefore drove upstate to the Simpson home at once. It only took two hours.

Olive Simpson was rather distraught, and there is no use in trying to tell you the story in her words. It took her awhile to tell it in a sensible way, especially since, as you can well imagine, there were numerous distractions in the way of medical men, funeral directors and even reporters, for Simpson, in a limited way, had been well-known. Let me summarize, then:

Simpson was not a frank and outgoing person, I recall, even in college. He had a tendency to be secretive about his work, and suspicious of his colleagues. He has always felt people were planning to steal his ideas. That he trusted me and was relaxed with me I attribute entirely to my nonmathematical bent of mind. He was quite convinced that my basic ignorance of what he was doing made it impossible for me to know what notions of his to steal or what to do with them after I had stolen them. He was probably right, though he might have made allowance for my utter probity of character as well.

This tendency of his grew more pronounced as the years passed, and actually stood in the way of his advancement. He had a tendency to quarrel with those about him and to make himself generally detestable in his insistence on maintaining secrecy over everything he was doing. There were even complaints that he was slowing company advances by preventing a free flow of ideas.

This, apparently, did not impress Simpson, who also developed a steadily intensifying impression that the company was cheating him. Like all companies, they wished to maintain ownership of any discoveries made by their employees, and one can see their point. The work done would not be possible without previous work done by other members of the company and was the product of the instruments, the ambience, the thought processes of the company generally.

Nevertheless, however much this might be true, there were occasionally advances made by particular persons which netted the company hundreds of millions of dollars and the discoverer, mere thousands. It would be a rare person who would not feel ill-used as a result, and Simpson felt more ill-used than anybody.

His wife's description of Simpson's state of mind in the last few years made it clear that he was rather over the line into a definite paranoia. There was no reasoning with him. He was convinced he was being persecuted by the company, that all its success could be attributed to his own work, but that it was intent on robbing him of all credit and financial reward. He was obsessed with that feeling.

Nor was he entirely wrong in supposing his own work to be essential to the company. The company recognized this or they would not have held on so firmly to someone who grew more impossibly difficult with each year.

The crisis came when Simpson discovered something he felt to be fundamentally revolutionary. It was something that he was certain would put his company into the absolute forefront of the international computer industry. It was also something which, he felt, was not likely to occur to anyone else for years, possibly for decades, yet it was so simple that the essence of it could be written down on a small piece of paper. I don't pretend to understand what it was, but I am certain now it was a forerunner of microchip technology.

It occurred to Simpson to hold out the information until the company agreed to compensate him amply, with a sum many times greater than was customary, and with other benefits as well. In this, one can see his motivation. He knew he was likely to die at any time and he wanted to leave his wife and two children well provided for. He kept a record of the secret at home, so that his wife would have something to sell to the company in case he did die before the matter was settled, but it was rather typical of him that he did not tell her where it was. His mania for secrecy passed all bounds.

Then one morning, as he was getting ready to get to work, he said to her in an excited way, "Where's my library book?"

She said, "What library book?"

He said, *"Exploring the Cosmos* I had it right here."

She said, " Oh. It was overdue. I returned a whole bunch of them to the library yesterday."

He turned so white she thought he was going to collapse then and there. He screamed, "How dare you do that? It was *my* library book. I'll return it when I please. Don't you realize that the company is quite capable of burglarizing the home and searching the whole place? But they wouldn't think of touching a library book. It wouldn't be mine."

He managed to make it clear, without actually saying so, that he had hidden his precious secret in the library book, and Mrs. Simpson, frightened to death at the way he was gasping for breath, said distractedly, "I'll go right off to the library, dear, and get it back. I'll have it here in a minute. Please quiet down. Everything will be all right."

She repeated over and over again that she ought to have stayed with him and seen to it that he was calmed, but that would have been impossible. She might have called a doctor, but that would have done no good even if he had come in time. He was convinced that someone in the library, someone taking out the book, would find his all-important secret and make the millions that should go to his family.

Mrs. Simpson dashed to the library, had no trouble in taking out the book once again and hurried back. It was too late. He had had a heart attack—it was his second, actually—and he was dying. He died, in fact, in his wife's arms, though he did recognize that she had the book again, which may have been a final consolation. His last words were a struggling "Inside—inside—" as he pointed to the book.—And then he was gone.

I did my best to console her, to assure her that what had happened had been beyond her power to control. More to distract her attention than anything else, I asked her if she had found anything in the book.

She looked up at me with eyes that swam in tears. "No," she said, "I didn't. I spent an hour—I thought it was one thing I could do for him—his last wish, you know—I spent an hour looking, but there's nothing in it."

"Are you sure?" I asked. "Do you know what it is you're looking for?"

She hesitated. "I *thought* it was a piece of paper with writing on it. Something he said made me think that. I don't mean that last morning, but before then. He said many times 'I've written it down.' But I don't know what the paper would look like, whether it was large or small, white or yellow, smooth or folded—*anything!* Anyway, I looked through the book. I turned each page carefully, and there was no paper of any kind between any of them. I shook the book hard and nothing fell out. Then I looked at all the page numbers to make sure there weren't two pages stuck together. There weren't.

"Then I thought that it wasn't a paper, but that he had written something in the margin. That didn't seem to make sense, but I thought *maybe*. Or perhaps, he had written between the lines or underlined something in the book. I looked through all of every page. There were one or two stains that looked accidental, but nothing was actually written or underlined."

I said, "Are you sure you took out the same book you had returned, Mrs. Simpson? The library might have had two copies of it, or more."

She seemed startled. "I didn't think of that." She picked up the book and stared at it, then said, "No, it must be the same book. There's that little ink mark just under the title. There was the same ink mark on the book I returned. There couldn't be two like that."

"Are you *sure?*" I said. "About the ink mark, I mean."

"Yes," she said flatly. "I suppose the paper fell out in the library, or someone took it out and probably threw it away. It doesn't matter. I wouldn't have the heart to start a big fight with the company with Oswald dead.—Though it would be nice not to have money troubles and to be able to send the children to college."

"Wouldn't there be a pension from the company?"

"Yes, the company's good that way, but it wouldn't be enough; not with inflation the way it is; and Oswald could never get any reasonable insurance with his history of heart trouble."

"Then let's get you that piece of paper, and we'll find you a lawyer, and we'll get you some money. How's that?"

She sniffed a little as though she were trying to laugh. "Well, that's kind of you," she said, "but I don't see how you're going to do it. You can't make the paper appear out of thin air, I suppose."

"Sure I can," I said, though I admit I was taking a chance in saying so. I opened the book (holding my breath) and it was there all right. I gave it to her and said, "Here you are!"

What followed was long drawn out and tedious, but the negotiations with the company ended well. Mrs. Simpson did not become a trillionaire, but she achieved economic security and both children are now college graduates. The company did well, too, for the microchip was on the way. Without me it wouldn't have gotten the start it did and so, as I told you at the beginning, the credit is mine.

And, to our annoyance, he closed his eyes.

I yelled sharply, "Hey!" and he opened one of them.

"Where did you find the slip of paper?" I said.

"Where Simpson said it was. His last words were 'Inside —inside—' "

"Inside the book. Of course," I said.

"He didn't say 'Inside the book,' " said Griswold. "He wasn't able to finish the phrase. He just said 'Inside—' and it was a library book."

"Well?"

"Well, a library book has one thing an ordinary book does not have. It has a little pocket in which a library card fits. Mrs. Simpson described all the things she did, but she never mentioned the pocket. Well, I remembered Simpson's last words and looked inside the pocket—and that's where it was!"

22

Never Out of Sight

Innumerable mysteries have involved the breaking of a "perfect alibi." Dorothy Sayers once had the solution to a mystery depend on the meshing together of railroad timetables to make it possible for some character to be at a spot where it seemed he could not possibly be. It was one of her duller stories.

Every other writer has attempted to produce ingenious ways of showing that a character supposed to be in one place could actually be in another. And that, in itself, poses a pretty problem. Can a writer think of a way of breaking an alibi that has never been used? Not having read every mystery ever written, I can't be sure I've found a new way, but certainly I have one that's not like any I've ever come across. And here it is.

I had arranged it with the other two, just to see what would happen. I walked into the Union Club library that Tuesday night with my copy of John Collier's *Fancies and Goodnights*, which I was re-reading attentively with a view to sharpening my style. Jennings arrived next with copies of *Time* and of

Newsweek, sat back, crossed his legs, and began to read in competition with me. Finally, Baranov showed up with a small chess set and took to working out combinations.

Not one of us said a word. Neither did we acknowledge each other's presence.

Griswold was there before any of us arrived, of course, as he always was. (Sometimes I think he lives in that library.) He was already dosing, and his hand, holding its scotch and soda, was resting on the arm of his tall armchair.

I watched out of the corner of my eye as he grew increasingly restless in the silence. There was no bet that he would speak, even though not one of us gave him a lead-in. We were all sure of that. The bet was: Which one of us would be the occasion?

Finally, Griswold cleared his throat interminably, opened his piercing blue eyes wide, and said, in his deep voice, "Conducting espionage operations is, of course, like chess," and Baranov won the five dollars.

As agreed, we continued our silence and, as we were certain, that did not stop Griswold.

As a case in point [said Griswold], we might consider the case of Sanford Brown. That is not his real name, of course, for I would not want to add to his troubles. He was a minor functionary in a particular government bureau, but even minor functionaries, by virtue of being on the spot, can become privy to matters that are not really for their eyes and ears, and can therefore become of interest to the other side.

The claim made by those who later dealt with the case was that he was recruited by the other side. Exactly what it was that gave the other side its handle, I'm not certain. Brown was underpaid, naturally, as are most government employees. It was possible he had grievances against those he worked with. He was out of sympathy with many of the stands taken by the government, as are all of us. That, however, is all rationalization. You must also allow for impulse, and for the kind of motive that is best described by "I don't know why I did it!", which, often enough, is literally true.

In any case, the Department put him under observation. Exactly what it was that first roused suspicion against Brown,

I don't know. I was never told and I never bestirred myself to find out, but agents began to investigate his background, to question in discreet fashion those who knew him, and to make sure they knew exactly where he was at all times and whom he talked to.

It was about this time that the Department became aware of a new enemy agent, a woman who was quite attractive and who spoke English perfectly. They wondered if this were a matter of sexual recruitment. That happens, too. It became clear, however, that the two had not ever met and yet—they might possibly meet in the future.

The Department went to great pains to give her full leeway, to make her seem free of all surveillance, but both were watched. And then Sanford Brown spent a day at an amusement park, which seemed out of character to him. The enemy agent entered the amusement park and, after a few hours, left the amusement park. It was difficult to keep both under constant watch at all times in the moving crowds and, although it was possible that the two had met, no one actually saw them together. However, she was arrested on emerging and she was not quick enough to destroy what she was carrying. It was microfilm that Brown was in a position to get and that she was otherwise in no position to have.

Brown was suspended from his post and the enemy agent was ordered out of the country. Brown, of course, denied everything, and found himself in limbo. The Department could not *prove* wrongdoing. There was no real evidence the microfilm had been in his possession or that he had transferred it to the enemy agent, but the circumstances of the case were too strong to allow him to continue in his position.

His lawyer came to visit me and brought with him a strikingly beautiful young woman, rather smolderingly Mediterranean in appearance.

The lawyer was an old friend of mine and I felt I had to disabuse him at once. I said, "My friend, I have no influence with the Department. I am in their perennial bad book, even though they come to me in an occasional emergency. They have not done so in connection with your client."

The lawyer said, "I have not come to you for influence, but for advice. If this thing comes to trial, he cannot be

convicted and the Department knows it, so they won't bring
him to trial. They will simply allow him to rest under suspicion and ruin his career and, quite possibly, his life. I want to
prove his innocence.''

"How? Is there someone else from whom the enemy agent
could have obtained the microfilm, and can you demonstrate
that?''

"No, but I can prove that she could not have obtained it
from Brown.''

"How?''

"This young lady is Carla Fuentes, and she is his fiancée.
She was with him in the amusement park that day.''

Carla spoke for the first time. Her soft voice had no accent,
but rather the shadow of one. It sounded as though there were
a faint, distant echo of Spanish that could not quite be heard
by the ear. I found it exceedingly attractive. She said, "And I
was with him all day. All day! He was never out of my
sight.''

"Indeed?'' I said, "When did you enter the amusement
park?''

"At 10 A.M. when it opened.''

"And how long were you there?''

"Till about 8 P.M. We had lunch there and dinner there and
then we left. We arrived together. We left together. In between arriving and leaving, we remained together.''

"And in all this time, Mr. Brown never spoke to anyone
else?''

"He might say, 'I beg your pardon,' when we bumped
someone, or ask, 'Where is the shooting gallery?', but I'm
told that the person with whom he is suspected of having
dealt was a fine-looking woman.''

"I've heard that,'' I said cautiously. "I haven't seen her.''

"Well, you can be quite certain, he spoke to no fine-
looking woman. Had he done so, I assure you I would have
been aware of it. From 10 A.M. to 8 P.M. he was never out of
my sight and he spoke to no woman at all, especially no
fine-looking woman.''

"Tell me,'' I said. "Why were you at an amusement park
for ten hours? Is that a usual way of spending the day for
either of you?''

"Of course it isn't—but we had just gotten engaged. We were in love. For a day, we were mad and we spent it madly—rides and games and trying to win foolish prizes and walking hand in hand and laughing our way through the tunnel of love. For one day we were children and it was marvelous. We would never have such a day again and on that day his life was blasted—" She looked uncommonly close to tears.

I had to go on, however. "The tunnel of love. Darkness. Could it be that your fiancé used the day for another purpose as well? A quick transfer in the dark? Something disposed on his person in such a way that his pocket might be picked?"

The lawyer said quickly, "That is not likely. The government itself admits that the enemy agent and Mr. Brown had never met. She would have to identify herself. Brown, if he were guilty, could scarcely allow a transfer to anyone but a known and identified agent, and for that there was no opportunity."

"None," said the young lady flatly. "I have asked for a lie-detector test and have passed."

"That is correct," said the lawyer.

"Then what is the problem?" I asked.

"The government will not accept it," said the lawyer. "Their attitude is that Miss Fuentes, as the accused man's fiancée, is not a trustworthy witness; that she would lie to save him."

"Wouldn't you?" I asked her point-blank.

Her chin lifted. "Whether I would or would not is not in question. The fact is, I am telling the truth, and the lie detector bears me out."

The lawyer said, "If the matter came to trial, we are convinced the jury would believe Miss Fuentes. Her background, her character, her manner would all speak for her. We cannot force a trial, however. Mr. Brown is not being punished. He is merely being relieved of his position and is left under a cloud."

"That is punishment. You could sue, could you not?"

"It would take years. The expense would be inordinate. Reinstatement by that means would come too late."

"What can I do?"

"Griswold, you are a clever man. Can you think of no way that would convince the government that Miss Fuentes is telling the truth, that her account should be accepted, that Mr. Brown should be reinstated now?"

I leaned back in my chair. My sympathies were entirely with Miss Fuentes. I believed that she was dreadfully in love and I envied young Brown, who (I felt very strongly) did not deserve her. I believe that she believed her story and that the lie detector had correctly recorded her belief.

But what could I do?

I said, "Miss Fuentes, you were at the amusement park from 10 A.M. to 8 P.M.?"

"Yes."

"You did not in this interval leave the park?"

"No."

"You did not at any time go to your apartment, or to his?"

"No."

"You did not go to any private home?"

"No."

"And he was in your sight during all this time?"

"Not only in my sight, but in my grasp almost all the time. I do not recall even letting go of his arm or his hand or his waist for more than a moment or two. On the carousel, to be sure, we were on separate but adjacent horses."

"Miss Fuentes," I said, "there is nothing I can do. The alibi you offer, though sincere, and apparently airtight, can be broken easily by any lawyer who thinks a bit; by your own even."

She and her lawyer asked, simultaneously and with equal indignation, "How?"

I had to tell them. It was no pleasure for me. And, of course, it broke them. My feeling is that Brown *was* guilty, but the government never pursued it and he is fortunate to be left merely under a cloud. I remain terribly sorry for Miss Fuentes, however, who, thanks to social convention, did not realize her testimony was patently false.

I said indignantly, "How did you know her testimony was false, you old fraud?"

Griswold said calmly, "I don't expect *you* to see that. But bend your feeble brain to the matter. Miss Fuentes was in a public place for ten consecutive hours. One doesn't speak about such things in polite society, so one forgets—honestly forgets. Did she never have to urinate? Did she never visit the ladies' room in the course of the ten hours?''

''Oh,'' I said, abashed.

''Of course she did,'' said Griswold, ''and perhaps more than once. And he visited the men's room, though that's less important. When Miss Fuentes was forced to the ladies' room in a public place, he simply could not accompany her. They *had* to be separated. She was young. She was in love. She wanted to look lovely and lovable. She adjusted her makeup. She fiddled with her hair. She would take ten minutes. In that time, if the enemy agent kept him in view, she could approach him, identify herself, and make off with the microfilm. Our own agents might miss that meeting and there you are.''

There was silence and then Baranov said, ''But how does that illustrate the fact that conducting espionage operations is like chess?''

And Griswold said haughtily, ''Who said anything about chess?''

23

The Magic Umbrella

Some years back I bought a cheap umbrella that was so small I could put it into my raincoat pocket. After a year or so, I couldn't help but notice that whenever I carried this umbrella, it never rained. It rained when I didn't carry it or when I had another umbrella, but not when I carried it. I took to calling it my "magic umbrella" and boasted about it in a manner entirely unsuitable to someone who was as proud of his rationalist philosophy as I am.

Eventually, of course, I did get rained on and, after withstanding the raindrops for quite a while because I didn't want to spoil my magic umbrella's record, I was forced to open it up.

I made up for the disappointment, however, by writing a story about a magic umbrella.

Jennings was the last to arrive, and he shook his hat with an air of disgust. Water sprayed this way and that.

"It started raining just three minutes ago," he said. "It was just in time to catch me in the last couple of blocks.

Naturally, it was when I decided to walk, and naturally, I didn't have my umbrella."

I had looked out the tall windows of the Union Club library just before he had walked in—in fact, I saw him making the last block in an undignified run—and I said, "It's just a shower. It won't last long." (I was hoping I was right, for I didn't have an umbrella either.)

Baranov said with disgusting smugness, "I always carry a folding umbrella at the least sign of rain. It fits into my raincoat pocket and is no trouble at all. It's small, of course, and just fits one, so I can't offer either of you a corner." He sounded exactly like Aesop's ant admonishing the grasshoppers for having loafed away the summer.

Jennings, still brooding on the injustice of the universe, said, "I swear that there's a full-time flunky in heaven who has nothing to do but notice when I leave home without an umbrella, so that he can make it rain."

That gave me a chance to take out my irritation on him. "Have you kept a statistical account? I'm sure you didn't carry an umbrella yesterday when you left your place, and it was brilliant sunshine all day."

At that moment Griswold stirred in his tall, winged arm-chair, brought his scotch and soda to his lips, wiped his mustache, and said, "I knew of a magic umbrella once."

"A *magic* umbrella?" I said.

His ice-blue eyes pierced me and he said, "I see you are all dying to hear the story of the umbrella that kept off the rain and never had to be opened."

"Actually, we aren't," said Baranov.

Since you insist [said Griswold], let me tell you the story of the umbrella that kept off the rain and never had to be opened.

Actually, it is the story of two old men, who had been fast friends for forty years and who quarreled unreasonably over a petty matter with the unforgiving fury that only those who have been fast friends for forty years could show.

And one of them came to me. This was not surprising. In those days, I was much more active than I am now and it somehow became well known that I was helpful to the police now and then. (One wonders how such news manages to leap mysteriously from person to person; certainly *I* never said anything.) Some even thought I was a detective myself and would come to me with some small problem. And when I helped them, as I sometimes did, the tale would spread and my reputation would become even more exalted.

I was sitting on a park bench, reading, on a late autumn day when the air was unseasonably mild and the sun's warmth was welcome, and then one of the old men took his seat next to me. It was Mr. Levy. I knew him well. We had encountered each other in the park often and, on occasion, I had watched him playing at chess with his perennial opponent— the other old man. They kept meticulous records and I think the score at that time was something like 1,234 to 1,205—I don't remember in whose favor. They were very well matched and, though they were not very good chess players, they played with the concentration and ferocity of grand masters, so that it did one's heart good to watch them and to listen to their picturesque threats of chessboard slaughter as they moved their pieces.

Levy said diffidently, "Mr. Griswold, I have a problem. Maybe you could help me."

"I can try," I said cautiously, putting down my book. "What's the problem?"

"It's Myerson, that idiot, that bum—"

"You mean your friend? The one you've played thousands of chess games with?"

"For years we've been playing chess. Why I wasted my time on him, I'll never know. A foolish person, you have no idea. How his two sons can both be doctors is a mystery."

"Well, what has Myerson done?"

"He's got a magic umbrella, can you imagine? That's what he calls it, a magic umbrella. Last spring—this is what he says—he was going somewhere and it suddenly looked like rain and he didn't have an umbrella, so he bought a small, cheap folding umbrella with an aluminum handle, and it cost only four dollars. So it kept on looking like rain, but it didn't rain, and he never had to open the umbrella. A clear waste of four dollars, it sounds like to me."

"At least he had a feeling of security. That's worth something."

"Security? Listen, that idiot is so insecure that—But never mind. I'm talking about the umbrella. He carried it a few more times when it looked like rain, and it never rained, and finally he began talking about it. It was a magic umbrella, he said. It kept off the rain. He said he *never* had to open it; he just put it in his pocket or under his arm and it didn't rain. Never, he said. It was all he would talk about, day and night. Such a bore!

"Sometimes it would get cloudy when we were playing chess in the park. Some dinky little cloud would get in the way of the sun. Right away, he would say, 'It's all right, Levy. I've got my magic umbrella. Don't try to get out of this game because it's not going to rain. Stay right here and be slaughtered.'

"Magic umbrella here; magic umbrella there. He would get me so nervous with this silly talk, I would lose the game sometimes, just from nervousness. That's why he did it. He has no decency, that Myerson."

I said, "Sometimes when you played and it got cloudy, did it actually start to rain, even though he had this umbrella of his?"

Levy looked chafed. "No, not actually. It encouraged his foolishness each time that happened."

"Surely, there are times when it actually does rain. We haven't been suffering any drought, you know."

"Of course it rains. So when it rains, Myerson doesn't go out of the house. Or if he does, he carries a regular umbrella. I saw him once in the rain with a regular umbrella, and I said to him, 'Aha, Myerson, and what's with the magic umbrella? It's suddenly not magic?' And he said, 'It's magic to keep the rain away, not to stop it after it has started to rain.' "

"Actually," I said, "there's no magic involved. You are old and experienced men who have been living in this city all your lives. You know when it looks *sure* that it will rain and when it looks as though, even with clouds, it won't rain. What's more, there are weather reports to listen to. I'm sure that Myerson only carries his magic umbrella in cloudy weather when he is quite certain it won't rain."

Levy shook his head. "You know that and I know that, but how are you going to explain to Myerson? Anyway, I'll tell you what I did. A few weeks ago, I came across umbrellas exactly like Myerson's in a department store. So I bought one. And it only cost me three dollars and fifty cents, a clear saving of half a dollar. After that, I had a magic umbrella, too. And listen, I've never had to open it. I never even touched it. I made them put it into my portfolio where I keep my chess board, and it's been there ever since. I haven't even looked at it. It's just there. And, to tell you the truth, I haven't been caught in the rain since I bought it. So I tell Myerson I have a magic umbrella, too. Naturally, it irritates him, and *good*. He *should* be irritated."

"So what is the problem, Mr. Levy?"

"So last week, Myerson was caught in the rain."

"When he was carrying his magic umbrella?"

"Absolutely. That stubborn idiot wouldn't open it and he got good and soaked, and when I found out, I laughed. Wouldn't *you* have laughed, Mr. Griswold?"

"Possibly," I said.

"So he got mad. Very mad. Listen what he says. He says I bought the umbrella, and when he wasn't looking, I switched them, so that now *I* have the magic umbrella and he has a piece of trash. He won't speak to me now, he won't play chess, and good riddance, except—" He looked to the right and left to make sure he wouldn't be overheard. "Except, I miss the chess—and him, too, the idiot he is."

"Did you by any chance switch umbrellas?" I asked.

He stared at me with a hurt expression. "Mr. Griswold, my word of honor. The same umbrella I bought is in my portfolio right now. I haven't even looked at it, let alone touched it. For all I know, I can't even open it, or it will fall apart if I lift it out. I did *not* switch."

"And you're sure it's the same umbrella in appearance."

"Yes. That's why I bought it. They're *precisely* the same. How can one be magic and the other not? That Myerson is a foolish man."

"Is it possible that Myerson stained his, or tore it, or put a chip in the handle?—something that can distinguish between the two."

Levy shook his head. "I don't think so. He never opened his either, not even when he was caught in the rain, that stupid moron."

"Well, what is it you would like me to do, Mr. Levy?"

"Explain to him, somehow, I didn't switch and let's be friends again. It's my curse. With him, I have to be friends."

"If he doesn't want to believe it, Mr. Levy, if his feelings are badly hurt, there may be nothing we can do. Perhaps you should just say you switched them, and then exchange umbrellas. Then he'd be happy and—"

But Levy's eyes opened wide and he said, "Never! I wouldn't give in like that. I did *not* switch, and I will not say I did. You don't know the man. He will hold it over my head for the next fifty years, we should only live so long."

I sighed. "Well, let's try. There's one chance. Is he in the park?"

"Where else? He sits here so when I pass he can move to one side like he doesn't want my shadow should fall on him. If I believed in the evil eye—"

We found Myerson without trouble. He looked at Levy with contempt and said, "Watch out, Mr. Griswold. If you deal with *certain* people in this park, you better count your change when you're finished."

I had a hand on Levy's elbow and a tightening of pressure kept him from answering hotly. I said, "Mr. Myerson, I am told by Mr. Levy that you suspect him of switching his umbrella with yours."

"*Suspect?* He *did.*"

"Suppose I prove to you that he did not switch. Will you both dismiss the whole matter, promise never to refer to it, and be friends again? It is silly to abandon forty years of friendship over such a small matter."

"It's not a small matter," said Myerson intransigently, "and how are you going to prove he didn't switch?"

"I'll leave it to you," I said. "Mr. Levy says he has never touched his umbrella from the moment that he bought it—"

"Not *even* when I bought it. Plain and simple, I never touched it. I have no fingerprint on it," said Levy.

I said, "So you take it out, Mr. Myerson and look at it. If

you're satisfied it is Mr. Levy's umbrella, let that be the end of it.''

Myerson sneered. "So let me see the nudnick's portfolio."

I handed it to him. It was a gamble, of course, but it paid off. Myerson had no choice but to admit error, and it did my heart good to see them shaking hands while trying to hide their tears. When I left, Levy had taken out his chessboard, and they were setting up their pieces and each was vowing checkmate in ten moves. I believe they remained fast friends till their dying day, and neither ever referred to a magic umbrella again.

Baranov said, "I thought you said both umbrellas were identical."

"They were," said Griswold.

"Then how could Myerson tell they weren't switched?"

Griswold finished his scotch and soda and shook his head pityingly. "I told you that Levy had sworn he had never touched the umbrella, even when he bought it. The salesman had placed it in his portfolio. I took the chance that he was telling the truth. In that case, it was very likely that the price tag was still on it. I told you that Myerson had spent four dollars for his umbrella, but that Levy had managed to get his for three dollars and flfty cents.

"When Myerson took it out and found a three-fifty price tag on it, he had to admit it wasn't his umbrella. Could anything be simpler?"

24

The Speck

Altogether, Gallery published thirty-seven of my Union Club mysteries in thirty-seven months, but then there was a change of editor and of publisher and the new people knew not Joseph. They decided they had had enough of me and said they didn't want any more.

It didn't matter to me. I could go back to my Black Widowers (which I had neglected because of the necessity of turning out a monthly mystery) and I could even continue to write an occasional Union Club mystery and sell it to EQMM also.

This I did. I have now sold no fewer than nine Union Club mysteries to EQMM, and the following is one of them, written, as you can guess, after I had visited Montreal on a speaking engagement.

Jennings pointed it out within five minutes of my arrival at the Union Club that night.

"You've got a speck on your shirt," he said. "Looks like tomato sauce.—It's right in front. Your jacket doesn't hide it," he added gratuitously.

I scowled at him. "I know it's there. A fresh shirt, too. I put it on just before going to dinner this evening. And I've had comments on the matter from my wife, thank you. She wanted me to change again."

Baranov said, "And you very rightly told her that you were going to spend your usual evening with your friends and it didn't matter how filthy-sloppy you were and, of course, she agreed."

They were baiting me, obviously. I knew they were, and yet I couldn't help responding. "It's a tiny speck," I said heatedly, "lost amid acres and acres of fresh and gleaming shirtfront. Why the devil make a fuss about it? Even with the speck, my shirt is probably cleaner than any other in the room. Look at Griswold," I said, pointing to where the old man nodded in his chair, his scotch and soda held firmly in his hand by reflex action. "He must have a pint of scotch and soda soaking various parts of his shirt."

That was pure slander, of course, since no one had ever seen Griswold spill a drop of any drink he held, but I had to strike out, if only because I was furious with myself. Could I never eat dinner without sending a droplet of sauce or gravy flying in my own direction?

Griswold, to my total lack of surprise, had heard it all. One blue eye opened under its shaggy white eyebrow and he said to me, "A speck, however small, can be of key importance. Not in your case, of course, for you probably have, on your clothes, the finest collection of gravy drenchings in the world and one more doesn't matter. In other cases, however—" He shrugged, sipped with exaggerated care at his drink, and composed himself as though to sleep again.

"Are you thinking of something specific?" said Jennings unwarily, and both Griswold's eyes snapped open at once.

Since you ask and seem interested [said] Griswold, let me tell you the matter I have in mind.

It dates back to the year after World War II, when in the first flush of enthusiasm, the victorious Allies were trying to find various people who had been involved in the slaughter of the innocents. Not all the villains were Germans, as it happened, and not all the victims were Jews. With a stretch of the imagination and allowance for ingrained bitterness, one could even understand the motivation for the villainy, in some cases.

The British had on their list, for instance, someone who had brought about the deaths of several dozen British prisoners of war. That villain had been smuggled into the camp as a French prisoner with the rank of lieutenant, a part he apparently played to perfection. He initiated the plan for escape, and played a leading part in it all the way through while keeping the Germans completely informed. The escape was entirely unsuccessful and the supposed Frenchman actually shot a few of the British himself. The Nazis had what they wanted. So spectacular was the failure that there were no further attempts at escape from that particular camp for the remainder of the war.

Identifying the villain, this Lieutenant Nobody, as he was called, was not easy. He had been removed from the camp after the aborted escape. Descriptions were vague and he had been, in any case, disguised. The records uncovered at the camp were incomplete, naturally, between the ravages of war and the deliberate destruction by those in charge who wanted no trouble with vengeful victors.

About all that could be found out, as it happened, was that the supposed Frenchman was not a Frenchman, but a Canadian—a French-Canadian, of course—who had lived most of his life in Montreal. There was no more than that. We had no record of his actual name, no photograph—not even a blurred snapshot—of his face, no details of any kind.

It made sense, you see. As a Montrealer, it was quite possible he was thoroughly bilingual. He could pass as a Frenchman, who could speak enough English to communicate; and he could also speak English well enough to pass as an American. There was some evidence, of a rather feeble nature, that he had indeed served the Nazis in the role of an American among American prisoners of war.

What's more, as a French-Canadian, it was quite possible that he had resented the ruling Anglo majority (who, in those days, controlled the Quebec economy totally) to the point of casting his lot in with the Germans.

The Americans were rather in a quandary, then, when an

American noncom of superlatively innocent appearance was identified as Lieutenant Nobody.

It was not much of an identification. The accuser was a British soldier who had been a prisoner at the camp in question and who had been one of the very few who had survived the attempted escape. Two years had elapsed since he had last seen the man and all he could say in support of his contention was, essentially, "I tell you that's the face, that's the face."

It could have been the face, of course, since it's not uncommon for one person to resemble another, but it was not anything one could sensibly use. The American was questioned, of course. He, too, had been a prisoner of war, so that the accuser might possibly have seen him quite innocently at one time or another. People were occasionally shifted from one camp to another to break up any groupings that might be troublesome.

The American had his dog tags, had a history, both military and premilitary, which he could reel off. It checked with army records, as far as they went, but it was always possible that Lieutenant Nobody had been fitted out with the personality and records of a real American noncom who had died in combat—just enough of a possibility to make some people uneasy.

In the ordinary course of affairs, the noncom was sent back Stateside. Yet though the accusation was insufficient to warrant his being detained overseas, it was enough to worry the Department here in the United States.

They called me in. I was a young fellow then, and a civilian, but I already had a reputation for being able to see the horizon on a clear day, which made me rather a phenomenon among the usual cloudy-eyed individuals that filled the Army then—as they do now.

I was called before a colonel who, generally speaking, had no use for me—which didn't bother me, since I had no use for him.

He said, "See here, Griswold, you speak to this guy and tell us whether he's an American or a Canadian."

I had been told the story, so I said, "Why not just take him back to the hometown and check with his relatives?"

The colonel said, "He doesn't have any close relatives. He

was brought up by an uncle who was a recluse and who is dead now. He claims he doesn't know anyone out there very closely and vice versa. We checked and that's so. Of course, it's possible that he had met a look-alike some years ago, found out that the background was sufficiently obscure, and then took it over.''

"Take him back to the hometown and see if he knows his way around. He'd know where the town drugstore was, wouldn't he?"

The colonel looked impatient. "That takes time and money, and I need both for better things than this—unless you can give me reason to believe there's something to this accusation.''

I said, with just a touch of sarcasm, "Does he know who won the World Series in 1941?''

The colonel said, "Listen, Griswold, *I* don't know who won the World Series in 1941, so don't waste my time. You just do what I say. Talk to him and look for a speck, just one speck of Canadian in him. If you come back with that, we'll see to it that he's turned inside out and emptied—but we need that speck to justify the trouble. You understand?''

I understood. "Yes, sir," I said. I knew how those things worked. If I found out something useful, the colonel would use it and take the credit. Still, I had no choice but to go ahead.

The noncom was a Sergeant Drisack. He had the kind of beaten, anxious look you would expect in a longtime prisoner who suddenly found himself under suspicion after his release for something he couldn't understand. Yet it seemed to me that underneath that there was a vein of hard shrewdness, which didn't really show. I knew very well it might be my imagination.

There was nothing to do but engage him in conversation. I said, "Do you remember your address in Iowa, sergeant?''

"Ohio, sir.''

"Sorry. Do you remember the address?''

"Yes, sir.''

"You know how to write, of course.''

"Yes, sir.''

I placed a piece of paper before him, then handed him a

pencil, putting it near his left hand, but he reached over with his right hand and took it.

"Just write it for me, will you?"

He did, and I took the paper from him and looked at it. It was the kind of writing one would expect of someone with a sixth-grade education, which was all that Drisack had had—if he were Drisack.

I said, "Can you write 'Des Moines'?"

He looked puzzled. "How do you spell it?"

"Oh yes," I said. "You're not from Iowa." (It seemed to me he looked amused, though I could see no clear sign of it.)

"Have you traveled much?"

He shook his head. "Only while I was in the Army. They took me to France. Then I got captured and the krauts took me to Germany."

"Can you speak German?"

"I can say 'halt' or 'marschieren.' Like that."

"Can you speak French?"

"Polly-voo, that's all."

"Ever been to Mexico?"

"No, sir."

I shoved the paper at him. "Write 'Guadalajara.'"

"What?" He looked completely blank, but his eyes seemed to glitter, or so it seemed to me.

"Well—write 'Mexico.' "

He did, quite quickly. He was not stupid—only uneducated, or appearing so.

"Ever been to Canada?"

"No, sir."

"You sure now? You never lived in Canada?"

He looked startled and shook his head.

"You never lived in Montreal?"

He shook his head. "No, sir."

"You've heard of it, haven't you?"

"Yes, sir. It's in Canada, isn't it?"

"You never lived at 721 Sherwood Street in Montreal?"

He hesitated, "No, sir."

"Well, is there a Sherwood Street in Montreal?"

"I don't know, sir," he said humbly.

I shoved a new piece of paper at him. "Write '721 Sherwood Street, Montreal.' Go ahead!"

He looked utterly confused, but did so. As soon as he had finished, I took the paper and pencil from him and nodded to the guard, who took him away.

I then went to colonel and said, in a leisurely way, "I found the speck, Colonel, and I explained. Our so-called American noncom was Lieutenant Nobody, of course, as a thorough going investigation eventually proved, and the British hung him about six months later."

I said suspiciously, "What gave him away—if anything?"

"You ought to be able to figure that out," said Griswold austerely. "I had him write 'Montreal,' didn't I?"

"So?"

"So it has two pronunciations, totally different, with respect to all three vowels. The *o* is short to English-speaking Canadians, long to French-speaking Canadians. The *e* is a long *e* to the English, a long *a* to the French. The *a* is pronounced like *aw* to the English but is short to the French."

"Yes, but he wrote the word. He didn't pronounce it."

"Well, I acted like such a jackass in the interrogation; I was so bumbling and transparent in my questions that he couldn't help but relax, so he lost that fine grip on himself and wrote as though he were a French-Canadian. When an *e* in French is pronounced *ay* it has an acute accent above it, a straight line moving from lower left to upper right, so that you have 'Montréal.' The supposed noncom couldn't keep himself from making a speck over the *e* in 'Montreal,' and that speck gave him away. No uneducated American could have done it."

PART III

MISCELLANEOUS MYSTERIES

25

The Key

In the 1960s, I was deeply involved in nonfiction, and wrote very little fiction. However, The Magazine of Fantasy and Science Fiction (F&SF) *was planning a special "Isaac Asimov issue" and they wanted to include a new original story by me. I was not proof against flattery, and so I wrote the fourth and last of the Wendell Urth stories, and the most elaborate of them. (In fact, it is the longest story in this book.)*

I was very pleased (and more than a little relieved) that I could still write fiction and I am celebrating that great discovery by including the story here.

Karl Jennings knew he was going to die. He had a matter of hours to live and much to do.

There was no reprieve from the death sentence, not here on the Moon, not with no communications in operation.

Even on Earth there were a few fugitive patches where, without radio handy, a man might die without the hand of his fellow man to help him, without the heart of his fellow man to pity him, without even the eye of his fellow man to discover the corpse. Here on the Moon, there were few spots that were otherwise.

Earthmen knew he was on the Moon, of course. He had been part of a geological expedition—no, selenological expedition! Odd, how his Earth-centered mind insisted on the "geo-."

Wearily he drove himself to think, even as he worked. Dying though he was, he still felt that artificially imposed clarity of thought. Anxiously he looked about. There was nothing to see. He was in the dark of the eternal shadow of the northern interior of the wall of the crater, a blackness relieved only by the intermittent blink of his flash. He kept that intermittent, partly because he dared not consume its power source before he was through and partly because he dared not take more than the minimum chance that it be seen.

On his left hand, toward the south along the nearby horizon of the Moon, was a crescent of bright white Sunlight. Beyond the horizon, and invisible, was the opposite lip of the crater. The Sun never peered high enough over the lip of his own edge of the crater to illuminate the floor immediately beneath his feet. He was safe from radiation—from that at least.

He dug carefully but clumsily, swathed as he was in his spacesuit. His side ached abominably.

The dust and broken rock did not take up the "fairy castle" appearance characteristic of those portions of the Moon's surface exposed to the alternation of light and dark, heat and cold. Here, in eternal cold, the slow crumbling of the crater wall had simply piled fine rubble in a heterogeneous mass. It would not be easy to tell there had been digging going on.

He misjudged the unevenness of the dark surface for a moment and spilled a cupped handful of dusty fragments. The particles dropped with the slowness characteristic of the Moon and yet with the appearance of a blinding speed, for there was no air resistance to slow them further still and spread them out into a dusty haze.

Jennings' flash brightened for a moment, and he kicked a jagged rock out of the way.

He hadn't much time. He dug deeper into the dust.

A little deeper and he could push the Device into the depression and begin covering it. Strauss must not find it.

Strauss!

The other member of the team. Half-share in the discovery.
Half-share in the renown.

If it were merely the whole share of the credit that Strauss
had wanted, Jennings might have allowed it. The discovery
was more important than any individual credit that might go
with it. But what Strauss wanted was something far more,
something Jennings would fight to prevent.

One of the few things Jennings was willing to die to
prevent.

And he was dying.

They had found it together. Actually, Strauss had found the
ship; or, better, the remains of the ship; or, better still, what
just conceivably might have been the remains of something
analogous to a ship.

"Metal," said Strauss, as he picked up something ragged
and nearly amorphous. His eyes and face could just barely be
seen through the thick lead glass of the visor, but his rather
harsh voice sounded clearly enough through the suit radio.

Jennings came drifting over from his own position half a
mile away. He said, "Odd! There is no free metal on the
Moon."

"There shouldn't be. But you know well enough they
haven't explored more than one per cent of the Moon's
surface. Who knows what can be found on it?"

Jennings grunted assent and reached out his gauntlet to take
the object.

It was true enough that almost anything might be found on
the Moon for all anyone really knew. Theirs was the first
privately financed selenographic expedition ever to land on
the Moon. Till then, there had been only government-conducted
shotgun affairs, with half a dozen ends in view. It was a sign
of the advancing space age that the Geological Society could
afford to send two men to the Moon for selenological studies
only.

Strauss said, "It looks as though it once had a polished
surface."

"You're right," said Jennings. "Maybe there's more about."

They found three more pieces, two of trifling size and one
a jagged object that showed traces of a seam.

"Let's take them to the ship," said Strauss.

They took the small skim boat back to the mother ship. They shucked their suits once on board, something Jennings at least was always glad to do. He scratched vigorously at his ribs and rubbed his cheeks till his light skin reddened into welts.

Strauss eschewed such weakness and got to work. The laser beam pock-marked the metal and the vapor recorded itself on the spectrograph. Titanium-steel, essentially, with a hint of cobalt and molybdenum.

"That's artificial, all right," said Strauss. His broad-boned face was as dour and as hard as ever. He showed no elation, although Jennings could feel his own heart begin to race.

It may have been the excitement that trapped Jennings into beginning, "This is a development against which we must steel ourselves—" with a faint stress on "steel" to indicate the play on words.

Strauss, however, looked at Jennings with an icy distaste, and the attempted set of puns was choked off.

Jennings sighed. He could never swing it, somehow. Never could! He remembered at the University— Well, never mind. The discovery they had made was worth a far better pun than any he could construct for all Strauss's calmness.

Jennings wondered if Strauss could possibly miss the significance.

He knew very little about Strauss, as a matter of fact, except by selenological reputation. That is, he had read Strauss's papers and he presumed Strauss had read his. Although their ships might well have passed by night in their University days, they had never happened to meet until after both had volunteered for this expedition and had been accepted.

In the week's voyage, Jennings had grown uncomfortably aware of the other's stocky figure, his sandy hair and china-blue eyes and the way the muscles over his prominent jaw-bones worked when he ate. Jennings, himself, much slighter in build, also blue-eyed, but with darker hair, tended to withdraw automatically from the heavy exudation of the other's power and drive.

Jennings said, "There's no record of any ship ever having landed on this part of the Moon. Certainly none has crashed."

"If it were part of a ship," said Strauss, "it should be smooth and polished. This is eroded and, without an atmosphere here, that means exposure to micrometeor bombardment over many years."

Then he *did* see the significance. Jennings said, with an almost savage jubilation, "It's a non-human artifact. Creatures not of Earth once visited the Moon. Who knows how long ago?"

"Who knows?" agreed Strauss dryly.

"In the report—"

"Wait," said Strauss imperiously. "Time enough to report when we have something to report. If it was a ship, there will be more to it than what we now have."

But there was no point in looking farther just then. They had been at it for hours, and the next meal and sleep were overdue. Better to tackle the whole job fresh and spend hours at it. They seemed to agree on that without speaking.

The Earth was low on the eastern horizon, almost full in phase, bright and blue-streaked. Jennings looked at it while they ate and experienced, as he always did, a sharp homesickness.

"It looks peaceful enough," he said, "but there are six billion people busy on it."

Strauss looked up from some deep inner life of his own and said, "Six billion people ruining it!"

Jennings frowned. "You're not an Ultra, are you?"

Strauss said, "What the hell are you talking about?"

Jennings felt himself flush. A flush always showed against his fair skin, turning it pink at the slightest upset of the even tenor of his emotions. He found it intensely embarrassing.

He turned back to his food, without saying anything.

For a whole generation now, the Earth's population had held steady. No further increase could be afforded. Everyone admitted that. There were those, in fact, who said that "no higher" wasn't enough; the population had to drop. Jennings himself sympathized with that point of view. The globe of the Earth was being eaten alive by its heavy freight of humanity.

But *how* was the population to be made to drop? Randomly, by encouraging the people to lower the birth rate still farther, as and how they wished? Lately there had been the slow rise of a distant rumble which wanted not only a population drop but a selected drop—the survival of the fittest, with the self-declared fit choosing the criteria of fitness.

Jennings thought: I've insulted him, I suppose.

Later, when he was almost asleep, it suddenly occurred to him that he knew virtually nothing of Strauss's character. What if it were his intention to go out now on a foraging expedition of his own so that he might get sole credit for—?

He raised himself on his elbow in alarm, but Strauss was breathing heavily, and even as Jennings listened, the breathing grew into the characteristic burr of a snore.

They spent the next three days in a single-minded search for additional pieces. They found some. They found more than that. They found an area glowing with the tiny phosphorescence of Lunar bacteria. Such bacteria were common enough, but nowhere previously had their occurrence been reported in concentration so great as to cause a visible glow.

Strauss said, "An organic being, or his remains, may have been here once. He died, but the micro-organisms within him did not. In the end they consumed him."

"And spread perhaps," added Jennings. "That may be the source of Lunar bacteria generally. They may not be native at all but may be the result of contamination instead—eons ago."

"It works the other way, too," said Strauss. "Since the bacteria are completely different in very fundamental ways from any Earthly form of micro-organism, the creatures they parasitized—assuming this was their source—must have been fundamentally different too. Another indication of extraterrestrial origin."

The trail ended in the wall of a small crater.

"It's a major digging job," said Jennings, his heart sinking. "We had better report this and get help."

"No," said Strauss somberly. "There may be nothing to get help for. The crater might have formed a million years after the ship had crashlanded."

"And vaporized most of it, you mean, and left only what we've found?"

Strauss nodded.

Jennings said, "Let's try anyway. We can dig a bit. If we draw a line through the finds we've made so far and just keep on . . ."

Strauss was reluctant and worked halfheartedly, so that it was Jennings who made the real find. Surely that counted! Even though Strauss had found the first piece of metal, Jennings had found the artifact itself.

It *was* an artifact—cradled three feet underground under the irregular shape of a boulder which had fallen in such a way that it left a hollow in its contact with the Moon's surface. In that hollow lay the artifact, protected from everything for a million years or more; protected from radiation, from micro-meteors, from temperature change, so that it remained fresh and new forever.

Jennings labeled it at once the Device. It looked not remotely similar to any instrument either had ever seen, but then, as Jennings said, why should it?

"There are no rough edges that I can see," he said. "It may not be broken."

"There may be missing parts, though."

"Maybe," said Jennings, "but there seems to be nothing movable. It's all one piece and certainly oddly uneven." He noted his own play on words, then went on with a not-altogether-successful attempt at self-control. *"This* is what we need. A piece of worn metal or an area rich in bacteria is only material for deduction and dispute. But this is the real thing—a Device that is clearly of extraterrestrial manufacture."

It was on the table between them now, and both regarded it gravely.

Jennings said, "Let's put through a preliminary report, now."

"No!" said Strauss, in sharp and strenuous dissent. "Hell, no!"

"Why not?"

"Because if we do, it becomes a Society project. They'll swarm all over it and we won't be as much as a footnote when all is done. No!" Strauss looked almost sly. "Let's do all we can with it and get as much out of it as possible before the harpies descend."

Jennings thought about it. He couldn't deny that he too

wanted to make certain that no credit was lost. But still—He said, "I don't know that I like to take the chance, Strauss." For the first time he had an impulse to use the man's first name, but fought it off. "Look, Strauss," he said, "it's not right to wait. If this is of extraterrestrial origin, then it must be from some other planetary system. There isn't a place in the Solar System, outside the Earth, that can possibly support an advanced life form."

"Not proven, really," grunted Strauss, "but what if you're right?"

"Then it would mean that the creatures of the ship had interstellar travel and therefore had to be far in advance, technologically, of ourselves. Who knows what the Device can tell us about their advanced technology. It might be the key to—who knows what. It might be the clue to an unimaginable scientific revolution."

"That's romantic nonsense. If this is the product of a technology far advanced over ours, we'll learn nothing from it. Bring Einstein back to life and show him a microprotowarp and what would he make of it?"

"We can't be certain that we won't learn."

"So what, even so? What if there's a small delay? What if we assure credit for ourselves? What if we make sure that we ourselves go along with this, that we don't let go of it?"

"But Strauss"—Jennings felt himself moved almost to tears in his anxiety to get across his sense of the importance of the Device—"what if we crash with it? What if we don't make it back to Earth? We can't risk this thing." He tapped it then, almost as though he were in love with it. "We should report it now and have them send ships out here to get it. It's too precious to—"

At the peak of his emotional intensity, the Device seemed to grow warm under his hand. A portion of its surface, half-hidden under a flap of metal, glowed phosphorescently.

Jennings jerked his hand away in a spasmodic gesture and the Device darkened. But it was enough; the moment had been infinitely revealing.

He said, almost choking, "It was like a window opening into your skull. I could see into your mind."

"I read yours," said Strauss, "or experienced it, or en-

tered into it, or whatever you choose." He touched the
Device in his cold, withdrawn way, but nothing happened.

"You're an Ultra," said Jennings angrily. "When I touched
this"—And he did so. "It's happening again. I see it. Are
you a madman? Can you honestly believe it is humanly
decent to condemn almost all the human race to extinction
and destroy the versatility and variety of the species?"

His hand dropped away from the Device again, in repug-
nance at the glimpses revealed, and it grew dark again. Once
more, Strauss touched it gingerly and again nothing happened.

Strauss said, "Let's not start a discussion, for God's sake.
This thing is an aid to communication—a telepathic amplifier.
Why not? The brain cells have each their electric potentials.
Thought can be viewed as a wavering electromagnetic field of
microintensities—"

Jennings turned away. He didn't want to speak to Strauss.
He said, "We'll report it now. I don't give a damn about
credit. Take it all. I just want it out of our hands."

For a moment Strauss remained in a brown study. Then he
said, "It's more than a communicator. It responds to emotion
and it amplifies emotion."

"What are you talking about?"

"Twice it started at your touch just now, although you'd
been handling it all day with no effect. It still has no effect
when I touch it."

"Well?"

"It reacted to you when you were in a state of high
emotional tension. That's the requirement for activation, I
suppose. And when you raved about the Ultras while you
were holding it just now, I felt as you did, for just a moment."

"So you should."

"But, listen to me. Are you sure *you're* so right. There
isn't a thinking man on Earth that doesn't know the planet
would be better off with a population of one billion rather
than six billion. If we used automation to the full—as now the
hordes won't allow us to do—we could probably have a
completely efficient and viable Earth with a population of no
more than, say, five million. Listen to me, Jennings. Don't
turn away, man."

The harshness in Strauss's voice almost vanished in his

effort to be reasonably winning. "But we can't reduce the population democratically. You know that. It isn't the sex urge, because uterine inserts solved the birth control problem long ago; you know that. It's a matter of nationalism. Each ethnic group wants other groups to reduce themselves in population first, and I agree with them. I want my ethnic group, *our* ethnic group, to prevail. I want the Earth to be inherited by the elite, which means by men like ourselves. We're the true men, and the horde of half-apes who hold us down are destroying us all. They're doomed to death anyway; why not save ourselves?"

"No," said Jennings strenuously. "No one group has a monopoly on humanity. Your five million, trapped in a humanity robbed of its variety and versatility, would die of boredom—and serve them right."

"Emotional nonsense, Jennings. You don't believe that. You've just been trained to believe it by our damn-fool equalitarians. Look, this Device is just what we need. Even if we can't build any others or understand how this one works, this one Device might do. If we could control or influence the minds of key men, then little by little we can superimpose our views on the world. We already have an organization. You must know that if you've seen my mind. It's better motivated and better designed than any other organization on Earth. The brains of mankind flock to us daily. Why not you too? This instrument is a key, as you see, but not just a key to a bit more knowledge. It is a key to the final solution of men's problems. Join us! Join us!" He had reached an earnestness that Jennings had never heard in him.

Strauss's hand fell on the Device, which flickered a second or two and went out.

Jennings smiled humorlessly. He saw the significance of that. Strauss had been deliberately trying to work himself into an emotional state intense enough to activate the Device and had failed.

"You can't work it," said Jennings. "You're too darned supermannishly self-controlled and can't break down, can you?" He took up the Device with hands that were trembling, and it phosphoresced at once.

"Then *you* work it. Get the credit for saving humanity."

"Not in a hundred million years," said Jennings, gasping and barely able to breathe in the intensity of his emotion. "I'm going to report this now."

"No," said Strauss. He picked up one of the table knives. "It's pointed enough, sharp enough."

"You needn't work so hard to make your point," said Jennings, even under the stress of the moment conscious of the pun. "I can see your plans. With the Device you can convince anyone that I never existed. You can bring about an Ultra victory."

Strauss nodded. "You read my mind perfectly."

"But you won't," gasped Jennings. "Not while I hold this." He was willing Strauss into immobility.

Strauss moved raggedly and subsided. He held the knife out stiffly and his arm trembled, but he did not advance.

Both were perspiring freely.

Strauss said between clenched teeth, "You can't keep it—up all—day."

The sensation was clear, but Jennings wasn't sure he had the words to describe it. It was, in physical terms, like holding a slippery animal of vast strength, one that wriggled incessantly. Jennings had to concentrate on the feeling of immobility.

He wasn't familiar with the Device. He didn't know how to use it skillfully. One might as well expect someone who had never seen a sword to pick one up and wield it with the grace of a musketeer.

"Exactly," said Strauss, following Jennings' train of thought. He took a fumbling step forward.

Jennings knew himself to be no match for Strauss's mad determination. They both knew that. But there was the skim boat. Jennings had to get away. With the Device.

But Jennings had no secrets. Strauss saw his thought and tried to step between the other and the skim boat.

Jennings redoubled his efforts. Not immobility, but unconsciousness. Sleep, Strauss, he thought desperately. Sleep!

Strauss slipped to his knees, heavy-lidded eyes closing.

Heart pounding, Jennings rushed forward. If he could strike him with something, snatch the knife—

But his thoughts had deviated from their all-important concentration on sleep, so that Strauss's hand was on his ankle, pulling downward with raw strength.

Strauss did not hesitate. As Jennings tumbled, the hand that held the knife rose and fell. Jennings felt the sharp pain and his mind reddened with fear and despair.

It was the very access of emotion that raised the flicker of the Device to a blaze. Strauss's hold relaxed as Jennings silently and incoherently screamed fear and rage from his own mind to the other.

Strauss rolled over, face distorted.

Jennings rose unsteadily to his feet and backed away. He dared do nothing but concentrate on keeping the other unconscious. Any attempt at violent action would block out too much of his own mind force, whatever it was; too much of his unskilled bumbling mind force that could not lend itself to really effective use.

He backed toward the skim boat. There would be a suit on board—bandages—

The skim boat was not really meant for long-distance runs. Nor was Jennings, any longer. His right side was slick with blood despite the bandages. The interior of his suit was caked with it.

There was no sign of the ship itself on his tail, but surely it would come sooner or later. Its power was many times his own; it had detectors that would pick up the cloud of charge concentration left behind by his ion-drive reactors.

Desperately Jennings had tried to reach Luna Station on his radio, but there was still no answer, and he stopped in despair. His signals would merely aid Strauss in pursuit.

He might reach Luna Station bodily, but he did not think he could make it. He would be picked off first. He would die and crash first. He wouldn't make it. He would have to hide the Device, put it away in a safe place, *then* make for Luna Station.

The Device . . .

He was not sure he was right. It might ruin the human race, but it was infinitely valuable. Should he destroy it altogether? It was the only remnant of non-human intelligent life. It held the secrets of an advanced technology; it was an instrument of an advanced science of the mind. Whatever the danger, consider the value—the potential value—

No, he must hide it so that it could be found again—but only by the enlightened Moderates of the government. Never by the Ultras . . .

The skim boat flickered down along the northern inner rim of the crater. He knew which one it was, and the Device could be buried here. If he could not reach Luna Station thereafter, either in person or by radio, he would have to at least get away from the hiding spot; well away, so that his own person would not give it away. And he would have to leave *some* key to its location.

He was thinking with an unearthly clarity, it seemed to him. Was it the influence of the Device he was holding? Did it stimulate his thinking and guide him to the perfect message? Or was it the hallucination of the dying, and would none of it make any sense to anyone? He didn't know, but he had no choice. He had to try.

For Karl Jennings knew he was going to die. He had a matter of hours to live and much to do.

H. Seton Davenport of the American Division of the Terrestrial Bureau of Investigation rubbed the star-shaped scar on his left cheek absently. "I'm aware, sir, that the Ultras are dangerous."

The Division Head, M. T. Ashley, looked at Davenport narrowly. His gaunt cheeks were set in disapproving lines. Since he had sworn off smoking once again, he forced his groping fingers to close upon a stick of chewing gum, which he shelled, crumpled, and shoved into his mouth morosely. He was getting old, and bitter, too, and his short iron-gray mustache rasped when he rubbed his knuckles against it.

He said, "You don't know how dangerous. I wonder if anyone does. They are small in numbers, but strong among the powerful who, after all, are perfectly ready to consider themselves the elite. No one knows for certain who they are or how many."

"Not even the Bureau?"

"The Bureau is held back. We ourselves aren't free of the taint, for that matter. Are you?"

Davenport frowned. "I'm not an Ultra."

"I didn't say you were," said Ashley. "I asked if you were free of the taint. Have you considered what's been happening to the Earth in the last two centuries? Has it never occurred to you that a moderate decline in population would be a good thing? Have you never felt that it would be wonderful to get rid of the unintelligent, the incapable, the insensitive, and leave the rest. *I* have, damn it."

"I'm guilty of thinking that sometimes, yes. But considering something as a wish-fulfillment idea is one thing, but planning it as a practical scheme of action to be Hitlerized through is something else."

"The distance from wish to action isn't as great as you think. Convince yourself that the end is important enough, that the danger is great enough, and the means will grow increasingly less objectionable. Anyway, now that the Istanbul matter is taken care of, let me bring you up to date on this matter. Istanbul was of no importance in comparison. Do you know Agent Ferrant?"

"The one who's disappeared? Not personally."

"Well, two months ago, a stranded ship was located on the Moon's surface. It had been conducting a privately financed selenographic survey. The Russo-American Geological Society, which had sponsored the flight, reported the ship's failure to report. A routine search located it without much trouble within a reasonable distance of the site from which it had made its last report.

"The ship was not damaged but its skim boat was gone and with it one member of the crew. Name—Karl Jennings. The other man, James Strauss, was alive but in delirium. There was no sign of physical damage to Strauss, but he was quite insane. He still is, and that's important."

"Why?" put in Davenport.

"Because the medical team that investigated him reported neurochemical and neuroelectrical abnormalities of unprecedented nature. They'd never seen a case like it. Nothing human could have brought it about."

A flicker of a smile crossed Davenport's solemn face. "You suspect extraterrestrial invaders?"

"Maybe," said the other, with no smile at all. "But let me

continue. A routine search in the neighborhood of the stranded ship revealed no signs of the skim boat. Then Luna Station reported receipt of weak signals of uncertain origin. They had been tabbed as coming from the western rim of Mare Imbrium, but it was uncertain whether they were of human origin or not, and no vessel was believed to be in the vicinity. The signals had been ignored. With the skim boat in mind, however, the search party headed out for Imbrium and located it. Jennings was aboard, dead. Knife wound in one side. It's rather surprising he had lived as long as he did.

"Meanwhile the medicos were becoming increasingly disturbed at the nature of Strauss's babbling. They contacted the Bureau and our two men on the Moon—one of them happened to be Ferrant—arrived at the ship.

"Ferrant studied the tape recordings of the babblings. There was no point in asking questions, for there was, and is, no way of reaching Strauss. There is a high wall between the universe and himself—probably a permanent one. However, the talk in delirium, although heavily repetitious and disjointed, can be made to make sense. Ferrant put it together like a jigsaw puzzle.

"Apparently Strauss and Jennings had come across an object of some sort which they took to be of ancient and non-human manufacture, an artifact of some ship wrecked eons ago. Apparently it could somehow be made to twist the human mind."

Davenport interrupted. "And it twisted Strauss's mind? Is that it?"

"That's exactly it. Strauss was an Ultra—we can say 'was' for he's only technically alive—and Jennings did not wish to surrender the object. Quite right, too. Strauss babbled of using it to bring about the self-liquidation, as he called it, of the undesirable. He wanted a final, ideal population of five million. There was a fight in which only Jennings, apparently, could handle the mind-thing, but in which Strauss had a knife. When Jennings left, he was knifed, but Strauss's mind had been destroyed."

"And where was the mind-thing?"

"Agent Ferrant acted decisively. He searched the ship and the surroundings again. There was no sign of anything that was neither a natural Lunar formation nor an obvious product of human technology. There was nothing that could be the mind-thing. He then searched the skim boat and its surroundings. Again nothing."

"Could the first search team, the ones who suspected nothing—could they have carried something off?"

"They swore they did not, and there is no reason to suspect them of lying. Then Ferrant's partner—"

"Who was he?"

"Gorbansky," said the District Head.

"I know him. We've worked together."

"I know you have. What do you think of him?"

"Capable and honest."

"All right. Gorbansky found something. Not an alien artifact. Rather, something most routinely human indeed. It was an ordinary white three-by-five card with writing on it, spindled, and in the middle finger of the right gauntlet. Presumably Jennings had written it before his death and, also presumably, it represented the key to where he had hidden the object."

"What reason is there to think he had hidden it?"

"I said we had found it nowhere."

"I mean, what if he had destroyed it, as something too dangerous to leave intact?"

"That's highly doubtful. If we accept the conversation as reconstructed from Strauss's ravings—and Ferrant built up what seems a tight word-for-word record of it—Jennings thought the mind-thing to be of key importance to humanity. He called it 'the clue to an unimaginable scientific revolution.' He wouldn't destroy something like that. He would merely hide it from the Ultras and try to report its whereabouts to the government. Else why leave a clue to its whereabouts?"

Davenport shook his head, "You're arguing in a circle, chief. You say he left a clue because you think there is a hidden object, and you think there is a hidden object because he left a clue."

"I admit that. Everything is dubious. Is Strauss's delirium meaningful? Is Ferrant's reconstruction valid? Is Jennings' clue really a clue? Is there a mind-thing, or a Device, as Jennings called it, or isn't there? There's no use asking such questions. Right now, we must act on the assumption that there is such a Device and that it must be found."

"Because Ferrant disappeared?"

"Exactly."

"Kidnapped by the Ultras?"

"Not at all. The card disappeared with him."

"Oh—I see."

"Ferrant has been under suspicion for a long time as a secret Ultra. He's not the only one in the Bureau under suspicion either. The evidence didn't warrant open action; we can't simply lay about on pure suspicion, you know, or we'll gut the Bureau from top to bottom. He was under surveillance."

"By whom?"

"By Gorbansky, of course. Fortunately Gorbansky had filmed the card and sent the reproduction to the headquarters on Earth, but he admits he considered it as nothing more than a puzzling object and included it in the information sent to Earth only out of a desire to be routinely complete. Ferrant— the better mind of the two, I suppose—did see the significance and took action. He did so at great cost, for he has given himself away and has destroyed his future usefulness to the Ultras, but there is a chance that there will be no need for future usefulness. If the Ultras control the Device—"

"Perhaps Ferrant has the Device already."

"He was under surveillance, remember. Gorbansky swears the Device did not turn up anywhere."

"Gorbansky did not manage to stop Ferrant from leaving with the card. Perhaps he did not manage to stop him from obtaining the Device unnoticed, either."

Ashley tapped his fingers on the desk between them in an uneasy and uneven rhythm. He said at last, "I don't want to think that. If we find Ferrant, we may find out how much damage he's done. Till then, we must search for the Device. If Jennings hid it, he must have tried to get away from the hiding place. Else why leave a clue? It wouldn't be found in the vicinity."

"He might not have lived long enough to get away."

Again Ashley tapped, "The skim boat showed signs of having engaged in a long, speedy flight and had all but crashed at the end. That is consistent with the view that

Jennings was trying to place as much space as possible between himself and some hiding place.''

"Can you tell from what direction he came?''

"Yes, but that's not likely to help. From the condition of the side vents, he had been deliberately tacking and veering.''

Davenport sighed. "I suppose you have a copy of the card with you.''

"I do. Here it is.'' He flipped a three-by-five replica toward Davenport. Davenport studied it for a few moments. It looked like this:

$$XY^2$$
$$PC/2$$
$$\overline{\overline{F/A}}$$
$$SU$$
$$C\text{-}C$$
$$H^0$$

Davenport said, "I don't see any significance here.''

"Neither did I, at first, nor did those I first consulted. But consider. Jennings must have thought that Strauss was in pursuit; he might not have known that Strauss had been put out of action, at least, not permanently. He was deadly afraid, then, that an Ultra would find him before a Moderate would. He dared not leave a clue too open. This''—and the Division Head tapped the reproduction—''must represent a clue that is opaque on the surface but clear enough to anyone sufficiently ingenious.''

"Can we rely on that?'' asked Davenport doubtfully. "After all, he was a dying, frightened man, who might have been subjected to this mind-altering object himself. He need not have been thinking clearly, or even humanly. For instance, why didn't he make an effort to reach Luna Station? He ended half a circumference away almost. Was he too twisted to think clearly? Too paranoid to trust even the Station? Yet he must have tried to reach them at first since they picked up signals. What I'm saying is that this card, which looks as though it is covered with gibberish, *is* covered with gibberish."

Ashley shook his head solemnly from side to side, like a tolling bell. "He was in panic, yes. And I suppose he lacked the presence of mind to try to reach Luna Station. Only the need to run and escape possessed him. Even so this can't be gibberish. It hangs together too well. Every notation on the card can be made to make sense, and the whole can be made to hang together."

"Where's the sense, then?" asked Davenport.

"You'll notice that there are seven items on the left side and two on the right. Consider the left-hand side first. The third one down looks like an equals sign. Does an equals sign mean anything to you, anything in particular?"

"An algebraic equation."

"That's general. Anything particular?"

"No."

"Suppose you consider it as a pair of parallel lines?"

"Euclid's fifth postulate?" suggested Davenport, groping.

"Good! There is a crater called Euclides on the Moon—the Greek name of the mathematician we call Euclid."

Davenport nodded. "I see your drift. As for F/A, that's force divided by acceleration, the definition of mass by Newton's second law of motion—"

"Yes, and there is a crater called Newton on the Moon also."

"Yes, but wait awhile, the lowermost item is the astonomic symbol for the planet Uranus, and there is certainly no crater—or any other lunar object, so far as I know—that is named Uranus."

"You're right there. But Uranus was discovered by William Herschel, and the H that makes up part of the astronomic symbol is the initial of his name. As it happens, there is a crater named Herschel on the Moon—three of them, in fact, since one is named for Caroline Herschel, his sister, and another for John Herschel, his son."

Davenport thought awhile, then said, "PC/2—Pressure

times half the speed of light. I'm not familiar with that equation."

"Try craters. Try P for Ptolemaeus and C for Copernicus."

"And strike an average? Would that signify a spot exactly between Ptolemaeus and Copernicus?"

"I'm disappointed, Davenport," said Ashley sardonically. "I thought you knew your history of astronomy better than that. Ptolemy, or Ptolemaeus in Latin, presented a geocentric picture of the Solar System with the Earth at the center, while Copernicus presented a heliocentric one with the Sun at the center. One astronomer attempted a compromise, a picture halfway between that of Ptolemy and Copernicus—"

"Tycho Brahe!" said Davenport.

"Right. And the crater Tycho is the most conspicuous feature on the Moon's surface."

"All right. Let's take the rest. The C-C is a common way of writing a common type of chemical bond, and I think there is a crater named Bond."

"Yes, named for an American astronomer, W. C. Bond."

"The item on top, XY^2. Hmm. XYY. An X and two Y's. Wait! Alfonso X. He was the royal astronomer in medieval Spain who was called Alfonso the Wise. X the Wise. XYY. The crater Alphonsus."

"Very good. What's SU?"

"That stumps me, chief."

"I'll tell you one theory. It stands for Soviet Union, the old name for the Russian Region. It was the Soviet Union that first mapped the other side of the Moon, and maybe it's a crater there. Tsiolkovsky, for instance. You see, then, the symbols on the left can each be interpreted as standing for a crater: Alphonsus, Tycho, Euclides, Newton, Tsiolkovsky, Bond, Herschel."

"What about the symbols on the right-hand side?"

"That's perfectly transparent. The quartered circle is the astronomic symbol for the Earth. An arrow pointing to it indicates that Earth must be directly overhead."

"Ah," said Davenport, "the Sinus Medii—the Middle Bay—over which the Earth is perpetually at zenith. That's not a crater, so it's on the right-hand side, away from the other symbols."

"All right," said Ashley. "The notations all make sense, or they can be made to make sense, so there's at least a good chance that this isn't gibberish and that it is trying to tell us something. But what? So far we've got seven craters and a non-crater mentioned, and what does that mean? Presumably, the Device can only be in one place."

"Well," said Davenport heavily, "a crater can be a huge place to search. Even if we assume he hugged the shadow to avoid Solar radiation, there can be dozens of miles to examine in each case. Suppose the arrow pointing to the symbol for the Earth defines the crater where he hid the Device, the place from which the Earth can be seen nearest the zenith."

"That's been thought of, old man. It cuts out one place and leaves us with seven pinpointed craters, the southernmost extremity of those north of the Lunar equator and the northernmost extremity of those south. But which of the seven?"

Davenport was frowning. So far, he hadn't thought of anything that hadn't already been thought of. "Search them all," he said brusquely.

Ashley crackled into brief laughter. "In the weeks since this has all come up, we've done exactly that."

"And what have you found?"

"Nothing. We haven't found a thing. We're still looking, though."

"Obviously one of the symbols isn't interpreted correctly."

"Obviously!"

"You said yourself there were three craters named Herschel. The symbol SU, if it means the Soviet Union and therefore the other side of the Moon, can stand for any crater on the other side: Lomonosov, Jules Verne, Joliot-Curie, any of them. For that matter, the symbol of the Earth might stand for the crater Atlas, since he is pictured as supporting the Earth in some versions of the myth. The arrow might stand for the Straight Wall."

"There's no argument there, Davenport. But even if we get the right interpretation for the right symbol, how do we recognize it from among all the wrong interpretations, or from among the right interpretations of the wrong symbols? Somehow there's got to be something that leaps up at us from this card and gives us so clear a piece of information that we can tell it at once as the real thing from among all the red herrings. We've all failed and we need a fresh mind, Davenport. What do you see here?''

"I'll tell you one thing we could do," said Davenport reluctantly. "We can consult someone I—Oh, my God!" He half-rose.

Ashley was all controlled excitement at once. "What do you see?"

Davenport could feel his hand trembling. He hoped his lips weren't. He said, "Tell me, have you checked on Jennings' past life?"

"Of course."

"Where did he go to college?"

"Eastern University."

A pang of joy shot through Davenport, but he held on. That was not enough. "Did he take a course in extraterrology?"

"Of course, he did. That's routine for a geology major."

"All right, then, don't you know who teaches extraterrology at Eastern University?"

Ashley snapped his fingers. "That oddball. What's-his-name—Wendell Urth."

"Exactly, an oddball who is a brilliant man in his way. An oddball who's acted as a consultant for the Bureau on several occasions and given perfect satisfaction every time. An oddball I was going to suggest we consult this time and then noticed that this card was *telling* us to do so. An arrow pointing to the symbol for the Earth. A rebus that couldn't mean more clearly 'Go to Urth,' written by a man who was once a student of Urth and would know him."

Ashley stared at the card, "By God, it's possible. But what could Urth tell us about the card that we can't see for ourselves?"

Davenport said, with polite patience, "I suggest we ask him, sir."

Ashley looked about curiously, half-wincing as he turned from one direction to another. He felt as though he had found himself in some arcane curiosity shop, darkened and dangerous, from which at any moment some demon might hurtle forth squealing.

The lighting was poor and the shadows many. The walls seemed distant, and dismally alive with book-films from floor to ceiling. There was a Galactic Lens in soft three-dimensionality in one corner and behind it were star charts that could dimly be made out. A map of the Moon in another corner might, however, possibly be a map of Mars.

Only the desk in the center of the room was brilliantly lit by a tightbeamed lamp. It was littered with papers and opened printed books. A small viewer was threaded with film, and a clock with an old-fashioned round-faced dial hummed with subdued merriment.

Ashley found himself unable to recall that it was late afternoon outside and that the sun was quite definitely in the sky. Here, within, was a place of eternal night. There was no sign of any window, and the clear presence of circulating air did not spare him a claustrophobic sensation.

He found himself moving closer to Davenport, who seemed insensible to the unpleasantness of the situation.

Davenport said in a low voice, "He'll be here in a moment, sir."

"Is it always like this?" asked Ashley.

"Always. He never leaves this place, as far as I know, except to trot across the campus and attend his classes."

"Gentlemen! Gentlemen!" came a reedy, tenor voice. "I am so glad to see you. It is good of you to come."

A round figure of a man bustled in from another room, shedding shadow and emerging into the light.

He beamed at them, adjusting round, thick-lensed glasses upward so that he might look through them. As his fingers moved away, the glasses slipped downward at once to a precarious perch upon the round nubbin of his snub nose. "I am Wendell Urth," he said.

The scraggly gray Van Dyke on his pudgy, round chin did not in the least add to the dignity which the smiling face and the stubby ellipsoidal torso so noticeably lacked.

"Gentlemen! It is good of you to come," Urth repeated, as he jerked himself backward into a chair from which his legs dangled with the toes of his shoes a full inch above the floor. "Mr. Davenport remembers, perhaps, that it is a matter of—uh—some importance to me to remain here. I do not like to travel, except to walk, of course, and a walk across the campus is quite enough for me.''

Ashley looked baffled as he remained standing, and Urth stared at him with a growing bafflement of his own. He pulled a handkerchief out and wiped his glasses, then replaced them, and said, ''Oh, I see the difficulty. You want chairs. Yes. Well, just take some. If there are things on them, just push them off. Push them off. Sit down, please.''

Davenport removed the books from one chair and placed them carefully on the floor. He pushed the chair toward Ashley. Then he took a human skull off a second chair and placed the skull even more carefully on Urth's desk. Its mandible, insecurely wired, unhinged as he transferred it, and it sat there with jaw askew.

''Never mind,'' said Urth, affably, ''it will not hurt. Now tell me what is on your mind, gentlemen?''

Davenport waited a moment for Ashley to speak, then, rather gladly, took over. ''Dr. Urth, do you remember a student of yours named Jennings? Karl Jennings?''

Urth's smile vanished momentarily with the effort of recall. His somewhat protuberant eyes blinked. ''No,'' he said at last. ''Not at the moment.''

''A geology major. He took your extraterrology course some years ago. I have his photograph here, if that will help.''

Urth studied the photograph handed him with nearsighted concentration, but still looked doubtful.

Davenport drove on. ''He left a cryptic message which is the key to a matter of great importance. We have so far failed to interpret it satisfactorily, but this much we see—it indicates we are to come to you.''

''Indeed? How interesting! For what purpose are you to come to me?''

''Presumably for your advice on interpreting the message.''

''May I see it?''

Silently Ashley passed the slip of paper to Wendell Urth. The extraterrologist looked at it casually, turned it over, and stared for a moment at the blank back. He said, ''Where does it say to ask me?''

Ashley looked startled, but Davenport forestalled him by

saying, "The arrow pointing to the symbol of the Earth. It seems clear."

"It is clearly an arrow pointing to the symbol for the planet Earth. I suppose it might literally mean 'go to the Earth' if this were found on some other world."

"It was found on the Moon, Dr. Urth, and it could, I suppose, mean that. However, the reference to you seemed clear once we realized that Jennings had been a student of yours."

"He took a course in extraterrology here at the University?"

"That's right."

"In what year, Mr. Davenport?"

"In '18."

"Ah. The puzzle is solved."

"You mean the significance of the message?" said Davenport.

"No, no. The message has no meaning to me. I mean the puzzle of why it is that I did not remember him, for I remember him now. He was a very quiet fellow, anxious, shy, self-effacing—not at all the sort of person anyone would remember. Without this"—and he tapped the message—"I might never have remembered him."

"Why does the card change things?" asked Davenport.

"The reference to me is a play on words. Earth—Urth. Not very subtle, of course, but that is Jennings. His unattainable delight was the pun. My only clear memory of him is his occasional attempts to perpetrate puns. I enjoy puns, I adore puns, but Jennings—yes, I remember him well now—was atrocious at it. Either that, or distressingly obvious at it, as in this case. He lacked all talent for puns, yet craved them so much—"

Ashley suddenly broke in. "This message consists entirely of a kind of wordplay, Dr. Urth. At least, we believe so, and that fits in with what you say."

"Ah!" Urth adjusted his glasses and peered through them once more at the card and the symbols it carried. He pursed his plump lips, then said cheerfully, "I make nothing of it."

"In that case—" began Ashley, his hands balling into fists.

"But if you tell me what it's all about," Urth went on, "then perhaps it might mean something."

Davenport said quickly, "May I, sir? I am confident that this man can be relied on—and it may help."

"Go ahead," muttered Ashley. "At this point, what can it hurt?"

Davenport condensed the tale, giving it in crisp, telegraphic sentences, while Urth listened carefully, moving his stubby fingers over the shining milk-white desktop as though he were sweeping up invisible cigar ashes. Toward the end of the recital, he hitched up his legs and sat with them crossed like an amiable Buddha.

When Davenport was done, Urth thought a moment, then said, "Do you happen to have a transcript of the conversation reconstructed by Ferrant?"

"We do," said Davenport. "Would you like to see it?"

"Please."

Urth placed the strip of microfilm in a scanner and worked his way rapidly through it, his lips moving unintelligibly at some points. Then he tapped the reproduction of the cryptic message. "And this, you say, is the key to the entire matter? The crucial clue?"

"We think it is, Dr. Urth."

"But it is not the original. It is a reproduction."

"That is correct."

"The original has gone with this man, Ferrant, and you believe it to be in the hands of the Ultras."

"Quite possibly."

Urth shook his head and looked troubled. "Everyone knows my sympathies are not with the Ultras. I would fight them by all means, so I don't want to seem to be hanging back, but—what is there to say that this mind-affecting object exists at all? You have only the ravings of a psychotic and your dubious deductions from the reproduction of a mysterious set of marks that may mean nothing at all."

"Yes, Dr. Urth, but we can't take chances."

"How certain are you that this copy is accurate? What if the original has something on it that this lacks, something that makes the message quite clear, something without which the message must remain impenetrable?"

"We are certain the copy is accurate."

"What about the reverse side? There is nothing on the back of this reproduction. What about the reverse of the original?"

"The agent who made the reproduction tells us that the back of the original was blank."

"Men can make mistakes."

"We have no reason to think he did, and we must work on the assumption that he didn't. At least until such time as the original is regained."

"Then you assure me," said Urth, "that any interpretation to be made of this message must be made on the basis of exactly what one sees here."

"We think so. We are virtually certain," said Davenport with a sense of ebbing confidence.

Urth continued to look troubled. He said, "Why not leave the instrument where it is? If neither group finds it, so much the better. I disapprove of any tampering with minds and would not contribute to making it possible."

Davenport placed a restraining hand on Ashley's arm, sensing the other was about to speak. Davenport said, "Let me put it to you, Dr. Urth, that the mind-tampering aspect is not the whole of the Device. Suppose an Earth expedition to a distant primitive planet had dropped an old-fashioned radio there, and suppose the native population had discovered electric current but had not yet developed the vacuum tube.

"The population might discover that if the radio was hooked up to a current, certain glass objects within it would grow warm and would glow, but of course they would receive no intelligible sound, merely, at best, some buzzes and crackles. However, if they dropped the radio into a bathtub while it was plugged in, a person in that tub might be electrocuted. Should the people of this hypothetical planet therefore conclude that the device they were studying was designed solely for the purpose of killing people?"

"I see your analogy," said Urth. "You think that the mind-tampering property is merely an incidental function of the Device?"

"I'm sure of it," said Davenport earnestly. "If we can puzzle out its real purpose, earthly technology may leap ahead centuries."

"Then you agree with Jennings when he said"—here Urth consulted the microfilm—" 'It might be the key to—who knows what? It might be the clue to an unimaginable scientific revolution.'"

"Exactly!"

"And yet the mind-tampering aspect is there and is infinitely dangerous. Whatever the radio's purpose, it *does* electrocute."

"Which is why we can't let the Ultras get it."

"Or the government either, perhaps?"

"But I must point out that there is a reasonable limit to caution. Consider that men have always held danger in their hands. The first flint knife in the old Stone Age; the first wooden club before that could kill. They could be used to bend weaker men to the will of stronger ones under threat of force and that, too, is a form of mind-tampering. What counts, Dr. Urth, is not the Device itself, however dangerous it may be in the abstract, but the intentions of the men who make use of the Device. The Ultras have the declared intention of killing off more than 99.9 per cent of humanity. The government, whatever the faults of the men composing it, would have no such intention."

"What *would* the government intend?"

"A scientific study of the Device. Even the mind-tampering aspect itself could yield infinite good. Put to enlightened use, it could educate us concerning the physical basis of mental function. We might learn to correct mental disorders or cure the Ultras. Mankind might learn to develop greater intelligence generally."

"How can I believe that such idealism will be put into practice?"

"*I* believe so. Consider that you face a possible turn to evil by the government if you help us, but you risk the certain and declared evil purpose of the Ultras if you don't."

Urth nodded thoughtfully. "Perhaps you're right. And yet I have a favor to ask of you. I have a niece who is, I believe, quite fond of me. She is constantly upset over the fact that I steadfastly refuse to indulge in the lunacy of travel. She states that she will not rest content until someday I accompany her to Europe or North Carolina or some other outlandish place—"

Ashley leaned forward earnestly, brushing Davenport's re-straining gesture to one side. "Dr. Urth, if you help us find the Device and if it can be made to work, then I assure you that we will be glad to help you free yourself of your phobia against travel and make it possible for you to go with your niece anywhere you wish."

Urth's bulging eyes widened and he seemed to shrink within himself. For a moment he looked wildly about as though he were already trapped. *"No!"* he gasped. "Not at all! Never!"

His voice dropped to an earnest, hoarse whisper. "Let me explain the nature of my fee. If I help you, if you retrieve the Device and learn its use, if the fact of my help becomes public, then my niece will be on the government like a fury. She is a terribly headstrong and shrill-voiced woman who will raise public subscriptions and organize demonstrations. She will stop at nothing. And yet you must not give in to her. You must *not!* You must resist all pressures. I wish to be left alone exactly as I am now. That is my absolute and minimum fee."

Ashley flushed. "Yes, of course, since that is your wish."

"I have your word?"

"You have my word."

"Please remember. I rely on you too, Mr. Davenport."

"It will be as you wish," soothed Davenport. "And now, I presume, you can interpret the items?"

"The items?" asked Urth, seeming to focus his attention with difficulty on the card. "You mean these markings, XY^2 and so on?"

"Yes. What do they mean?"

"I don't know. Your interpretations are as good as any, I suppose."

Ashley exploded. "Do you mean that all this talk about helping us is nonsense? What was this maundering about a fee, then?"

Wendell Urth looked confused and taken aback. "I would like to help you.

"But you don't know what these items mean."

"I—I don't. But I know what this message means."

"You do?" cried Davenport.

"Of course. Its meaning is transparent. I suspected it halfway through your story. And I was sure of it once I read the reconstruction of the conversations between Strauss and Jennings. You would understand it yourself, gentlemen, if you would only stop to think.''

"See here," said Ashley in exasperation, "you said you don't know what the items mean.''

"I don't. I said I know what the *message* means.''

"What is the message if it is not the items? Is it the paper, for Heaven's sake?''

"Yes, in a way.''

"You mean invisible ink or something like that?''

"No! Why is it so hard for you to understand, when you yourself stand on the brink?''

Davenport leaned toward Ashley and said in a low voice, "Sir, will you let me handle it, please?''

Ashley snorted, then said in a stifled manner, "Go ahead.''

"Dr. Urth," said Davenport, "will you give us your analysis?''

"Ah! Well, all right.'' The little extraterrologist settled back in his chair and mopped his damp forehead on his sleeve. "Let's consider the message. If you accept the quartered circle and the arrow as directing you to me, that leaves seven items. If these indeed refer to seven craters, six of them, at least, must be designed merely to distract, since the Device surely cannot be in more than one place. It contained no movable or detachable parts—it was all one piece.

"Then, too, none of the items are straightforward. SU might, by your interpretation, mean any place on the other side of the Moon, which is an area the size of South America. Again PC/2 can mean 'Tycho,' as Mr. Ashley says, or it can mean 'halfway between Ptolemaeus and Copernicus,' as Mr. Davenport thought, or for that matter 'halfway between Plato and Cassini.' To be sure, XY^2 could mean 'Alfonsus'—very ingenious interpretation, that—but it could refer to some co-ordinate system in which the Y co-ordinate was the square of the X co-ordinate. Similarly C-C would mean 'Bond' or it could mean 'halfway between Cassini and Copernicus.' F/A could mean 'Newton' or it could mean 'between Fabricius and Archimedes.'

"In short, the items have so many meanings that they are

meaningless. Even if one of them had meaning, it could not be selected from among the others, so that it is only sensible to suppose that all the items are merely red herrings.

"It is necessary, then, to determine what about the message is completely unambiguous, what is perfectly clear. The answer to that can only be that it *is* a message, that it *is* a clue to a hiding place. That is the one thing we are certain about, isn't it?"

Davenport nodded, then said cautiously, "At least, we think we are certain of it."

"Well, you have referred to this message as the key to the whole matter. You have acted as though it were the crucial clue. Jennings himself referred to the Device as a key or a clue. If we combine this serious view of the matter with Jennings' penchant for puns, a penchant which may have been heightened by the mind-tampering Device he was carrying—So let me tell you a story.

"In the last half of the sixteenth century, there lived a German Jesuit in Rome. He was a mathematician and astronomer of note and helped Pope Gregory XIII reform the calendar in 1582, performing all the enormous calculations required. This astronomer admired Copernicus but he did not accept the heliocentric view of the Solar System. He clung to the older belief that the Earth was the center of the Universe.

"In 1650, nearly forty years after the death of this mathematician, the Moon was mapped by another Jesuit, the Italian astronomer, Giovanni Battista Riccioli. He named the craters after astronomers of the past and since he too rejected Copernicus, he selected the largest and most spectacular craters for those who placed the Earth at the center of the Universe—for Ptolemy, Hipparchus, Alfonso X, Tycho Brahe. The biggest crater Riccioli could find he reserved for his German Jesuit predecessor.

"This crater is actually only the second largest of the craters visible from Earth. The only larger crater is Bailly, which is right on the Moon's limb and is therefore very difficult to see from the Earth. Riccioli ignored it, and it was named for an astronomer who lived a century after his time and who was guillotined during the French Revolution."

Ashley was listening to all this restlessly. "But what has this to do with the message?"

"Why, everything," said Urth, with some surprise. "Did you not call this message the key to the whole business? Isn't it the crucial clue?"

"Yes, of course."

"Is there any doubt that we are dealing with something that is a clue or key to something else?"

"No, there isn't," said Ashley.

"Well, then—The name of the German Jesuit I have been speaking of is Christoph Klau—pronounced 'klow.' Don't you see the pun? Klau—clue?"

Ashley's entire body seemed to grow flabby with disappointment. "Farfetched," he muttered.

Davenport said anxiously "Dr. Urth, there is no feature on the Moon named Klau as far as I know."

"Of course not," said Urth excitedly. "That is the whole point. At this period of history, the last half of the sixteenth century, European scholars were Latinizing their names. Klau did so. In place of the German 'u', he made use of the equivalent letter, the Latin 'v'. He then added an 'ius' ending typical of Latin names and Christoph Klau became Christopher Clavius, and I suppose you are all aware of the giant crater we call Clavius."

"But—" began Davenport.

"Don't 'but' me," said Urth. "Just let me point out that the Latin word 'clavis' means 'key.' *Now* do you see the double and bilingual pun? Klau—clue, Clavius—clavis—key. In his whole life, Jennings could never have made a double, bilingual pun, without the Device. Now he could, and I wonder if death might not have been almost triumphant under the circumstances. And he directed you to me because he knew I would remember his penchant for puns and because he knew I loved them too."

The two men of the Bureau were looking at him wide-eyed.

Urth said solemnly, "I would suggest you search the shaded rim of Clavius, at that point where the Earth is nearest the zenith."

Ashley rose. "Where is your videophone?"

"In the next room."

Ashley dashed. Davenport lingered behind. "Are you sure, Dr. Urth?"

"Quite sure. But even if I am wrong, I suspect it doesn't matter."

"What doesn't matter?"

"Whether you find it or not. For if the Ultras find the Device, they will probably be unable to use it."

"Why do you say that?"

"You asked me if Jennings had ever been a student of mine, but you never asked me about Strauss, who was also a geologist. He was a student of mine a year or so after Jennings. I remember him well."

"Oh?"

"An unpleasant man. Very cold. It is the hallmark of the Ultras, I think. They are all very cold, very rigid, very sure of themselves. They can't empathize, or they wouldn't speak of killing off billions of human beings. What emotions they possess are icy ones, self-absorbed ones, fe ings incapable of spanning the distance between two human beings."

"I think I see."

"I'm sure you do. The conversation reconstructed from Strauss's ravings showed us he could not manipulate the Device. He lacked the emotional intensity, or the type of necessary emotion. I imagine all Ultras would. Jennings, who was not an Ultra, could manipulate it. Anyone who could use the Device would, I suspect, be incapable of deliberate cold-blooded cruelty. He might strike out of panic fear as Jennings struck at Strauss, but never out of calculation, as Strauss tried to strike at Jennings. In short, to put it tritely, I think the Device can be actuated by love, but never by hate, and the Ultras are nothing if not haters."

Davenport nodded. "I hope you're right. But then—why were you so suspicious of the government's motives if you felt the wrong men could not manipulate the Device?"

Urth shrugged. "I wanted to make sure you could bluff and rationalize on your feet and make yourself convincingly persuasive at a moment's notice. After all, you may have to face my niece."

26

A Problem of Numbers

This is the first mystery story I ever sold to EQMM. I had received one or two rejections from the magazine, but I had shrugged them off. After all, I was a science fiction writer, not a mystery writer. However, by 1969, I had written enough mysteries of one sort or another to feel like a mystery writer, too.

In November of that year, I was going through the magazine and read one of their "First Stories." EQMM routinely had one or two stories representing the first sale of a particular author and they were usually pretty good, too.

And I said in exasperation, "Well, if they can sell a story to EQMM, then I can, too, or what's the use of being Asimov?" So I sat down without delay and wrote a story and had it in the mail within an hour of having walked to the typewriter.

The story was accepted and a year after it appeared the magazine asked me for another one and I wrote my first Black Widower and was off and running.

Professor Neddring looked mildly at his graduate student. The young man sat there at ease; his hair was a little on the reddish side, his eyes were keen but calm, and his hands rested in the pockets of his lab coat. Altogether a promising specimen, the professor thought.

He had known for some time that the boy was interested in his daughter. What was more to the point, he had known for some time his daughter was interested in the boy.

The professor said, "Let's get this straight, Hal. You've come to me for my approval before you propose to my daughter?"

Hal Kemp said, "That's right, sir."

"Granted that I'm not up on the latest fads of youth—but surely this can't be the new 'in' thing." The professor thrust his hands into his lab coat pockets and leaned back in his chair. "Surely, young people aren't taking to asking permission these days? Don't tell me you'll give up my daughter if I turn you down?"

"No, not if she'll still have me, and I think she will. But it would be pleasant—"

"—if you had my approval. Why?"

Hal said, "For very practical reasons. I don't have my doctor's degree yet and I don't want it said that I'm dating your daughter to help me get it. If you think I am, say so, and maybe I'll wait till after I get my degree. Or maybe I won't and take my chances that your disapproval will make it that much harder for me to get my degree."

"So, for the sake of your doctorate, you think it would be nice if we were friends about your marriage to Janice."

"To be honest, yes, Professor."

There was silence between them. Professor Neddring thought about the matter with a certain creakiness. His research work for some years now had dealt with the coordination complexes of chromium and there was a definite difficulty in thinking with some precision about anything as imprecise as affection and marriage.

He rubbed his smooth cheek—at the age of fifty he was too old for the various beard styles affected by the younger members of the department—and said, "Well, Hal, if you want a decision from me I'll have to base it on something, and the only way I know how to judge people is by their reasoning powers. My daughter judges you in *her* way, but I'll have to judge you in *mine*.''

''Certainly,'' said Hal.

''Then let me put it this way.'' The professor leaned forward, scribbled something on a piece of paper, and said, ''Tell me what this says, and you will have my blessing.''

Hal picked up the paper. What was written on it was a series of numbers:

6966371726337683304 7

He said, ''A cryptogram?''

''You can call it that.''

Hal frowned slightly. ''You mean you want me to solve a cryptogram and if I do, then you'll approve the marriage?''

''Yes.''

''And if I don't, then you *won't* approve the marriage?''

''It may sound trivial, I admit, but this is my criterion. You can always marry without my approval. Janice is of age.''

Hal shook his head. ''I'd still rather have your approval. How much time do I have?''

''None. Tell me what it says *now*. Reason it out.''

''*Now?*''

The professor nodded.

Hal Kemp shifted in his chair and stared at the row of numbers in his hand. ''Do I figure it out in my head? Or can I use pencil and paper?''

''Just do it. Talk. Let me hear how you think. Who knows? If I like the way you think, I may give my approval even if you don't solve it.''

Hal said, ''Well, all right. It's a challenge. In the first place, I'll make an assumption. I'll assume you're an honorable man and would not set me a problem that you knew in advance I couldn't solve. Therefore this is a cryptogram which, to the best of your judgment, is one I can solve sitting in this chair and almost on the spur of the moment. Which in turn means that it involves something I know well.''

''That sounds reasonable,'' agreed the professor.

But Hal wasn't listening. He continued, deliberately, ''I know the alphabet well, of course, so this could be an ordinary substitution cipher—numbers for letters. Presumably, it would have to have some subtlety if it were, or it would be too easy. But I'm an amateur at that sort of thing and unless I can see at once some peculiar pattern in the numbers that gives the whole thing meaning, I'd be lost. I notice there are five 6's and five 3's and not a single 5—but that means nothing to me. So I'll abandon the possibility of a generalized cipher and move on to our own specialized field."

He thought again and went on, "Your specialized field, Professor, is inorganic chemistry and that, certainly, is what mine is going to be. And to any chemist, numbers immediately suggest atomic numbers. Every chemical element has its own number and there are one hundred and four elements known today; so the numbers involved would be 1 to 104.

"You haven't indicated how the numbers are divided up. There are the one-digit atomic numbers from 1 to 9; the two-digit ones from 10 to 99; and the three-digit ones from 100 to 104. This is all obvious, Professor, but you wanted to hear my reasoning, so I'm giving it to you in full.

"We can forget the three-digit atomic numbers, since in them a 1 is always followed by a 0 and the single 1 in your cryptogram is followed by a 7. Since you've given me twenty digits altogether, it is at least possible that only two-digit atomic numbers are involved—ten of them. There might be nine two-digit ones and two one-digit ones, but I doubt it. Even the presence of two one-digit atomic numbers could result in hundreds of different combinations of places in this list and that would surely make things too difficult for an instant or even a quick solution. It seems certain to me, then, that I am dealing with ten two-digit numbers, and we can therefore turn the message into: 69, 66, 37, 17, 26, 33, 76, 83, 30, 47.

"These numbers seem to mean nothing in themselves, but if they are atomic numbers then why not convert all of them into the names of the elements they represent? The names *might* be meaningful. That's not so easy offhand because I haven't memorized the list of elements in order of their atomic numbers. May I look them up in a table?"

The professor was listening with interest. "I didn't look up anything when I prepared the cryptogram."

"All right, then. Let's see," said Hal slowly. "Some are obvious. I know that 17 is chlorine, 26 is iron, 83 is bismuth, 30 is zinc. As for 76, that's somewhere near gold, which is 79; that would mean platinum, osmium, iridium. I'd say it means osmium. The other two are rare earth elements and I can never get those straight. Let's see—let's see—All right. I *think* I have them."

He wrote rapidly and said, "The list of the ten elements in your list is thulium, dysprosium, rubidium, chlorine, iron, arsenic, osmium, bismuth, zinc, and silver. Is that right?—No, don't answer."

He studied the list intently. "I see no connections among those elements, nothing that seems to give me any hint. Let's pass on then and ask if there is anything besides the atomic *number* that is so characteristic of elements that it would spring to any chemist's mind at once. Obviously, it would be the chemical *symbol*—the one-letter or two-letter abbreviation for each element that becomes second nature to any chemist. In this case the list of chemical symbols is"—he wrote again—"Tm, Dy, Rb, Cl, Fe, As, Os, Bi, Zn, Ag.

"These might form a word or sentence, but they don't, do they? So it would have to be a little more subtle than that. If you make an acrostic out of it and read just the first letters, that doesn't help, either. So if we try the next most obvious step and read the second letters of each symbol in order, we come out with 'my blessing.' I presume that's the solution, Professor."

"It is," said Professor Neddring gravely. "You reasoned it out with precision and you have my permission, for what that's worth, to propose to my daughter."

Hal rose, turned to leave, hesitated, then turned back. He said, "On the other hand, I don't like to take credit that's not mine. The reasoning I used may have been precise, but I offered it to you only because I wanted you to hear me reason logically. Actually, I knew the answer before I began, so in a way I cheated and I've got to admit that."

"Oh? How so?"

"Well, I know you think well of me and I guessed you would want me to come up with a solution and that you wouldn't be above giving me a hint. When you handed the cryptogram to me, you said, 'Tell me what this says, and you will have my blessing.' I guessed that you might mean that literally. 'My blessing' has ten letters and you handed me twenty digits. So I broke it down into ten pairs at once.

"Then, too, I told you I hadn't memorized the list of elements. The few elements I did remember were enough to show me that the second letters of the symbols were spelling out 'my blessing,' so I worked out the others from among those few that had the proper second letters in *their* symbols. Do I still make it?"

Professor Neddring finally smiled. He said, "Now, my boy, you *really* make it. Any competent scientist can think logically. The great ones use intuition."

27

The Little Things

The New York Times *asked me for a short mystery for an experimental page they were planning to start in their* Magazine *section. I wrote the following story and they rejected it. I was astonished. I thought it was a sure sale and, as it happened,* EQMM *took it at once when I sent it to them.*

It would have made more of a splash in the New York Times *if it had appeared there, but I'm philosophical about such things There's no accounting for tastes. Besides, if I don't get a rejection every year or so, I'm liable to become conceited and I wouldn't want that to happen to a wonderful fellow like me.*

Mrs. Clara Bernstein was somewhat past fifty and the temperature outside was somewhat past ninety. The air-conditioning was working, but though it removed the fact of heat it didn't remove the *idea* of heat.

Mrs. Hester Gold, who was visiting the twenty-first floor from her own place in 4-C, said, "It's cooler down on my floor." She was over fifty, too, and had blond hair that didn't remove a single year from her age.

Clara said, "It's the little things, really. I can stand the heat. It's the dripping I can't stand. Don't you hear it?"

"No," said Hester, "but I know what you mean. My boy, Joe, has a button off his blazer. Seventy-two dollars, and without the button it's nothing. A fancy brass button on the sleeve and he doesn't have it to sew back on."

"So what's the problem? Take one off the other sleeve also."

"Not the same. The blazer just won't look good. If a button is loose, don't wait, get it sewed. Twenty-two years old and he still doesn't understand. He goes off, he doesn't tell me when he'll be back—"

Clara said impatiently. "Listen. How can you say you don't hear the dripping? Come with me to the bathroom. If I tell you it's dripping, it's dripping."

Hester followed and assumed an attitude of listening. In the silence it could be heard:—*drip—drip—drip—*

Clara said, "Like water torture. You hear it all night. Three nights now."

Hester adjusted her large faintly tinted glasses, as though that would make her hear better, and cocked her head. She said, "Probably the shower dripping upstairs in 22-G. It's Mrs. Maclaren's place. I know her. Listen, she's a good-hearted person. Knock on her door and tell her. She won't bite your head off."

Clara said, "I'm not afraid of her. I banged on her door five times already. No one answers. I phoned her. No one answers."

"So she's away," said Hester. "It's summertime. People go away."

"And if she's away for the whole summer, do I have to listen to the dripping a whole summer?"

"Tell the super."

"That idiot. He doesn't have the key to her special lock and he won't break in for a drip. Besides, she's not away. I know her automobile and it's downstairs in the garage right now."

Hester said uneasily. "She could go away in someone else's car."

Clara sniffed. "That I'm sure of. *Mrs* Maclaren."

Hester frowned, "So she's divorced. It's not so terrible.

And she's still maybe thirty—thirty-five—and she dresses fancy. Also not so terrible.''

"If you want my opinion, Hester," said Clara, "what she's doing up there I wouldn't like to say. I hear things.''

"What do you hear?''

"Footsteps. Sounds. Listen, she's right above and I know where her bedroom is.''

Hester said tartly, "Don't be so old-fashioned. What she does is her business.''

"All right. But she uses the bathroom a lot, so why does she leave it dripping? I wish she *would* answer the door. I'll bet anything she's got a decor in her apartment like a French I-don't-know-what.''

"You're wrong if you want to know. You're plain wrong. She's got regular furniture and lots of houseplants.''

"And how do you know that?''

Hester looked uncomfortable. "I water the plants when she's not home. She's a single woman. She goes on trips, so I help her out.''

"Oh? Then you would *know* if she was out of town. Did she tell you she'd be out of town?''

"No, she didn't.''

Clara leaned back and folded her arms. "And you have the keys to her place, then?''

Hester said, "Yes, but I can't just go in.''

"Why not? She could be away. So you have to water her plants.''

"She didn't tell me to.''

Clara said, "For all you know, she's sick in bed and can't answer the door.''

"She'd have to be pretty sick not to use the phone when it's right near the bed.''

"Maybe she had a heart attack. Listen, maybe she's dead and that's why she doesn't shut off the drip.''

"She's a young woman. She wouldn't have a heart attack.''

"You can't be sure. With the life she lives—maybe a boyfriend killed her. We've *got* to go in.''

"That's breaking and entering," said Hester.

"With a *key?* If she's away, you can't leave the plants to die. You water them and I'll shut off the drip. What harm?

—And if she's dead, do you want her to lie there till who knows when?''

''She's not dead,'' said Hester, but she went downstairs to the fourth floor for Mrs. Maclaren's keys.

''No one in the hall,'' whispered Clara. ''Anyone could break in anywhere, anytime.''

''Sh,'' whispered Hester. ''What if she's inside and says, 'Who's there?' ''

''So say you came to water the plants and I'll ask her to shut off the drip.''

The key to one lock and then the key to the other turned smoothly and with only the tiniest click at the end. Hester took a deep breath and opened the door a crack. She knocked.

''There's no answer,'' whispered Clara impatiently. She pushed the door wide open. ''The air conditioner isn't even on. It's legitimate. You want to water the plants.''

The door closed behind them. Clara said, ''It smells stuffy, in here. Feels like a damp oven.''

They walked softly down the corridor. Empty utility room on the right, empty bathroom—

Clara looked in. ''No drip. It's in the master bedroom.''

At the end of the corridor there was the living room on the left with some plants.

''They need water,'' said Clara. ''I'll go into the master bath—''

She opened the bedroom door and stopped. No motion. No sound. Her mouth opened wide.

Hester was at her side. The smell was stifling. ''What—''

''Oh, my God,'' said Clara, but without breath to scream.

The bed coverings were in total disarray. Mrs. Maclaren's head lolled off the bed, her long brown hair brushing the floor, her neck bruised, one arm dangling on the floor, hand open, palm up.

''The police,'' said Clara. ''We've got to call the police.''

Hester, gasping, moved forward.

''You musn't touch anything,'' said Clara.

The glint of brass in the open hand—

Hester had found her son's missing button.

28

Halloween

This was written on order. I do a regular column for American Way *(the in-flight magazine of American Airlines) on what the future might be like in one way or another. I have done 160 of these articles so far, but every once in a long while the magazine asks for a piece of fiction from me.*

This is the mystery story I wrote for them. This was written before I had begun my Union Club mysteries, but, in my opinion, this could have become one of them with very little in the way of change.

Sanderson looked troubled and grew sulky. "That was a mistake on our part. We took him so for granted that we didn't see him. Human error." He shook his head.

"And what was the motive?"

"Ideology," Sanderson said. "He got the job just to do this. We know because he left a note behind, couldn't resist crowing over us. He was one of those who feel that nuclear fission is deadly; that it will lead to the bigtime theft of plutonium, to the making of homemade bombs, to nuclear terrorism and blackmail.''

"I take it he was out to show it could be done?"

"Yes. He was going to publicize it and rouse public opinion.''

"How dangerous is the plutonium he stole?" Haley asked.

"Not at all dangerous. It's a small amount. You could hold the case in your hand. It wasn't even meant for the fissioning core. We were doing other things with it. There's certainly not enough to build a bomb with, I assure you.''

"Could there be possible danger to the individual holding it?"

"None if it's left in its case. If you took it out, there would be damage eventually to anyone coming in contact with it.''

"I could see where public alarm would be justified," Haley said.

Sanderson frowned. "But it proves nothing. It was a mistake that will never happen again and, in any case, the alarm system worked. We were after him at once. If he hadn't managed to get to this hotel; if we didn't fear alarming the people here . . .''

"Why didn't you inform the Bureau at once?"

"If we could have gotten him ourselves . . .'' Sanderson mumbled.

"Then the whole thing could have been hidden, even from the Bureau. Mistakes and all.''

"Well . . .''

"But you did inform us in the end. After he died. I take it, therefore, you don't have the plutonium?''

Sanderson's eyes drifted furtively away from Haley's steady glance. "No, we don't.'' Then defensively, "We couldn't operate too openly. There were thousands of people here and if the notion arose that there was trouble—if it were pinned to the station . . .''

"Then you would have lost and he would have won, even if you caught him and retrieved the plutonium. I understand that. How long was he here then?" Haley looked at his watch. "It's 3:57 A.M. now."

"All day. It was only when it got late enough to allow us to work more openly that we trapped him on the stairs. We tried to rush him and he tried to run. He slipped—hit his head against the railing, after tumbling a flight, and fractured his skull."

"And he didn't have the plutonium on him. How do you know he had it with him when he entered the hotel?"

"It was seen. One of our men almost had him at one point."

"So during the hours he managed to evade you in this hotel, he could have hidden this thing, a small box, anywhere on the twenty-nine floors, in the ninety rooms on each floor—or in the corridors, offices, utility sections, basement, roof—and we have to have it back, don't we? We can't allow plutonium to float about the city, however small the amount. Is that right?"

"Yes," Sanderson said unhappily.

"One alternative is to take a hundred men and search the hotel—floor by floor, room by room, square inch by square inch—until we find it."

"We can't do that," Sanderson said. "How would we explain it?"

"And what is the alternative?" Haley asked. "Do we have a hint? The thief said something. Halloween?"

Sanderson nodded. "He was conscious a few moments before he died. We asked him where the plutonium was and he said, 'Halloween.'"

Haley took a deep breath and let it out slowly. "Is that all he said?"

"That's all. Three of us heard him."

"And it was definitely 'Halloween' you heard? He didn't say 'hollow ring,' for instance?"

"No. 'Halloween.' We all agree."

"Has the word any significance to you? Is there a Project Halloween at the station? Is the word used to mean something in an 'in' way?"

"No no. Nothing like that."

"Do you think he was trying to tell you where the plutonium was?"

"We don't *know*," said Sanderson agonizingly. "His eyes were unfocused. It was a dying whisper. We don't even know if he heard our question."

Haley was silent for a moment. "Yes. It could have been a last fugitive thought of anything at all. A childhood memory. Anything—except that yesterday was Halloween. The day on which he hid in this hotel and tried to evade you for long enough to get the story to the newspapers was Halloween. It could have had some significance to him."

Sanderson shrugged.

Haley was thinking out loud. "Halloween is the day on which the forces of evil are abroad and he must surely have been considering himself to be fighting those forces."

"We are not evil," Sanderson said.

"What counts is what *he* thought—and he didn't want himself caught, and the plutonium, too. So he hid it. Every room is vacuumed, every room has its sheets and towels changed at some time during the day, and when that is happening the door is open. He would pass an open door and step in—one step and a quick placing of the box where it wouldn't be readily seen. Then he could come back later to retrieve it; or if he was caught, the box would eventually be noticed by some guest or some employee, taken to the management, and recognized with or without having done damage."

"But *what* room?" Sanderson agonized.

"We can try *one* room," Haley said, "and if that doesn't work, we will have to search the hotel." He left.

Haley was back in half an hour. The body had been removed, but Sanderson was still there, deep in dejection.

"There were two people in the room," Haley said. "We had to wake them. I found something on top of the shelf above the coatrack. Is this it?"

It was a small cube, gray in color, heavy in the hand, the top held down by wing nuts.

"That's it," Sanderson said with barely controlled excitement. He loosened the wing nuts, lifted the top a crack, and put a small probe near the opening. The sound of crackling could be heard at once. "That's it. But how did you know where it was?"

"Just a chance," said Haley, with a shrug. "The thief had Halloween on his mind, judging from his last word. When he saw a particular hotel room open and being cleaned, perhaps it seemed like an omen to him."

"*What* hotel room?"

"Room 1031," Haley said. "October the thirty-first. Halloween."

29

The Thirteenth Day of Christmas

I also write a series of mystery stories for young people, stories in which my detective is a junior high school student named Larry. I don't do them often and have only eleven of them so far.

Usually, they run in Boys Life *magazine. This one, however, was rejected by them for some reason, but it was snapped up by EQMM, even though it was patently juvenile.*

It was my favorite Larry story and I had even been so vain as to read it aloud to my daughter (ordinarily, I never let anyone see my stories before acceptance), which meant I was all the more taken aback at its rejection.

However, it is still my favorite and here it is.

This was one year we were *glad* when Christmas Day was over.

It had been a grim Christmas Eve and I had stayed awake as long as I could, half listening for bombs. And Mom and I stayed up until midnight on Christmas *Day*, too. Then Dad called and said, "Okay, it's over. Nothing's happened. I'll be home as soon as I can."

Mom and I danced around as if Santa Claus had just come and then, after about an hour, Dad came home and I went to bed and slept fine.

You see, it's special in our house. Dad's a detective on the force and these days, with terrorists and bombings, it can get pretty hairy. So, when on December twentieth, warnings reached headquarters that there would be a Christmas Day bombing at the Soviet offices in the United Nations, it had to be taken seriously.

The entire force was put on the alert and the FBI came in, too. The Soviets had their own security, I guess, but none of it satisfied Dad.

The day before Christmas was the worst. "If someone is crazy enough to want to plant a bomb and if he's not too worried about getting caught afterward, he's likely to be able to do it no matter what precautions we take." Dad's voice had a grimness we rarely heard.

"I suppose there's no way of knowing who it is," Mom said.

Dad shook his head. "Letters from newspapers pasted on paper; no fingerprints, only smudges. Common stuff we can't trace and a threat that it would be the only warning we'd get. What can we do?"

"Well, it must be someone who doesn't like the Russians, I guess," Mom said.

Dad said, "That doesn't narrow it much. Of course, the Soviets say it's a Zionist threat, and we've got to keep an eye on the Jewish Defense League."

"Gee, Dad," I said. "That doesn't make much sense. The Jewish people wouldn't pick Christmas to do it, would they? It doesn't mean anything to them; and it doesn't mean anything to the Soviet Union, either. They're officially atheistic."

"You can't reason that out to the Russians," Dad said. "Now, why don't you turn in, because tomorrow may be a bad day all round, Christmas Day or not."

Then he left. He was out all Christmas Day, and it was pretty rotten. We didn't even open any presents; just sat listening to the radio, which was tuned to the news station.

Then at midnight when Dad called and nothing had happened, we could breathe again, but I still forgot to open my presents.

That didn't come till the morning of the twenty-sixth. We made *that* day Christmas. Dad had a day off and Mom roasted the turkey a day late. It wasn't till after dinner that we talked about it at all.

Mom said, "I suppose the person, whoever it was, couldn't find any way of planting the bomb once the Department drew the security strings tight."

Dad smiled, as if he appreciated Mom's loyalty. "I don't think you can make security that tight," he said, "but what's the difference? There was no bomb. Maybe it was a bluff. After all, it did disrupt the city a bit and it gave the Soviet people at the United Nations some sleepless nights, I'll bet. That might have been almost as good for the bomber as letting the bomb go off."

"If he couldn't do it on Christmas," I said, "maybe he'll do it another time. Maybe he just said Christmas to get everyone keyed up and then, after they relax, he'll . . ."

Dad gave me one of his little pushes on the side of my head. "You're a cheerful one, Larry. No, I don't think so. Real bombers value the sense of power. When they say something is going up at a certain time, it's got to be that time or it's no fun for them."

I was still suspicious, but the days passed and there was no bombing and the Department gradually went back to normal. The FBI left and even the Soviet people seemed to forget about it, according to Dad.

On January second, the Christmas–New Year vacation was over and I went back to school. We started rehearsing our Christmas pageant. We made an elaborate show out of the song "The Twelve Days of Christmas," which doesn't have any religion to it—just presents.

There were twelve of us kids, each one singing a particular line every time it came up and then coming in all together on the "partridge in a pear tree." I was number five, singing "five gold rings" because I was still a boy soprano' and I could hit that high note pretty nicely, if I do say so myself.

Some kids didn't know why Christmas had twelve days, but I explained that if we count Christmas Day as one, the twelfth day after it is January sixth, when the Three Wise Men arrived with gifts for the Christ child. Naturally, it was on January sixth that we put on the show in the auditorium, with as many parents there as wanted to come.

Dad got a few hours off and was sitting in the audience with Mom. I could see him getting set to hear his son's high note for the last time because next year my voice changes or I'll know the reason why.

Did you ever get an idea in the middle of a stage show and have to continue, no matter what?

We were only on the second day with its "two turtle-doves" when I thought, "Oh my, it's the *thirteenth* day of Christmas." The whole world was shaking around me and I couldn't do a thing but stay on the stage and sing about "five gold rings."

I didn't think they'd ever get to those stupid "twelve drummers drumming." It was like having itching powder on instead of underwear. I couldn't stand still. Then, when the last note was out, while they were still applauding, I broke away, went jumping down the steps from the platform and up the aisle, calling, "Dad!"

He looked startled, but I grabbed him, and I think I was babbling so fast he could hardly understand.

I said, "Dad, Christmas isn't the same day everywhere. It could be one of the Soviet's own people. They're officially atheist, but maybe one of them is religious and he wants to place the bomb for that reason. Only he would be a member of the Russian Orthodox Church. They don't go by our calendar."

"What?" said Dad, looking as if he didn't understand a word I was saying.

"It's *so*, Dad. I read about it. The Russian Orthodox Church is still on the Julian Calendar, which the West gave up for the Gregorian Calendar centuries ago. The Julian Calendar is thirteen days behind ours. The Orthodox Christmas is on *their* December twenty-fifth, which is *our* January seventh. It's *tomorrow*."

He didn't believe me, just like that. He looked it up in the almanac; then he called up someone in the Department who was Russian Orthodox.

He was able to get the Department moving again. They talked to the Soviets, and once the Soviets stopped talking about Zionists and looked at themselves, they got the man. I don't know what they did with him, but there was no bombing on the thirteenth day of Christmas, either.

The Department wanted to give me a new bicycle for Christmas after that, but I turned it down. I was just doing my duty.

30

The Key Word

This is another Larry story.

Some reviewers seem to think that Larry is an insufferable kid and wonder how his father can stand him. As a matter of fact, anyone that smart is bound to be insufferable, and I make it quite plain that his father, in between being proud of him, tends to get exasperated with him.

It doesn't bother me. I was that bright when I was a kid, and quite insufferable, and I managed to survive—and my father even liked me part of the time, I think.

Ordinarily, Dad keeps his temper pretty well around the house and he never loses it with me—almost never. I like to think it's because I'm a good kid, but he says it's because I'm smart enough to stay out of his way when he's mad.

I sure didn't stay out of his way this time. He swooped down on me, all red in the face, and snatched the New York *Times* right out from under my hand. "What do you think you're *doing?*" he said. "Don't you have any *brains?*"

I just stood there with my pencil in my hand. I wasn't doing *anything*.

I said, "What's the matter, Dad?" I was just plain astonished.

Mom was hurrying over, too. I guess she wanted to make sure her one and only son wasn't smashed beyond repair.

"What's the matter?" she asked. "What's he done?"

Dad stood there, getting even redder. It was as if he couldn't think what I had done. Then he said, "Doesn't he know better than to touch the paper? That's not our paper."

By that time I sort of got indignant. "Well, how am I supposed to know that, Dad?"

And Mom said, "How *is* he supposed to know? If that's something important, dear, you might have said so. You needn't have left it on the dining room table."

Dad looked as if he wanted to back down, but didn't know how. He said to me, "You didn't tear anything, throw anything away . . ."

I guess he had become so angry when he saw me at the *Times* that he didn't see what I was doing. "It's in perfect shape," I said.

He walked back and forth in the room, breathing hard, and we just watched him. I figured he must be on a hard case, and when a detective is on a difficult case, you can't blame him for breathing hard.

Then he stopped. He had worked it all out of his system and he was himself again when he turned to me. "I'm sorry, Larry," he said. "I was wrong. It wasn't important. We have the paper microfilmed anyway. . . . I just can't make anything out of it."

Mom sat down and didn't say anything, because Dad isn't really supposed to talk about his cases at home. I knew that, but I just put a blank look on my face and said, "Out of what, Dad?" And I sat down, too.

Dad looked at us and *he* sat down and threw the paper back on the table. "Out of that. The paper."

I could tell he wanted to talk, so I kept quiet and let him.

After a while, he said, "There's a . . . Well, never mind what there is, but it's pretty worrisome, and there's a code involved and we can't break it."

"That's not really your job, is it?" Mom asked. "You don't know anything about codes."

"There's something I might do."

I said, "All codes can be broken, can't they?"

"Some not as easily as others, Larry," he said. "Sometimes a code is based on a key word that changes every once in a while, maybe every day. That makes it hard, unless we can find what the key word is, or, better yet, what system they use to change the key word."

"How do you do that?" said Mom.

With a grim look on his face, Dad said, "One way is to pick up somebody's notebook."

"Surely, no one would put it in a notebook for people to find," she said.

I butted in. "They would, Mom. You can't rely on remembering a complicated system, and you can't take chances on forgetting. Right, Dad?"

"Right," he said. "But no one has found a notebook or anything else, and that's it." The tone of his voice told me that was the end of the discussion. "Have you done your homework, Larry?"

"All except some of the geography." Then, to keep from being chased out of the room, I said, "What's the *New York Times* got to do with it?"

That took Dad's mind off the homework. "One of the men we had our eyes on was mugged last night. He managed to fight off the mugger, but he was hurt and we brought him to the hospital. That made it easy to search him very carefully without getting anyone suspicious and scaring them into changing their system or lying low. We got nowhere. No notebook."

"Maybe the mugger got away with . . ." I said.

Dad shook his head. "We had a good man following him. He saw the whole thing. *But* the man being mugged had a *New York Times* on him and he held onto it while he was fighting. I thought that was suspicious, so I had the paper microfilmed and brought it home. I thought there might be some system of picking out one of the words—in a headline on some particular page—last word in some particular column—who knows? Anyone can carry the *Times* It's not like a notebook. There's nothing suspicious about it."

"How could you tell from the paper what the system was?" I said.

Dad shrugged. "I thought there might be a mark on it. He might look at the key word and just automatically, without even thinking, check it off. No use. There's not a word in the paper that's marked in any way."

I got excited, "Yes, there are!"

Dad gave me that look I always get when he thinks I don't know what I'm talking about. "What do you mean?"

"That's what I was doing when you yelled and grabbed the paper," I said, showing him the pencil I was still holding. "I was doing the crossword puzzle. Don't you see, Dad, it was partly worked out. That's why I started on it, to finish it off."

Dad rubbed his nose. "We noticed that, but what makes you think that has any meaning? Lots of people work on crossword puzzles. It's natural enough."

"Sure, that's why it's a safe system. This one was worked out in the middle, Dad, just a little patch in the middle. No one just does a part in the middle. They start at the upper left corner, with number one."

"If it's a hard puzzle, you might not get a start till you reach the middle."

"It was an easy puzzle, Dad. One across was a three-letter word meaning 'presidential nickname' and that's got to be Ike or Abe, and one down. . . . Anyway, this guy just went straight to that part and didn't bother with anything else. Twenty-seven across was one of the words he worked out and the paper is for yesterday, which is the twenty-seventh of the month."

Dad waited a long while before answering. Then he said, "Coincidence."

"Maybe not," I said. "The *Times* crossword puzzle always has at least sixty numbers every day, twice as many on Sunday. Every day of the month has a number and for that day the key word is the one in that number in the crossword puzzle. If there are two words, across and down, maybe you always take the across."

"Hmm," said Dad.

"How much simpler can it be? Anyone can remember that, and all you have to do is be able to work out crossword puzzles. You can get all kinds of words, long or short, even phrases, even foreign words."

Mom said, "What if a crossword puzzle happens to be too hard to work out just in the crucial spot?"

Now Dad got excited. "They could use each day's puzzle for the day after, and check with the solution to make sure." He had his coat on. "Except Sunday, for which the solution comes the next Sunday. . . . I hope the pencil you used made a different mark from his, Larry."

"He used a pen," I said.

. . . That wasn't all there was to the case, but they did break the code. Dad got a bonus and he put it in the bank toward my college education.

He said it was only fair.

31

Nothing Might Happen

Sometimes a mystery story isn't a mystery story in the literal sense of the word. There is no puzzle, merely the outline of some criminal or near-criminal course of behavior. You might call it simply a "crime story."

Alfred Hitchoock's Mystery Magazine (AHMM) is very strong on that sort of story and it occurred to me to write a story for them because, for one thing, the editor, Cathleen Jordan, is one of my favorite people. Naturally, I had to write a crime story, which is atypical for me, but I'm sort of pleased with the way it turned out, and here it is.

Samuel Gelderman had been working quite diligently for five years toward the goal of becoming a millionaire. Many people do so with varying degrees of hope, some in one way, some in another. Sam's hope was high, but his method of achieving his goal was exceptionally tedious, for he served as secretary and odd jobs man to his uncle, the well-known writer of espionage-suspense novels, Ralph Gelderman.

Ralph was not a flashy bestselling writer. His books did not explode onto the scene in sprays of obvious money-making.

He might even be considered rather obscure. This did not displease Sam, however, for Ralph was something better than a bestselling writer: He was a prolific one whose books were smooth and reliable. Each one sold moderately steadily, remaining in print for a long time, and gathering paperback editions, foreign sales, and movie options along the way.

If Ralph had been more obviously successful, he might have slowly collected a large staff about himself and he might then have developed numerous ways of spending a large percentage of his money before he passed from this earthly scene.

As it was, his professional advance had been so gradual that it had never occurred to Ralph to be anything but a one-man production machine. Nor did it occur to him to alter his generally frugal way of life. The result was that each year the number of his books in print accumulated, and each year he made a little more than the year before, and each year his investments and assets increased appreciably. He remained a bachelor, too, showing no signs of any impatience with his marital status as his years advanced.

And Sam, the orphaned son of Ralph's older brother, was Ralph's only close relative and his obvious sole heir.

Five years ago, Ralph had finally been persuaded by his accountant to form a small corporation, with himself as president and treasurer. He needed a second officer and it was then that he asked Sam to become, officially, what he had been on and off in an informal way for quite a while—his secretary. That became Sam's corporation title.

The duties were tedious, for Sam had to take care of accounts, of publishing records, of correspondence, of routine dealings with publishers, editors, and agents, and also with a certain querulousness on the part of his uncle.

On the brighter side, he received a moderately decent salary, which, with the small inheritance he had received from his father, enabled him to live with his wife and teenage daughter in modest comfort, if not in splendor. Much more to the point, his position enabled Sam to know the exact nature of his uncle's income, investments, and assets and he was astonished. It was far greater than he had imagined—and it enabled him to bear with his uncle's occasionally unreasonable whims with the patience of a saint.

It was, moreover, a source of gratifying reassurance to Sam to know that, as the only other officer of the corporation, he would at once have its assets available to him on his uncle's decease—as well as inheriting, in more tedious fashion, the precorporation earnings.

What was a source of deep chagrin to Sam, however, was that the happy denouement was not imminent. Ralph Gelderman was sixty, but in robust health. He might well live on for another quarter century. Sam himself was forty-two and was, he had to admit, *not* in robust health. Even if he survived his uncle, he might well be an old and sickly survivor, unable to get much use out of his inheritance. To be sure, the older Ralph grew, the larger the estate would be, but what if, as senility approached, he grew suddenly enamored of some charming young lady who found his wealth and his shortening life expectancy irresistible? Sam would find himself cut off with a small legacy.

Under such circumstances, Sam could not help but meditate on how convenient it would be if a kindly Providence were to carry Ralph off in the very near future; if a building cornice were to fall on him, or an automobile were to collide with him, or some virus were to attack him with unaccustomed ferocity.

It might have seemed logical for Sam to ruminate on the possibility of helping Providence along by some action of his own, but he did not like to think of such things. He was not a vicious man, he told himself, but above and beyond that, as sole heir, he himself would be the immediate and obvious suspect if anything untoward happened to Ralph. He could not possibly withstand that. Nor could he avoid it by faking a faultless alibi, or by working out a murder method that would look like suicide or accident. He just didn't have that kind of mind.

He couldn't even go through the unthinkable process of hiring a paid killer to do the job for him. Aside from lacking the funds for it, or the knowledge of how and where to find such a person, he did not wish to put his life into the hands of a potential blackmailer.

He sighed and realized he would simply have to content himself with hoping that Providence would do the job for him, and to watch, wistfully, as the years slipped away.

And then, much to his own astonishment, he thought of a perfect method for murder, the *perfect* murder—not a flaw in it, not a danger, not a care.

It happened this way. . . .

The intercom signal had sounded one day, two years ago, and Sam had picked up the receiver and said, "Yes, Uncle."

"Sam, come up here."

The voice in Sam's ear was testy, but Sam felt no cause for alarm. He had just skillfully managed to cancel a potential photography session and Ralph had grumped his thanks for it. Ralph detested photographers and cameras, and never yielded to the necessity of having his picture taken except under conditions of overwhelming force.

To Sam's gentle suggestion that this sort of personal publicity might help sales of his books, Ralph growled impatiently and said, "I don't want that kind of sale. I want my books to be successful on their own. I want *them* well known, not me."

It was for that reason that Ralph Gelderman never became a household face, so to speak, and that his photographs on book jackets tended to be old ones, taken before middle age and continued success had hardened his stubbornness.

So Sam, following instructions, as he always did, had quashed the photography matter, and was surely in favor now.

He climbed the flight of stairs to Ralph's neat and well-organized writing room (always referred to as his office), and said, "Yes, Uncle?"

Ralph thrust a letter at him with a discontented air. "Why am I plagued with this?"

Sam tightened his lips slightly in chagrin. It was well understood that fan mail (except for those unusually intelligent and complimentary items that Ralph rather enjoyed reading) was to be kept away from him. Sam, by long practice, could take care of it himself, knowing which should be answered and which not. Those he answered, he knew exactly how to answer, and then he would take those answers to Ralph for his signature. Nor did Ralph bother to read them. He merely signed.

It was not really a safe procedure, and Sam had at one time made the careful observation that it was not good practice to sign anything without reading it.

Ralph had put down his pen. "If I can't trust you, I'll have to fire you. Can I trust you?"

"Of course, Uncle. I was merely making a general statement." But for a while, it had scared him out of making such general statements.

And now he had accidentally allowed a fan letter to reach his uncle, and it was one of the "crackpot" items; a careless oversight.

"Here's a man," said Ralph, peering at the signature, "named Lawrence K. Leghorn, who seems to be convinced that there is an active Communist conspiracy affecting the grade schools in his town out in Long Island somewhere, and he wants me to join him in squelching it. Apparently he confuses me with my fictional characters and wants to meet me for dinner, which, by the way, he doesn't offer to pay for. Am I getting many letters like this?"

"One or two, Uncle. Not many."

"Well, I don't want to see the letters. And I certainly don't want to see the writers of such letters. Just send them a polite squelch. Make sure it's polite, but make sure it's a *squelch*."

"That's exactly what I try to do, Uncle. This won't happen again."

"Good. See to that!"

Sam nodded and turned. As always, Ralph looked depressingly vigorous and a good ten years younger than his age. His full head of hair was dark and unfrosted, as Sam's was, and the distinct family resemblance was all in the older man's favor.

Sam sighed, went to his own office on the lower floor of the duplex apartment on Manhattan's Upper East Side, and read the letter again.

It was clearly the work of a paranoid personality. A surprising number of them wrote letters to Ralph Gelderman. Perhaps it was the spy-suspense that drew them out of the woodwork; there was no question but that espionage tales fostered paranoia.

The proper reaction to letters by such people was inaction. There was no point in replying to a paranoid personality. Any reply was a provocation.

Occasionally, though, they would write again—and even again. They would complain that their letters were being stolen by post office employees, or rerouted by malign influences working through long-range radio beams. It then became necessary to send a very brief note to the effect that their letters had been received.

And in the case of this Mr. Leghorn, Ralph had specifically ordered an answer to be sent, and he would expect to sign it.

Sam sighed again, and set himself to the job of thinking out an answer. A polite one: "Dear so-and-so—heavily overextended—deadlines—no time whatever—deeply regret cannot meet with you—not a matter in which I can concern myself—"

It had to be done very delicately, for there was no telling what a paranoid personality might do, once affronted. If they thought you were part of the conspiracy . . .

It was at that moment that Sam achieved his blinding insight.

Of course! No telling what they might do. They might, unbribed and of their own accord, impelled by their own madness, serve the role of the falling cornice or of any of the other convenient accidents Sam dreamed of.

Why, then, be polite to this Leghorn? Why not be provocative—without being blatantly so, of course?

Excitedly, he scribbled out a note in longhand. "Dear Sir: Any meeting between ourselves is quite out of the question. Please do not waste your time in repeating this request, as it is clear to me that your suspicions with regard to conspiratonal activity are quite without foundation."

Good! Short, even curt! And a distinct sneer, too.

Uncle Ralph would sign it and off it would go. Leghorn would then find himself with a deep grievance against Ralph Gelderman and, in all likelihood, something of a suspicion that Ralph was himself part of the dangerous Communist conspiracy. If he wrote again, Sam would answer again—appropriately.

It was perfect. Sam could use similar tactics on every letter of the sort that came in—one or two a week, usually.

For two years now, Sam had followed this procedure—and he had enjoyed it. Each day's mail was an adventure. Would a new letter come from an old name? Would a new crackpot make his appearance?

Some stopped, but others started, and there were always half a dozen in being, with emotions to be played upon skillfully. Sam grew to admire his own light touch, his ability to irritate these people without seeming to be doing so deliberately. He didn't answer too soon or too harshly, and he rejoiced every time he elicited an unreasonable response. The more unreasonable, the more he could hope.

Leghorn himself, the first case, was the best. There were times when for a month at a time there would be nothing from him. Sam would decide that the crackpot had tired of the game, but then, eventually, there would come the familiar envelope with the hand-printed address.

Nor did Ralph ever read the answers. He merely signed. He was so uninterested that he spoke of having a rubber stamp designed so that Sam could manage it all. Always, though, Sam put in a quiet objection to that. After all, Sam said, the actual authentic signature was precious to his readers. They should not be deprived of that. Ralph snorted, but complied.

Sam, after all, needed the authentic signature. It must always be a reasonable assumption that Ralph had dictated the letters—there was the neatly-typed "RG/sg" at the lower left—that he read the answers once they were prepared, and that he signed them with his own hand. A stamp would ruin everything.

And, after all, ninety-nine out of every hundred letters that were sent off to readers over his signature were totally harmless.

Sam made sure that, at parties, he entertained different friends with stories of the odd letters Ralph received. Such stories were authentically amusing, and the friends laughed. Then, turning sober, Sam would, ever so gently, deprecate Ralph's tendency to be cruel or cutting in his answers. He himself (he explained) did his best to soften the answers, but Ralph always objected to that.

Sam did not do this too often. He did not overdo. Just once in a reasonable while; just enough to make it likely that someone would remember if the time should come when such remembering would be useful. It would all tend to indicate that it was clearly all Ralph's fault—over Sam's objections.

At one time, a friend said, on such an occasion, "Isn't that sort of thing dangerous? What if one of these crackpots gets mad enough to try to beat up your uncle? The return address must be on the stationery."

Sam rejoiced inwardly at that. He shook his head and said, "I do worry about that on occasion, but most of them live far away and the letters they write tend to blow off steam and reduce their internal pressure, I suppose. Just the same, I did try to warn Uncle Ralph once about that very point, and he all but bit my head off. I can't cross him too much, you know. He's the boss."

It was *perfect*. What if someone with murder in his heart *did* come to see Ralph? And if Ralph were killed?

How on earth could any blame be attached to Sam in that case? He could produce the entire body of correspondence, and it would all pile the guilt on Ralph himself. Sam, everyone would say, had actually tried to save Ralph from himself.

It was not just his own statements to his friends, either. On several occasions, Sam had written two letters, one blatantly and crudely provocative, and the other more diplomatic by several notches—yet not actually designed to cool the fires. Only the first was signed, but only the second, milder one was mailed, with a scrawled initial "G." Copies of both remained in the files, and Sam could explain that he had hesitated to send the first, and had sent the second instead, on his own responsibility and at the risk of his job, and that he had scrawled the "G" himself.

Far from being blamed, Sam would be overwhelmed with assurances that it was not his fault and that he must not blame himself. Even the police would surely say so.

And the best part of this plan for the perfect murder was that *nothing might happen*. No madman might appear with the desire to kill gnawing at his heart. Ralph might safely live on indefinitely. This meant that Sam need not live on for years with the gnawings of conscience poisoning his life. He was just playing a game—not an innocent, harmless one, perhaps, but one that would probably turn out to be so in fact, if not in intent. It had, after all, been harmless for two years now.

Indeed, the game did Ralph a service, for it kept Sam from longing uselessly for his uncle's death, and perhaps being drawn to murder, eventually. As it was, the game gave Sam the feeling of doing something about his problem, and made him happy. It made it unnecessary for him to do anything else. In a way, it might be saving Uncle Ralph's life, and it was that thought that enabled Sam to turn to the day's mail with a light heart and to continue the game without feeling shame.

He was about to turn to the mail now, when the house phone rang.

Sam picked it up. Ralph was away at his publisher's office, but it would have been Sam's job to pick it up even if Ralph had been in his office upstairs.

"Yes?"

"Delivery, Mr. Gelderman, from Prime Publishers."

Sam groaned inwardly. It would be another bound galley of a book for which Ralph would be asked to compose a promotional statement. Ralph never did so, but neither did publishers ever give up. And it would be up to Sam himself to compose a tactful reply for the hundredth time. It wouldn't do to irritate a publisher.

"Is the delivery man still there?"

"Yes, Mr. Gelderman."

"Well, send him up."

The doorbell sounded its subdued chime two minutes later, and Sam went to the door.

The delivery man at the door, middle-aged, nondescript, held out the package. "Mr. Gelderman?"

"Yes," said Sam impatiently. "Do you want me to sign something?"

He was suddenly aware that the package, whatever it was, was empty. It squeezed together without resistance under his fingers. "What is this?—Hey what are you doing?"

The delivery man had stepped inside, shouldering Sam to one side, and closed the door behind him.

He said, "My name is Lawrence Leghorn, and I'm here to see you, Mr. Ralph Gelderman."

Sam's stomach tightened. The crackpot! Possibly intent on assault and battery! He said huskily, "You're wrong. I'm not Ralph Gelderman. I'm his secretary. Mr. Gelderman is not in."

Leghorn's eyes narrowed, and he seized Sam's wrist in a surprisingly strong grip. "The doorman called you Gelderman, and you just told me you were Gelderman."

"I'm *Sam* Gelderman."

"You just said you were his secretary."

"I *am* his secretary. I'm also his nephew, so I have the same name. On the letters it says 'RG/sg.' I'm 'sg.' "

Leghorn hesitated for a moment. Then he said, "It's your picture on the books."

"It's an old picture and there's a family resemblance, but he's twenty years older than I am," said Sam, wildly.

Leghorn thought for a moment. Then he said, "I don't believe you!" He pulled a handgun out of his pocket and fired—not at all wildly.

About the Author

Isaac Asimov has written over 340 books on subjects as diverse as the Bible, Shakespeare, math and alien encounters. He is perhaps the best known—and certainly the best loved—of all science fiction authors. Dr. Asimov lives in New York City.